BIRCH

Mind of the Dragonflies

Jon P. Roth

Bright Bridge Communications

Bearing witness, even when it comes via genetic memory, carries the responsibility of knowing, tested by the question of our human relationship with intelligence (do we embody intelligence, or does intelligence embody us?) From what complexity does the shape of consciousness emerge, and how does that shape rebalance the forces of love and fear?

Except for the point, the still point, There would be no dance, and there is only the dance.

-T.S. ELIOT, BURNT NORTON, FROM FOUR QUARTETS

For Elizabeth, Anna, and Mary
You are the inspiration behind all that I do

He watched the wall of rain, topped by nimbus eruptions roiling skyward, like a lumpy brain the size of two counties, gaining mass as the winds gathered in strength, lightning flashing like neurons from within it, nonstop, thoughts forming as it rose in wakefulness, the bright flashes and smears chained, frenetic, organized. What was it thinking? It was the largest thing he'd ever seen over the land, covering the horizon and towering higher than the mountains he used to hike in California. He craned his head back to try to understand its scale, the strain on his neck intensified by the angle and the wind pushing against his helmet.

The road shot him toward the storm like a needle injecting him into a vein. He unconsciously slowed the motorcycle, glancing left to the north and right to the south for any other direction to go. There was none, except back, and that thought jabbed his raw senses with a rush of fear.

He twisted the throttle, regaining speed, and the wet wind slapped against his face shield, sending tiny droplets racing across his vision.

The first few big drops hit him in the shoulders like musket balls.

Two weeks prior...

Birch took a deep breath and glanced at the temperature and fan controls. He dialed down the temp a couple degrees, eased the volume on the breeze-and-surf loop he used to quiet his tinnitus, and lowered the LEDs to help focus. Then he took his hands away from the keyboard, resting them in his lap, and closed his eyes.

Seconds later he had his hands back on the keyboard, walking his mind into the algorithm. He spent the next 118 minutes refactoring the code and editing comments. He knew that the engineer who wrote this module—a guy named Lars, who'd recently come over from one of the big video sharing companies—would pore over the code branch and pay special attention to the comments. It was one of the "evolve" modules that gave the game characters personalities and the ability to learn. *Lars still doesn't trust simple ideas,* Birch thought. *Nice-looking code, solid comments, easy to work with, but he wants to keep too much control and do too much thinking ahead of time, like he's worried he'll miss something if he just lets it run.*

Birch took the code from 3,300 lines to four hundred and change.

The game, *Zongo Bongo*, had started as a typical, networked role-player adventure. Robin Turcek, the company founder and CEO, had planned to stake his territory with insanely high-resolution graphics and audio. He'd convinced his venture capitalists that arresting eye candy and stellar soundtracks laid over a playable storyline would win serious market share and set them up to grab share in the virtual reality space.

That strategy was eclipsed soon after Birch answered one of Zongo Inc.'s ads and joined the team as a junior developer. At twenty-six, it was Birch's first full-time job out of college after a series of contract gigs. Robin welcomed him to the team after a few interviews and tests, turned him over to Melanie, the engineering lead, and parked him at a station on the floor to start coding. Within a couple months, Birch demoed a game character that could operate off-script by learning and remembering the other characters and the environment, and even anticipate the moves of human players. A few months after that, he launched a more compelling version of this first-person character, one that could learn the player's habits and keep up an internal dialogue, either through speech recognition or the keyboard.

BETA players were spooked by it at first, claiming that their character knew what they were thinking before they did. More than a few of the early testers yanked their goggles and headphones off, gaping at the game controller or some nearby random object to reorient themselves in concrete reality. The testers found, however, that the spookiness wore off, and the players became passionate about their characters, identifying with them so closely that they played twice as long as the average. They talked about them outside of the game incessantly, referring to them as they referred to themselves, and even built their avatar's appearance to resemble themselves more honestly than the typical player, who tends to "upgrade" their self-image.

Robin noticed what was going on and saw huge dollar signs and market domination. No longer did graphics rule at Zongo: Robin was going to make his mark as the CEO of the valley's premier Artificial Intelligence game maker.

It took Robin only twenty minutes of highly animated talk, with another ten or so to demo one of Birch's game characters, to froth up his venture capitalists and convince them to open the money spigot wider. Within a couple more months, Robin promoted Birch to senior level, then to engineering lead. The staff doubled, then tripled soon thereafter. Robin drew up plans to expand the building with the increase in venture funding, and the culture took on the enriched quality of a more mature company.

Now, *Zongo Bongo* was about to launch. Robin was frantic with excitement, and he had the staff stretched thin and exhausted.

Birch ran his tests, went back through to fix a few fails, and then, as a courtesy, sent Lars a pull request to review the changes. He knew Lars would approve it and tag it for integration.

Birch turned his LEDs back up, switched off the breeze-and-surf loop and started a playlist he'd designed to lower his heart rate. Then he slacked a message to Robin. "As soon as Lars approves the merge, it's ready."

Thirty seconds later a message came back from Robin: "WOOOOOOT!!!!WOOOOOOT!!!! ::))"

Even through the insulated walls of his personal harbor —a cylindrical, enlarged phone booth-like structure designed to provide coders a distraction-free environment—Birch could hear a commotion growing out on the development room floor. He arrowed up the music volume to cover the outside noise and levered back his chair to rest a while longer. Another message from Robin arrived on his screen. "So are you ready to start work on DASHER? TOMORROW?!? ::))"

Birch shook his head and reached forward to type his response. "I wish we could do something less violent."

Fifteen seconds later Robin sent back: "YOU'RE NOT THE ONLY GENIUS IN THE VALLEY BIRCH!" Then another twenty seconds after that: "If you think you can DICTATE POLICY to this company, YOU are SO WRONG!! :((("

Birch leaned back and closed his eyes again, feeling the familiar tension and pain in his chest like a heavy stone. He was amazed at how the stress could dull his thoughts to the point where they seemed like rocks tumbling away from him down a slope.

Birch heard and felt the palms of two hands attach themselves like suction cups to the curved door to his harbor, and knew it would be Robin wanting to apologize in person. The door began to slide open, hissing like a purging airlock as the composite surface slid between two felt liners into the wall cavity. The sound of general commotion slopped in from the main room. Robin's salt-and-pepper crewcut accompanied his ruddy face through the door, then his pink tie swung through the gap into Birch's work space.

"You know I didn't mean that. Right?" Robin smiled to show professionally whitened teeth, his eyes darting and flashing with fear. Birch could smell M&M's and some ghastly energy drink on Robin's breath. He saw people milling around outside past the margin of his doorway and the edge of Robin's linen jacket. He pulled his attention back to watch Robin's eyes twitch nervously in their sockets.

Birch nodded once, then turned to his computer screen and pulled his long blond hair back into a ponytail, securing it with an elastic hair tie he took from his wrist. "Of course,

Robin," he said.

"Good. Well," Robin continued, "this is a big day for Zongo Inc. Let's relax a little."

Robin removed himself from Birch's doorway and shouted to the room at large, "HEY, someone want to order some FOOD for chrissake?"

"Party!" voices shouted from the far end of the room, and a migration of employees surged through the desks and cubicles.

Birch got up from his chair and stepped out of his harbor. People clapped and smiled at him. He smiled back. Some of the senior coders on the opposite side of the room had their harbor doors open and were sitting in their chairs, each dangling a leg into the room, jawing with others sitting at stations among the open desks. They stopped when Birch emerged, looked his way and waved. Melanie gave him a nod and a fist pump. A couple of the interns drifted through his path: "Hi," he said as he walked by. "Hi Birch," they said back, and looked at each other.

Birch went first to Lars' desk. "Thanks Birch," Lars said, rising and shaking his hand. "Easy approval."

"Hey Lars," Birch said, and smiled. "Yeah. I liked working with your stuff. It was good. You made my job easy." Lars beamed and nodded.

A man and two women from marketing came over to them. One of the women wore jeans and a white blouse, the other a silk suit. The man, a forty-something with a brown bowl cut, wore expensive blue jeans and a black turtleneck with the sleeves pushed up. "Congratulations, Birch," he said. "Great job, you guys. This should be big, a real paradigm shift for our stakeholder engagement and synergized narrative immersion!"

The group looked at him for a beat. While the guy prattled on about alignment to core values and agile KPI optimization, the woman in the white blouse turned and said, "Yeah, great work. We're going to rule the marketplace with this one. Check out the blog comments piling up from the beta players already, and they haven't even seen Birch's latest deploy."

Robin hovered behind the marketing people, then tapped the woman in the suit on the shoulder. They walked off together.

Birch peeked into Melanie's harbor and saw a scale model of a white '66 Ford Mustang convertible with red interior on her desk. He hadn't seen that before. The sight of it triggered an image of a white mustang of the horse variety, hooves flying over rock, mane and tail whipping in the wind, nostrils flaring. "Hey Melanie," Birch said. "You into Mustangs now?" It was a baited question. He knew she drove a pimped-out Mini Cooper and loved it with a passion.

He watched her eyes glint back at him through her wire aviators. Birch and his former roommate from Berkeley, Angel, had written software that, by definition, were viruses. They designed them to copy themselves from server to server across a network, but always remove the previous copy, so they would never accumulate like a true virus. They came up with their own term for the digital creatures, calling them mustangs. They wrote them as pranks for fun and to see what they could do, never intending them to do significant damage. Their mustangs roamed undetected around the internet, gathering information and then returning home. They wrote them to masquerade as processes normally found running on busy servers so that administrators wouldn't easily notice them. A mustang would target a host server, explore it from the outside to determine its environment and security, and if the server was vulnerable put on the appropriate cloak and go in, installing itself on the new host before erasing itself from its previous host. Birch and Angel were careful to keep their mustangs light and quiet. They didn't want a mustang to slow a server down by eating up too much CPU or by stealing too much memory. What they were after was amusement and mental exercise, to see how far they could take mustang evolution. They'd gotten them to the point where they could learn and adapt, essentially rewrite themselves as they roamed.

What Birch and Angel were doing was strictly illegal, and if a mustang were ever caught and traced back to the originators, they would make the headlines and wind up spending years in jail. After all, federal prosecutors sent Andrew Auernheimer away for four years just for hacking one of AT&T's unprotected URLs. If the legal system could find Auernheimer the guilty party for stepping through a wide-open door—instead of AT&T the guilty party for leaving it wide open in the first place—then what would they do with Birch's and Angel's mustangs? The very thought, every time it occurred to him, punched Birch in the gut like fresh news of a death in the family. Releasing something onto the net was not something you could undo, but so far they'd been lucky; their mustangs had roamed through countless university systems, military and government systems, corporate networks and foreign networks undetected, at least as far as they were aware.

Because of the high risk of getting caught, Angel had stopped writing them when he went to work for the national lab in Los Alamos. And while Birch had reviewed mustang code plenty of times at home while thinking about his autonomous game characters, he'd not written a new mustang since the last one he'd created with Angel. The possibility that one had been discovered somewhere, however, always lurked below the surface of Birch's consciousness, spooking him every time he heard of a hacker getting arrested.

Birch wondered about Melanie, if somehow she knew about them. She was sharp. She didn't say much, but watched the world with a wry smile. She wrote excellent code. Maybe she'd snagged one of their old mustangs somehow, deconstructed it and recognized Birch's style. She'd certainly reviewed thousands of lines of his code over the past months.

Melanie laughed. "Yeah," she said. "I like Mustangs." Her green eyes caught his and he felt the heat of worry begin at the back of his neck. He turned his eyes away and reached back to adjust his ponytail.

He also worried about Robin. When he'd first joined the company, it seemed to him that Robin immediately acted as if he "had something" on Birch. He'd never experienced that before. Robin was constantly claiming that he had friends in high, unassailable places who could do anything to anyone with impunity. Birch saw Robin use that to threaten some people, but not others. Birch experienced it directly when he was new, but Robin backed off once he saw that Birch was creating valuable self-learning game characters. Now Birch watched Robin treat others to that psychological violence, which he began to see as only a ruse of Robin's ego. But you never know for sure, until you know.

"Food's here!" someone called out from the center of the room.

Caterers unpacked recycled-paper plates and plant-starch utensils onto the round tables in the open meeting area. Employees emerged from cubicles, harbors, and programming tables to drift toward the area, following the steamy scents of curried chicken, samosa, and palak paneer wafting from freshly opened containers.

Birch, Melanie, and the other engineers joined the herd, browsing the tables and filling plates. Birch wondered if Robin would try to "optimize" the food experience by gathering them up to toss out some rah-rah while they stood there with bits of fried dough and spiced potato falling from their lips. He filled a plate with three samosas and a dollop of Hari Chutney, picked up a cup of iced green tea, and looked for Melanie. She, Lars, and five other coders had settled themselves at a round table at the edge of the meeting area, so Birch joined them and half-listened to their talk about frameworks, open source projects, and working at various companies up and down the West Coast. He took a bite of a samosa and peered inside, imagining the cells that composed the potato fragments, the spices and oils, then the molecules, then the atoms. He took a long whiff of the warm, humid air floating up from the crater he'd bitten into the side of the Indian dumpling and imagined the scent particles and vapor droplets rising to his nose. *Billions of them,* he thought, *trillions of molecules, and in each of those, form, energy, intelligence.*

He took another bite and imagined the collection of intelligence sitting on his plate. *The same natural law exists in each of these vapor droplets as in this whole building, the planet, the universe.* He recalled things Angel had said while part of a team working with organic logic gates and molecular computers at the national lab. Theoretically, Birch's half-eaten plate of samosas contained more raw computing power than was currently used in all of the equipment running in northern California, if only humanity had the knowledge and talent to organize and use it. *What would we be like if we could harness that much computational power? What if we could draft the DNA molecules in these potato bits to function as usable storage? What would life become?*

Birch imagined the new levels of thinking that would become possible, the collective intelligence, the global problems that would become solvable. He closed his eyes and rubbed the center of his forehead.

"Birch," someone was saying. "Hey, Birch."

He opened his eyes. "Yes?"

It was one of the new junior engineers, a fellow with a brown beard, black-framed glasses, and a hopeful look on his face. He was asking him what he thought of a JavaScript framework. The others were looking at Birch.

"Oh," Birch said. "I haven't worked with that one much yet. If there's a project with it, I'm happy to try it out."

The other coders went back to chatting. Birch didn't want to talk about that stuff. He sipped his tea and mused about software that would enable nanobots to build things from carbon molecules harvested from the environment.

The phone in Birch's pants pocket buzzed. He took it out and looked at it. A Slack message from Robin: "We need U my office."

The stone in his chest dropped into his gut. What did Robin want now? Birch was always afraid that Robin, or one of his "friends in high places," had come across one of their mustangs somehow. That would be terrifying. Birch had seen Robin try to own people plenty of times, and more than a few lines of code pioneered in mustang form had wound up deployed in *Zongo Bongo*, mostly in the learning modules. Birch thought he and Angel had been careful, but with a few years of perspective out of college, he also realized that they'd held a pretty high opinion of their abilities at the time.

Another chat: "Jeremy + Scott R here."

Ahh. Robin had the venture capitalists there and, Birch was sure, wanted to beat some dead horses. He slid the phone back into his pocket and sat for a moment before getting up with his plate and cup.

"Where are you off to?" Melanie asked.

"Robin and the VCs," Birch said softly.

Melanie sighed. "Sorry."

Birch tossed his plate and cup into a recycling bin, then went to his harbor, slid open the door and leaned in without fully entering. He watched the fractals grow and fade on his screensaver. He didn't have anything particular he wanted to do there other than feel the darkness and quiet. He slid the door closed and walked along the far edge of the development floor, past the party in the meeting area and down a long corridor lined on both sides by tall windows and sliding glass doors leading out to alternately sunny stone gardens or shaded moss gardens with waterfalls and redwood benches.

At the end of the corridor he turned down a hall of office doors and walked through the last doorway without knocking. He entered a large, glass-walled office with grass rugs and mahogany furniture. Robin looked up from his desk and the two venture capitalists got up from their chairs. One was a fit man in his thirties, wearing a black suit and purple silk tie. The other man was slightly pudgy, with gray around his ears. He wore a cashmere sweater and gray silk slacks. The woman in the suit from marketing remained in her chair in front of the desk, but turned and smiled at him as he entered the room.

"Birch!" the older man said, and extended his hand. The younger man patted him on the back. "Nice work getting Bongo ready today!"

"Hi guys," Birch said.

Robin got up from behind his desk and led them to a large coffee table circled by a couch and four suede chairs. Birch and Robin took the couch while the others each took a chair.

"Carolyn thinks it's going to be vital to follow Bongo pretty closely with Dasher, Birch," Robin said, then cleared his throat. "And, obviously, the engineering team won't get it done on the schedule we need without you taking the lead."

Birch knew this. He also understood that subscription sales of Dasher would be much higher if Bongo was as popular as they'd projected, and if Dasher came out while Bongo still had the buzz. Birch's problem was that the designers had made Dasher even more violent than Bongo. It was to be a shooter/slasher with both modern and medieval weapon play, which Birch didn't favor, but beyond that it featured male and female warriors that could gang up and tear each other to pieces. The graphics he'd seen so far were astonishing, the resolution shocking, the design the best, but the concept and the potential game situations sickened him.

One of the early storyboards showed two warrior thugs decked out in full leather and spikes on either side of a shapely female warrior wearing rags and a few leather straps, pulling her arms and legs and tearing her open at the pelvis. The artists had done an amazing job. The detail singed the ends of Birch's nerves. They even showed a peek of intestine and a thicker organ he thought was her uterus where her belly skin was ripped. Birch was shocked into staring at it, like at a traffic accident, and felt a ball of leaden sorrow in his stomach. He felt the tearing nerve fibers in her skin as if it were his own memory, brought to the surface from a long past darkness.

There were her guts, the center of emotion, the second brain that makes us fully human, being desecrated with no sense of remorse, brutalized for sick entertainment and profit. Cold stones of self hatred, fear of Robin, and a feeling of defeat by whatever allowed a group of people to enthusiastically produce something like this video game weighed inside him.

An old demon haunted him the night he first saw the story boards. Since he was thirteen he'd had a recurring nightmare of a black-haired woman pursued across a dark, grassy landscape, caught from behind by a soldier in a blue uniform and a couple of cowboys. They held her down and thumped their fists into her, sick, muffled sounds punctuated by her staccato shrieks. The soldier unsheathed a knife and ripped through the fabric of her dress, while one of the cowboys yanked away her shawl and tore off a beaded belt at her waist. One by one they put their dusty bodies on top of hers. In the dream Birch was a teenager watching from behind a short rise on the plain. The men didn't know he was there. He wanted to get up and run at them, rescue the woman, punish the men, kill them, but he lay paralyzed in the tall grass, fear and darkness holding him down as if under a stifling weight. The woman let out one more longer shriek when the man with the knife got up on his knees, drew his elbow back and repeatedly plunged the blade into her belly. Birch had shocked awake then, back in his condo in California, no longer a teenager hidden somewhere on the dark plains, but he knew the kid's fear deep in his cells. The pain was real and present, carrying with it the terrifying echo of memory.

That was weeks ago, but Birch had realized then that he couldn't be a part of any more projects like Bongo or Dasher.

"That's right. The release date is going to be super important on this one," Carolyn said.

"And," the guy in the suit added, "we think with Dasher and Bongo both strong in the marketplace, we'll get significant interest from Microsoft and Sony. Could be a bidding war. We don't want to mess this up."

Birch pulled his lips into his mouth and reached back to hold his ponytail with both hands. They all watched him. He looked at the ceiling, fighting off feral shadows and heat flashes from the nightmare. *Ignorant parents will buy this game for their kids, legions of growing humans taught to hate and devalue each other with maximum skill and violence, but without any sense of consequence.*

"Can we make any changes to the game content?" Birch asked. He'd asked this question no fewer than twenty times over the past three weeks.

They all looked at each other, wondering who would take it this time. Robin rubbed his hands together and looked at the floor, gritting his teeth. "We've been across that plain. I don't think we can do that," Carolyn finally said. "The research is too clear." Birch turned toward Robin. Robin didn't look up.

"Microsoft and Sony, Birch," the guy in the suit said.

The stones hung heavy in his chest. These people were just doing what they knew how to do to make money. They didn't wake up today, or any day, and wish to hurt anyone. They were part of a system that relied on money and profit as its prime imperatives. He saw their eyes watching him, wondering.

Birch sighed. "Okay, let me sleep on it," he said.

That broke the tension in the room. They were relieved that he didn't say "no." The man in the sweater stood up. "Okay, Birch. Take your time. Tomorrow's fine. We really need you on this, but we want you to be on board with it, not halfway."

Back in the glass corridor, Birch stopped to watch a man and a teenaged boy working in one of the moss gardens. They wore shorts and sweat-stained t-shirts from a landscaping company. Birch stood with his hands on the glass and watched them use hand clippers to trim the moss borders. He could see them talking to each other, but he couldn't hear anything through the thick glass. They wore peaceful expressions, every now and then pausing to wipe a brow or look up at the sky. The man said something, and the boy laughed.

He knew that he was energy, that the glass was energy, and the garden, the clippers, the man and the boy, the air, the trickling water in the electric impeller-driven waterfall. They all were ripples in a sea of energy, organized tendencies among particles, waves and charges. He should be able to hear them through his hands flat on the glass, absorb and decode their thoughts. He should have access to the patterns of information that composed them, like data over a wireless network, but he felt the barrier of his own ignorance, a wall of separation through which only the coarsest chunks of information could pass. He felt like an animal in a glass cage whose senses have been dulled by long captivity. *This is not how it's supposed to be,* he thought.

"Birch?"

He turned to find Banni Sharma looking up at him. A tiny grain of crystal glinted from the side of her nose. Banni was his favorite among the current interns. She was a senior at Stanford, interning at Zongo to learn project management. Though five years younger than he, Birch found Banni more mature than some of the full-time staff. She maintained unusually long eye contact, listening deeply when in conversation. She hung with the pack, but seemed to have an extra measure of ambition and inspiration. He was impressed by her work.

She watched him from deep brown eyes.

"Hey Banni."

"Hi."

"What's up?"

"Well, I'm doing feasibility research for Dale and the story team for some forks in Dasher, and I need to talk with you about it, to determine if some of the features they are considering are, you know, possible."

He looked at her, exhaled. "I'm going home early today, and possibly working from home tomorrow. Do you think Melanie, or maybe Jayvon or Lars, could help you with that?" His eyes danced quickly to the coffee skin of her throat, back to her eyes.

She dropped her eyes to his sandals, his linen chinos, up to his hemp hoodie, before returning to his face. "Dale said it has to be you, and she needs it done by tomorrow. Robin told her so, apparently."

Birch could see her bracing for disappointment and frustration. If he said no, there would be nothing she could do except complain to a higher up. It was the same look his mother gave him when he'd failed to observe some manner or other as a kid, or if he let it be known that he found the lessons of Sunday School illogical, allegorical, or anything other than the literal truth. It was a look that tried hard not to reveal itself, but by that effort affected him even more.

"Seriously? She only gave you one day to do this? How many features are we talking about?" He would feel phony talking about the specs for Dasher. He needed another day just to think about it himself. He reached back with both hands and adjusted the band holding his ponytail. Banni unconsciously mirrored his gesture, gathering up her long, straight black hair for a second, hands then sliding down the back of her neck to drop at her sides.

"I could come to your condo," Banni blurted. She cleared her throat. "I mean, not to invite myself, but, if it's okay. I wouldn't take much time, and I can call Gina to come get me when we're done."

"You don't have a car?" Birch asked, noting she somehow knew that he had a condo. She shook her head.

Part of him wanted to sit alone at home and think. If he took Banni back to his place, he wouldn't get much thinking done. She twisted on her spine with her hands clasped in front. He worried that he was taking too long to answer.

"Okay," he said. "See you in the parking lot in five?"

"Okay, great, thank you." She smiled and nodded, then hurried off down the corridor to retrieve her laptop and knapsack.

Birch went out to sit in his Subaru and wait for her.

Robin had had the groundskeepers mark out a special parking space for Birch with low shrubs and fronted by a paper birch sapling. Robin had thought the idea cute, but the tree wasn't thrilled about the climate—or about having a one and a half ton car sitting over its roots all day. It wasn't thriving.

Banni walked out through the front door into the sunshine and slipped dark glasses over her eyes. Birch could see a few of the interns watching from the second landing of the yellow-painted metal stairs snaking up the inside of the glass building. He popped the passenger door and she climbed in, setting her knapsack at her feet.

"I can put that in the back for you," he said.

"No, it's fine," she said.

As they drove, he could see her in his periphery checking out the interior of the Subaru. It was a brand new STI he'd bought for cash, a bonus Robin gave him after his game characters made such an impact on the VCs. He'd given the car a stage-three tune and after-market exhaust, savoring the throaty roar and visceral boost in those rare occasions when he wasn't in thick traffic.

"After Dasher, this will probably be a Maserati or something," Banni joked.

"I don't know," Birch said.

He watched the streets and she watched the houses and condo developments go by.

They pulled into his garage, the garage door closing behind them. Inside the condo, Birch said, "Put your stuff down anywhere you like. Make yourself at home." He went to the kitchen, grabbed two bottles of mineral water from the refrigerator and poured them into glasses, cutting a lemon slice into each. He carried the glasses back into the living room, where Banni was looking at the stereo equipment.

Birch took one end of a mission couch. Banni took the other end and sipped her mineral water. She exhaled deeply and appeared to be searching for something to say.

I suppose we'll have to talk about that wretched computer

game at some point, he thought.

He imagined her naked and sliding her body over his, immediately feeling inappropriate and then itchy. Thoughts of Robin invaded his consciousness, and the stress stone took all his wind away, ruining his flash fantasy about Banni.

"Do we really have to talk about Dasher?" he asked. "I'm not even sure I'm going to work on that project. I'd rather play tic-tac-toe." He drew an imaginary tic-tac-toe board on the couch cushion between them and put an "x" in one corner.

Banni looked him in the eye and frowned. "What do you mean you're not sure you'll work on Dasher?" Then she reached out her finger and drew an "o" in the opposite corner. They played the game to a draw, each noting that the other kept perfect track of the invisible board. Banni drew another board. They played to another tie, then to five more, throwing moves down with increasing speed. Finally, during the eighth game, Banni drew a line down one side and yelled, "Ha! Now you have to work on Dasher!"

Birch leaned back and smiled uneasily. He felt untethered and confused.

"I can't," he said. "It's too violent." At the sound of his own words he felt stupid and inept for bringing her here, for wasting her time in this way. He saw her eyes darken like planets in deep space whose star just went cold and blinked out. He imagined she had contemplated making love with him and thought he should test for signs, but figured that ship had already sailed. He felt overwhelmed and embarrassed by his own presumptuousness.

"Banni, I'm so sorry for wasting your time like this. I'm being an ass."

She reached toward him, saying, "No. I asked to come here. I'm the one wasting your time."

"No. Look. I need to get you back to the office. I'm so sorry."

Banni was quiet during the drive in, and Birch thought about her research project for Dale. "I don't know what all is on your list, but I do know this: fortunately, or unfortunately, it'll all be possible. You might as well report that to Dale," he said.

"You sure you won't work on Dasher?" she asked.

He guided the car through traffic and pulled up to a red light.

"If I could learn how to build a stronger autonoetic intelligence into the game characters, I would do Dasher," he said. He glanced at her and could tell he'd lost her. "Here's what's got me concerned," he continued. "I've created these electronic copies of humans, terribly incomplete but which can be infinitely replicated. Human players stick their minds and awareness into these game characters for hours at a time, repeatedly over long periods. And these characters don't have any facility to be able to care about anything. They look like humans, they move like humans, sound like humans, I *think* they remember something like humans and even reason a bit like humans, but they don't care like humans. I'm worried that I'm contributing to this sea change in humanity's diminishing ability to care. It feels like erosion on a mass scale. Hard to see without altitude, but happening just about everywhere around us. I also think more people are going to be playing these games with VR rigs. The immersion is just going to make it worse."

Birch glanced at Banni again as they accelerated from the stop light. She frowned, staring through the windshield with her lips bunched.

He turned the Subaru into the drive at Zongo Inc., steering past a row of shining SUVs and sports cars at the edge of the lot. He rolled past the last cement wheel block and headed over the grass toward his spot in front of the building. He saw the birch sapling, the low shrubs and irrigated green grass. He saw where his wheels had left ruts and killed the grass between the shrubs—yellow and brown blades squashed into the dirt in two long parallel patches. He stopped short of the space to let Banni out.

"Thanks, Birch," she said. "I'll tell Dale that what she wants is feasible." She hoisted her rucksack and laptop case and got out of the car.

Birch looked again at the blades of grass he'd killed with his tires and saw in each one his own lack of care. Each blade was an email he'd never bothered to return, a person standing in line somewhere he didn't acknowledge. Each blade was another person on the freeway driving back and forth like a pendulum, most of them keeping time to an existence they barely bothered to think about, much less understand. Each blade was that woman warrior being torn apart in the storyboards for Dasher. There were too many of them. He couldn't see the order. He could only see the mash of blades, crushed and torn, empty of life, flattened husks of dead cells.

He put the car in reverse and headed back out to the road. His unconscious guided the car toward his condo while his upper mind still worked on decoding the flattened grass. The grill of a tall red pickup truck appeared in his rear-view mirror and stayed there along El Camino Real, spreading the truck company logo larger in his mirror at each stop light. Birch paid it no particular interest, as impatient tailgaters were the norm on these streets. Finally, the driver of the truck found space in the lane beside him and pulled up next to his car, passenger window rolled down. "Hey IDIOT!" the guy hollered. He sported a shaved head and wrap-around dark glasses, the arms of which pressed into the pink flesh at his temples. He directed a thick finger toward Birch. "We don't have all goddamn day for a nice drive! Why don't you get a MOVE ON and stop holding people up, ASSHOLE!" With that he squealed his rear wheels to speed away, but then had to slam on his brakes and skid as the car in front of him decided to stop for a yellow light.

The heat in Birch's neck was instant. He had a flash fantasy of chasing the guy down, smoking that stupid truck with his STI, bumping the dude's fat head while dragging him out of the driver's-side door and pounding the sides of that shiny bald melon with his fists. Birch pulled up and glanced over to see that the guy had rolled his window up and was angrily slapping at his steering wheel. The guy saw Birch looking his way and stuck his middle finger up in the passenger window, keeping it there as the light switched green. Birch turned off at the next corner to take an alternate route home. He felt the after-burn of road rage like a virus invading his bloodstream as he pulled into his garage.

He went to sit in a folding chair on his backyard deck between two potted orange trees and stared at the sunny blur that was his tiny, private, fenced back yard. He closed his eyes and swung back at the disturbing thought that fear was winning over love. He imagined the generations of people moving like herds westward from all corners of the country, the world, streaming here to make a better life, competing with each other at every step, building their toughness and savvy to be ever more effective in the grab for resources. The climb and clamor over each other to get to—what? Peace? Security? Longer life? More people? He saw the population growing, the spaces shrinking, the heat and pressure building, the fear, anger, and mistrust compressing, becoming ubiquitous and dense, culminating in this hostile in-your-face road rage. That guy in the truck might have gotten to his destination half a minute sooner if he'd been able to speed the way he wanted, and somehow he equated that with status, a better position to sustain himself, or better to procreate. But he failed to factor in the stop lights and other structures the culture had built up around him. *Why don't people do the math?*

Birch opened his eyes and stared at the grass in his yard. He let out a long breath. *I wonder what Angel is up to.* It seemed like forever since they'd spoken. They'd been in touch regularly after graduation, video chatting at least every week, swapping notes on their first jobs, helping each other with code ideas, and even managing to arrange hikes and camping trips on a few occasions, but that sturdy cadence of contact began to loosen and unravel as they became more absorbed in work, job changes, and the accumulating details of daily life over the following few years.

Birch felt a pang of worry that time was busy rolling along while he wasn't paying attention, and he was losing touch with what really mattered. He pulled his phone from his pocket and opened his Telegram app. Angel's user was at the top of his chat list, as they'd exchanged comments on some tech news four weeks ago, and other than pinging Angel now and then, Birch didn't much open the app. He tapped Angel and typed "hey man I need a ketchup when you have time" and sent it. He closed the app and put the phone back in his pocket.

He closed his eyes again and sat imagining what he'd feel like if he no longer had his job. Finding a new one would likely not be difficult given his circumstances, but finding a better one was always a gamble. He'd miss most of his co-workers. Money wasn't an issue at present. *What if I got out of software, or at least out of games?* And, he felt strange about Robin, like he could be one of those things that unexpectedly ruins your life somehow, or ends it. Robin was that thing that at first seems so shiny and bright, but you soon understand has a dark core, a darkness that you can not measure, one that causes you to gaslight yourself, to wonder if you were paranoid, or if it would be stupid not to be afraid of what he might do.

Ten minutes later his pocket buzzed. It was Angel's reply. "yo still at work lets roscoe at 7 your time".

Just that much was enough to lift Birch's spirits. He pushed up from the chair and walked the perimeter of the tiny yard repeatedly, checking his phone for the time, eager for the afternoon to pass into evening. After a few circuits he realized that he was pacing and would be silly to wear a path into his lawn for the next four hours, so he diverted back over the deck and in through the sliding door.

He felt momentary pressure to open his work laptop, start the VPN, and check Slack, but his mind and body were in the wrong gear. He rationalized it away and told himself that his work for the day was done.

Instead he surfed for cajun chicken recipes on his phone

while sprawled on the living room couch and when he found one moved to the kitchen where he attempted to speed up time by dramatically slowing his own motions as he went through his dinner preparations.

He finished eating and cleaned up right about time to talk with Angel.

He went into the spare bedroom where his work station sat on an old scratched up wooden desk that his father had used as a boy growing up in Colorado Springs.

He woke the computer and launched an app from his desktop that he and Angel had built for fun and decided to maintain on one of Angel's cloud servers since it worked as well as any other video chat app they'd used.

His image filled one of two video windows while he waited for Angel, and he sat watching himself inspect his own face. The man he looked at appeared tired, the narrow jaw he used to see a little thicker, the blonde stubble a little ragged, a wrinkled knot between his eyebrows where he'd never noticed one before. He lifted his brows and moved his jaw to smooth it out. Faint creases remained. "Why are YOU so worried?" He said. "What do you see from there? You don't even have to breathe, or sleep, or worry about your heart not beating." He turned his head from side to side, keeping his eyes on the screen, checking the length of his ponytail. "What good is all this money I'm making if I can't be you?"

The blank window next to his brightened, and then Angel's round face and thick black curly mane resolved, taking up most of the rectangle. "Hey man! Long time!"

"Hey buddy! What's going on down there in New Mexico?" *Okay, Angel looks a touch older too, still one big smile though.*

"Funny you should ask," Angel said. "You must have caught a synapse on the collective mind. I'm starting a new job next week. Quasi private sector. Might even be making damn near as much as you now."

"Damn! Congrats! Got tired of working for the gov

mint?"

"Government contractor this time. I'll be leading a team coding for a military system. Recruiters came right into NatLab and scooped me up with one other guy. Like, here's what we want you to do, and obviously you will accept our offer."

"Huh. Do you know what you'll be building yet?"

"Sort of, not really. The security is uber tight. They're actually kind of weird about it. The money is sick though, so sick that when I heard, I was scared not to take it, like, I don't want whatever this shit is going on without me knowing about it." Angel laughed. Birch noticed that his normal spark dimmed for a microsecond.

"Well, damn! I hope it turns out well for you."

"Hey Birchy," a woman's voice came through the speakers, and Angel leaned to the side, saying "Here's Winnie." Angel's girlfriend appeared in the rectangle pushing her bright dimpled face in next to Angel. The sight of her short, sandy hair, hazel eyes, and the soft sound of her voice gave Birch an oxytocin hit.

"Oh my god you look great!" She said. "How ARE you?"

"Good, good."

"How's your mom and dad?"

"Oh, good. Same ole same ole, both still teaching at City College, doing great."

"How's you sister?"

"June's a senior this year. Graduating with a degree in education, following in Mom and Dad's footsteps."

"Oh that's great! Good for her. So, are you dating any of those interns at your work?"

Birch laughed and looked off camera for a beat. "Umm, nah."

"Well find yourself a nice girlfriend, Birch. You deserve it. It's so great to see you!"

Angel slid back into the center of the rectangle. "Well, hey, buddy. You said you needed to catch up. What's going on in your world?"

"I'm considering a possible career move too," Birch said. Angel raised his eyebrows. "No idea where I'm headed yet, but I'm starting to have nightmares about what I'm building. It's eating at me too much."

Angel cocked his head and squinted. "Really. I thought you were having fun over there. And you were making north of three hundred right?"

"Yeah, it's nothing about the money, and I like most of the people I work with, good coders, good team, plenty of challenge. I just think it's making me sick, the game violence, way intense."

"You can't carve that off and leave it at work? Is it that recurring nightmare you used to have?"

"That, yeah. Feels like my breathing stops and I can't start it again. And. I don't know if I'm just being paranoid, but I want to take your pulse on something."

Angel waited. Birch looked down and then back up.

"So, Turcek, the CEO." Birch looked off to the corner of the ceiling.

"Yeah?"

"I don't know. It's like he holds you hostage, in a way. He's nasty, super rough on some people. Not on me, currently, he used to be when I started. But, he jokes about having had people killed, and then makes it like he's not joking, and then gets all chummy. It's weird. Super cringe. I don't know."

Angel mashed his lips under his nose. "He openly threaten anyone?"

"He's good at plausible deniability. Makes it sound like he's saying something else, but you know what he means."

"You don't think he's just a blowhard? Probably a malignant narcissist."

"I don't know. He's got money. He acts like he can do whatever he wants. He thinks he owns people. He probably is a narcissist, psychopath too, likely. I'm scared to stay and scared to leave."

"Chances are it's all a show. But, I would endorse your leaving that place. You should be able to find something good."

Birch imagined leaving, caught in the collisions of too many competing thoughts, no space left for him to say anything.

Angel continued, "but, yeah, definitely keep your wits. If he tried something, obviously, have him arrested."

"Yeah," Birch said, "I have to figure out how to safely leave."

"Speaking of weirdos," Angel said, "the background check for this contractor role was over the top. I never even heard of anything like it, way more than for the national lab. They were asking me detailed questions about stuff I'd forgotten, and their device security policy, comms security policy, everything, nuts. So I may be hard to reach for a while. I'm expecting a very tight leash. Probably have to nuke the Roscoe server, definitely have to wipe the mustang repo. They knew about the existence of both of them and were asking me about what's on them."

"Shit, dude. You don't think they found any mustangs do you? What would that look like?"

"That would be worse than bad," Angel said. "I'm thinking they haven't run across any, otherwise they never would have talked to me. I'm not sure we still have any roaming around out there do we?"

"I think we were pretty careful, but, I mean, it IS possible. Server gets powered down, then powered back up after long enough."

"Texting, chatting, all my email accounts. They had the full list, but I don't think they pulled content, but seems like they could. I sort of want to come up with a test for that."

"What about your mom?"

"I told her about it. I think sanitized phone calls are probably okay, but mostly I said I'd visit her more often. El Paso isn't too far. But you and I, we'd have to talk in code on a phone call. I don't trust them not to snoop. In fact, I'm not a hundred percent sure they haven't found the socket for this video right now. They aren't supposed to do that, but I don't trust them."

"Huh." Birch pondered this. "How's Winnie with all of this?"

Winnie's voice piped in, sounding like it was coming from a room away, "I think he knows what he's doing, Birchy."

"Let's hope so anyway," Angel said.

"Well," Birch spoke slowly, his thoughts still churning, trying to imagine solutions to their dilemma between each word, "I'd say I'll keep you posted, and you do the same, but I'm not sure exactly how we'll do that if you are going radio silent, and I'm going who knows where."

"I tell you what." Angel paused to get it straight in his mind, closed his eyes, and then spoke slowly and methodically. "Mustangs, Klondike, server-less, temporary prefer unwitting host couriers, mime-cloaked fingerprint, local origin, preferably dedicated machine, same door out, same door back. Path stays encrypted in Klondike. Return is triggered by message status. Good?"

Birch ran it back and forth in his mind a couple times and repeated it back to Angel. It was like a reverse flea-flicker called on fourth down. "I love it! My god it's good to hear your voice and see your face! Okay. Be careful out there, and please be well my brother."

"You as well. I love you man. Nuking the server right after we're off here."

They looked at each other's image for another beat and then exited the app.

The contact with Angel and Winnie left Birch feeling like he'd gained a couple life points, a little better supplied and encouraged to make a decision.

If I can't figure out how to write the code so that love learns how to win over fear, I'd just be contributing to what all these other games are doing: codifying and normalizing the stuff of road rage.

2

Angel lifted his plastic badge, showing it to the uniformed woman in the security booth. After a long look, she nodded through the green glass and hit the buzzer. The first door slid open and disappeared into the block wall. Angel let his badge dangle from the lanyard around his neck. Stu put his hand on Angel's back to shepherd him through, the door shushing closed behind them as they walked along the corridor.

"You might as well give me that," Stu said. "You won't be needing it anymore. You'll love these new chips. Never have to worry about where your badge is. Good timing joining the team."

Angel lifted the lanyard from his neck and over his black curls, handing it to Stu. They arrived at the second door and stood in front of it. Stu glanced up at the camera ball and then at the door. "New system," he said as they waited. "Reading my chip. They'll get it speeded up. It's the face rec that's slowing it down I think. Look up at the ball, would you?"

Angel glanced up, and the door slid open. Stu put his hand on Angel's back again and they walked through. The hallway was wider and lit by LEDs. Closed doors lined each side. Men and women in military uniforms walked among others wearing white lab coats. Two men in gray suits and an army officer crossed the hall in front of them. One of the men looked at Stu and Angel and said, "Why hello, Stuart."

Stu gave him a two finger salute. "Alister."

They stopped at a door and Stu opened it for Angel. The

two entered a small, sparely equipped medical office. "Howdy Doc," Stu said. The doctor, who sat on a rolling stool, turned from his desk.

"Good morning, Stu. Hello, Mr. Oleastro. Come for your credentials I see."

Angel regarded the doctor and didn't say anything. He was not happy about the chip, had nearly refused the position because of it. He'd heard from colleagues that once injected, the chip would migrate—not far, but far enough to make it difficult to find and painful to remove should you not want it anymore. His curiosity about the project and the unusually high salary tipped the scale for him. The doctor motioned, and Angel settled in a chair next to the desk. Stu stood leaning back against the wall with his arms folded.

Angel had known Stu only ten minutes and already felt a growing dislike for him. He was one of those tall guys with a square jaw and fortunate looks who seemed to assume the world had been built for them. He'd already mentioned, twice, that he'd played tight end for Yale. Angel had always felt short and dumpy next to guys like that, which made him cranky.

The doctor retrieved a tiny glass vial with a scan code label on the side. He held the vial between his thumb and forefinger and passed the label in front of a laser scanner. The scanner beeped, and his computer woke and loaded a registration screen. He typed into the fields and moved to the next screen. "Your code, Stuart," he said. Stu leaned over, typed a password and pressed the enter key. Another screen loaded showing a progress bar with an antenna metaphor extending its signal toward the shape of a human. The progress bar completed its journey. The doctor picked up the vial and inspected it. It contained a clear liquid and one black speck the size of a large grain of sand. He put the vial down and retrieved a syringe from another box on the desk, tearing open the plastic wrapper before sinking the needle into the upturned vial cover. He held the vial and syringe close, watching as liquid and speck were sucked into the needle, then turned to

Angel and said, "Okay, Mr. Oleastro."

Angel bent his head to the side. The doctor rubbed an alcohol swab near the base of his neck, then stuck the needle into the moist spot. He pulled the needle out and tossed it into a safety bin, holding the swab over the spot on Angel's neck where he'd injected the chip. He applied pressure for a moment, then took his finger away to inspect the spot. "Good," he said. He turned to his computer and clicked a button with the mouse. They all watched the screen as the antenna metaphor reached for the human. A dialogue box appeared displaying "Oleastro, Angel" in the top line, an ID number next, and latitude and longitude data below. The box had a drill-down button that the doctor did not click. "Okay, we gotcha. Good to go," the doctor said. He patted Angel on the back.

"Excellent," Stu said. "Let's go, Oleastro."

They continued down the hallway. "So," Stu said, as his hand again found the center of Angel's back, "you will still get your paycheck from Uncle Sam, but you officially work for the company now. Let's go take a quick look at the production room before the meeting."

They walked through double doors at the end of the hall and turned right down another corridor where they entered an elevator that took them five levels below ground. Angel noted that the bank of buttons showed another five levels below that. The doors opened, and they stepped into a hallway sparsely populated compared to the one at ground level, just a couple of guys in lab coats talking outside a door. Stu led Angel to a door with an eight-inch square window of reinforced glass at eye level. He looked up at a camera ball above the door. A buzz-click sounded in the latch and he pushed the door open. Stu lifted a dimmer switch on the wall to bring up the LEDs. Six clusters of four work desks filled the long, windowless space. Each desk had a flat screen monitor and keyboard. Everything was white except for the black enameled desk legs and the blue plastic chair backs and cushions. A huge whiteboard covered each long wall. Blue markers lay capped on the trays. "Well, here it is," Stu said. *So there will be twenty-four of us,* Angel thought.

"Okay, meeting time," Stu said. "Let's go." He darkened the room and held the door for Angel. They took the elevator back up to ground level, traversed the corridor and went through another door, Angel crossing the threshold with Stu's hand again planted on his back. This room held a long conference table with high-back chairs, wooden paneling on the walls instead of whiteboards. A thick-jowled man in a gray suit sat at the end of the table, finishing a guffaw as he said, "This is the best thing we've come up with since discovering oil!" Angel noted the man's pink face. The laughter must be hard work for his heart. Angel thought he saw frosted lipstick or something on the guy, but realized it was just that his lips were bloodless. A couple of men in military uniforms and half a dozen in dark suits lined both sides of the table. Angel noted a small white cylinder on the table next to the man at the end. The cylinder had a transparent nose cap, like a personal oxygen bottle, hand-lettered words he couldn't make out written on masking tape running its length.

"Hello, Stuart," the pink-faced man said. Stu pulled a chair out for Angel and then went around the table to take the one across from him.

"Hello sir," Stu responded in a surprisingly full baritone.

The pink-faced man said, "So this is the guy who's going to get the drones all figured out for us? I didn't know these guys were into computer stuff."

"Yes, this is Angel Oleastro," Stu said. "We just brought him over from the national lab."

"Are you going to get him a lab coat so we know who the hell he is? I thought these guys were landscapers and shit," the man said.

Angel flinched. This wasn't the first time he'd sat in a meeting room full of white dudes, but he had not been openly disrespected for his ethnicity since his college days, and even then it was by those known to be arrogant and generally drunk. He suppressed a pang of alarm.

"The hardware guys wear the lab coats," one of the dark suits said.

"Oh," the pink-faced man said. "Why don't the programmers wear them too? How the hell are we supposed to know who they are?" He looked around the table.

"Angel's done exceptional work over at the national writing code for their super-computing program, and since then as one of the lead engineers for the nano program," Stu said.

The pink-faced man said, "Get him his binder."

Angel watched pink splotches move across the man's forehead, chased by pale patches. He wrinkled his brow and moved his cheeks as he spoke. Angel imagined the man's head stuffed with salsa and sour cream, then a giant thumb and finger descending from above to squeeze that puffy head like a carbuncle. One of the suits produced a black-covered binder and passed it down the table to him. "This is your security and secrecy directive," he said. "You'll need to be versed in these rules before you begin work on the project. Any breach, intentional or not, is grounds for prosecution."

Angel opened the binder and thumbed through the stack. There were 200 pages of black type in block paragraphs in sections and subsections, appearing to contain an epic list of detailed thou shalts and shalt nots. He'd seen plenty of such documents in his time with the government, but none to this extent. He scanned the table of contents as the suit continued speaking.

"Turn to the back page, and you'll find the signature lines. Please sign and date in the spaces indicated by the tabs." Angel glanced at the man and flipped to the back page. Stu smiled and slid a pen across the table to him.

Angel picked it up hesitantly. "Do you want me to read it before I sign?" he asked, looking around the table.

The speaking man paused and regarded the pink-faced man. The pink-faced man said nothing, but some whitish patches drifted across his forehead, red darkening around his cheek bones. The speaking man turned back to Angel, who could see that he'd somehow confused the process. Finally, the man resumed, "You'll have time to read it later. We're still hiring the rest of the engineers. We need your signature now. It's required before any further discussion about the project."

Angel looked more closely at the signature page. By signing, he was agreeing to the contents of the binder, to its two hundred pages of this's and that's. Its convoluted, nested parade of provisions and prohibitions and requirements, by and large and hereinafter under penalty of law of these United States and the great state of New Mexico, etc. etc. and so on and so forth. *Really,* Angel thought. He drummed the pen on the paper a couple times. It was a heavy pen. This was no public school pen, not even a government service-grade pen. You wouldn't see a pen like this walking around with the census or filling out an intake form for veterans' benefits. This was the pen of a group of people who expected to make a fuckload of money at something and didn't intend to suffer trivial distractions or bothersome scrutiny while they did so.

Meh, Angel thought. *By signing this thing, I'm only moving an antique line-making apparatus around on pressed and bleached wood pulp. This line of ink, perhaps eighteen centimeters long were I to stretch it out straight, adds nothing of value to this document, creates nothing that exists apart from the ink particles on the pulp. These are the kind of people who do what they want regardless, so while this line of ink I am about to draw might make them feel slightly better or somehow justified about what they may eventually do, it certainly won't change any real outcomes.*

He uncapped the pen, looped "Angel Oleastro" onto and around the signature line and then dated it. The mood in the room seemed to lighten. Angel capped the pen and slid it back to Stu.

"Okay, then," the man who did most of the talking said. "You will be reporting directly to Stuart. Stuart has the requirements for the system we need and will brief you on them. We expect to have the remaining programmers hired by the end of this week, so…I guess we're ready to roll."

"Excuse me," Angel interjected. "These programmers that you're hiring. They will be working for me, as I understand it?"

"Yes."

"Shouldn't I be part of the hiring process then?"

"That's all taken care of, Mr. Oleastro."

Angel knotted his brow and looked at the binder on the table. Stu pulled the binder across to himself, popped open the spine and removed the signature page, passing it to another suit at the table who slipped it into a folder. He closed the binder and slid back his chair to leave. "Let's go, Oleastro. I'll show you the specs." Stu flashed his teeth at him, then thought of something and said, "Oh, almost forgot." He reached into his suit pocket and pulled out two devices, setting one down on the table in front of Angel. It was a PalmPilot. "We have a schedule," Stu said. "Here's how you and I will communicate what we're doing and track the schedule and project specs. These two devices will be the only point of contact between the executive network and your development network, which will remain entirely quarantined until we're ready to deploy to production."

Angel picked up the device. "They don't even make these anymore, do they?" He flipped up the lid and pressed the power button. The screen blinked a bright lime color.

"They've been customized for our purposes, the only two in existence. I have a power cord and sync cradle for you as well."

Angel pulled his smart phone from his pocket and said, "Why don't we just select tracking software to plug into our IDE?"

"You'll see in the security policy that we don't permit the use of anything open source or any publicly available software packages or integrated development environments," Stu said, and tapped the binder with his forefinger. "You won't be able to make any reference to the project, or in fact that you even work for the company, in any networked communications outside of the immediate infrastructure here. You and I will sync these devices using the infrared connection between them. That will be the only permitted connection. They've been uniquely keyed with two pairs of encryption keys, one for information moving from my to your device and one for information going from yours to mine and from yours to your work station in the production room. You'll be required to keep the device secure on your person at all times while in the compound." Stu set his device on the table with the infrared port facing Angel's. He pressed a button and watched the screen. A smile widened on his face, forming dimples. The screen on Angel's device brightened and displayed a moving arrow illustrating the fact that data was moving into his device via the infrared port. "Okay," Stu said. "That's our first sprint. Remember that you'll need to have this with you at all times. It's either on you or it's sitting in the sync cradle at your machine in the production room with your butt in your chair." Stu retrieved his PalmPilot from the tabletop and dropped it into his suit pocket, rose and stepped toward the door. Some of the others at the table were inclined toward each other in private conversation. Others were scrolling on their phones.

"We don't want to poll the new hires and find out what their favorite tools are? And, you're already defining the sprints for me?" Angel asked.

"No," Stuart replied. "We've made those determinations. And, yes, I just defined the first one. I'll expect you to take it from there, but keep us current with syncs multiple times each day. You and I will be seeing a lot of each other."

Angel grabbed his PalmPilot and followed Stuart from the meeting room. This was an odd practice. It seemed an obvious choke point, overboard on the security to the point of being paranoid but, he understood, paranoia would be normal here. After all, the kind of people they would be hiring to fill the programming room would be the kind with the skills to hack through their own network and into the executive network. The company clearly did not want that possibility.

Stu led Angel through another set of double doors, into a shorter corridor and then a darkened room. Angel knew that it would grate on him that this building had no outside windows. He needed natural sunlight to be happy.

"Be right back with your sync cable," Stu said, and walked through an interior door to a smaller room. Angel waited, watching a small band of men and women sitting with their faces whitewashed by the glow from their monitors. Angel noted that they were not arranged to interact with each other, but were penned in their cubicles, all facing the same direction. He also noted the lack of keyboard sound. In a programming room, where the inhabitants were building something or figuring things out, you could close your eyes and get a sense of how things were going from the chatter and flurry of typing. You could hear the surging storms of troubleshooters trying to fix something that had crashed, or the steady patter of engineers building something close to production, or the intermittent gusts of code explorers finding their way into new territory.

This room didn't have any of those sounds, only the occasional brief clatter of keys mixed in with periodic taps and mouse clicks and the faint grinding of scroll wheels. These people were sitting and watching. Angel paused by the opening to one cubicle and looked over the silhouetted shoulder of the man sitting there. The man's screen showed part of a building schematic with path lines drawn along the corridors and into rooms. Angel frowned and shifted on his feet to get a better look. The path lines appeared organic, like tracking lines rather than design lines. The man clicked his mouse. The schematic was replaced by another similar one. Stu came out of the interior room, saying, "Found it. Here's your power cord. Let's head to the programming room and bust open the specs."

Angel followed him back into the corridor and toward

the elevator, the image from the man's screen following him. He wasn't certain, but the schematic and path line looked like it could have been tracking Angel's own journey through the building. If that was the case, then that grain of silicon in his neck was more than just a toll booth chip to let him pass through secured doors.

"What are those people working on in there?" Angel asked as they descended in the elevator.

"Oh," Stu said. He drummed his fingers on the button bank of the elevator while the floors ticked down. "They monitor the project and prepare progress reports for management."

"That's it?" Angel cocked his head at him.

"Yeah," Stu said, without looking at Angel. "Here we are."

Back in the programming room, he brought the lights up and walked to the first cluster of work tables, pressing the power button on the machine at the corner table. "This is your station. You'll find your login credentials in a note I beamed you on your PalmPilot. Go ahead and log in, and I'll show you where to find the project specs. There is no outside connectivity here at all. The repos, dev environment, staging, integration—everything is locked down on prem."

Angel rolled out and sat in the chair. As the screen lit up he felt under the keyboard tray for the adjustment knobs and loosened them, tilted and moved the tray just so, then retightened the knobs. He opened his PalmPilot and was logged in and looking at his new work space in a few moments. Stu reached for the mouse to direct Angel to the network drive where he would find the project specs, but Angel grabbed it at the same instant, causing an awkward moment when Stu's hand sat on top of Angel's like a starfish. Stu tried to move the mouse anyway. Angel resisted and looked up at him, at the generous nose and taut jaw skin reflecting blue from the screen. Stu swiveled his eyes to return the glance, pulled his hand away and resorted to pressing his finger on the screen to show Angel where he wanted him to click to locate the documents.

"Okay, well. I'll leave you to review these. There's also a copy of the security agreement you signed in this folder here. You should read that too. Remember that you cannot copy anything onto removable or transportable media or transfer any digital assets outside of the network. We prosecute those actions as felonies. I'll check in with you first thing tomorrow morning and we can go over the schedule and talk about any questions you have about the project. The rest of the staff should start arriving just after the weekend. Okay?" Stu clapped his hands together, causing Angel to flinch in his chair. "I'm stoked to get this rolling."

That evening Angel sat at his kitchen table typing on his laptop. He wanted to figure out what he had gotten himself into. The late afternoon sun slanted across Pajarito Mountain and angled over the mesa into his condominium through the glass slider to the balcony. The beam of sunlight cast an irritating glare onto his screen, showing him all the dust particles and fibers that would not leave even though he kept a lens cloth at hand and periodically wiped it down. He got up to pull the drapes closed.

Angel sat back down and searched Google for anything on Stuart Pitt and the company he now worked for, an entity called Idemoxi, which for some reason didn't appear on his paycheck. All he could find out about Idemoxi was that it had formed. Its name resided on documents that were filed... somewhere. It had shareholders...somewhere, obscured by LLCs, trusts, and other entities, but was apparently not public. He had only a little more luck with Stuart. He found that he'd gone to Yale for undergrad, held an MBA from Syracuse, had a pending legal case with a car dealership in Seattle, had lived in Seattle and Baker, California, and now in Los Alamos. He also owned a house in Taos and had a number of profiles on various social networking sites.

The front door to the condo opened and then closed. Angel's girlfriend, Winnie, breezed in, set her canvas bag down and buried her face in Angel's black curls, nibbling behind his ear. "How was your first day?"

"Weird." He cocked his head to give her more of his neck and ear. "Check this out." He brought his finger up to show her the red spot on the back of his neck. She pushed his thick hair up and squinted at it.

"You got a mosquito bite?" She tried to pop it, but he brushed her hands away.

"Chip. It gives me access to the new building. Tracks me too, I think."

She stood back from him and made a face. "What the hell? Is it sending signals right now?"

Angel closed his laptop, stood up from the table and shrugged.

They chopped peppers and onions, sliced mushrooms, and put quinoa on the stove. Winnie started tortillas warming in the oven. Angel got out Tabasco and some paprika and cumin, then checked on a pot of red beans that had been soaking overnight. He told her about Stuart, the programming room five floors below ground, the meeting room, and the odd project requirements he'd started reading. He was careful not to talk specifically about the contents of the specs, but told her that this was going to be one crazy project and that he was glad he would be able to see it from the inside. "I'm not sure I'd want this thing happening somewhere else without me knowing about it," he said.

She told him about an eighty-year-old lady she'd worked with at the natural health center, how the lady had been rigid as a board on the table and looked scared to death, but then had opened up and started bawling when Winnie worked around her heart chakra. "It was like she had eight decades of crust in there," she said, holding her fajita.

Later they wrestled slowly in bed, as was their favorite

game. Winnie glided all over his body, twisting and swirling her way between his arms while he held her above him and mock fought her off, his arms and legs moving like a slow motion taffy machine against her happy, relentless pursuit. She won, as she always did, and pinned him to the mattress, warming him with the length of her body, moving herself onto him. Then she started laughing and he looked up, startled.

"Oh my god! I think I'm getting your signal! From that thing in your neck!"

The next morning five more people were in the programming room—two women and three men—all looking around at the bare whiteboards and periodically scratching at the backs of their necks.

Angel recognized a couple of the new hires from the national lab. He had them all grab chairs and roll into a corner of the room where they could circle up to get to know each other and talk about approaches to writing code and tests. Stuart remained standing outside of the circle with his arms folded.

"One of the first things I'd like to do," Angel said, "is to rearrange the furniture a bit in here so that we can use flexible pairs programming and also have a single integration station. We'll want to set up a corner where we can have some refreshments, too, and some more casual seating." The engineers concurred, looking around the room, and one of the women mentioned that her previous engagement had the programming floor set up that way as well.

Angel looked at Stu and asked, "Can we requisition some alternative seating for that?"

Stu frowned. "We've assumed that each engineer would have an assigned station. I'm not sure about the additional seating." Then he added, "We do have a lunch room here, as you know."

"We can talk about that." Angel regarded him and then went back to discussion within the circle. He assigned each programmer a station, thinking he would work on changing the arrangement later—hopefully before the rest of the room was filled—and then started story lists on one of the whiteboards. With Stu's help, he got each of the new hires logged into a station and looking around the network and programming environment.

Stu pulled Angel aside and said in a low voice, "By the way. You don't need to research who I am or who the company is. We'll tell you everything you need to know in order to get this project done. Need-to-know only, got it?"

Angel looked up at him, shocked. He didn't say anything, but stood still and watched Stu's teeth move up and down. Stu continued, "We'll provide every resource and all the required information internally. You should have no reason to explore anything related to this project outside the confines of this room and this network, and in fact are prohibited from doing so." Stu stopped speaking. Angel searched his short-term memory. Then Stu said, "Do you understand that?" Angel nodded, feeling himself redden. "Good. I'm off to a meeting now. I'll leave you to get the team started. We'll have another group in tomorrow, should have the full team in another few days."

Angel looked at the lists he'd started on the whiteboard, then wheeled his chair over to his work station to sit and think. He took an inventory in his mind of his searches and interactions the night before, wondering how Stu became aware of them. He immediately suspected the chip, but wondered what channel it could use to pass that type of information to his employers. Did it sniff the wireless signal in his condo and thus observe his internet traffic? No way would it have enough power to send that much usable information… unless it could somehow harvest electricity from his body… but still. Maybe it just sent a control code back to his ISP…but then, they'd have to be in collusion with these guys, somehow.

Was it able to pick up audio and send it somewhere? Did it send data via his wireless connection? Or did it have its own? Or could it read his brain activity and interpret his thoughts?

Angel felt a moment of panic bubble-wrap his forehead. He had no idea what the chip was or what it could do. He set his face into his hands and his elbows onto his desktop and tried to think empty thoughts, tried to rake every thought away to keep it out of reach of the snooping chip. This quickly grew frustrating. *Okay, okay, if they're monitoring my thoughts, I'll give them thoughts.* He thought of punching Stu's teeth in, then took a few breaths and imagined bringing plastic explosives duct-taped to his body through the security doors and into the programming room. Then he carefully imagined connecting wires to a handheld detonator, inserting batteries and then checking the connection screws, tugging on the wires, preparing to press the detonator switch. Then he started counting down in his mind. He expected armed guards to come bursting through the door any second. He felt a growing anxiety and anticipation, and one cycle of his mind, the observer cycle, congratulated himself for its realism. I'M ABOUT TO BLOW UP THIS BUILDING LIKE A MISSILE SILO SUNK IN THE DESERT!

No guards came running in. Angel finished the countdown. He wiped his brow and looked up. The new hires were clicking and scrolling, staring at their screens, reading policy stuff and getting oriented to the network. *Okay, so maybe the chip doesn't siphon off my brain patterns. What could it be then? How did Stu find out about my searching?* Maybe it wasn't even the chip. Maybe they had software remotely monitoring his various accounts: email addresses, web connection, social network accounts, keyloggers monitoring his keystrokes at home. That wouldn't be too difficult. He'd written stuff more complex and nefarious himself.

What if it was Winnie? What if they'd gotten to her somehow and she was acting as their agent? *That's ridiculous,* Angel thought, *yet possible.* He couldn't eliminate that out of hand. How much would they offer her? *But, she doesn't care about money anyway.* What was it? Did they threaten her?

He decided that he needed to calm down and devise some tests. He'd take his time and figure out exactly how they were able to monitor him. He already knew that they could track his movements within the building. He would find a way to get back into that office, or access his profile over the network, to see how far the chip could track him. Then he'd systematically try each channel to see what got a response from Stu.

3

Birch looked at his wall of books, at the stack of stereo equipment, the tall black speakers standing in the corners, the furniture. He thought of his mortgage. *What if I wimp out and agree to work on Dasher,* he thought as he picked up the water glasses from the coffee table from the day before. *How can I say no to that much money?*

As soon as that thought formed, the images of the woman running through the twilight broke into his consciousness. He stopped between the living room and the kitchen. He stood holding the two glasses, staring with dry, itching eyes at the countertops, espresso machine, and the brushed steel of the refrigerator, staring without blinking, but not seeing them, only seeing the woman running, falling, the men falling upon her. He saw things that he hadn't noticed before in the dream, but from where? A torn leather thong on her right moccasin, its leather wrap falling away from her shin, beads from her belt cast into the grass like stones hoofed from a dry river bed in a dash of panic.

He closed his eyes and breathed. *I'm awake. Why is this happening now?*

He set the glasses down on the counter.

I don't want this condo anymore, he thought, *or any of the stuff in it. This is all just energy, but it's in the wrong form. It's making me sick.*

He saw an image in his mind of his condominium empty, and of himself walking out of the city on a rising road somewhere, toward unpopulated hills. It was a sudden flash of an image, but something about it pulled up in him a deep feeling that he couldn't shake even after the vision faded. *Angel would approve.*

His phone dinged and buzzed on the butcher block top of the kitchen island. He picked it up and saw that it was a text message from Robin: "Birch! Please read your email. ::))"

Birch didn't open his email. Instead he opened the web browser and searched for real estate agents in Palo Alto. He scrolled through a few, tapped one and tapped the phone number. "Yes, I want to list my condo," he told the guy. He gave him his address and told him to come look at the place as soon as he had time.

Hanging up with the agent, Birch opened Craigslist and walked around the rooms entering classified ads for his furniture and possessions. Then he opened Ebay and started auctions for a few of the larger items, like the Subaru, stereo, and dining room furniture.

Robin sent three more text messages within a span of five minutes, each more urgent than the last and with longer, more harrowing emoji parades. Birch ignored them until he finished his last Craigslist ad. His phone battery was drained, so he plugged in, sent Robin a brief response: "I'll check email this afternoon", and set the phone down on the kitchen island to charge. It immediately dinged and buzzed, skating around on the butcher block, yanking against the charging cord. Birch glanced at it and saw that Robin had sent a longer message, apparently pasting in some of the contents of the email messages Birch hadn't yet retrieved.

Birch went to lean in the doorway to the back yard. The neighbor's cat sat crouched next to a flower bed by the privacy fence. Birch watched the cat flick its haunches and level its head, then leap up into the low branches of a cedar and smack a gray junco fluttering to the ground. The bird flapped and lifted off from the flowers, and the cat leaped again and swatted it out of the air onto the lawn and dove on top of it. The bird did its best to yell and fight in the cat's fangs. Birch thought of running into the yard to startle the cat and save the bird, but he stayed rooted in the doorway, letting the thought come and then go. The cat made quick work of the junco and walked off through the bushes with it in its mouth, leaving a spray of gray and white feathers in the grass.

Birch gazed at the pattern of feathers and imagined the cat in the shadows of the shrubs eating the bird. He imagined the bird's fuel moving into the cat in the form of its molecules. The mass of the bird's material was conserved in the cat, but its memory and intelligence, the patterns of perception it accumulated throughout its brief life, were lost.

That is what makes the moment a brutish one, Birch thought. *If everything the bird did and remembered were also transferred into the cat, we'd see things differently. The bird's time spent in that form would remain as part of a whole. Eventually the cat's intelligence, with all of its birds and mice, would pass into the whole as well, like bumps and ripples in life's field flattening out, pulled smooth as new bumps and ripples form elsewhere. As it is, we lose all but the tiniest sliver of the bird's experience. If we're lucky we keep that sliver when the bird reproduces and passes along its genetic code before it's eaten. Maybe we don't even get to keep that. That was a young-looking junco, probably never had a chance to mate.* Birch supposed that the bird contributed something by not passing along its genetic code, but even so, the moment felt wasteful and this part of the universe crude.

The chat messages from Robin were rants and pleadings, growing progressively more intense and threatening. The venture capitalists might withhold the next round of financing if Birch didn't commit to Dasher. Birch could get a bad reputation in the valley if he didn't stick by his founder CEO and support the company plan. Robin knew Birch's feelings about Dasher and was willing to adjust his compensation to sweeten the deal accordingly. Robin had sunk everything he had, and everything lots of other people had, into this company, and by god he was not going to see it compromised by one developer with morals. Robin would be happy to do whatever it was he needed to do in order to persuade Birch to work on Dasher. Anything! Robin was sorry, that last message sounded a little extreme. Robin reconsidered his last message, he WOULD be willing to do whatever it took.

Birch scrolled through the messages and couldn't think of a reply. They left him with a sick feeling. He imagined Robin coming after him with a baseball bat. He saw it happen in his mind and rehearsed how he would defend himself and get away, then, despite telling himself that he was being irrational, continued the scenario, imagining Robin actually hiring thugs to come after him, to surprise and overwhelm him. He began to feel powerless and truly scared while simultaneously ridiculous.

He looked at the characters in the words, the pixels in the characters, and imagined the bits in the pixels, his sick feeling beginning to dissipate. He closed his eyes and thought of different ways a bit can be stored, comforted to be imagining electrons in different states instead of reading Robin's words. He opened his eyes and pulled in a full breath, feeling the nitrogen, oxygen, argon, and carbon dioxide molecules filling his lungs, wondering why these molecules should be so much less bothersome than those lining up to form the pixels of his phone display. *Of course it's not the molecules; it's the patterns that organize them.* The pattern in his lungs was simple and useful for moving oxygen into his bloodstream. Not so the patterns on his phone display. They were complex and overlapping, and gave people like Robin access to push their codified emotions into the device where Birch would have to experience them.

The sick feeling came back. He owed Robin a reply. The obligation sat on his countertop like a burn mark. Robin represented the kernel of what was reacting inside Birch like a massing virus; hours, days, months of his thinking and best creative skills turned into meaningless, unproductive violence.

When faced with confusion, Birch had learned that the only thing he could finally rely on was plain honesty, no matter how inelegant it may be. He sent his reply to Robin. "I can't participate in Dasher. I'm very sorry. I know you'll probably have to let me go." He laid the phone back on the kitchen island, rinsed the breakfast dishes and put them into the dishwasher.

Birch saw the agent in the late morning through the front window, a tall man dressed in expensive slacks and a white button-down, walking around the common yard and looking up at the roof. He saw him shoot some photos with a smartphone and then come to the door to knock. Birch invited him in.

The agent pocketed his phone and slowly strolled around the living room with his hands clasped behind his back, looking over the bookshelves, the framed posters, and the finish on the floor. "I like your place," he said in a polished British-sounding accent. "Very nice. What brings you to put it on the market?" Then Birch's phone buzzed and slid on the butcher block in the kitchen. "Sounds like someone's after you," the agent said. "Do you need to get that?"

Birch ignored the phone. "I'm in the process of converting all of this into a simpler, more useful form of energy," he said, "one that will better serve my life path." For the first time that day, he felt like he was getting somewhere. He felt like sunlight was finally reaching him.

The agent glanced at Birch while continuing his tour into the kitchen. He cocked his head with a closed-lipped smile, bright eyes set off by his dark black face. He raised his eyebrows. "That's a first," he said.

Birch sat in the living room while the agent snapped photos in the kitchen, then went down the hall to snap some more in the bathroom and bedroom. He came back out and said, "You know, we may be able to move this pretty fast. I have a buyer who's been dying to get into this neighborhood. Young family, first child."

The agent went to his car and came back with a briefcase. He sat with Birch on the couch and prepared the listing agreement on the coffee table. Birch signed, and the agent organized his papers and got up to leave. "When can I start showing it?" he asked.

"Any time," Birch said. The phone buzzed on the butcher block again.

"Boy, somebody's really trying to get your attention. Well, you straighten up a bit back there, and I'll get a couple more pictures and get your listing done. I'll contact my buyer and maybe bring him around tomorrow or the day after."

They shook hands, and Birch showed him out.

Birch held himself under the armpits and stood shaking his head in the doorway for a moment. He felt suddenly lighter. *I guess I'm moving,* he thought, and smiled. He went back into the house and started removing all of his possessions from drawers and shelves, arranging things on the floor in each room in groups to see what was there. He found a few more items that he wanted to put on Craigslist, so went to the kitchen to grab his phone. Another message from Robin was on the screen. "Birch!!! This is SERIOUS!!!! ::((DO NOT think you can IGNORE ME!!"

Birch left the phone there, feeling the stone in his chest, and walked back to the den to use a desktop computer instead. He logged on and entered a few more ads, then sat back in his desk chair and glanced around the room. *I don't need any of this,* he thought. He entered more ads for the computer on which he typed, the stack of external hard drives connected to it, the rack of flat panel monitors, a plasma monitor on his wall, a couple laptops and a netbook on the credenza behind him, a subwoofer and set of speakers on the shelf opposite his desk. Everything, except the files stored on the external hard drives.

He opened a new browser tab, searched cloud hosting services, and chose one that offered burly Linux servers for cheap rates. He registered with an anonymous Gmail address, ordered a large one with a healthy supply of RAM, and prepaid for a year using an untraceable credit card number from his Slang account. Then he shelled into his new virtual server and began uploading the contents of his hard drives. He deleted extraneous files that he didn't need, but kept the code libraries he and Angel had developed while writing mustangs in college.

When the uploads completed, he closed his terminal and web browser and set the computer to erase and reformat the external hard drives, then the internal drives. He fired up the laptops and erased and reformatted them too. He decided to take it a step further and, prior to erasing the netbook, deleted all of his Gmail accounts except for the one he'd just created for his cloud server and one other he needed for his Slang and PayPal accounts and Craigslist transactions. Then he erased and reformatted the netbook. *I don't need any of this now. The only person I really care to contact now is Angel, and none of this will help with that anyway.*

He went to the garage and brought back a collection of cardboard boxes, broken down and neatly folded from his move into the condo. He set them up and began filling them on the living room floor.

The agent came back the next day to snap some more pictures. He looked at the boxes accumulating in the living room. "This isn't what I had in mind when I said 'straighten up a bit.'" He mentioned that he had an interested buyer he wanted to bring by that afternoon and probably wouldn't need to bother with a for sale sign. Birch promised him that he'd move the boxes to the garage.

"Good," the agent said, "and put that nice-looking car out in the drive. Park it off to the side at a slight angle so you can see room in the drive, one full garage door, and so you can see the side of the car."

Birch complied. The boxes began to line up in the garage. People began to respond to the Craigslist ads, and a couple showed up to cart things away. One lady with an Amazon store came with a van to take away all of his books at pennies on the dollar. Birch was happy to let them go. The lady was happy to add them to her store, saying she'd make a nice profit on them as they were in good condition. She got out her smart phone, sent Birch a PayPal payment, and the deal was done.

The agent pulled up in his Range Rover later that afternoon. A slim man in his late thirties got out of the passenger side. The agent rang the doorbell, and Birch invited them in.

"This is Alex Pierpont."

Birch greeted him and shook his hand, saying, "Nice to meet you."

Pierpont stared up at Birch's face. "You're Birch from Zongo," he said.

Birch nodded.

"I'm Alex Pierpont from IGT Capital Group. Wow. It's a pleasure to meet you. You know, we've been following your work. We've been trying to get an appointment with Robin Turcek, but he's tough to get ahold of."

Birch didn't know what to say. "Yes, he's always in motion. You might try him again now though."

He led them into the living room, and the agent began talking to Pierpont about the condo. Pierpont kept his focus on Birch. "So, you're moving? Are you staying in the area? You're not leaving Zongo, are you?"

"My plans are uncertain at this point," Birch said.

"Wait a minute!" Pierpont stopped. "So you are going somewhere." He inclined his head and considered Birch for a moment, then pulled out a business card. "If you're leaving to do a startup, will you please contact me and at least talk to me about it? Will you do that?"

Birch took the card and stuck it in a pocket. "Sure," he said.

The agent stood taking in the exchange. Pierpont looked at Birch a moment longer, then began looking around the room. He said to himself, "Birch's condo."

The agent caught that lob and gestured to the maple ceiling beams with enthusiasm. "You're looking at rare craftsmanship here," he said to Pierpont.

"Of course," Pierpont said, looking up at the ceiling.

While the agent led Pierpont around the rooms, Birch left them and carried more boxes out to the garage. Another Craigslist person showed up to take a pair of black walnut chairs and increase the balance in Birch's PayPal account. When the agent and Pierpont were leaving, the agent leaned in to Birch and said softly, "He likes it. I think we're going to see an offer."

Birch saw them out and went into the kitchen to chop up some vegetables and put rice on the stove. He dribbled olive oil into his steel wok and started it heating on another burner. Reaching into a cupboard for a small glass bowl to hold a measure of sliced almonds, he found the cupboard empty, the bowl already carried to the garage. "Ha," he said to himself, then dumped a small pile of almond slices onto the cutting board. He hadn't planned any of this, and though he felt on new ground, starting something rolling like this without thinking it through to various possible conclusions, he also felt warm and bright. He felt suffused by a lightness he hadn't known since childhood.

The following day was a Saturday. Robin texted a message saying that "THIS IS FUCKING SERIOUS!!!! NOT A FUCKING GAME!!!!!!!" and that he was coming up to see Birch first thing Sunday morning. The irony of Robin's message was not lost on Birch, though a pang of fear rattled him. What would Robin do? What if CEOs had some dark net database somewhere where they stored dirt on people they wanted to control? Some private forum where they got together to laugh about all the people they owned. What if Robin had evidence of a mustang and could connect Birch to a cybercrime? What if he was just waiting for the right moment to send in the federal agents to pick him up?

That's crazy, Birch thought. *I'm just being paranoid. If there was such a thing, I could find it. I could write a mustang to go out and discover it, breach it and expose the entire database. But I've never looked. It could exist. And even if I hacked into it, some bells would have rung that could not be un-rung. Robin would know things.* Birch's face flushed as much from embarrassment at his own thoughts as from the fear of their potential truth.

I can make things up out of thin air, he thought, *and then be afraid of them. I must not be well.*

Birch spent the rest of the morning carrying boxes and intermittently thumb-typing answers to questions posed by people interested in his Craigslist ads or his auctions.

He didn't have boxes for the computers and office equipment, but set them up on a workbench on the back garage wall. By early afternoon the only things left in the house were rugs, furniture, some kitchen implements and dishes, and some boxes of clothes that he hadn't yet carried out to the garage.

He expected more people to come by, including one lady who offered to take his spare clothes to the Goodwill station. She sent him an email saying that she would be leaving within the hour.

Birch felt happy to give his clothes away, but the woman's impending arrival caused him to think about what he needed to keep. All that he wanted now was basic maintenance, simplicity. He again imagined himself walking into hills somewhere and decided that simplicity meant whatever he could fit into a backpack.

He went to an upper shelf on the wall adjacent to the workbench, pulling down his backpack and camping gear. He hadn't used them much since his college days when he and Angel and other friends would take weekends from Berkeley to backpack on the Pacific Crest Trail. They'd put in miles and miles treading through the Sierras, camping in meadows and drinking water filtered from streams, but since graduation and starting work his pack and gear spent their time in moving boxes and on shelves. He carried the gear, still dusty from his last trip, into the back yard and laid it out on the grass. He emptied the pack, unrolled the sleeping bag and foam pad, spread out the tent, disassembled the cook set and stove, and opened up the stuff sacks, releasing old campsite odors, to give them some air and sun. Eyeballing the interior of his pack to remember how much it could hold, he then went back inside to select clothes to keep. He set aside what he could fit into his pack or wear, putting the rest in boxes or leaving them on hangers in his closet. He carried the keepers —his favorite white hemp pants with draw cord waist, a pair of hiking shorts, white cotton hoodie, wind jacket, some socks and underwear, t-shirts and a couple flannel button-downs— out to the yard and folded them into stuff sacks, then into the backpack. He fluffed the sleeping bag and tent to make sure they were getting air and went back in to carry the clothes boxes to the garage.

The woman who came from Goodwill was thrilled with all that he gave her. He helped her load the boxes into her van and laid armloads of suits, shirts, and sweaters still on hangers on top of the boxes. Then he grabbed his coats, hats, and shoes from the hall closet and loaded those in as well.

The garage was looking like a warehouse at the end of a going-out-of-business sale. A few more people came by toward evening to enlarge Birch's PayPal balance (which he periodically emptied into his online bank account) and drive away with golf clubs, laptops, a piece of furniture or two, random tools or outdoor equipment. A young couple drove up in a pickup truck to buy his bed and dresser. He got an email message from the shop that did the mods and tune on his Subaru saying that they'd seen his auction on eBay, remembered the car and wanted to come look at it, were sure they could find a buyer for it.

Birch set up the tent in the back yard and moved his camping gear inside. He crawled in to look over the gear. In the dim orange light filtering through the nylon walls, he sat imagining Robin with a bloodthirsty scowl, dressed as one of the warriors in his games, holding a poleaxe and sneaking up behind the tent. This butane stove, these aluminum pots, these nylon walls, would not protect him from a rampaging Robin. The thought freaked him out, and he made haste out of the tent and stood up in the twilight, instantly feeling ridiculous.

4

The seat cushions in the programming room were each compressed and warm now. The clicking rain of the keyboards was intermittent, a brief flurry now and then separated by long silences. It was the rain of a team coming together and sorting itself out, just beginning to see what it was it would be making.

Angel stood at the whiteboard with a blue marker attended by a group of four circled up with their rolling chairs. A couple of them looked at notes in their laps, a couple up at the boxes and lines on the board. Angel asked a question of his group and rubbed out a line on the board, replacing it with a different one. Stu entered the room and leaned in the corner by the door, watching. Angel saw him but studiously ignored him to keep the conversation thread from breaking, something he was convinced Stu was incapable of comprehending, like an object colored in a part of the spectrum his sight could not perceive.

Stu pushed himself off the wall and circled the room, looking at screens as he drifted by. He saw numbered lines of colored characters on some screens, and some divided up into different views of smaller windows with numbered lines next to windows with lists of files and windows with shapes and lines with arrows. He saw one or two screens displaying what he recognized as the development network file system. He kept his hands clasped behind his back and pushed his lips together and nodded, though no one looked at him. He stopped along the wall near Angel and leaned his shoulder against it, facing Angel, then stood up to check his shoulder for blue ink, realizing that the entire wall was whiteboard, now with notations and diagrams clustered in various places.

Angel concluded the conversation to his satisfaction and sent the four programmers rolling back to their stations, then turned to Stu. Stu pulled his PalmPilot from his pocket and pointed it toward Angel. "I have a schedule and spec update for you," he said.

Angel lowered his eyelids slightly, pulled his PalmPilot from his pocket and pointed it toward Stu's. Stu tapped with the stylus and then punched the sync button, watching his screen as the circling arrows indicated his calendar file was jumping out of the infrared port across the air to Angel's, while Angel's was updating and jumping back to his. When the arrows stopped and the devices beeped, Stu smiled and looked up at Angel. "Oh," he said, "and, again, the ban on outside communications explicitly includes email. I thought I told you that yesterday. Okay?"

He waited. Angel raised his eyebrows and nodded. "Oh, certainly, yes, very sorry." Stu nodded back and turned to exit the room.

Angel smiled. He would only have a few more tests to do now. With this admonishment from Stu, Angel felt confident that Stu's mind operated close to the surface most of the time, and that any stimulus from Angel to the boundaries of the company's rules would result in a similar response. The intensity of this response was not qualitatively different from the first one he'd gotten after his web searching session, or from the one he'd gotten yesterday. He thought of repeating some of his stimuli three or four times to test for a progressive response, but for now, the important tests were designed to uncover the company's surveillance channels. He'd started by gossiping to Winnie about the project specs and bad-mouthing the mission. He was predisposed to think that she couldn't be involved, that were she on the company payroll somehow, his heart would break. But the other side of that coin made it ever more important to use solid methodology to gain as much certainty as he could. No mention from Stu after he talked Winnie's ears off, and such a chatter session was part of their relationship anyway, talking about politics, their jobs, friends, parents, anything at all. Angel was relieved. That session also tested for any audio capabilities of the chip in his neck. He had trouble imagining the technology that would enable that, but then again, he'd seen some freaky stuff. This company had plenty of military resources kept on floors he was not permitted to access.

Stu turned back toward Angel before walking through the door. "Looks like things are moving along pretty well in here," he said. Angel nodded. "Say," Stu continued, "these IRs should be able to sync through glass, right?"

Angel thought, and nodded again. "We could test that," he said.

"What I thought," Stu said. "Well, you can come to my office down on seven at noon every day now, and I'll have updates for you. Things are getting busy so I won't be coming up here as often. If I'm in with someone, we'll just shoot it through the window."

The next night Angel shut off his internet connection by pulling the plug on his cable modem and then disabling the WiFi on his laptop, since a couple of his neighbors' WiFi signals leaked into his condo. He wrote some text documents with inflammatory language hypothetically planning to subvert the project, saved the documents, moved them from his desktop to other directories on his laptop's file system and back to his desktop, reopened them and closed them again. Then he opened his web browser and viewed a cached form even though it wasn't connected to the internet, and typed the same language into that. This all to test for screen phreaking. Maybe they had a radiation sensor installed somewhere, or maybe it was that damned chip, recording whatever rendered on his laptop's screen. If so, then they would be able to record the contents of his open documents even though he'd shut off his internet connection.

No mention from Stu the next day. That was also a relief. That one would be tough to work around. Just to be sure that they didn't have a software mole that could keep his internet connection alive yet hidden, without him detecting it, he took his laptop out of the condo and walked into the desert to where he could pick up no data signal with his phone, then powered down his phone and tried the experiment again. Again, nothing from Stu.

He'd used his Gmail address for the next test. He made up an unlikely Yahoo address and sent it an innocuous hello message, waiting for the bounceback from the Yahoo mail servers to confirm that the address didn't exist. Then he sent it another message, pretending he was writing to a friend, bragging about his great new job. He got a bounce for that message too, and an admonishment from Stu the next day. Then he took his show on the road, using the public WiFi at a cafe in town for the same experiment to test whether the surveillance was localized to his condo. He'd left his phone home just to be sure they weren't tracking its location to sleuth out which WiFi connection he might be using. Today, another admonishment. So it wasn't just in his condo. Somehow they were monitoring the internet traffic leaving his laptop when he was connected at home or elsewhere.

He thought about the next few tests he would do. He'd have to perform the email experiment using another machine, maybe a public work station at the library, to eliminate malware on his laptop, though he'd scoured the system looking for any signs of rogue processes and found nothing. He wasn't in a hurry. He was more interested in being thorough. After he tested on a public computer, he'd repeat the test using a burner email service with a new address.

Angel tapped his chin and turned to gather up his next group of programmers to talk about the module they were building.

That night at home, Angel sat with his fingers quietly tapping the Formica top of the kitchen table, thinking through what he was about to do as Winnie sat meditating on the living room futon.

He and Winnie had spent this past weekend up north in Boulder. Winnie had hoped to get in a hike up around the Flatirons while they were there, but she'd had to take that walk herself. Angel headed straight for the university library after the seven-hour drive and began researching PalmPilot hacks. He wanted to be sure he was well out of range of the chip while in a place with resources where he could access the net anonymously. He spent all of Saturday afternoon on a library terminal while Winnie went out for her hike, then later amused herself in a few shops before they closed after checking on Angel. She brought him a sandwich and bottle of iced tea for a late dinner, and when it became clear he was in for an all-nighter she kissed him and left to go find a campground to set up their tent. She returned early Sunday morning to discover him parked at the same work table with a stack of papers he'd printed on one of the library lasers. The librarian had caught sight of him burning through half a ream and required three dollars cash since he didn't have a student ID card. Winnie also saw a new used laptop covered in band-and-skateboard stickers sitting on the table next to the printouts. Angel blearily told her that he'd bought it for cash from a student the night before and promptly installed his favorite flavor of Linux on it, wiping the other operating system off, then cracking open the case to remove the WiFi antenna. This laptop would be fulfilling a specialized mission that required strict separation from any networks.

Now it sat on the kitchen table with its hard drive whirring and a split-veined set of wires dangling from one side of a serial port adaptor with micro alligator clips at the ends.

Angel carefully clipped the alligators onto the power and data tabs at the bottom of the PalmPilot. No window opened on his laptop screen, and nothing came to life on the PalmPilot's screen, as the laptop had no software that was familiar with this primitive device, though the LED on the PalmPilot indicated it was accepting an electrical charge.

Angel opened a terminal window and began navigating through his file system, visiting directories and their subdirectories he'd cabled over from his other laptop, reviewing the lists of files, looking through his libraries of code —copied, adapted, and written from scratch over the years— with a calm demeanor, something like a watchmaker setting out and inspecting his tools.

Were he a college kid exercising his curiosity with this old device, this task would be an amusing hobby he could pursue while watching a movie or sports on TV. This was different, however. He was an employee with a lucrative and strict contract working for serious, dangerous people, and this was not mere curiosity. He was about to open the classified contents of a device that did not belong to him but was specifically modified for his use in fulfillment of his contracted duties, and was governed by the security policy he had signed.

By the time Winnie had finished her meditation and was deciding which scents of candles she wanted to light, Angel had gained access to the PalmPilot's file system. He saw that it was a modified version of PalmOS 1.0. He discovered how the applets were organized and integrated with the operating system. He saw how the company had modified it to add their own encryption and access rules, though he also saw how they could have done a better job. He looked for logging or any mechanism or flag he would have to switch to thwart any attempt by the company to detect his tampering. Using a pair of hacked PalmPilots as the single point of communication between the executive network and the development network still baffled Angel. It was either the stupidest thing he could imagine, or it was pure genius. It worried him that they didn't check him for it when he left the compound at night. They must really trust their modifications. He decided his only option was to trust in his own ability to reverse engineer this thing. He moved on to looking for the screen interface controls.

By the time the mingling fragrances of spruce, pine, and vanilla (which Winnie had chosen as an experiment, thinking it might conjure an upland, snowy hillside when mixed with the spruce and pine) drifted from the living room into the kitchen, Angel had figured out the controller interface for the touch screen and was exploring the interface that caused the tiny piezo disk to make all of its adorable beeps and chirps to signify the various stages of syncing and other such events.

Winnie retrieved a woven bear grass basket from a corner and sat cross-legged on the living room floor with it, sifting through its contents of scraps of all manner of fabrics, suedes, and leathers, picking out odd shapes, colors, and textures that fit with her current feeling of a mountain meadow near the end of a spring melt. She imagined the scene and then watched it assemble, layer by layer, as she set a piece of green wool next to a torn swatch of denim, those underlapped with a piece of deer suede, arranged with a frayed piece of burlap and another of white cotton muslin. She set out, arranged, lapped, turned, folded, swapped, slid dozens of pieces, lightly sketching a curve or a line on some with a grease pencil where she thought she might cut, seeing the slope and the sky, a green bough tipped with new growth in the foreground, a streak of melting snow far in the distance. After a while she stood to view the scene from higher altitude, the triad of candle scents drifting past her nose. She returned to ground level, lifted steel scissors from the basket, and set their edges to the fabrics and leathers.

Angel had stubbed out and mostly filled in an app to use the piezo disk in reverse. Rather than sending instruction to it to vibrate and create sound, it would detect vibrations and log them to a file. He used a small cluster of pixels in the lower corner of the PalmPilot's screen to trigger the app when tapped; it would run and log data until the cluster was tapped again. He built an encoder and used perceptual noise shaping to compress the volume of data, but even so set a limit on the file size so that the app wouldn't use all the storage capacity of the device and raise Stu's suspicion if he couldn't sync their calendars. He also had to exclude the log files and app from the syncing directories so he didn't accidentally move them onto the company network when dropping the PalmPilot into its cradle at his work station. Angel checked the alligator clips and tapped the lower corner of the screen with the plastic stylus.

Winnie called from the living room, "Honey, come tell me if you get new life on a mountain from this."

Angel tapped the corner again, anxious to copy off the log file to his laptop and view the contents. He pulled the file over and opened it in his text editor, a rush of satisfaction washing through his blood as he saw the headers and evidence that his encoder had at least made an effort to capture and encode vibrations sensed by the little disc. He closed the file and then opened it again in an audio conversion utility, running it through a couple of cycles to clean it, and tried to play it as an mp3. The speakers in his laptop hissed softly and then, amid some static and other artifact sound that Angel had yet to account for, said, "Honey, come tell me if you get new life on a mountain from this."

Angel put his palms together in an oft-repeated, reflective gesture of thanks, then opened them and rested his face in his warm hands before getting up from the kitchen table. He let his hands glide down his roughly bearded cheeks. He stepped into the living room and stood next to Winnie, who was up again, looking down at the scene on the floor. He rested the full weight of his hands on her shoulders and looked down at the scene with her. The warm blend of spruce, pine, and vanilla was stronger, filling his sinuses. The scene on the floor took him straight to one of his favorite alpine meadows in the Sierras, a place he used to backpack along the Pacific Crest Trail.

"Yes, absolutely, I get that," he said.

Angel left the programming room and headed to the elevator. He looked up at the camera ball, then punched the down arrow and waited for the door to open. Inside his finger missed floor seven and punched six by mistake. The panel buzzed a staccato warning at him and failed to light up. He wasn't cleared for access to floor six, only to four, five, seven, and ground level. He realized his mistake and punched seven. The panel lit and the doors slid closed.

Angel stood outside, looking through the glass-paneled door at Stuart having an animated conversation with another suit. He pulled his PalmPilot from his pocket, tapped the pixel cluster in the corner and held the infrared port against the glass. He stood like that for a few minutes before Stuart looked over and noticed him. Stuart said something to the other man, who glanced back at Angel for a second before returning to their conversation.

A guy in an MP uniform walked by in the hallway. Seeing Angel, he stopped and called out, "You waiting for someone?"

Angel turned and looked at him. "Waiting for Pitt," he said. Stuart had walked to the door and tapped the glass. Angel turned and moved his infrared port to be opposite Stuart's. Stuart pressed his sync button, and the two PalmPilots lit up, syncing through the glass. The MP watched for a few seconds, then shrugged and moved on down the hallway.

Stuart continued his conversation over his shoulder.

Angel watched his mouth move but heard no sound. The sync finished, and Stuart, still talking, turned without looking at Angel and walked back to his chair. Angel put his PalmPilot back into his pocket and headed toward the elevator.

That night Angel sat at his kitchen table poring through the data file, running it repeatedly through filters, tweaking them, and running it again. When he listened to the filtered file he heard plenty of humming and buzzing, high-pitched hisses, and rhythmic thrumming. He closed his eyes and concentrated, trying to visualize what he was hearing. This building, or bunker, or subterranean cavern, whatever this strange structure where he spent his days was properly called, vibrated with a miasma of crossing frequencies and activity. What appeared to Angel so sterile and mundane in its design and on its surfaces was, when examined in this way, infused with an eerie cacophony alarming in its hissing planes and distant muffled screams.

Angel pinched his eyes tighter and bowed his head, trying to push his hearing and attention deeper into each run of the filters. He thought he heard faint human voices emerging from this boiling soup of noise. He worked through the interference, slicing through it layer by layer, until he was sure he did hear voices. He kept at it until Winnie had finished her torn fabric painting, started the night before, and came in to say that she was going to bed. Finally, after working through perhaps a hundred variations of filter combinations, he amplified the sound that was left and heard the deep, scratchy voice of Stu Pitt, talking with another man.

"...need every bit of electricity we can pull from the grid for this. It'll take more than we used for HAARP. Way more. That was just practice. We got to get a microwave out twenty miles to the nearest drone, then it has to build it up and fire it off to the next one, and so on. That way the whole network stays powered in the air, never has to touch the ground, never has to come home. But the electricity is just fucking crazy. In fact, here's my guy. I gotta shoot him some changes for this. Hold on."

"The software ape? Won't those people talk? I mean, shit, they have to be able to figure out where this is going. They're building it for chrissakes."

"Be surprised what the mind will do when you throw enough money at it…all we gotta do is keep sick money on 'em, keep 'em moving fast, and maybe make an example out of one or two of 'em. They'll be quiet as mice. We've been there before. HAARP ran the same way. A few of those people are gone, but most are still taking our money. They never talk. We make sure of that."

Angel stared at the shuttle bar moving across the sound graph.

Over the next weeks he made a habit of going down to Stu's level a few minutes early. He didn't wave or otherwise draw attention to himself. He just stood, with his PalmPilot touching the glass window of Stu's door, and waited while Stu jabbered at someone, or at his phone. The MP got used to him being there, and to the unusual infrared exchange through the glass, just nodding as he walked by on patrol.

Angel couldn't wait to get home each night and run the sound file. He was often disappointed to learn nothing more than that Stu Pitt still held a very high opinion of himself, but over time he did learn that the company was involved with planning public relations campaigns to reduce electricity consumption in areas where they intended to install microwave facilities to power the drone network. He heard him lecturing a guy who was apparently responsible for a campaign in the southern and western states. "Gotta tag electricity un-American. Especially electric cars. Those fuckers will kill us when we need the most juice. Tag 'em un-American and liberal elite. Somehow connect plug-in cars with 'They're coming for your guns,' and all that shit. Play the environment angle at the same time. That will confuse the fuck out of them. Get it out through news and ads, social media. Movies too, where you can. Okay, here's what we want Americans doing: barbecue outside, cook with gas, burn the fuck out of fossil fuels all day fucking long and all fucking night, spend all day driving their fat stack diesels to feel powerful and safe, cart the family around in their minivans and live out of those things as much of the day as possible, long commutes, store the kids, watch their movies, have their dinner, charge their phones, all so they don't have time to use up the grid-tied electricity. Make that the right lifestyle, that everybody wants. Got it? We need every kilowatt we can get to pump out to the drones. We're working on getting something on Canada too, so they have to let us build a transmitter near one of those dams."

5

The neighbor's cat slipped into the yard and crept along the privacy fence, stalking in and out of the flower beds. She came into Birch's view, a moving shadow as he lay with his chin on his laced hands, looking out through the patio door at the light beginning to accumulate on the grass. The cat stopped beneath a sword fern and waited.

Birch had slept fitfully in the tent for a few hours before taking his sleeping bag into the house. Now he was warm and snug in the bag on the floor inside. He used his hoodie as a pillow, and the smell of it and the goose down bag had given him pleasant dreams for once, dreams of the Sierras. He tried to recall and savor the dreams while watching the light particles accumulate on the grass outside. His dreams were the fragile edges of memory from trips with Angel and their friends, and he tried to hold on to the edges, gently loosen them from the stack to bring more of them out where he could see them in greater resolution.

The cat sprang from beneath the fern and split a stand of tiger lilies. Birch saw the tall stems wave, then the cat picked her head up with a struggling mouse in her jaws. The cat looked around the yard, looked at the tent, and then trotted off.

A knock sounded on the front door. Birch unzipped his sleeping bag and crawled out, found his pants and shirt and pulled them on. Too early for someone to come by from a Craigslist ad. It was Sunday morning.

The knocking repeated. Birch pulled the door open.

Robin stood there in his suit with a professionally dressed woman standing behind him. Birch thought he recognized her from some company happening the year before. She looked like she might be his age, not far from the beginning of her career, whatever that was, but her expression said she was sure of her business and not likely to suffer fools. Birch stepped aside, pulling the door wider, and motioned for them to come in.

Robin walked in ahead of her, saying, "What the fuck!" Birch could see he was jumpy. He walked onto the wood floor and turned to motion toward the woman. "This is Pam, Birch. She's helped us in the past. I'm worried about you."

Birch nodded. Pam said, "It's my pleasure to meet you, Birch." She looked him over. Robin stepped into the living room and looked across the empty shelves and bare walls. He frowned and turned in a circle, cocking his head at the corner of the room where the stereo should have been.

"Birch? What the fuck is going on here? Where's all your stuff?" Robin touched his forehead with his fingers and strode into the kitchen. Pam stood observing Birch. Birch followed Robin with his eyes.

"Holy FUCK, Birch! How long have you been living this way?"

Birch started walking toward the kitchen. Pam followed.

"Shall we go sit down and talk?" Pam asked.

Robin walked back into the living room. "Sit?" he said. "Where can we sit? There's no furniture! Holy FUCK!"

"We can sit out on the deck chairs," Birch said.

Pam motioned to Robin. "Let's go out to the deck," she said.

The sun was up above the foothills, jousting with a few low clouds. Birch arranged three folding chairs on a corner of the deck where the sun made it past the clouds. He sat facing the orange light. Pam took a chair adjacent to him, and Robin dragged his chair a few feet into the shade. He sat with his elbows on his knees, then leaned back and crossed his arms in front of his chest. Birch had his eyes closed and his face in the sun. He turned toward Pam.

"So, you're a coach of some sort?" he asked.

"Yes," Pam said, "a business counselor."

Birch smiled at her.

"Birch," Robin began. "You haven't been into work since the middle of last week, and you haven't been communicating with me. Now I come here and find you like this. We have a lot riding on your performance, a huge amount." Robin paused, leaned forward again and looked at his shoes.

Pam interjected, "What's with the empty condo? Are you experimenting with minimalism, or survival or something?"

Birch looked at Pam's face. Her cheeks were high and smooth. He liked how the sun fell sandy and gold on them. "I've been thinking about fractals, and Calabi-Yau spaces," he said.

Robin sat up and tilted his head back, closing his eyes with a pained look.

Pam looked at Robin for an explanation, got nothing, then looked back to Birch.

"So are you doing some kind of experiment?" Robin asked with his eyes still closed, struggling to remain calm, hoping that Birch would say something to wash his fears away and make this whole episode the inconsequential joke it deserved to be, hoping with all the sweat-drenched hairs on his head.

Birch didn't answer. Inside his own head he yelled, however. He yelled that this was no experiment. This was no game. *All you have to do is sense, even if only for a split second, that everything in the universe is interconnected. Afterward, how can you dedicate the best parts of yourself for months at a time to creating intense violence and trivialized, re-bootable hatred without rendering yourself truly sick? Then to top that, you watch how those in charge of creating this digital violence actually treat living people with the same cold indifference and cruelty as the characters that simply restart themselves after running out of "life points.*" No, this was no game. Birch had been part of inventing a new form of cancer, one where you repeatedly train yourself to kill and then laugh about it. No, this was no experiment. He was sick and trying to find a cure.

"What books are on your night table these days?" Pam asked.

Birch had given his night table to the young couple who bought the bed and dresser. All of his books were gone too, except for the ebooks he read on his phone.

Robin opened his eyes and gestured to the tent in the middle of the yard. "Is this some kind of camping trip? Are you planning on coming into work tomorrow?"

Pam looked at Robin and frowned. She looked back toward Birch and brushed her fingers across her lips. "Birch, I understand that you were very upset by some of the content and themes in the next Zongo Inc. project. Is that right?"

"Very," he said.

Robin said in a low voice, "The VCs won't fund it if you're not the lead developer. They know that would kill the timing, if not the product. Doesn't that mean ANYTHING TO YOU? How am I supposed to get this done in any reasonable time if I have to BRING SOMEONE ELSE UP? What's more, how can I do it WITHOUT CAPITAL? We FUCK this up and we MISS our WINDOW!"

Pam held her hand up to Robin. "Can we talk about what made you upset?" she asked.

Robin reached into his inside jacket pocket and pulled out a folded, clipped stack of paper. "Birch, look at this clause in your contract." He unfolded the paper and held it out to Birch, pointing at a paragraph near the center of the page. "I can fire you for this, obviously. Read it. You know I can also SUE YOU if I find anything that looks like sabotage. I could sue your ASS OFF! You also have a non-compete. That would be IT! FUCKING YOUR ASS IN THAT GRASS!"

Birch raised his eyebrows, looking at the paper. Fear stabbed him in the throat. What could be construed as sabotage? Probably anything that Robin didn't like. How would he prove it? How would you put code in front of a judge and get her to say it was sabotage or not? All it would take would be one of his old mustangs left on a server somewhere, discovered by some persistent sleuth and traced back to him, and he would be living out his days in prison. The thought slapped him, and he began going over old inventory in his memory, mentally fingering back through code, wondering if he could have ever been that careless. What if he'd used something from his and Angel's libraries and forgotten to edit out the comments? What if Robin and Melanie were in cahoots? What if Melanie had already discovered a mustang?

"Robin," Pam said.

"You can't want to throw away your career like that," Robin pleaded. "Look at what you've got. And you're thinking about fractals! Listen. What if I DOU-BLE YOUR SAL-ARY?"

"Robin, please," Pam said. "Let me work here." Robin refolded the contract and stuffed it back inside his suit jacket. The doorbell rang inside the house. They looked at each other.

"Excuse me," Birch said, and went in to answer the door, his head feeling woozy from thoughts of prison.

The agent waltzed in, leading with a fist bump. "Whoo hoo," he said. "Look what I got, and on a Sunday no less."

Birch absently returned the bump.

"Who's that?" Robin called from the deck. He got up and stepped into the house. Pam sat for a long moment, then decided to go in too.

The agent looked at Birch, saying, "Hey, you're busy. I won't keep you," and plopped down a stack of papers in a binder on the kitchen island. "Here ya go, offered the asking price."

"What's this?" Robin said, peering over their shoulders. Birch glanced down at the signed offer. The agent handed him a pen and pointed to the line where Birch was to sign to accept the offer. Robin leaned in, squinting to get a better look. "You're moving to a new house?" he cried, voice rising a few notes.

The agent looked up at Birch. "Friends over, I see," he said.

"Alex Pierpont's buying it," Birch said as he put the pen onto the paper. "He works at one of the VCs. Been trying to get in touch with you, apparently."

"I know Pierpont," Robin said in a lowered voice. "It's not me he's after. So where are you moving to? Where's your new place? You're not talking to Pierpont about a new venture, ARE YOU?" Robin's face was growing progressively more red.

Birch signed and handed the pen back to the agent, who collected the papers into his binder and gave Birch a wide smile. "I'll let you know when we can schedule closing, okay?" He offered Birch another fist bump, which Birch accepted before walking with him to the front door.

"Birch! WHERE ARE YOU MOVING TO?" Robin demanded.

Birch said goodbye to the agent at the door and then turned back into the room. "I don't have another place, Robin."

"What? Oh my god! PAM!" Robin pointed a trembling finger at her. "You gotta figure out what the FUCK IS GOING ON HERE! He's talking to PIERPONT about something! He just sold him his damned CONDO for god's sake. How much, Birch? Just tell me what they're offering you."

Birch turned to Robin and frowned. "For the condo?"

"NO not the fucking condo. I don't care about the fucking CONDO," Robin said. "The venture! I'll match it. I'll beat it. Fucking POACHERS! Not NOW!" Robin gripped the edge of the kitchen island as if to yank off the top. He yelled, and his body gave a wild shudder, causing Birch and Pam to flinch. Robin released it, then slammed both fists down on the countertop, making the glasses jump. He closed his eyes, then turned toward Birch and blinked them open. "How much, Birch?" he growled through clenched teeth. "How much of my fucking money will this require?"

Birch stood shocked for a moment. Pam was silent, observing from a few more steps back. "I'm not talking to

Pierpont," Birch said. "He's just buying the condo."

Robin let out a long breath. "I'm confused," he said. "Who is it then?" His phone dinged in its belt holster. He unclipped it and glanced down at it. He looked up at the ceiling, pinched his eyes closed hard, then looked at Pam. "I gotta go," he said. "You get to the bottom of this, and have him drive you wherever you need to go. Birch," Robin turned to him. "I hope you're not talking to someone else. If you're not my lead programmer on Dasher, then number one it doesn't get funded by our guys; I gotta go hunting again. Number two, we don't have a prayer of making our release date. This is our shot, Birch. I can't have those clowns over at Xinda beating Dasher to market. I'm taking good care of you, right? RIGHT?" He looked at them a moment, then strode over to Pam and leaned in, whispering in her ear, "Whatever it takes. I don't care what it costs." He let himself out, then paused on the threshold. He kept his body still but turned his neck and locked eyes with Birch. "You have no idea," he said in a low growl, "how easy it would," then he stopped himself. He looked at the ground, screwed up his face, then walked out, leaving the door open. Pam strode the few steps to push it closed after him.

They heard Robin spin the tires of his Tesla at the end of Birch's driveway.

"How easy it would be to what?" Pam asked.

"I don't know, but I suspect nothing good," Birch said, eyes on the door.

Pam stepped around the island to stand next to him. She looked up at the light gold stubble shading his cheek and jaw, at the thick blond hair falling in unkempt twists to his shoulders. Soil stained the elbows of his white linen hoodie pullover. His hemp trousers were wrinkled, and the draw chord at his waist hung untied. "You haven't showered in a couple days, have you?" she said.

He glanced at her, wondering if her question was designed to throw him off balance or locate the door knob to intimacy. She had an intriguing presence, but even the brief wonder brought back thoughts of Banni and the strange disconnectedness he felt the other day, mixing uncomfortably with the harsh echoes of Robin's threats and sudden departure. He let the wondering cease at the surface of her silk jacket. "Sorry," he said. "Hope I don't offend you with my musk."

"No," she said. "Just curious about what you're doing. This isn't how Robin described you."

"I guess we'll have to sit out on the deck again," he said.

She followed him. The sun was higher. He arranged two of the chairs facing out to the yard. She sat next to him.

"Okay," he said. He had to take a few deep breaths to let the residual fear of Robin subside. Even so, an image of Robin looping in Birch's imagination, busting back in and coming for him, kept him glancing at the deck door.

"Robin tells me you're an up-and-coming rock star programmer, a ten X he called you, well known in the valley, a well-off guy on the brink of being truly rich. Where IS all of your stuff?"

"Sold most of it already," he said. "I might have sold my car, too, by the way. The shop guys could come by at any time, so I may not be able to drive you into town." He looked at her apologetically.

Pam considered him a moment. "Well, we'll figure that out when I'm done with you. I can always Uber. So, tell me. Why are you getting rid of everything?"

"CEOs hire you to make sense of their engineers? Is that a rewarding vocation?"

"Quite." she said, looking out to the yard. She worked on commission now and spent most of her time convincing people that they wanted to do what they first thought they did not want to do, and then extracted signed agreements from them for her employers. Amazing how people will turn once you find their trigger. She'd left Oxford four years ago with a fresh graduate degree in experimental psychology and came home to California, hoping to teach at a university. She'd thought she was on track to her dream job when an instructor spot opened at Davis, but after only two semesters she was downsized, and nothing else surfaced in her specialty. She took an HR job at a big tech firm to keep paying on her student loans, thinking she'd keep her eyes out for the next research and teaching gig. She soon forgot about teaching, however, once her employer discovered how effective she was at convincing and began to remunerate her accordingly. It dawned on her that making the explosive talent in the valley do what employers and financiers wanted could be lucrative business. She imagined herself the personnel counterpart to all of those patent attorneys running around colonizing and building forts in intellectual territories for their corporate masters. She left the HR job, printed up business cards, and was immediately hired back as a consultant pulling down per month what she had been making in half a year. By the time she met Robin the student loans were long gone, and she entertained a stout list of well-paying clients.

She looked back at Birch, hunted for his eyes. She had a large fee at stake here, maybe larger than she'd first discussed. She needed to start figuring him out, and she needed eye contact to do it.

"Will you answer my question? Why get rid of everything?"

"I started seeing it all for what it is: energy in a form not useful to me," he said.

His answer pushed her off the rails of her routine. Normally, with men, she looked in the usual places: sex, money, power, fame, roughly in that order. She couldn't trace Birch's answer back to any of those. *Unusual.* Normally every answer to one of her questions could be somehow tied to one of the big four. She'd have to take it one level back and try to figure out if his motivation was coming from love or fear. And, she still needed eye contact.

"Birch," she said, and waited. She was hoping it was fear. It's always easier to gain control of someone who is chased by fear.

He turned toward her. *Good.* She slipped her eyes onto his. Once she felt he'd stay with her, she began imagining herself having sex with him, loving him, adoring him. She peered deeper into his green-gray eyes and felt the love in herself, magnified it, forced it to bloom and intensify. It felt good, easy with this subject. She could feel the familiar changes in her body chemistry. She could feel the skin of her cheeks flush with warmth. She looked for a sympathetic response in him, looked for his mirror neurons kicking in. "What do you mean, 'not useful' to you?" she asked. She needed to soften him, get him talking, about anything, didn't matter what.

He was at first alarmed by her gaze, then curious. He hadn't really noticed how alluring she was before, attractive in sort of a surprising, not obvious, way. He tried to recall what she was asking about. "What?" he asked.

"What do you mean," she repeated more slowly, smiling inside and keeping her eyes on his, conjuring the warmth of love, "in a form of energy not useful to you?"

"Oh," he said, and took his eyes away to look at the grass. She reached over and lightly touched his thigh with a fingertip, smiling at him when she got his eyes back. She stroked a six-inch line down his thigh as she withdrew her finger, watching his eyes and wondering if perhaps this might be an ASMR trigger for him. *No tremble around his jaw or ears, must be someplace else.*

Birch continued, "I was starting to get confused."

"Yes?" she prompted, the pleasure of confidence building behind her eyes. Confusion was a good indicator, his primal motivation must be fear.

"All of my possessions, all of these things that I've purchased with my time, my work; they are distracting me and clouding my thoughts. I'm trying to figure something out now, and I need clarity. So I've decided to get rid of everything."

Pam kept her eyes on his for only another second, deciding that her own confusion wouldn't help here. He didn't go where she expected. She couldn't make out if this was love or fear. She looked out to the grass for a moment, attempting to process what he'd just said. He looked out too, and was silent.

"What are you trying to figure out?" she finally asked.

"Intelligence. How intelligence lives and moves. What our role is relative to intelligence," he said. "Whether it lives in us, or we live in it."

Her go-to was to seek eye contact again, but she held herself away. She felt doubt, and couldn't afford to transfer that to Birch. She needed him to feel clarity and resolve, but only toward the points spelled out in the document waiting in the inside pocket of her jacket, on which Birch's signature would allow her to collect her large fee. She needed to move away from his thoughts about intelligence toward something simpler with which she could gain traction, begin to maneuver.

She kept her eyes directed toward the yard. "Tell me about Zongo's new project, Dasher. Has that contributed to what's going on with you now?"

"Dasher is needlessly violent and minimal in meaning. Nothing about it is constructive," Birch replied in a monotone. "Okay, maybe some of the tech in the characters could be useful, but not in that context."

Pam decided that she needed footing. She touched the back of his hand to get his eyes back. Maybe money could reveal a path.

"But Robin pays you a lot of money to develop these projects, correct? Zongo has made you a rich man. How do you feel about that?"

Birch let his eyes take in her full face, then her posture. He let his peripheral vision travel her frame before returning to her eyes. He thought she looked uncomfortable. She looked like she wasn't taking full breaths, and like she was stiff.

"Does that really make a difference to you?" he asked.

"It's important to a lot of people, most people, I'd say. The question is: is it important to you?" Pam already knew the answer to that. She felt like a rookie posing that question, like she was randomly moving chess pieces to buy time to think of a strategy, not sure if she was already caging herself on the board or not. She looked away and rolled her eyes. She could feel the clammy heat of embarrassment beginning to rise from her lower back. Maybe what she did for a living was immoral, and this guy was an agent of some higher power sent to bring her under a light. *Stop,* she told herself. *Stop thinking. If I get paranoid and start doubting myself, then that will transfer to him, and he'll never get near a pen.*

She composed herself and decided to go for all of it; she'd commit to a strategy, and a risky one with which she had no experience yet. She'd been researching a line of questioning, part of a study in the mid-90s, that was purported to make people who could slog through them fall in love with each other. The danger, or course, was that the effect develops mutually. She would have to be strong enough to fall in love, get his compliance, but then get back out in one piece.

Pam adjusted her chair to face him more directly, then reached across her knees to touch his arm. "Forget about work," she said. "Let's just chat. I can see you thinking in there, and I feel like you're my long lost brother or something." She smiled at him and waited for him to return it. She wished that they were on a couch together, where she could more easily hunt for his ASMR triggers, but these chairs would have to do. She sat back as comfortably as the chair would allow. "I can tell thinking is one of your favorite things. Me too," she said. "What else do you like doing? What would be a perfect day for you?"

Pam hadn't worked with the questions long enough to be confident in the sequence, or practiced at working them naturally into conversation, but she knew them well enough to hold Birch's curiosity and keep him talking. He maintained an amused expression while listening to her. The method required both parties to answer the questions, and Birch paid polite attention, half-wondering what she was up to and half at the fluttering feeling around his ears and jaw as she spoke in a near whisper, now and then tapping her tongue against the roof of her mouth.

Before long, they were sitting leaned toward each other, looking into each other's eyes as they listened or spoke. Birch scooted his chair closer so he didn't have to lean so far. Pam rested a couple fingers on Birch's leg. She felt the warmth of his breath as he spoke, unconsciously mirroring her whispered tones.

Thirty minutes in, she marveled at how she felt she could love him, maybe did already love him. *So, this shit really works,* she thought. She concentrated on her breath to calm it down, even it out. *If it's working for me, is it working for him?* She felt her heart beating faster and warmth behind her cheeks, up the back of her neck and down her spine, a thin mist of perspiration forming around her temples. She forgot what she was there to do, momentarily recalled the folded papers in her jacket pocket, then forgot them again as she watched his eyes while he related the last time he cried by himself.

He told her a story of waking up after one of his nightmares about the woman on the plains. She listened to him, glancing up and down from his lips to his eyes, feeling a broad shift in her being, a widening of undefined space, like a nameless, borderless land where whole weather systems of vulnerability formed and spun together. He finished his story and said, "Okay, now your turn. What happened the last time you cried by yourself?"

Pam stared at him and could no longer think. She couldn't remember. She could only remember his face. She closed her eyes, then opened them, tears forming in a rush. He leaned back from her with a concerned expression. "Pam?" She turned her head away and let out one sob, slipped off her jacket and draped it over her chair back.

"I can't remember the last time," she sobbed. "I can only remember right now."

Birch sat in his chair with raised eyebrows. Her sobs

continued quietly. His first thought was to comfort her. *This woman is fighting something big here,* he thought. *She probably can't tell me what it is with words; words are too coarse for that. We need a more finely grained language. If we were a more advanced and perceptive species, I would be able to decode the message through my fingers, through this thin layer of silk, through the vibrations emanating from her and moving through space.*

Whatever it was she fought existed as a pattern stored in her brain and nervous system. It was a pattern that must have established in a way that the language code and logic we all use was insufficient to solve it. Yet she sought to solve it that way, not knowing any alternative. She studied the strategic use of words and ideas in order to solve it, becoming a psychologist as a result. She apparently earned her living that way, yet the tools she'd gained were not enough.

Birch pulled out his phone and contacted an Uber driver for her. Later, after she climbed into the back seat, she rolled down the window and gave him a long, thoughtful look. Her eyes were heavy. "You're leaving Zongo, aren't you," she said, a statement more than a question.

He thought a moment, then nodded.

He went back to the yard to rest and think. She'd only been there a couple hours, but he was strangely exhausted by it. He laid down on the grass in the sunshine. He set the phone on his chest with the solar cells from the case facing the sun and let his arms and legs spread out. He drifted into sleep and dreamt about the space between subatomic particles. He entered the point of view of a single particle, was starting to feel the composition of the space between himself and other particles. It was something like knowing push attraction computation, and he could feel how the space everywhere was all one thing. There weren't different spaces, and the space near him knew everything about the space everywhere else, around every other particle in existence. It knew itself. It was a single thing.

The phone buzzed and dinged on Birch's chest, waking him. He felt the warmth of a mild sunburn on his face as the shreds of the dream rolled off of him like dried pine needles. He lifted the phone and saw a text from Melanie. It was still Sunday. People were in the office, and someone had said they'd seen Robin slapping his desk until his hands were red. He'd been pacing around angry with everyone. She'd heard him through his office door leave a message for a headhunter firm to try and poach some engineers from Google. Melanie wanted Birch to know. He texted her back, informing her he was leaving the company and that he thought she should be the lead programmer. "Tell Robin I said that" he typed. He then took the phone inside and plugged it in to charge it faster.

The agent called to say they could get the inspection done first thing Monday morning and probably close the next day at the title insurance office in Palo Alto. Pierpont didn't need financing and was ready to go. He mentioned that Birch would probably want to have the place cleaned before the inspection.

Birch got out the vacuum and cleaning supplies, deciding to take care of that himself. His decision to leave Palo Alto with no destination in mind had felt incomplete, like a thought experiment in progress. As he followed the vacuum from room to room, lifting particles of soil, sand, and dust, listening to their gritty sling up the suction tube, sometimes believing he could almost hear the scrape and percussion of individual particles as they turned the corner at the handle and slammed into the bag, the idea that he was leaving gained mass.

He dusted and wiped into the evening, cleaning all of the rooms save the kitchen down to their roots. It grew too dark to do the windows, so he stopped for the night, felt the soreness of fatigue, and crawled into his sleeping bag.

With the sun he was up, wiping the hard viscous film of industrial age atmosphere, mixed with information age and road rage atmosphere, from the outsides of his windows, the cloth and cleaning spray circling together in squeaks and cries as the film softened and left the glass.

He moved to the insides of the windows. The inspector came and went through her list. Nothing but routine. The place was functionally new.

He took pleasure in clearing the window glass, shining it to invisibility. He was buffing the living room window when his phone dinged on the kitchen counter. He walked over to glance at it. A text from Robin, not surprising.

"What the hell did you do to Pam? You BASTARD!!! DON'T think that life is FREE! YOUR BILL might be coming DUE!!! You will not be getting OUT OF THIS FOR FREE!!!!"

Birch would have let the shock subside and gone back to wiping the windows, except this text included a link to Quora, which made him curious. He tapped it, and his browser opened to a Quora page asking the question: "Are there really hired hitmen?" Birch's face felt instantly hot and his chest became heavy with pain. The answers asserted that certainly there were—with enough money you could pretty much get anyone killed. It looked like some of the people answering had worked for the government. Numerous comments referenced the Jeffrey Epstein case. He stopped reading, closed the browser and put the phone down, a damp sweat breaking out on his forehead. He went to look in each room and peer out each window, feeling halfway ridiculous, but half expecting to see someone sneaking toward him. He locked the front door and rear slider.

He desperately wanted to talk to Angel and thought about trying to call him, maybe trying to speak in code. He went over in his mind the mustang sequence Angel had laid out the last time they'd spoken. It was a little too elaborate for a moment of panic. *What the hell.* He picked up his phone and tapped Angel's contact info and dialed his number. The phone rang and rang. No answer, then a click and a message saying that Angel's voicemail had been deactivated. *Fuck!*

He took Ziplock bags from a kitchen drawer and filled

them with greens, oatmeal, cheese, beans, crackers, summer sausage, dried apricots, and rice. He paused by the rear slider and scanned the yard, staring for a long time at the tops of the tall pickets of the privacy fence, then quietly unlocked the slider and moved it open just wide enough to slip through. He took the filled baggies out to the tent and cached them in the drawstring food bag in his backpack, feeling the hair on the back of his neck prickle as he crawled into the tent. He went back into the condo and re-locked the slider, then compressed a loaf of bread to a quarter of its size and grabbed some plastic spice bottles, collecting these on the counter with the bread ball. He filled a food tube from his camping collection with peanut butter, another with vegetable oil, grabbed a few apples and pears from the refrigerator, gathered those with the bread and spice containers, unlocked the slider again, and took everything out to the tent. He came back in, moving quickly and lightly, and looked into the wine fridge, deciding to leave the few random bottles as a housewarming gift for Pierpont.

He called the Salvation Army and walked from room to room, telling the woman what he had and that if they sent a large truck before the end of the day they could have it all as a donation. Then he set to washing the remaining dishes and implements and cleaning the kitchen. He left the knives lined up on the counter in case he needed to grab one quickly, then imagined how that might go if he found himself face-to-face with some sort of professional, and put them back into the drawer with a shudder.

A cloud front pushed across the foothills, darkening the sky and spilling rain for a few hours. Birch went outside, as the first drops fell, to organize his gear in the tent and zip up the tent fly. The rain beat down heavily, rinsing off the deck, the driveway, and the building. Later in the afternoon the sun returned, pulling wisps of steam up from the lawn.

The Salvation Army truck rolled in around mid-afternoon. A wiry guy with tattoos and a sleeveless black t-shirt and a burly guy with a white faded Hard Rock t-shirt and oil-stained bluejeans started carrying out the remaining contents of Birch's condo.

Birch left them to their work but kept tossing wary glances at them, thinking about that Quora link Robin had sent. He sat with his phone on the edge of the deck, turned to face the house, and ordered a butane cartridge for next-day delivery for his backpacking stove. He then entered the condo through the slider with a camp cup and water bottle, going to the sink to fill them. The Salvation Army guys came down the hall. "You guys all set?" Birch asked, capping the water bottle.

"Yeah, we got all of it," the wiry guy said.

"Thanks," Birch said.

"You need a donation receipt for your taxes?" the wiry guy asked.

"No thanks."

The guys left through the front door.

Birch heard the truck engine start and the gears grind as the truck pulled out of his driveway.

It looked like rain again that night, so Birch draped his clothes on the outside of the tent to get drenched and slept naked in his sleeping bag, in the tent this time, to the sound of the drumming droplets.

In the morning he wrung out his clothes, shook them and put them on. He shivered in the clammy cloth, but knew he'd be walking soon and would dry quickly. He broke down the tent and packed up his gear. He put on clean socks and his hiking shoes, shouldered the pack and walked through the empty condo one last time, exiting out the front door. He made sure that he had both sets of keys and locked the door, then walked around his driveway with the pack on to check the load, waiting for the FedEx driver with his butane cartridge.

His clothes were mostly dry by the time his cartridge arrived. He checked the time on his phone and decided that he could make the closing if he walked instead of calling an Uber, so headed out the driveway and turned right toward Palo Alto. With his eyes he cased the windows of the neighboring units to see if anyone appeared to be watching him. He didn't think Robin would expect him to be walking anywhere, and wouldn't be on the lookout for someone with a backpack, but at the same time he felt being vigilant didn't lose him anything. As he walked he kept his eyes moving and scanning, searching his memory for stories of lunatics full of bluster who turned out to be the real deal. He seemed to recall many of the dozens of school and theater shootings peppering the news had that component, the guy no one expects to actually snap, thinking him troubled but basically harmless, until the day he loses it and sprays a group of innocents with his AR-15. It's only with hindsight that people say they should have known based on the crazy stuff in his Instagram stories or his Facebook posts. Birch didn't want that same regret about Robin.

When he arrived at the title agency on Cowper Street an hour an a half later, the agent and Alex Pierpont were already in the conference room with the title agent and Pierpont's lawyer. Birch left his backpack in the waiting room and joined the others. They sat at the table and passed papers back and forth to scribble their signatures, with Pierpont's lawyer periodically stopping the flow to ask a question or request a word change. Birch didn't object to anything the lawyer suggested, so the closing completed in half an hour. The agent calculated the difference between Birch's mortgage payoff and the buying price, and asked Birch if he had a new address where he'd like a check sent from the escrow service.

"I don't," Birch told him.

"We can also send you an email when the funds clear escrow," the agent said, "and you can come in to pick it up."

Birch told him he'd rather the funds were simply wired into his account. He gave the agent his routing and account numbers, handed the keys over to Pierpont, shook everyone's hands, and said goodbye. He shouldered his pack in the waiting room and headed out to the street.

6

Angel concluded the meeting by drawing a line on the whiteboard under the last objective in the list, "domain name services," and saying, "We'll unwrap this one in the next meeting, but the preview is that we are to make the network fully compatible with the commercial internet." The programmers kept their eyes on him, waiting for him to finish as they began to drift back toward their work stations. He was going to say more but then didn't bother. He let them roll back, glancing at each other, to get their hands on their keyboards and eyes back to their screens, to sit there and type and think, figure out adequate solutions to micro problems so granular and obscure that they could expand those mental puzzles to fill the entire scope of their daily lives, ignoring the bigger picture while they spun the time they spent into their ample paychecks.

One woman stood with her hands on her chair back and looked at him. "I know what this—is about," she said. Her name was Erin. She was one of the last coders to join the team. She was also one of the youngest, in her early twenties, and showed crazy raw talent. Her thoughts flowed smoothly through her hands on the keyboard, but they banged into each other when she spoke, building pressure behind her mouth and coming out in awkward bursts as part of her brain wanted to push the thought out while another part of her brain found it ridiculous that we still express ourselves with such primitive apparatus. Her glasses slipped on her nose and her wide ears batted black curls back and forth as her head spasmed, pushing each phrase past her teeth. Angel liked her but hadn't had much time to get to know her. He had been preoccupied trying to get the teams organized and on task while privately working to deconstruct how the company's surveillance worked. He tried to send her a signal with his eyes that she shouldn't say any more.

"This isn't about national defense," Erin said, "or battlefield comm. Those last modules are strictly for commerce. And—now we're going to make it all compatible with global DNS?" She glared at him. "Look at this." She swept one hand in a circle, indicating the whiteboards on all four walls of the cavernous room, all covered with lists and diagrams and process flows. "We're spending taxpayer dollars to build," her head jiggled, "a system to compete with and absorb as much of the existing internet—as possible. I'm sure —nobody here minds." She flashed her eyes wide and squeezed her lips together. "We're getting—paid like five times what a normal developer would get. That's—quiet money!"

Angel blinked his eyes and lightly shook his head at her, causing Erin's face to blush with frustration. "Someone plans to—own this," she went on, "to—control it. It's obviously —designed to mock open systems—to fool—whoever the users are—who I think are supposed to be—the public— not soldiers—while being tuned—for centralized control— surveillance. That logging bit is crazy with everything else we're building. It would make sense in a closed temporary network, but not with this. So—we're writing for special chips, creating our own flavor of Linux, our own scripting language, going—nuts on power and memory management. I get that, battlefield drones, battery life, sure. But what's this?" She gestured toward a section of one whiteboard. "What battlefield operation needs—a payment gateway? And this? It's—a back door to let someone snoop more easily. Look. And those are—virtualizations—of every service that runs the world wide web! And, every one is designed to use the exact same protocols as the commercial internet. Why wouldn't soldiers have proprietary—devices to connect to a proprietary network? So that the wrong people CAN'T connect to it, and so we could write efficient code that IS better on memory and CPU. This is designed to allow anyone to connect and use it just like the commercial internet. Who is this—for—anyway?"

He put his hand on her shoulder and nodded his silent agreement to her. She continued to glare at him, not understanding. "We can't talk about that right now," was all he could think to say.

"What do you mean we can't talk about it?" she asked. "We're building it!"

"Not here," he tried to mouth silently to her. She cocked her head at him and squinted behind her wire glasses. Her whole body spasmed, and she rolled back to her desk and slumped. The other engineers glanced up now and then, but kept their focus on their screens.

Angel was impressed by her. In a short time she had taken in all the pieces and understood the big picture, even though the company had him deploy the group in separate teams that worked under difficult deadlines focused on separate pieces. He had thought that he was the only one in the room who was getting how the whole design fit together. Now they were all probably wondering. Angel felt disjointed, even wrong, working this way, but he let it happen, subconsciously believing that he was protecting them from the truth, and believing that he had to keep a grip on the tiger's tail until he could figure out what to do about the teeth and claws. If not him, then who?

It wasn't long before Stu strode through the door. Angel was back at his desk, provoked by Erin's protest to try to stitch together in his mind where the money for this project actually came from. He hadn't thought about that angle much, but he recalled the Federal Reserve pulling such shenanigans as blowing fourteen trillion dollars into existence and then shipping it off to Great Britain to accounts unknown and then refusing to provide any detail, the Fed chairman claiming that to reveal same would be "unproductive." Angel imagined that if you could pull that off in broad daylight, then it wouldn't be too difficult to flip funds around to some black budget somewhere controlled by people who don't feel the need to answer to anyone. The irony of his situation became just a little more clear. The federal withholding on every paycheck in this room was more than the average American's total salary, and it, along with everyone else's tax dollars, was flowing like a river into a system that deigned itself less accountable every year, free to peel off black budgets for projects like this one that were designed to make a few people huge profits.

"I didn't expect to see you up here," Angel said. Stu pointed his PalmPilot at him, and Angel picked up his and pointed the infrared port at Stu's.

"Everyone working on what they're supposed to?" Stu asked while watching the spinning sync icon on his screen. The devices simultaneously beeped.

"Yes," Angel said. He opened the calendar and notes on his PalmPilot to see what Stu had added before dropping it into the cradle wired to his work station.

"Good," Stu said. He stuffed his PalmPilot into his jacket pocket, walked over to Erin's desk and leaned down to speak with her. She looked up and frowned. A few of the nearby programmers watched as Erin got up from her chair and followed Stu from the room. Angel took a few steps toward them, but Stu held up his hand without looking at him, stopping his advance. *Damn it,* Angel thought.

The next day, when Erin did not appear at her desk, he asked Stu where she was. Stu's eyes appeared to glaze and darken. "Human resources determined that she should pursue opportunities elsewhere," was all he would say.

A couple weeks later it was the last Saturday in October, and the weather promised to be clear and warm. Angel and Winnie took their coffees before dawn, loaded up their day-hiking gear and drove east across the valley to Santa Fe and on up to Apache Canyon. Winnie guided their little pickup bouncing up the rutted forest road, pulling into the trailhead lot at the Baldy gate just as sunrise painted the very tops of the pine trees. A few other vehicles rimmed the dirt lot. Winnie and Angel got out, stretched and shook themselves loose. Angel yawned and swung his arms. He spotted a guy from his programming staff clipping on a belt pack and locking up his Subaru.

"Mornin' Chad!" Angel called across the lot to him.

The guy turned and recognized Angel. "Hey!" he said, and walked over. Angel introduced Winnie as they were shouldering their day packs.

"Looks like a beautiful day for Thompson Peak," Chad said. Winnie smiled at him, and Chad looked around like he was distracted, commenting on the weather and scenery. Angel could see in his face and eyes that Chad was in the same muzzled communication mode that they all used at the office, feeling that itch in the back of their necks and assuming that everything they said was being monitored and recorded. They talked with each other like cyborgs rather than people and limited their subject matter to acceptable work topics, behaving like they were in a small dictatorial state dropped into the middle of what was supposed to be the vast freedom of America.

Angel laughed at Chad's platitudes and laid his hand on his back, touching the back of his own neck with his other hand. "Chad, listen. Don't worry. These fucking chips don't work this far from the complex."

Chad stopping talking and looked at Angel.

"Seriously," Angel continued. "I've done a series of tests to figure it out. I've used our own Stu Pitt as my main testing device, and either he's a genius student of human behavior or these chips lose their connection about halfway across the valley to Santa Fe."

Chad's whole body visibly relaxed, his shoulders dropping a full six inches toward the earth. He let out a long breath and nodded, then slowly shook his head and smiled.

"It's crazy," he said.

"Yeah," Angel said. "They track our butts real close in the complex and around town, and just so you know, all your email, social net stuff, web browsing from home, they're pretty good at that. But the signal drops off around thirty miles. As long as you're not using your phone, they got nothing out here."

The three walked together past the gate and started climbing the trail, rounding the shaded slope into the sunlit pines. "You sure about the signal?" Chad asked.

"As sure as I can be," Angel said.

"Well," Chad continued, "I'm worried something bad happened to Erin."

"Hmm?" Angel wondered too, but wanted to learn what Chad knew.

"Yeah. I knew her from before. Really sharp. After she left, I emailed her personal account to see how she was doing and got a bounceback, capacity full. That would never happen. She's nuts about in-box hygiene. The only way that would ever happen is if she's not able to check her mail, or if someone else got control of her account."

Angel frowned, staring at the trail ahead of them. They were silent for many steps, the only sounds a sliding breeze and the crunch of sand and ancient clay under their boots. They had opened the lid a crack, but neither really knew if he could fully trust the other. Angel caught Chad's eye as they walked and held his gaze, trying to decide if this guy was a plant or could be an ally.

Angel then looked ahead along the trail and said, "Dammit. I don't know. Fuck!"

"I don't think I like this company," Winnie said.

They skirted a slope for a mile or so before turning uphill toward a hilltop, where they stopped to drink from their water bottles and take in the view.

Chad turned to Angel and said, "You know, that Stu is a

total weirdo."

"No joke," Angel said.

"You know he visits porn sites from his office?"

"Really? His office in the compound?"

"Yeah. One of the IT guys, Dave Pacineki, used to work with me at Oak Ridge, told me he's seen Pitt's network address come up in the proxy logs from their outside network hitting all these porn sites like every day. Can you believe he's that stupid? If any of us ever did that.... They must not scrutinize their VPN logs like they do ours."

He glanced over at Chad. "You're shittin' me, right?"

"Nope," Chad said. He leaned forward to look at Winnie. "Sorry Winnie," he said.

She waved him off. "I've heard worse," she said.

Interesting, Angel thought. They entered the trailhead and walked up Baldy Trail, stepping over a narrow gully and hiking between scrub pines through a crowning meadow toward mature woods at the apron of the mountain. Large air masses roamed slowly through the valleys and washed over the hills. The morning warmed as they entered the old pines at the turn.

"You know," Chad said, "what we're building. Seems pretty fucked up to me. I heard what Erin was saying before she disappeared. Brilliant, in some ways. But really fucked up. I can kinda see where they want to go with it. I'm actually thinking of quitting. You know? I mean, the money's incredible, but I'm just weirded out by it, especially with not being able to get in touch with Erin now."

They wound through tall tree trunks and passed a sign announcing that they were entering a watershed.

"I know," Angel said.

"It's fucked up, man. I feel like I'm taking blood money."

"Well," Angel said, "I'm staying in. Gonna try to figure something out."

After a few hundred more yards of trail, Chad said, "Wouldn't mess with them. They've got the military, CIA, NSA,

I'm sure the whole package. Don't know how you could do anything without them taking you out. I mean, where's Erin?"

"I hear you," Angel said. "You're gonna have to be careful if you leave, too."

They stopped to rest at a promontory looking out over the treetops toward Pecos Canyon, sitting with the rising sun at their backs, gulping water and nibbling granola and raisins, pulling in the fresh air.

"So, what do you think you can do?" Chad asked Angel.

Angel followed the horizon with his eyes and tried to imagine all of the evergreen needles within the scope of his view, envisioning how each needle did a small set of simple things, yet together they made a forest. "I think the OS," he said, "though, to keep us all safe, for what it's worth, maybe I shouldn't say any more." He glanced at Chad and then looked back at the horizon. He could tell Chad was curious, could feel him deciding whether to press.

"You know how they're planning on deploying the network, right?" Angel asked.

"I'm guessing small deploys of drones for remote areas like battlefields, like half a dozen or a dozen, something like that? I mean, that's even a pretty big communication area. And maybe piggybacking on satellites or the cell network? I'm still not clear on all that, but that's what I thought the DNS tie-in was for."

"No," Angel said. "The whole thing is going to be airborne. They've got a design for a drone made mostly of graphene-4 and resin, powered by a wafer battery that is recharged remotely with microwave. Super light, strong, able to repair itself in the field using nanobots and onboard material stores. They're planning on sending up something like six million of these things, each one a wireless node with a six-to-twenty mile range, router, and the host of our OS. They intend to wrap the globe inside this network. With our software, it will manage and repair itself, manage bandwidth, traffic, store data, run apps. It'll function like its own ISP for the entire globe."

Chad thought in silence for a few moments. Then, "Holy fuck," he whispered. "They think they're going to deploy that, give away service for free for awhile and put every other ISP out of business."

Angel nodded. "That's what it looks like. Then they control everything and can charge what they want."

"Crazy." Chad shook his head. "It'll never work."

"Wait 'til you see one of these drones. It'll blow your mind. If they figure out how to stamp those things out and launch them into the environment, holy fuck is right."

Chad looked at him. "So what's your plan?"

Angel took another gulp of water and then stood to continue the hike. "Just keep on building it. When they launch it, it won't be exactly what they intended." He chuckled to himself, but said no more.

Chad and Winnie stood also. Chad's eyes were on the trail ahead, but his thoughts were inside the code, trying to imagine what Angel had in mind and how he could pull it off.

Angel was thinking about Birch. How could he find him and contact him without the company's surveillance machinery sniffing him out?

"I'm not seeing how you can make much of a difference," Chad said as they strode along the trail.

"I know a guy who might be able to help," Angel said.

7

Birch thought about walking back up into the foothills, but then had an urge to head east toward the mountains. He pictured himself hidden on a mountainside somewhere, watching black SUVs tracing a road in a valley below. He walked along Cowper, stopping for a rest and to drink some water in the shade of the tall evergreens in Hoover Park. Then he continued east toward Mountain View. He stopped at a 7-Eleven to use the ATM and bought some beef jerky and a chocolate bar. As the cash flopped out of the ATM like a big green tongue, it struck Birch that by using his bank card he had just left a breadcrumb for Robin. On cue his phone buzzed in his pocket. It was Robin beginning his harassment for the day. Birch glanced at the message and deleted it, something about making sure he'd never work anywhere besides Zongo. A flash of fear clawed Birch's throat, and he resolved not to be so careless. He would only use his untraceable Slang account from here on.

Farther along the street, elementary school boys were practicing soccer in a field next to their school. Birch felt the sun on the back of his pants, seeing the shadows lengthen in front of him. It was a warm, mid-September day, and his back sweated beneath the snug backpack, though the air began to cool as the afternoon wore on.

Toward evening he stopped in a well-groomed neighborhood park in Sunnyvale, with picnic tables made from recycled plastic bottles and charcoal grills stuck in the ground in the shade of tall locust and spruce. Parents with jog strollers sat on benches around a redwood play structure while their children navigated the bars and columns and platforms above a thick bed of wood chips. In a field nearby, a group of four teenaged boys flew an electric radio-controlled airplane.

Birch felt tired from the walk. His knees, hips, and ankles were hot and sore. He hadn't taken a walk like this in a long time. Seven years earlier, he would have walked that far over mountains and only felt exhilarated by it. He felt he'd lost touch with his body over the years, but might now choose to get to know it again.

He swung his pack off and set it on the ground next to a picnic table and sat, leaning on an elbow on the tabletop. He pulled a water bottle from a mesh pocket on the side of the pack and drank while watching the kids play thirty yards away in what was left of the sunlight. He took his hiking shoes and socks off and propped his feet up on the picnic bench. The fatigue inside his body welled up as if a search bot were methodically visiting each muscle, ligament, and joint, each square inch of facia, to index how worn and tired it was, then publishing the results for him to experience.

He pulled out his phone and immediately regretted it. The litany from Robin included a message saying he knew that Birch had sold his Subaru, so Robin guessed he wasn't looking for that vehicle anymore but assured Birch that "we will still find you." *Who's "we?"* Birch wondered. He frowned and moved to a table backed by a row of evergreens, less visible from the street.

Some of the parents were packing up their kids and rolling out of the park. A few struggled with their kid's desire to stay longer. The high whining of seven-year-olds mixed with the lower whining of young parents, drifted over to the shaded picnic area. Birch opened the top of his pack and reached in for some beef jerky. Every now and then he would look up and catch one or another parent staring at him as if he were some sort of threat. Maybe he'd been there too long for their comfort.

The sun dipped behind the trees. Birch went on alert as he saw a ragged man with an unshaven gray face walk into the park with a black garbage bag slung over his shoulder, a greasy canvas tote in his other hand stuffed with gray matter that looked like bursting entrails but was probably a sleeping bag or blankets, perhaps a soiled quilt. He wore an insulated, oily black snorkel coat, way too hot for the weather but unzipped in front, revealing a dirty faded Berkeley sweatshirt stretched taut over a mound of chest and gut. He visited each trash barrel on his way in, setting down the tote and lifting the barrel lid to peer inside. He leaned deep into one, the top half of his body about disappearing and his rubber boots lifting off the ground, clunked around inside and came out with a paw full of cans. He lidded the barrel and dropped his harvest into his garbage bag. Birch glanced over toward the play structure and saw that the last of the parents had rolled their children away, the teenagers with the RC plane also having vacated the field.

The guy checked the last of the barrels on his way into the picnic area, setting his garbage bag and tote down at a table next to Birch's. The garbage bag settled to the ground with an extended clinking and clattering that made Birch think of a knight errant setting down his weaponry. Birch watched him closely and thought to pay special attention to his hands. The guy regarded Birch from his round, hairy face, and said, "Where you in from? You down I-5? Portland?" Birch shook his head. "You look like you have a place somewhere," the guy said. "You a journalist?"

"No," Birch said.

"You got a place?"

"No."

"Just new then," the guy said. "Your kit looks too nice. I'd watch it."

The sun continued its descent below the hills, and a languid breeze pushed along by the traffic in the street crept under the trees, cooling them. Another homeless guy walked along the edge of the park and approached the barrels. He noticed the guy sitting near Birch and saw his garbage bag on the ground. He vectored away from the barrels back out to the sidewalk and moved on.

"The more a guy's got to lose," the round-faced guy continued, "the more turtle he's got in him, and the less wolf. Everybody out here knows that. When you're hungry, you're the wolf, and you can pick at the turtles all day long until one leaves his leg or his head out too far. That pack of yours looks too nice. Unless you're trying to hitch somewhere. Then it might help."

Birch thought about where he might go, and whether it made a difference beyond getting somewhere Robin would not find him. It didn't matter to him where he took his body, only where he took his thoughts. "I don't know where I'm going yet," he said. "I'm thinking about east, the middle of the country somewhere."

The round-faced guy pondered that a moment. "I wouldn't go out there. Most guys are heading south to LA this time of year. Good restaurants all the way up and down, decent parks to sleep. You'd starve if you went east. Nothing out there. Cops don't have as much to do out there either. Hassle you like hyenas. Harder to get around."

Birch thought about what might be out there. Less distraction, he imagined. More space. He'd never been out there, but he knew he wouldn't starve if that's where he decided to go. He was different from this homeless man. Technically, Birch was also a homeless man, albeit temporarily, he supposed, but he guessed most homeless people considered it a temporary condition. But Birch had an electronic device in his pocket that allowed him to connect to the cloud. As long as he could access the cloud, he wouldn't starve. He had access to any information he could want. He had access to communication. He could call transportation to himself. He owned rights to accounts measured in numbers of dollars, and he could put those numbers into service for things that he needed. He could transfer some of his numbers to some other account and have a plane ticket in exchange, or clothes or food, a nice hotel room. He had his pack and sleeping bag, and his gear, and clothes, and his arms and legs and feet, but these were just tiny pieces of who he was and what he had. His thoughts, the patterns stored in his brain, his ability to access the cloud and do things there, to create patterns that could interact with other patterns and change them and store them, this was the larger part of who he was.

"You look skinny. You know how to eat yet? How long you been out?" the round-faced man asked him.

Birch didn't know what he meant by that. Of course he knew how to eat. "Just today," he answered.

"Holy smokes! First day! Boy do I remember. Let's make dinner," the man said. "I'll show you how it's done." He leaned over and plunged a thick hand into his tote among the folds of his blankets, mumbling, "First day! Gawd, pretty scary shit." He fished around and withdrew a yellowed plastic bag. From it he pulled a package of meat on a Styrofoam tray wrapped in cellophane. The grocery store bar code and price label were still on it. The man held it up for Birch to see. "Two days past the expiration," he said. "I'm going to share this with you, but only tonight, since you're new. Back of any grocery store. It's the law. They have to get rid of this stuff every day, but it's perfectly good." He began to unwrap the cellophane. "Dumpsters full of just about whatever you want. Cube steak for dinner, my friend." He raised the unwrapped tray to his furry face and sniffed. "Yup, perfectly good. See that playground over there? Go get me two big handfuls of wood chips. Smell 'em before you bring 'em over. Make sure there's no kid piss or dog shit in 'em."

Birch did as instructed. The round-faced man went back to the trash barrels and found some crumpled newspaper. "You have to check this too," he said. "No telling what people will wrap in newspaper to throw away." He wadded it up and stuffed it under the grate of one of the standing grills. He piled some wood chips onto the paper and pulled a book of matches from his pocket. He showed them to Birch. "Liquor stores give these away," he said, and lit the newspaper. As the flame spread and caught the chips, he said, "Here. You keep adding wood chips. I'll go get some more. We want a nice bed of coals."

They ate the steaks well-done, draped over a couple of sticks, chewing the edges until the meat was gone. "Not bad, eh?" the round-faced man said. "What's your name anyway?"

"Birch," he said, and immediately thought he shouldn't have used his real name. What if this guy was an informant, or happened to mention that he'd seen him?

"You a tree?"

Birch thought he detected a glint of amusement in the man's eye. He pondered a while. "Yes," he finally said.

"I'm Wolf," the man said. "Careful I don't pee on you."

Wolf got up from the picnic bench and walked over to a tall maple. Through the gray twilight Birch could hear a stream splashing against the trunk. Birch took his pack to the grass at the edge of the picnic area and pulled out his tent. He took it from the stuff sack and laid it out on the ground. Wolf's voice came from near the orange glow of the grill: "Number one, you can't set up a tent. That just makes you a turtle right off. The wolves will start to circle as soon as they see it. The cops too. You gotta get a dark tarp. You are not on a camping trip. Put that thing back in your pack."

A police cruiser crept along the curb, easing to a stop across a sidewalk and lawn opposite the picnic area. The darkening sky reflected opaque on the closed windows.

"See?" Wolf said. "Now we have to adapt. Put your pack away real tidy and lean it against that tree. We only have a minute if we want to avoid some real unpleasantness. Fuck. And if they saw me pee then I have to do some fast talking."

Birch did as instructed. Meanwhile Wolf shed his coat and peeled off the sweatshirt to reveal a rather clean, sporty looking track suit. He pulled a new ball cap with a GSI logo out of his tote and deftly arranged his mass of hair beneath it, then wrapped his coat inside out in a foil-backed space blanket and stuffed them into his tote bag. Lastly he pulled out a composition notebook while instructing Birch to take the dinner wrappings to a nearby trash barrel and then return to the picnic table.

By the time Birch had returned to the table, two police officers were walking across the lawn toward the picnic area. Birch considered grabbing his pack and heading out, but then thought it was too late not to look suspicious.

"You know," Wolf said in a low voice, "your clothes do look a tad dirty. You might want to have a clean set for encounters, and a durable set for traveling. That's what works for most of us."

The officers stopped at the edge of the table cluster. One gripped a long aluminum flashlight, sweeping its beam over the table where Birch and Wolf sat across from each other. They stood silently, taking in Birch and Wolf, the fading grill, the pack and tote by the base of the tree. Birch wondered why they needed the flashlight this early.

"Hello there," one of them finally called out.

Wolf looked up from his open notebook into the flashlight beam. "Thank you for the added illumination, officers. We were just about ready to attend to that need ourselves. Now, what can we do for you two gentlemen?"

The policemen looked at each other. Random unrelated squawks chirped from their mobile radios. "Park's closed," one barked. "Time to clear out."

Birch stared at the notebook pages, attempting to decipher their contents upside down, scanning slowly from the bottom, right to left. He saw what appeared to be dense algebra, diagrams, numbered lists, margin notes with reference lines, notes written upon notes, lines and notes scratched out, some with obvious vehemence. He looked up to see Wolf's eyebrows arch in the flashlight beam. Wolf slowly shifted his weight on the picnic bench and reached into the pants pocket of his track suit. Birch heard one of the officers behind him unholster his gun, then saw the alarm in Wolf's eyes. Birch cringed. "It's just a wristwatch, officers," Wolf said. He slowly lifted it to show them, then slid it onto his left wrist and gently snapped the clasp. Birch noticed that it appeared to be a Rolex and wondered if it was a fake. "I'm sorry. I wasn't aware that this particular park closed this early. In fact, I was under the impression that this one, since it doesn't have a designated dog area, doesn't have an official closing time. Am I mistaken on that particular point, officers?"

Birch turned to see the officer without the flashlight re-holstering his gun and snapping the strap in place. The one with the light trained it on Birch's face for a long moment before returning it to Wolf. "Don't make this difficult," the officer holding the flashlight said. "We'd like you guys to move along now. Clear out."

Wolf glanced at Birch. "Are we committing any crime? Do you have a complaint or a victim? I believe we're using this picnic ground for its intended purpose."

The policemen looked at each other and rolled their eyes. "Look buddy," the flashlight-wielding officer said, "if we need to take you to the station, we'll be able to figure that part out, but you don't want us to do that. You're homeless, right? Let's just be reasonable and move along now. We can do this the easy way, or the hard way."

"What about him?" the other officer said. "He look homeless?"

The beam swept onto Birch's face. "I need to see some ID," the officer with the flashlight said. Birch shifted nervously on the bench, glancing at Wolf.

Wolf dipped his eyes at Birch, covertly lifting the fingers of one hand from the table. "You don't need to show them ID," he said in a low voice. Birch remained still on the outside, his heart slamming blood and adrenaline around inside. In an instant he imagined handing over his driver's license, squawks through the police radios, his wrists cuffed behind his back, then Robin, or some thug hired by Robin, finding him somewhere left exposed, the cops having done their part in the capture and stepping back. Then the thug, no, Robin in person, hacking him down with a machete—he could feel the blade going deeper and deeper with each whack. He had to close his eyes and shake the image from his mind.

"Don't interfere with police business," the flashlight-brandishing officer barked. "You're impeding our investigation!"

"Um, did you just say I looked homeless?" Wolf said in a raised inquiring voice. The flashlight beam returned to his furred face.

Wolf looked into the beam a long moment. "You might as well have said you're Jewish, or Wiccan, or whatever group identifier you've chosen to disparage. I think Richard Flores is going to be very interested in your approach here." Wolf looked down at his notebook and turned to a blank page. He slipped a ballpoint from the rear cover and ceremoniously clicked it with his thumb, saying, "Now, we're, all four of us, located on the grounds of Hulver Park at 8:20 p.m. on September 24th." He wrote as he spoke. "Would you agree?"

He looked up at the policemen. They both looked at him, then each other. They passed a silent signal between them, turned without a word and walked back to the patrol car, snapping off the light beam.

Wolf followed them with his eyes. Birch turned to see them get into the car, then, breathing out his fear and tension, returned his focus to the notebook lying open on the tabletop.

"There you have it," Wolf growled. "That's modern America in a nutshell. Those clowns just realized that a FOIA request for their body cam footage would turn them into fifteen-minute Youtube stars, and they were beginning to gather I might know how that works. Such a waste. We fund those guys, at least I used to. We bestow on them power and authority, a hundred percent intended for the maintenance of public safety, yet they spend a high proportion of it just proving to themselves that they have it and trying to prove to the rest of us that they need more. Almost like politicians spending half their time trying to get reelected. Talk about inefficient systems! It's both disgusting and beautiful at the same time."

Birch raised his eyebrows. "The waste I mean," Wolf continued on his tear. "It's disgusting that mankind has become so wasteful and cares so little, yet beautiful that those willing and able to pay attention can live so well from others' lack of care. On the disgusting side you have guys like that spending their time and our resources trying to establish dominance over others when they should be spending all of that resource, all—of—it, keeping people safe. We're not endangering anybody sitting here! And I can guarantee you that if we were sittin' here looking like a couple of bros in clean white boy clothes or, better yet, off-duty cops, they never would have come over. Half the time, from a distance, they think I might be black; I'm a little dark, and with the beard at night and all. That has them marching over real quick, you can bet. The looks of disappointment when they figure out I'm not!" He shook his head and smiled. "But on the beautiful side, what we had for dinner tonight was already thrown out, for godsakes!"

"Who's Richard Flores?" Birch asked. "And, who are you?"

Wolf smiled. "Flores is their commissioner, and I'm Norm Klossman." He reached his hand across the table. "Pleased to meet you. I think I might know who you are, by the way. Are you Birch, the engineer, from that gaming company?"

"How?" Birch stuttered. "Yes, Zongo Inc."

"Ha! At least you were from Zongo Inc., until you decided to bug out. Unless you're just out on sabbatical."

Birch stuck his tongue through his teeth, shaking his head. "Wait, what? How did...?" Birch flicked his eyes over the GSI logo on Norm's cap. "And what happened to GSI? The medical software, right?"

"Yeah, you're catching up now. I'm sure you heard all

sorts of stories about that. I'll tell you what." Norm leaned in on his elbows to get his face closer to Birch's. "None of what the press reported is the real version. It was a classic scissors move, but stupid me! It was my first time, and only, as I've now decided, as CEO of a startup, so I never saw it coming. All because, just before we tried to go public, I invested heavily in Franz Simon's cancer treatment system. We were close to releasing a version of GSI designed to couple with Simon's system. It would have taken cancer out of the scare zone for the common folk. Well, big pharma got wind of what we were doing, and they hated it. I'll bet you never heard the part about the Simon system. Totally covered up. First came the PR blitzes, then a series of orchestrated short sells, and GSI was in receivership. Stock went through the floorboards. Their timing was good on that deal, I have to hand it to them. Ruthless, those bastards. Anyone gets near their billion dollar chemo business, and they come out for blood, literally! Fuckers! And Simon winds up selling his patents to a company that he believes is going to develop the technology and roll it out, but turns out, it's a shell company owned, get this, three levels deep by the same pharma jackasses that set up the short sell on me! They flat-out lied to him. So that technology is buried a mile deep in their circular vault for the next seventeen years, and you get cancer? You still have to have a jar lid installed in your chest and get bankrupted for the privilege of having gallons of poison washing through your body! And you wait! Seventeen years from now, watch them tweak those patents just enough to renew. And me? Lost everything. Every fucking thing!" He shook his head and laid his palms flat on the table. "I never imagined. Totally naive. How the fuck?"

Birch was shocked. "That's crazy! And you're," he hesitated, "actually homeless?"

"Hey," Norm said. "Don't think I'm the only guy from the valley to do this. Look around sometime. After I realized the extent to which getting more money is the only thing that matters to so many of these psychos, I was like, fuck this, I'm bugging out. Life's too short. I know, I'm weak, I couldn't handle the sheer fight of it all. Just knowing that a better solution to cancer is sitting there legally locked away just so a bunch of fat fucks can keep selling their chemistry at higher profits to a captive market drives me absolutely nuts. I'm basically sitting here having lost my fucking mind. I'm sure my body chemistry just from the stress alone is worse than their product. I'm probably full of cancer right now. Oh, the irony!" Norm shook his fist at the sky for dramatic effect. "You get the basic formula, right? Call it Formula A," Norm continued. "What I was doing, what I'll guess you were doing, was spending LIFE for the purpose of gaining RESOURCE. Does that seem at all fucked up to you? All the low-level sorting, the power games, the climb up the dominance ladder, the short sells those fucks pulled on me, those fucking cops trying to prove that they can move us around at their whim; it's a rivalrous system which doesn't do anything to advance humanity, engineered by shrewd people who want resources to flow to them in vast quantities to the exclusion of everyone else. For their system to work, they need the formula to be LIFE spent in pursuit of RESOURCE. Then they can influence how lives get spent and how the resources flow. List a thousand rules that apply to people or corporations, anywhere, list them at random, and then go down the list and see how many fit that formula. You'll see. Part of Formula A is that those who want it also make the rules that run it. Duh! When that dawned on me, drove me nuts. I said that day, I'm out. Call me a wimp. I was done with it. Now I've flipped the formula on its head and use Formula B. Instead of life is a means to resource, resource is a means to life. I'm basically back to hunter-gatherer. I feel better now than when I was driving my Audi around. And by adopting Formula B, I'm no longer contributing resource to those who engineer or maintain Formula A. Definitely feels better."

He returned his eyes to Birch. "And look at you. You're apparently bugging out for some reason, so it can't come as too much of a surprise that someone else chose this road. What's your beef?"

Birch looked at the dark plain of the picnic table. "I realized what I was spending my time building. I started to connect it with how I see people behaving toward each other."

Norm frowned. "So, why not just drop the shooter and blaster games and work on something that can help? Like Vonnegut said, do something that humanity can be proud of. You're still young, and I'm sure you're not in the same sort of financial shape I am. Though, the one plus for me was when my wife discovered that she could no longer go spending she dumped me like a bag of empty peanut shells, went to find some other money source."

"Well," Birch said, "when I refused to work on the next Zongo project, I think my boss actually may have put a hit out on me. So I'm just trying to get lost for awhile. Gotta get some perspective."

"Zongo?"

Birch nodded.

"Turcek?"

"Yeah."

"Hmm, okay. Maybe you should be a little careful. I've heard he's violent. Some say he scores highly on the Robert Hare test, so not much you can trust there. And he's definitely one of those psychos about money. I have a buddy who knows him. My gut tells me a hit, some sort of accident, is not entirely out of the question. A guy gets access to a whole lot of money or influence, and suddenly he thinks all the rules are different for him; you just can't be sure. Crazy shit. Not even really his money, I've heard."

Birch was quiet for a while. "I thought maybe he'd sent those cops to look for me," he said. "He's been escalating the threats on my phone."

Norm raised his shoulders and frowned. "Well, ditch the phone for god's sake. Don't make it easy for him."

Birch pulled his phone out and powered it down.

"It will take more than that if he's really hunting for you," Norm said, nodding toward Birch's phone. "You know they can turn those on remotely, right?"

Birch asked to look at Norm's notebook, and Norm was glad to let him page through it. He retrieved a small LED lantern from his tote bag, as the evening had darkened enough to make reading the pen marks a strain.

"What is this you're working on?" Birch asked.

"Trying to either prove or disprove what Tyson and others claim as a high likelihood—that our universe is a digital simulation. If they're right, it would explain a lot, to me at least."

Birch inspected the pages carefully, front and back, as he slowly unwound the story of Norm's thinking from the dense jungle of ink. He paused on a page of Venn diagrams to have Norm talk him through the reasoning. "Is this the only notebook?" Birch asked. "It looks like you started in the middle with this one."

"I toss them when I run out of pages, start a new one."

"You throw these out?" Birch asked in disbelief.

"Yeah, it's all progressive, I don't need the history. I just need the marker where I am, so I can move forward. I've already thrown out a bunch that were going nowhere anyway, or used them to start fires."

Birch paused again on a page detailing algorithms for generating rule sets designed to modify models representing the five common senses. "So, you're going to throw this notebook out?" Birch asked.

"Yeah, pretty soon. A few pages left to fill."

"Mind if I take this page?"

Norm looked over the page and lifted it to glance at the backside. "Go ahead," he said. "Don't need it."

Birch gingerly tore it from the book, folded it and slid it into his pants pocket. "Thanks." A few pages later Birch said, "So, your theory suggests that most of our knowledge and memory is not stored in our brains, is that right?"

Norm looked up toward the few stars bright enough to poke through the dim orange smear of street light spreading up into the night sky. "Right," he said. "I have no frikkin' clue where that information is actually stored, maybe in the dark matter of the universe somehow. Lots of people are working on that question, but I've noticed most of them appear to do the math so it works out that, hey, whatever the storage capacity of the human brain, that's how much data we appear to hold on to. That's just too convenient for me. I think we have access to considerably more information, and that the information we're consuming and processing is much higher resolution than other theories describe. No, while I think we use some temporary storage in the brain, it seems more suited to operate as an antenna and active data processor than a large and long-term storage system. Take the idea of expertise and experience, your violinist for example; she spends years practicing a progression of pieces, playing them thousands of times. Science knows that results in pathways among her neurons, right? She uses those pathways often enough, and the brain wraps them in lipids and proteins to strengthen and preserve them; you got your myelin sheaths, like insulating wires, right? Is that the data, the actual mechanics and music itself? No, what that is is an antenna finely tuned to receive pertinent data so your violinist can process it. A less skilled violinist has less finely tuned antennae, so the processing tends to be lower resolution. But notice, once that data is received and processed in one place, it's available elsewhere too. It's processed and returned to a field somehow where other antennae can receive it. When one violinist processes a piece to a given level of resolution, you'll find that another one, somewhere else on Earth, will begin rendering it at the same resolution. They each have an antenna tuned to that resolution. When a sprinter sets a new record on one side of the world, another will break it on the other side of the world. You've got Isaac Newton working on the ideas of calculus in England, and then there's Leibniz independently creating the whole system over in Germany, not known to each other until they started duking it out over who deserved the credit years later. See? Two antennae tuned for and working on the same data set."

"Do you need this page?" Birch asked. Pages brushed and crinkled as he turned them back and forth, trying to follow the logic. "And this one?"

Norm waved a hand over the table. "Nah, go ahead," he said. "Look," he continued, "those cops will be coming back in a couple hours to see if we're still here. We gotta move out. Talk about resource, it's not worth the expenditure to wrangle with them further. We've given them something to prove to themselves now. You should find someplace to sleep where you won't be seen until you get the routine down, and a dark tarp, I'm telling you."

Birch carefully tore a few more pages from the composition book and folded them into his pocket.

"And another thing: pastries," Norm said. "They're too tempting in the dumpsters. You'll find them by the dozens, one day expired, still beautifully wrapped, and now and then it's okay, but go for the vegetables first, otherwise you'll feel like crap and you won't have your strength for traveling. To keep your wits, you gotta stay strong, healthy, well-rested. Got it? My motto is SSWK, strong, smart, wise, and kind. It's the only thing that's worked for me in this life."

Birch nodded. He stood from the picnic table and went to shoulder his pack. Norm got up and went to his tote, retrieved his snorkel coat, shook it out and slipped it on. He picked up his tote and garbage bag full of cans, slung the bag over his shoulder with a great symphony of rattles and collisions, looked at Birch once, and then trudged off.

Birch walked east under the street lights for a couple miles before finding a cluster of dumpsters caged by a wooden privacy fence behind a massive Lutheran church. He stayed in the shadows under trees at the edge of the back lawn buffering the church from its parking lot, waiting to see if anyone was around or might see him if he snuck over to the dumpsters. He almost fell asleep waiting there, but a passing breeze brought him back to wakefulness with a feeling of sudden exposure and vulnerability. He listened to the cars hissing by on the street on other side of the church, then picked himself up and pulled up his pack by one shoulder strap, easing around the lawn's edge toward the dumpsters. He slipped past the open fence gate, the hair up on the back of his neck, afraid that he'd find someone already in there, and pulled the gate closed behind him, penning himself away from the eyes of any passersby. He was thankfully alone with the brown metal dumpsters and their aged stench. He set his pack down against the fence corner and sat on the asphalt, leaning back against the pack to drift off, wrapped in the strong smell of putrid trash.

He thought about his phone in his pocket. Norm was right. Even powered down, electrons still moved in there. Someone with resources and determination could still locate it. But he wasn't about to ditch the thing completely. It was a prosthetic lobe of his brain, his access to pretty much everything he had left in this life now. He had to come up with a better solution.

His brief episodes of sleep interlaced with hazy half-sleep were shadowy periods of confusion and soreness outside of time. He dreamt of soap bubbles, drifting through the air, taking on the color and image of the background, nearly invisible except for the lens effect distorting the imagery as they floated by.

Each time he woke he felt the quickly fading sense of an echo, presumably of the sound that woke him, but he could never place the sound and never heard it again, whatever it was. The putrid waft of the dumpsters hung on him like a wet cloud. He sensed the closeness of the dumpsters and the fence walls, barely visible in the ambient light, and rather than feeling protected by them felt like an animal caught in a trap, waiting to be discovered and clubbed.

What a dumb mistake, he thought. *Someone could have easily seen me come in here, and they would just send a simple text message to someone else to come finish the job.* He looked for the latch on the fence in case he needed to make a hasty exit but couldn't find it in the dark, despite it being only feet from his face, and couldn't be sure now of which wall it was on. He moved his head and his eyes, trying to pull sight through the darkness, and panic grew in him, filling his chest like wool, leaving no space for air. *I'm not cut out for this. I don't know what I'm doing.* He pushed himself as far into a corner as he could and gave into the exhaustion once again.

When he came fully awake, morning light was already sliding under the privacy fence from the parking lot and filtering down through the walnut limbs above him. His neck felt twisted and bruised, and his head throbbed. His lungs were weak from breathing the sour gaseous stench of trash all night. He was dizzy as he stood and fumbled for his pack straps. He steadied himself against the slats for a moment, listening, and then pushed out from the wooden cage and stumbled toward the trees at the edge of the church yard. He dropped his pack and sunk his hand in for a granola bar and bottle of water, his neck twisting this way and that as he scanned the environs for any sign of someone watching him.

He decided to leave his phone off as long as he could stand as an experiment. What he really needed this morning was a bathroom, some decent food, and an idea of how to make the next night better than the last.

He decided to travel randomly and spent the morning walking southeast, stopping when he noticed a coffee shop at the outskirts of Santa Clara University. He went in and gingerly tucked his pack between a small bistro table and the wall, where he sat for a few seconds in the rickety chair before getting up to find the restroom. The woman behind the counter flinched and followed him briefly with her eyes, dropping them in disgust. He knew it was his smell. He could tell from a quick glance at her body language that his presence was something she would endure despite being upset by it, probably angry about his smell wafting over the scones and coffee cakes in the glass case, tainting them for the other customers. He used the bathroom, washed as well as he could with brown, fibrous paper towel, and felt guilty using so many. He emerged and apologetically ordered a grande chai and a couple scones, paying with some of his cash. He shouldered his pack and left as soon as he could, skidding the chair and bumping the door with his swinging pack on his way out.

Walking across campus disheveled, with his orange pack so much larger than anyone else's nearby, sipping his chai and munching a scone, he felt he stood out in the flow of bodies streaming along the sidewalks and grassy areas en route to class buildings with laptop cases and knapsacks slung over their shoulders. He recalled his soap bubble dream and pondered being invisible, passing through a landscape, taking on the colors and texture as he went, still existing as himself, like a point of consciousness unseen. He imagined this right past the boundaries of the university and eastward toward San Jose. He considered powering up his phone to look for an actual bed and shower for the night, but immediately thought of Robin, imagined him telling lies and making deals with the carrier to put a track on Birch's phone. He began imagining a phone that could pass through the tower space like a clear soap bubble without broadcasting its location to the network. He saw himself walking right past Robin's bat-wielding goon undetected, free to go. How could that work?

His mind grew weary with the steps. The weight of his pack, pulling him down at the shoulders and waist, pressing his feet into the hot cement sidewalk, felt doubled since he started his walk the day before. It was late afternoon when he saw the King public library ahead and veered toward it.

The rush of air conditioning at the main entrance breathed a wave of hope through him. He found the coat room and hung his pack there, thinking he'd use the restroom and then find a quiet corner where he could sit in a comfortable chair and think of what to do next. Walking up the moving escalator steps to the second floor without the weight of the pack felt like luxury. The burned rot smell of the dumpsters from the night before lingered in the threads of his pants and shirt, though dimming as it mixed with his own sweat; as a result he felt nearly civilized. He thought of but didn't bother with a smile as he walked along stacks of books, instinctively letting any unneeded muscles hang slack to conserve energy.

He found two stuffed chairs flanking a small round coffee table in an unoccupied corner. He dropped himself into one of the chairs and immediately let his eyelids droop. Gravity pulled his head down to the arm rest. His spine bent into the intersection of seat and back.

He slept deeply for an hour or so, then wandered into that shadow zone between dreaming and wakefulness. His awareness rose high enough to wonder how long he'd been out, feeling a dry mouth and thirst, and curiosity at the tail end of patched-together dreams about floating soap bubbles again.

He reached into his pants pocket for his phone to check the time. The dark screen reminded him that he'd powered off the night before. *Screw it,* he thought, and powered back up. He watched the screen through bleary eyes as the phone booted. Immediately text messages, piled up at the gate while the phone was off, stormed the bell and shocked him with adrenaline. He grabbed for the volume button to mute the phone, nearly dropping it. The list of messages was mostly Robin, with a couple from other co-workers. Birch scrolled through them while the heat of fear grew behind the skin of his face, as if his skull were metal heating from the inside from a bad short. He looked up and scanned the room for any eyes on him, taking in the other chairs and tables, the stacks of books, the halls and stairwells within view. He decided that he'd been sitting in one place too long, especially since he'd been asleep. He got up to find another spot. Now that he'd gotten some rest, it was time to think.

As he followed a serpentine path through the book

stacks, he mused about becoming invisible. He came upon a computer station in a cubical intended for people working on job applications. He looked around and then took the seat. He set his phone on the table next to the keyboard and stared at it, fantasizing about creating a bubble of invisibility around him. He relaxed and conjured his dream fragments, and the bubble became a clear globe containing a projection of what it passed in front of, and Birch started to play it over and over in his mind. It appeared as a mirror reflecting toward him what was on its other side. He imagined it floating through the land, and he saw nothing there.

He picked up his phone and began tapping through the settings menus, looking at the various identifying numbers, the device ID of the phone, the device serial number, the ID identifying the SIM card that connected the phone to his account with the carrier. These ID numbers were like the reflective pigment that allowed a device to be seen. He opened a browser on the library computer and began researching. He found posts about IMEI numbers, ICCIDs, MEIDs, and IMSIs. He found examples of how the phone software worked and diagrams of how a single phone lived within the larger ecosystem of towers, terminal servers, WiFi networks, and carrier accounts. He opened the file manager app on his phone and began looking for data files, mostly configuration files, where un-encrypted or uncompiled readable values may be stored. He turned back to the library computer keyboard, opened a text file, and set to writing the first mustang he'd written in nearly two years.

Within two hours he had a mustang that could find and enter a network server at any of the city's public library branches, identify the network routers at the branch, the media access addresses of all devices accessing the network through each router, and return to him a list that mapped the current state of the network. He was thirsty and needed to use the restroom, but he didn't want to give up his computer station, so he stuck it out to keep working. In another hour and a half he was desperate to use the restroom, but had managed to add to his mustang the ability to spoof his own phone's MAC address, register to a WiFi hotspot within the library system, and then hop from one hotspot to another. He quickly saved his files, tucked them into a directory and hid it, then gingerly rose from his chair and limped toward a restroom.

When Birch returned, a woman with tan shoulders and a sleeve tattoo, making her arm look like a skeleton, had occupied the computer station and was slowly clicking through employment listings. Birch moved down the row of stations to an empty one that left him feeling exposed at his back, but the progress he'd made earlier had left its warmth in him, like a residual energy in his neck and shoulders, and the visceral memory of when he and Angel had written mustangs on a regular basis also roused in him a boldness he'd misplaced while working at Zongo Inc. He took the station, anxious to get back to work, and swiveled his head left and right to check the sight lines from behind him to his monitor screen.

He got back into the local network and found his files. He felt rusty, and the time it took him to do simple things left him itchy. He added to his mustang a sequencer and binder that would cause his phantom phone to move from hotspot to hotspot within the library system at varying speeds, making it look like he was strolling around the library, then sometime later appearing at one of the other library branches and strolling around that one, endlessly. He spent the rest of the afternoon adding a relay that would forward any messages or signals sent to his phone account to an anonymous service he could access from a secure browser later. He thought about building in some timers to make it look like he was remaining in one or another hotspot for long periods, perhaps sleeping, but decided against it, not wanting to leave a given hotspot "active" long enough for anyone Robin might send to thoroughly determine that he wasn't there.

He did a final code check, ran it through a compiler he'd downloaded from Github, and launched the mustang as a low-level service, light enough to live far down any process list on the library network servers, hopefully staying below the eyes of the system administrators.

Now that he'd made it appear as though he, or rather his phone, was forever roaming the library buildings, he had to deal with the fact that he needed his actual phone with him, operational, but without revealing his identity or location. That's where the soap bubbles came in. While working on the mustang, he'd allowed his dreams of floating bubbles to drift through the periphery of his thoughts. Now he walked back to the stuffed chairs where he'd taken his nap and sank into one, thumbs ready to type on his phone's keyboard. He opened a terminal app along with the file manager, and began navigating through his phone's operating system. The sooner he could figure this out, the sooner he could make his phone stop identifying itself to the carrier network, leaving only the mustang roaming the library network pretending to be him.

He found where the phone received a query from the carrier network and sent its device ID, SIM card ID, and device serial number back, navigating quickly with his thumbs as he'd just built a software agent to mimic this very process. He modified his phone to first query the carrier database to locate account holders near him. He found the names were encrypted, but was only interested in the device IDs anyway. Next he wrote a routine to select an account holder at random and temporarily "borrow" their IDs, sending them to the carrier instead of his own. To test it he specified his GPS location and added a short radius to see if he could find an account holder within range at the library. Bam! More than enough to play with. He didn't want any of their calls or texts; he only wanted to temporarily piggyback on their cell data connections. Texting and phone calling were over for him now. Any communicating he did, and he wasn't even sure with whom he would communicate at this point, would be strictly via apps and services.

He worked for a few more hours, getting up periodically

to change locations in the library, nervous that he was spending too much time focused on his phone screen and not paying attention to what was around him.

After saving and compiling one more time, he found that he could walk around the building and grab nearby cell connections at whatever interval he wanted. He started with twenty seconds, thinking that most of what he would need in the near term would be simple requests to web services. On his next trip to the restroom, he pulled the SIM chip from his phone and flushed it down the toilet. *Won't be needing that anymore!*

His last chore before heading downstairs to retrieve his backpack took him back to the employment application work stations. He shelled into the cloud server account he'd started before leaving home and wrote a simple API that would store requests from his library-roaming mustang in a database he could retrieve at some later date. He tested that, then found the mustang files and edited a configuration file to point requests to his cloud server. Now, any text messages or phone calls anyone tried to make to his old phone number would be recorded in his cloud server. His mustang wouldn't actually answer phone calls or reply to text messages, though he mused over how much time it would take him to work on that. The cost benefit didn't add up at this point, but he would at least have the meta data and caller ID from phone calls and the inbound messages from texts.

Feeling blurry-eyed but rather accomplished and certainly less visible now, he went downstairs, shouldered his backpack and headed out onto the sidewalk beneath the dull tungsten light of the street lamps. He turned east through the San Jose night, playing with his phone as if it were a new invention, grabbing cell signals from people standing in line to enter bars, people driving by on the street, people in their seats in restaurants.

He stopped to sit on a park bench along the sidewalk, drank some water and ate a bit of cheese. His next thoughts focused on how he might find a safe place to sleep tonight. Sure, his phone presence was gone; he was theoretically still wandering around the library system. But outside, he was still a tall skinny dude with long blond hair in a ponytail. Not too hard to spot if someone were hunting for him. Better not get cocky.

Birch sat on the sidewalk leaning back against a lamp post, watching the door of the motorcycle shop. He'd made it a few days out of Palo Alto to the east side of San Jose before the throbbing in his feet and knees grew omnipresent enough to throw him off-balance. His shoulders were numb and sore, his hips chafed from the belt on the backpack. This was not the part he remembered from his trips to the Sierras, and he'd never before had to contend with the exhaustion of constant fear and splintered attention.

He'd woken early that morning to the ripping thunder of small jets and the buzz-hammering of prop planes taking off directly over his damp, chilled head. The small, grassy park where he'd rolled out his sleeping bag under a clump of spruce the night before was situated just across Ocala Avenue from the departure ends of the Santa Clara County airport runways. After opening his eyes he stewed for a few minutes in the rank gasses accumulated in his sleeping bag from the drying layers of sweat on his skin and crusted into his clothes. He lingered in the fetid warmth of the bag, not yet wanting to expose the rest of his body to the damp cool settling on his face or confront the truth of whether the assassin he'd imagined crouched on the other side of the grove was truly there.

When he'd finally gotten to his feet, he shivered and looked out beyond the airport to the rising hills. His back and shoulders begged him not to hoist the backpack. The hills looked small from this distance, but Birch knew that would change as he reached them. He knew as he climbed they would grow in inverse proportion to his body's shrinking energy supply. He also knew from the map on his phone that they would turn into mountains not far beyond where he could see.

He had it in mind to traverse them, then continue across the San Joaquin Valley and up into the Sierras. He'd thought of walking through Yosemite and revisiting fond memories from his college days, simultaneously putting rock and distance between himself and Robin, but the idea had begun to crumble at the edges as his muscle fibers and connective tissues began to inflame and tear. He'd pictured himself taking his time, keeping himself hidden as he walked into the mountains, but the sight of the first column of hills and the aches roaming his body shifted the images he'd held in his mind. Now he saw himself trudging uphill with cold rain in his face, a wrinkled food bag full of empty wrappers twisted in among the contents of his pack. Layered on that was the nagging image of some vehicle, maybe Robin's Tesla, stalking him from behind, then closing faster than he could escape. Each time he'd borrowed someone's cell connection or nipped the edge of an unprotected WiFi network to check his server over the past couple days the messages from Robin poured in like a deluge. "They" were closing in on him; he had "chosen his fate." They would "finish the job" to "make things right." Birch's animal self was growing more concerned with the innuendo despite his rational self's suspicion that Robin was merely toying with him, only trying to extract some revenge via fear. His animal self was winning, felt exposed and vulnerable and too slow. Every direction he turned left him with the feeling of something behind him, closing the distance. *Then who knows? Blunt force? Bullet? Something worse?*

He'd wadded up his sleeping bag into its compartment, shouldered his pack and walked along Ocala, reinforcing the idea with each sore step that he would change his mode of travel, or at least disguise himself somehow to be harder to find. He'd thumbed the map on his phone to see how far it was over the hills, was about to enter search terms for a bus station when in his peripheral vision he spotted the motorcycle shop's icon on a side street. He'd turned toward it as though compelled by reflex. Motorcycles were never a part of his life; he had no connection to motorcycle culture. Perhaps this would be the perfect pivot to change his course, defy expectations, build some speed and get him out of here.

The hours sign on the glass door said they opened at nine, so he parked himself on the sidewalk against the building wall to wait and rest his feet. He watched the street in front of him, following the cars with his eyes, trying to notice the drivers and if any passengers looked at him.

At five minutes to nine a guy with a gray mustache and tattoos on his shoulders turned the lock in the door and pushed it open. Birch pushed himself up off the sidewalk and dragged his pack into the shop. The guy eyed him and said, "Can I help you?" in a voice full of grease and rusty chains. He had in a single earbud, wired to a phone stuffed into the tight front pocket of his jeans. Birch could hear the tinny thrash of some metal band escaping between the node of the tiny speaker and the guy's leathery ear.

Birch leaned his pack against the wall by the door and looked around the shop. A row of six brand new Harleys, decked out with chrome and black leather, leaned in formation at the front of the shop. A squad of brightly colored sport bikes occupied the floor behind the Harleys, with a collection of used bikes beyond those. Birch eyed the price stickers on the Harleys, smelled the new leather, looked at his reflection in the polished chrome. *Nice,* he thought. *If the closing money has landed in my account, I could buy twenty of these right now, but one will do.* He smiled to himself as he imagined roaring over the mountains, winding out the miles.

Racks of leather jackets, chaps, and riding pants, mostly black but with some other colors mixed in, stood on casters along a wall of boots, gloves, helmets, and goggles. Birch moved among the bikes, trying his hands on the grips, looking at the speedometers and engines.

"You lookin' for something particular?" the guy asked. The micro metal band thrashed a little louder as he approached.

Birch looked up at him. "Nothing particular, something that will get me over the mountains. These Harleys look nice."

The guy followed Birch with his eyes as he moved through the racks of leather, then sifted through a table of jeans and T-shirts with motorcycle brand logos on them.

"Those Harleys are nice," the guy said. "You buying today?"

"I'm buying right now," Birch said. He chose a shirt and pair of jeans, then pulled a thick black leather jacket from a hanger and took everything over to the checkout counter. "Do you have a changing room where I can try these?" Birch asked.

The guy looked alarmed and then shook his head. "Ah, no. We don't."

Birch went over and pulled out a box of tall square-toed riding boots, size eleven. He sat on a bench, unlaced his hiking shoes and pulled them off, releasing a cloud of stench that mingled with the rest of his body odor and wafted past his nose. He lifted the boots from the box, preferring their treated new leather smell to his own odor, and pulled them onto his feet, first the left, then the right. The guy stood behind him, frowning, and said, "You have money with you?"

Birch turned to look up at him, then got to his feet to try out the boots. He smiled, now looking down at the guy. "I'm sorry I stink. I'm on a bit of an odyssey. And, yes, I have more than enough money with me."

The guy's facial muscles cycled through a number of configurations as he reconciled Birch's words with his appearance, and then he visibly relaxed. "What kind of riding you do?"

"Never been on anything except a Vespa back in school," Birch said as he took the boots up to the counter. He added some Harley socks and boxers to his pile and went to look at the helmets.

"You'll want gloves too, if you're planning on going over the mountains," the guy said. Birch grabbed a pair of XLs and added them to his pile.

"You got your M-1 endorsement on your license? I guess that's a dumb question since you've never been on a real bike before."

Birch shook his head no.

"Well," the guy said, "about a third of the riders don't these days. Just don't get pulled over."

Birch gravitated to one of the new Harleys. He swung a leg over and sat, rested his hands on the grips, looked out over the windscreen. He turned to look at the store keeper. The guy dropped his head forward a moment, bounced his chin on his chest, and then looked up at Birch, walking over to him. "Look, Bud. I'd love to sell you a new bike today, really I would, but I can't do this. I don't even know you, but you'd be dead in a pile of hot scrap by the end of the day if you left here on that."

Birch frowned and looked at him.

"Seriously," he continued. "Riding one of these ain't a movie. You gotta know what you're doing. Riders normally work up to these." He considered Birch a moment. "Follow me," he said.

Birch got off the bike and followed him to the back of the store. The man stopped next to an older, gray-colored bike sporting hard gray saddlebags with slightly bent hinges. He gestured toward it and said, "Here. I wouldn't sleep at night if I sent you off on something you couldn't handle. This is what you want. It's a 1982 Silverwing, a Honda."

Birch looked it over. It was a friendly-looking bike, noticeably smaller than the Harleys. "1982?" Birch said. "This bike is older than I am."

"Yeah, it's no Harley," the guy said, "but it's in great shape for how old it is, low miles, solid, forgiving. It's the little brother of the Goldwing. My Harley pals would puke if they heard me say this, but they know it's the truth. This is one of the best-engineered bikes ever to take the road."

Birch threw a leg over and sat. It was clean, comfortable, and just 20,000 miles on the odometer.

"It's a V-twin," the guy said. "More giddy-up than you'd expect. Guys on the big bikes are often surprised by how one of these can keep up with them on the highway, but this one ain't going to bite you so hard when you mess up. And you will mess up, believe me. You been trained at all? Watch Youtube videos or anything?"

Birch shook his head and looked at the price tag, a creased, oil-smudged paper tag hanging from the handle bar by a dirty string. "$2100" was crossed out in blue pen, "$1750" written right below it. A far cry from the $24,000 he'd been about to plunk down for the Harley that would have killed him by the end of the day. "You take credit cards?" he asked.

He went to his pack to retrieve his wallet. He wouldn't be careless this time, leaving traceable transactions for Robin to hunt him by. He used his phone to log into his bank account, then transferred $2,500 into his Slang account, enough to cover the cost of the bike, the riding clothes, and whatever other fees the guy might need getting it ready for him. He heard the metal band suddenly cease in the guy's ear, and the guy pulled his phone out to look at it, tugging out the earphone jack and plugging it back in. *Ha,* Birch thought, *he must have been streaming that music, and I just hijacked his connection. Sorry brother, this won't take but a minute.* Birch logged into his Slang account, checked the balance, and initiated a new credit card number to be assigned to his Slang Visa card.

"You can gas it up for me now?" he asked as he handed the guy his card.

The salesman plucked the card from Birch's soiled fingers. "Yeah," he said, "I can get it all ready for you. So," the guy added, "you're traveling huh?" He keyed in the cost of the motorcycle, taxes, and preparation fees, then waded through the pile of clothes and helmet, adding up the total with a growing sense of satisfaction. He eyed the leather jacket and the jeans Birch had picked out. He took them back to the racks and brought back a similar-looking jacket and similar jeans. "CE-certified armor built in," he said. "You can hardly tell by looking at them, but I just think it's a good idea."

He finished the total and then ran the card. Seconds later the authorization came back, and the man smiled for the first time that morning. "You know," he said, "we do have a shower in the back." The music started up in his earpiece again, and he pulled his phone out to frown at it once more.

Birch took him up on the shower. He carried his pack and his newly purchased clothes through a door in the back of the shop, along the wall of the repair shop past another guy leaning over a disassembled cafe racer, and into a cement-floored bathroom. He stood in the dingy shower under steaming hot water and watched the dirt from his body cascade to the floor and swirl down the drain. He felt his muscles loosen in the steaming heat, his skin soften and relax. When he'd scrubbed himself dry, put on his new clothes, and pulled on the riding boots, he stood combing his hair out in the mirror, then shaved, feeling the dull throb of his body recovering itself in his legs, feet, and shoulders.

He looked at the pile of dirty white cotton clothes heaped wet on the bathroom floor, then scooped them up and dropped them into the trash can. Out on the repair floor his bike stood idling while the guy from the front squatted next to it with a screwdriver, slowly twisting while he listened to the engine. Birch unlatched the luggage bags and transferred the contents of his backpack, taking special care to fold and stash the notebook pages he'd gotten from Norm, into them while the guy worked on the engine. He couldn't fit the tent or sleeping pad, leaving them in the pack. He offered the pack and remaining contents to the guy, who said he'd give them to one of his employees, then stood up and declared the bike ready to go. "Throttle's here. Clutch here, one down, four up on the shifter there. Favor the front brake here. Foot pedal here is the rear brake. Even though it's a small bike, you'll wanna take it easy until you get a feel. Think you'll be okay?"

Birch said he'd be fine.

"And that plate. It expired years ago. You'll have to stop by the Secretary of State to get a new one, first thing. Or else by god don't get pulled over."

Birch slipped the jacket and gloves on, slid the helmet on without fixing the chin strap, and thanked the guy. The guy and his mechanic watched Birch kick up the stand and wheel the bike out through the overhead door, swing his leg over and test the throttle. "One down, four up!" the guy called out to him. Birch gave him a salute, grabbed the clutch, toe-slapped it into first gear, and feathered the clutch out a bit to feel it grab and begin to roll over the gravel. He worked the throttle and clutch back and forth gently against each other, rolling the bike along with his feet out wide, duck walking out the drive onto the street. He didn't look back, but knew the shop guys were watching him.

The bike was heavier than he'd expected. He jerked it pretty badly getting it into first, but felt the pressure of a car coming up behind him. He jerked it again, getting into second, but found a smoother place going into third, feeling the wind against his face under the lifted face shield of his helmet.

8

Angel stepped through his code. His success with the reverse piezo sensor had emboldened him to leverage this electronic antique further.

Winnie came in from the living room after spending the last hour and a half sitting on the futon playing SimEarth. She kissed Angel on the head, saying, "I'm going to bed."

Angel didn't look up from his text editor, but laughed a giddy, almost deranged laugh. "This fucker is actually going to work," he said as he copied files across the wire from his laptop to the PalmPilot. Then he looked up. "Okay. See you in the morning."

"Don't stay up too late," Winnie pleaded, and then went into the bedroom.

The next morning was Monday, and Angel slumped in his rolling chair, occasionally slopping coffee from a white porcelain mug under his mustache and into his mouth. He had stayed up too late. It had been his third night in a row since Friday, and the lack of sleep left bags under his eyes and a sore spine. He'd written his first mustang since he and Birch used to hack together in college. This one needed to be light, and perfect. He had to be certain that it would function as designed and remain undetected.

Angel signaled Chad over to talk about how they were

handling kernel updates. He'd assigned Chad as the lone coder on that project and made himself the only reviewer. Angel hadn't identified anyone else in the room who seemed to share his attitude about the project. Certainly there was plenty of skepticism and cynicism, but the production room culture was clipped and falsely congenial, clearly padded by their huge salaries while constrained by the chips and the agreements they were all forced to sign. People seemed happy enough to perform their expected roles, keep their heads down, take the money, and leave the room at day's end.

Angel had hopes for Chad, but didn't want to push too hard or put him in any danger he wasn't already in. Plus, how do you know when you can really trust someone? If Angel asked Chad to do something to the operating system that was clearly a breach of their specs, their contracts, and could be proven to be intended as sabotage, who's to say Chad wouldn't get scared and start worrying about his safety, or thinking about all that money?

Angel was too tired to formulate a complex plan just then, deciding to keep it simple and not involve Chad. He'd already finalized the key he wanted Birch to use, had it encoded into his mustang alongside a message, a unique token concatenated to the word "breeze" concatenated to another token and then encrypted. Birch would remember, and he'd know how and where to use the key just by its name. Angel determined that he would simply install the backdoor while reviewing Chad's final code and then keep everyone out from then on. He felt loopy from fatigue, distracted by the mustang waiting in his PalmPilot. He sat zoning out in his chair while Chad gazed into the empty space between diagrams on the whiteboard. The metal door buzzed open, and Stuart strode into the room, nodding and smiling at the backs of the engineers as he walked along the wall toward Angel and Chad. Angel lifted his head from his hand and watched Stuart approach.

Stuart stopped in front of him and frowned. "You look

sick." He pulled his PalmPilot out and pointed it at Angel.

Angel took a long breath. "Just tired. Long camping trip over the weekend. Do you need me? It's not noon yet." Angel lifted his PalmPilot from his shirt pocket and pointed its infrared port at Stuart's.

Stuart hit the button on his, and the swirling arrows appeared on both screens. "You guys getting it figured out?" Stuart asked.

Angel looked at Stuart's face. He really did remind him of a squirrel sometimes. "Yes," Angel said. "We've got it handled."

"Good," Stuart said. The PalmPilots spun longer than usual; Angel felt his face begin to flush and tried to fight it back.

"What's wrong with these things?" Stuart said.

Angel pushed his elbow out like he was repositioning his device, careful to keep the IR port pointed at Stuart's. "Sorry, didn't have it pointed right."

Finally the devices beeped. Stuart closed the lid on his and slipped it into his jacket pocket. "We want to test a prototype of the AAV with the controller you're working on. You'll see the flight date on the calendar."

Angel watched Stuart's front teeth as he spoke, and for the first time found some amusement and comfort in them. "I hope the AAV designers will increase the memory size. That's a long list of rules we have to process per second to keep those things flying and out of harm's way."

Stuart shrugged his shoulders and glanced at the whiteboard. "I'll make sure that's on our review list. Maybe you'll have to make that code more efficient. We'll see." Stuart pressed his bottom lip against his two front teeth and raised his eyebrows. "Okay guys, see you later."

Stuart turned and strode back out of the room. He stepped into the hallway and turned right toward his office. A group of four gray-haired Army officers and a couple senior VPs rounded the corner at the end of the hallway. The men spoke jovially with each other as they walked. One of the

VPs turned and nodded to Stuart as they passed, saying, "Pitt." Stuart nodded back and continued along the hall to the elevators.

Once back inside his office, Stuart let out a long breath. He took the PalmPilot from his jacket pocket and slipped it into the sync cradle connected to his work station. He sat and twisted in his chair for a few moments. It kept him anxious that he was responsible for a room full of programmers, all of whom he suspected had higher IQs than his, and he didn't really know how they did what they did. He had to use the language of non-coders to talk about code, relying on the calendar and his checklists to keep pace with his responsibilities. And he had to maintain an alpha demeanor, not only with his charges but also with his superiors, to hold onto respect. It felt good sometimes, when things were going well, but it could also be exhausting. He felt at the mercy of Angel Oleastro and that roomful of geeks. In order for him to look good, they had to come through. As long as Stuart was firm in his requirements, and as long as he kept Oleastro glued to the calendar, Stuart's bosses would have nothing to complain about.

He gripped his mouse and clicked open the calendar. The LED on the sync cradle brightened, and the swirling arrows appeared in the icon on his task bar. He opened his internal mail to see if he had any new orders to transfer to the specs and add to the calendar. That's one thing he knew he was good at which gave him a sense of accomplishment: keeping things organized.

No new orders. He saw a fresh keyword report in his inbox, however. That could keep him busy for an hour or so. He clicked it open and began to scan the report. He'd been able to reprimand Oleastro nearly a dozen times over the past couple months for minor breaks in the communications policy. He'd felt some power when doing that, and had enjoyed it. The breaches were never serious, always yellow list infractions, but it was clear that Oleastro and a few of the others continued to have difficulty adjusting to the company's restrictive policies. Stuart walked the line between coming down too harshly and alienating his talent verses letting them develop loose lips that could compromise the project. He felt he'd handled it well. They'd only had to remove one of the programmers so far, one who had shown up on the report every day since her first and had ranked in the red list repeatedly for keyword phrases that were critical of the company and the project. Not only had she ranked every day, but her channels were both internal and external: words spoken on the premises, words used on the internal private network, in email she'd sent outside from a Gmail account, words she'd typed into web forms on her home computer. It was one of the analysts who ran the reports that pointed the problem out to Stuart, though he'd had suspicions even before they said anything. That programmer wasn't adjusting, wasn't apparently influenced enough by the higher-than-normal compensation, and had to be removed. He'd felt bad about it for awhile, because she'd been there long enough to see too much detail, and the keyword matches suggested she was developing some opinions that could be dangerous to the project outcome, so his bosses had to really remove her. He was glad he didn't have to be involved in that end of things. You had to take care of the project, of course, but still.

Stuart was disappointed to see such a brief report this morning. Nothing to dig into and think about, just some random matches that didn't appear to go anywhere. He went over them again anyway just to be sure, then leaned back in his chair and thought about the public relations campaign he'd lost. He'd thought he had it nailed, had a good person working on it, thought he'd sounded confident and sharp giving the guy orders, but his bosses had taken it away and given it to someone else.

He stretched, closed his eyes and yawned, shuddering at the end of it. He opened his eyes and sat up. He reached for his mouse to open up the production checklist again, maybe check his internal mail again for new orders from his bosses, but by the time his index finger was ready to click he'd changed course, instead selecting the executive external network. His friend Dave from IT had shown him how to drop the internal network connection, leave the VPN, and select the "executive" network to bypass the proxy server and go outside to the internet. Stuart felt privileged and important every time he did that. He opened up his web browser and typed in the address of his favorite porn site, just to relax of course, making a mental note, as he did every day, to erase his browser history before switching back to the internal network.

He entered his user ID, 'Nutkin01,' and then his password. As he did so, an undetected piece of software took note of his keystrokes. It was a light, elegantly constructed program, autonomous and stealthy and carrying a brief, specific payload. It had just arrived on Stuart's C: drive via the sync cable connecting his PalmPilot to his work station. It had snuck across embedded in the calendar data. The anti-virus software running on Stuart's machine had missed it, seeing it only as a lengthy calendar note. But, of course, this was no virus; this creature was a mustang.

The first thing Stuart did after seeing his "Welcome Back, Nutkin!" notification was search the recent posts for 'Chippy.' He'd started following Chippy's posts about a week ago. He found himself intrigued by her profile. From Chippy's posts, he'd begun to think that she might be somewhere near Albuquerque. Maybe he could arrange to meet her, or run into her at a party. The idea made his heart beat faster. He'd sent her a private message but hadn't heard back, and he'd gotten jealous over conversations she'd had with some dude calling himself "Badger" on a public thread.

He decided to send her a picture of himself in another private message. Maybe that would elicit a response. He opened a new browser window and navigated to his photo sharing account. He logged into that with the same username and password, checked for new messages, and then began browsing his images, having posted a recent one that he particularly liked.

That's the JPEG I want. He downloaded it to his desktop, then switched back to the forum window and began composing a private message to Chippy. "Hey Chippy. This is Nutkin again. Here's a shot of me last week. What do you think? Give me a shout sometime. -Nutkin"

He read his message over. Not too forward, right? He wanted to keep it casual.

He clicked the "attach an image" button and navigated to his JPEG file. Seeing the file name in the upload field and mousing the cursor over the submit button made his heart beat faster again. He smiled and mentally crossed his fingers.

As he clicked the submit button, the mustang lurking on his C: drive was watching. It copied itself and embedded the copy with the JPEG uploading to the forum. The upload took longer than it would have otherwise, but Stuart didn't notice; he was thinking about Chippy, imagining that she might respond to his message, maybe say something nice about his picture.

The forum's web server sent back a "200" success response, so the mustang on Stuart's C: drive wrote a cookie, looking like any other cookie from any typical advertising network, left it in Stuart's web browser, edited a flag in the sync file to be picked up by Stuart's PalmPilot, and then erased itself. The mustang on the porn server extracted itself from the JPEG image, verified that it was on a public network, and then got down to the business at hand, which was to roam the internet, keeping its own record of where it went. Copy, confirm then erase from server to server, rinse and repeat, searching for one of its own kind using an algorithm originally developed on the eighth floor of Davis Hall to navigate and learn along the way, to search for another mustang, if one existed.

9

Birch sat straddling the motorcycle idling in the gravel at the side of the road, studying the map on his phone. He felt as if a nerve had fired in him a couple hours before, a long nerve in his spine or maybe at the base of his brain, causing a cascade of impulses that he never would have anticipated but that took on a new pattern, and now he sat on this motorcycle in new clothes wondering where he was going. Then another pattern, this one from higher up and forward in his brain, a pattern he'd felt a number of times recently, layered over the one from lower down, and he stopped wondering about where he was going, realizing that it was a silly thing to wonder about. He didn't need to know in advance where he was going to end up. He wasn't looking for anything in particular that he was aware of. He recalled one of his favorite quotes from one of the smartest beings he'd ever come across in the pages of a book, a little bear, in fact, named Pooh, who said, "I get to where I'm going by leaving where I've been."

Birch didn't expect to locate something. What he was doing didn't involve touching something that had a "where" about it. It was not even that he sensed something he wanted to feel more of, or that he wanted to reassemble a pattern from some memory. That wasn't it at all. He imagined that something *was* out there, something was, and he needed to find it not with "where" but with "how." He was not in a space where there existed one right thing to do, but he felt the best thing was to start with some simple rules, get his two tires rolling, and allow execution of this ethos to draw his path, course corrections occurring based on the rules. If necessary, he would allow new rules to form and sort into the existing rules, rules that weren't returning something better sorting to the bottom of the stack, maybe even falling away.

He decided on his starting rule set: open, toward center, fewer lanes, lower intersection density, lighter traffic. He wanted space. He wanted time to see what was around him, who might be approaching. He wanted to find trust. He wanted to rediscover connection, but connection without threat or malice.

In order to trigger the rules and allow them to guide him, he'd need gradients to descend. He decided he would start with trust, or call it instinct. He would pay attention to the whole of where he was, as well as he could, at each moment, hopefully getting better and better at it as he practiced, and allow his awareness of place to translate into any feeling it would. Let that feeling be an emotion in his other brain; he would trust his gut, ironically, above all else.

He put his phone into his inside jacket pocket, toed the bike into gear and rolled past the city's edge up into the hills on Quimby Road. The machine growled and hummed under him, and the altitude felt satisfying spooling into the wheel bearings as the road carved past horse ranches and twisted into the soft mass of hills. He took it slow at first, as linear time was not a factor, nor was destination part of the object. He was more interested in how the bike pressed into and took up the turns, how the frame and shocks, the flexing rubber and squeezed air in the tires registered the road's story, and how these forces translated through his body to assemble patterns in his mind.

He noticed dapples in the wind popping against his knees and shoulders as he loped through turns and swung through air pockets and currents drifting along the San Antonio Valley. He ran up toward a long line of tall cottonwoods leaning over, shading the road, and felt the rhythmic flutter of parceled air sliding sideways through the trunks across the weathered pavement. The thrum against the leather of his jacket told him how fast he was going, not in miles per hour, but in pressing through air.

Later he leaned around a long curve bounding a ranch and slapped into a sun-warmed air mass thick with the sweet dung of cattle and the tang of suspended dust. He wondered how much information was pooling at his surface unnoticed, then tearing away with the slipstream. How many cows? How many steers? How many bulls? What kind were they? Did the rancher love his land? Did his family live there, or was it a faceless corporate farm? The road straightened, then bent the other way and ramped uphill, the ranch smell disappearing behind him.

Near midday he rolled through velvet green grasslands covered with armies of almond trees in parallel columns under the sun. The road was straight and looked endless, its double yellow line drawn direct to the horizon, a softly wrinkled seam joining the distant hills to the brushed sky. He stayed on the line and rolled on the throttle to chase the horizon up a long slope, but it continued to pull away as if the land was taking a rising breath. Finally it began to exhale and settle, and he crested the rise to see the city of Patterson spreading out below him.

The horizon line tugged straight, and he coasted under the I-5 bridge and onto a boulevard lined on both sides by wide palms and the brown backs of condominium developments. He glided through the city center, past a big stucco library and grassy park. After stopping to fill the tank, he found a taqueria where he sat at a Formica table. The waitress brought him tacos and lemonade.

Rested and empty-minded, he followed the road out of Patterson and through Turlock, then turned north at Merced Falls, liking the look of the road on his phone map. The green seeped out of the grasses, leaving them a buff brown, and the sky dried of most of its clouds, turning from powder blue to fired white where it touched the desert. Scattered broad-crowned hardwoods ranged in groups near the horizon, looking like bison in the distance.

Through Granite Springs the road narrowed and smoothed, a single yellow line to follow with a Volvo coming this way and a pickup to pass now and then, always checking his rear-view mirrors for any vehicles that might be tailing him. The horizon folded in, and the bison-trees gathered near the road, becoming woods.

After Coulterville the road snaked upward, gaining altitude, and Birch had to lean hard into some of the turns and bleed off his speed, sometimes running wide and feeling his inexperience as a rider. The hardwoods gave way to tall pines crowding the road as it continued its ascent. The road ended at a pine-dotted brown hill, so he turned east toward the center of Yosemite.

He wound through the mountains, following a camper with a rack of four bicycles on the back for a few miles before finding a comfortable stretch to pass. Each time he passed, he felt one more large object between his taillight and whatever he imagined was back there trying to find him. The road lay notched into the slope, first to his left, then to his right as he crested a saddle or swung through a draw.

The air turned colder and tasted sharp with balsam over Tioga Pass. The spruce there were tall and thick at the roadsides, the ground dark and littered with jumbled forest debris. He rolled up behind a Mustang convertible with the top down. A guy in a baseball cap and a women with a tight headscarf fluttering in the wind were fishing the cool mountain air for the last tatters of summer. Birch pulled around them and glanced over as he passed. Their expressions were stone behind dark glasses. That left him feeling itchy, irrationally he knew, but he pressed on to create distance from the Mustang and his "what if" thoughts.

Boulders the size of bears leaned down from the mountainside toward the road. Fractured stones rested in the juniper on the downslope shoulder, putting rockslides in mind and adding a thrill to Birch's awareness. Moisture gathered in the air without his noticing, until he started missing the dapple of sun spots and tree shadows on the cracked pavement, realizing it had grown overcast. *Pay attention Birch. Notice more. Get better at this. Improve with each mile.* The farther he rode, the lower the gray clouds hung, looking uncannily like the hulking boulders walling the road.

He pulled off to rest on a wide shoulder at Tenaya Lake, went down to the lakeshore and splashed steel-cold water on his face, shaking his hands to toss off the icy burn while looking as far as he could ahead and behind. Across the road from the lakeside an unbroken hill of quartzite the size of a factory rose from the gravel shoulder. Birch wandered over and leaned against it, putting his palms flat on the rock and closing his eyes. The rough surface was warm to his alpine lake-watered hands. *The sun must have baked on this rock face at some point today.* He stood gathering the warmth and sensed something waiting inside the rock. He felt toward it with the nerves of his palms and fingers, thinking it felt like motion, not a gross motion like trembling or movement predictive of some quake or slide. This was the constant, gentler motion of being. And it felt to Birch like it was waiting patiently for something. What was in there? Was it the memory of the rumble of wagons, hooves cloven and shod, and leather boots that had passed this way going the opposite direction 150 years before? Was it also the motion of lives that moved through here long before the wagons rolled by? And did it also take in the quiet rumble of the V-twin engine as he pulled up?

Birch stood a while longer, wanting to interact with it, to communicate, to know. He felt something organizing and rising, or thought so. Then he opened his eyes and took his hands away. Something there to wonder about. And the pursuing threat of Robin felt dulled just a bit. *Good. Thank you, Silverwing. Continue.*

He followed the pass road, pressing into the turns a bit

for the feel of it and to make some time under the low light. He approached the national park road and spun passed it, none of his rules urging him to make that turn. He crossed the Tuolumne River on a rock bridge and swung through a broad meadow into some light traffic from late-season vacationers leaving a small parking lot. He briefly considered staying the night in the park lodge, but thought he had enough of the day left to keep going and wanted to feel more turns on the motorcycle.

The peaks near Ellery Lake scraped the bellies of the clouds for fresh snow that blended with pocket glaciers spotting the faces below. By the time he reached the intersection with Highway 395 near Mono Lake the altitude and cold had packed a heavy fatigue onto him, and the Silverwing felt sluggish as well. He was ready to descend to seek warmth and rest. He followed the road nearly another hour downslope into the falling evening, into an opening valley of sage flats, leaving the cold sodden sky back in the mountains.

As the sun set somewhere behind him, he rounded a curve with a white rail fence and saw a sign for a bed and breakfast. He coasted to the entrance, making an awkward turn, and rolled gingerly into the dusty drive in front of a ranch building with a hood-light hanging next to the front door. A couple European sports cars shared the lot with a row of four well-loved Harleys. He added his Honda at the end of the row and removed his helmet, staggering a bit in the sandy lot as his feet tingled against the ground and a plume of warmth from his core vented downward toward the cold bones of his legs. He stretched his arms and back, saw stars blinking through the purple sky directly above and to the east.

Inside, a waft of gravy and potatoes greeted him and led him to a pine-paneled dining room where an oak slab table for twelve, only partially cleared of plates, glasses, and serving platters, looked recently vacated after a festive meal. Iron-handled utensils lay scattered among leather place mats, on which sat thick clay plates and bowls. A stout woman, with dark hair and wearing an apron, walked in from the kitchen rubbing her hands together. She jumped when she noticed Birch.

"Howdy," she said, looking at him with a cocked head.

"Hi," Birch said.

"You stayin' with us?"

"I just saw your sign on the road. I came over from San Jose."

"That's some miles. Well, sorry, but you missed dinner. I can warm some up for you though. I'll have to make the room up too. We weren't expecting anyone else today."

She turned and poked her head back toward the kitchen. "Jenny! I'll take care of this now. You go make up the double room. We have another guest." She led him to a counter off of the entrance hall, wrote in a book and took his debit card to slide through the terminal, punching some buttons to make it beep. "Take a seat at the table," she said. "I'll bring you your dinner while Jenny gets your room up, long as you don't mind me clearing the other stuff while you eat."

Birch didn't mind at all. He sat against the chair back with a forkful of roast beef and a clay mug of lager, looking around the room at weathered ranch tools and mule deer heads mounted on the walls for decoration, and felt a vast, wide relaxation, like an empty land inside of him. The innkeeper went back and forth from the kitchen, clearing away the other guests' dinner debris and making idle chatter. Birch heard laughter moving through the walls and outside the dining room window in the yard. He realized that after a full day through the mountains on a motorcycle, which he was only just learning how to ride, he felt more relaxed and positive than he had the entire time he'd worked for Robin.

When he was done with dinner the innkeeper showed him to his room, explaining as they walked about the hot springs and various pools of hot sulfur water located on the grounds. Birch went out to the lot to retrieve his things from the Honda's saddlebags, then lay on the bed a moment, letting the pull of gravity drag away a layer of thought and fatigue.

At length he decided to go for a soak, stripped down to his boxers, grabbed a towel and donned a white, flannel robe that lay folded on the foot of the bed. So attired, he wandered out back to the grounds, following a trail of flagstones lit by dim solar lights stuck into the dusty soil. Stars beamed down from above, flickering brightly like fire through pinholes in a barrel stove. The air was cool, soon smelling of warm sulfur as he approached the shadow of a huge willow, hearing bubbling talk and laughter beyond.

"Wadda we got here?" a woman's voice rasped, an image of Peppermint Patty flashing through Birch's mind. Beyond the willow he discovered a steaming tile-lined pool the size of two sofas, set flush with the ground and aproned with a deck of random slate tiles. A bald, heavy man with a gray beard and two women who appeared around the man's age bobbed at the sides of the pool, slowly moving their arms at the steaming surface, looking up at him. "Bring it, cowboy," the raspy woman said.

"Mind if I join you?" Birch said.

"Feel free," the man said.

Birch noticed a foot bucket and dipped his feet, one then the other, to wash off the dust. The bearded man said, "So THAT's what that's for. I thought it was to put the fire out!" The three of them cackled like geese with sore throats. Birch dropped his robe on the slate deck and dipped a toe into the water. "Nice," the raspy woman said. "He looks like Wild Bill Hickok without the beard," the other woman said. "Mind if we call you Wild Bill?"

Birch laughed briefly and worked more of his foot into the water. It was hot. He sat on the edge and started on his other foot, got in up to his knees and then stayed there a moment.

"That must be you on the Honda," the thin woman bobbing beside the bald man said, shaking out her salt-and-pepper hair as she spoke.

"That is me," Birch said.

"You should be riding a Harley," the woman said.

"Yeah, the best vibrators on the road," the raspy one said, and the women cackled again and splashed the water.

Birch levered off the edge and slowly slid into the water. "Fhooooo," he exhaled. "Yah."

"There you go, Wild Bill," the thin woman said.

The man reached back into the shadows on the deck, then leaned toward Birch with his meaty fist wrapped around the neck of a wine bottle. "Now cool your insides with a slug of this," he said.

Birch took the bottle and tipped it up, taking in a big swallow of tepid chardonnay, then handed the bottle back. "Thanks," he said.

The sulfur heat saturated him quickly and rose up his neck, cupped his ears and streamed into his nostrils. The bald man introduced himself as Dave and the thin woman next to him as his wife, Suzanne. He was a recently retired physician, while Suzanne worked as a tax auditor at a law firm in Reno. Dave mentioned that they were road-tripping, "with a couple of deadbeats who are already in asleep."

Suzanne laughed and added, "Well, Brad's probably sitting poking his finger at his phone."

The raspy woman introduced herself as Calypso. "My friends call me 'Lips,'" she said. She worked as a registered nurse at the Reno hospital Dave had recently retired from. Birch introduced himself and said he was traveling solo, taking some time off from software.

"We're still calling you Wild Bill," Suzanne said, and they laughed again.

"You're wondering where my old man's at?" Calypso said.

Birch didn't say anything.

"Well, I dumped his self-centered ass. Now I'm the one who rolls on the throttle."

Dave reached back for the wine again and passed it over to Calypso. "Yeah baby," Suzanne said as Calypso pointed the bottom of the bottle up at the stars.

Calypso tilted the bottle back down and handed it over to Birch. "You got some catchin' up to do," she said.

"We got more," Dave added.

Birch leaned back against the earth-heated tile, watched the stars and imagined the planetary veins carrying the heat and water to the springs that fed the pool. His three companions joked and drank wine. Every now and then the bottle would come his way, and he'd take a slug and pass it back, offering up a joke he knew or tossing in an observation on whatever they were batting about. He felt buoyed and suspended by the hot swirling minerals, let his head rest on the tile and closed his eyes, feeling micro currents in the bath brushing over his skin. *Some of the currents must be from the vein that feeds the pool,* he thought, *and some from the motions of my companions.* He let his body and mind quiet, listening to see if he could discern which current was which.

When the wine bottle was drained, and another after that, Dave said, "Well, I'm ready to call it." Birch felt a tidal surge in the pool as Dave turned and lifted himself to crawl up to the deck. Birch opened his eyes on what looked like two dripping white hogs perched atop thick bridge stanchions as Dave bent down to pick up his robe. Birch felt his eyebrows involuntarily raise, had the urge to close his eyes again but didn't.

Suzanne followed Dave, standing and stepping out of the pool like a naked woods sprite. She scooped up her robe from the ground and turned to look at Calypso, robe dangling from her hand and breasts pointing to the center of the earth. "You coming?" she asked.

Calypso glanced at her and said, "I'm not leaving Wild Bill out here to drown by himself. He might need some medical attention."

Suzanne looked at her a moment and then turned,

saying, "Okay, Lips, see you at breakfast." Her white form receded along the dim path.

Birch felt another, gentler surge in the water, and Calypso was sitting next to him looking at his face. "I don't need to say anything," she said.

Birch was immediately, awkwardly alarmed. He very much *did* feel the need to say something, but had nothing ready. He smiled uneasily, turned and lifted himself from the pool. Calypso frowned and said, "You sure? Aww shucks, Wild Bill," as he toweled off quickly and walked back to his room.

The next morning Birch filled himself with biscuits, gravy, sausage, a large omelette, coffee, juice, and fresh fruit, sitting at the table with his three companions from the night before plus the two who'd been in their room. Dave and Calypso joked with him about parking his Honda in a line of Harleys. The innkeeper and her helper circled the table, warming up coffee mugs and serving dishes. The guests clanked forks and knives on their clay plates, everyone looking freshly scrubbed and rosy in the morning sun beaming past the gingham curtains. Birch enjoyed his appetite. He also enjoyed the lightness of the banter, how unattached and unworried it was. He looked at Calypso, could see that she was nothing and neither was he. No weight. Nothing to carry. In fact her scratchy laugh was buoyant as she chatted about the day's upcoming ride.

Birch was the first to fire his bike into life and roll out of the dusty lot. He was sore from the prior day's ride, but he figured not nearly as sore as he would have been without the mineral bath.

The morning was cool but warmed quickly as he descended toward the state line. At the junction of Route 6 he stopped to consult the map on his phone. He had assumed he would be turning right, but pinching the map out to a higher view showed left was the turn that would lead toward center. Center of what? Center of the thought pattern he occupied, toward some nucleus he felt but didn't understand. He had many patterns at play, sliding in and out of his present space like cells moving through a fluid sea. Some new patterns, like his near miss idea of Calypso, swirled and touched edges with patterns he'd had for a longer time, like the idea of Calypso from the old Greek story, which in turn swirled and touched edges with denser patterns related to Banni and other interns. The pattern of Zongo Inc. and violence, of Robin, skated through his space. He saw them float past. The motorcycle had become a pattern. The sound of the motor, his body's points of contact, the foot pegs, the grips, the seat cushion, his knees holding the gas tank in the curves, the vibration, the wind, the sound of the tires tugging on pavement, the petroleum smell, the warmth of the exhaust pipe by his right lower leg, the stiffness of his leather jacket, all layered into the pattern and broadened as he rode. The road surfaces and landforms wove into a pattern laminated beneath the motorcycle pattern, filling details of geography into his overall pattern of America, this place he thought of as home.

The map, when pinched out to a high altitude view, gave him the shape he needed to follow his centering rule. He turned left to head north and then east. After a few miles he thrummed over a cattle grate built into the road surface, lifting himself off the seat a touch to unweight the bike as he flew across, and found himself in a flat, sage-dotted range. The road drew a straight line due east to somewhere beyond the horizon. Unless he turned his head slightly to look more directly at the sage winding by in his view, the scene ahead of him, the road, the peripheral blur, the blue sky, didn't much change. It was as if the bike hummed in place, the seconds ticked away, yet nothing like distance happened; that intersection between the idea of travel and progress wasn't present.

Birch recognized this as a moment requiring his faith and trust. He hadn't much thought about faith since he was a kid going to church with his parents, yet here he sat on this buzzing contraption in this sparse scene new to his consciousness, alone save for the occasional pickup truck and the assumed hidden hare or rattlesnake, with the dim knowledge that he could jerk his hands mere inches one way or the other without even thinking about it and instantly turn himself into a pile of bloody coyote food soaking into the hot sand.

Faith was what had put him here, and faith was what kept his hands relaxed on the bars. Sitting with his sister in the pew between their parents, faith had started as two tall bodies that created this magnetic field of love and acceptance he was allowed to inhabit, and the trust that they would continue to create that field. Of course the minister told them faith was something they had to have, in a way that accused them of not having it. Maybe trusting in that magnetic field wasn't really faith. Listening to the minister over the years, he got the impression faith was a kind of arrival. Once you had it, you were done, saved. You no longer had to continue trying to refine your understanding of things. You were officially relieved of that human responsibility. You had faith. You could hold it up like a badge or diploma. You could rest now, sit around waiting to croak so you could be invited into someplace they called Heaven, though no one seemed to agree on how to describe it. That faith felt like the piece of paper he'd gotten from his kinder music class, his certificate of participation. He lost his interest in faith then.

Years later at the university he hung out with scientists who had not given up their desire to refine their understanding of things. They were hungrily seeking knowledge and intelligence, and Birch saw faith over and over in their quests. His interest rekindled. There he recognized faith as a powerful connective bridge, one that defied paper and certificates, and one without which science would stall and rust. He saw it used as a placeholder to allow seekers to continue the process of refining and increasing knowledge despite gaps in the continuum of our collective understanding. Faith allowed the seekers to use imagination as an ingredient in an environment that demanded evidence and proof. Birch learned the art of faith in his programming, and quickly gained access to territory he had not previously imagined.

Now, sitting on this motorcycle, Birch needed faith. He needed faith so that he could trust the quality of his rules, and the quality of his perceptions should he need to sort or alter his rules. Faith let him turn toward center and feel the value in that. It let him seek the point at the center where nothing turns, where patterns and their preconceptions cease to exist.

He stopped in Tonopah for gas in the early afternoon. Heat rose from the desert in languid ripples as he stood by the pumps. He inserted his Slang debit card into a pump slot, wondering how hot it would have to get before the softening plastic of the card would fuse with the plastic edges of the slot. He grabbed the nozzle and clanged it against the steel collar of the gas tank, squeezing the trigger handle with one hand while resting the other on the black vinyl seat to prop up his slumping back, feeling soft and weakened by the soaking heat. Nothing came out. He frowned and glanced at the pump readout. His card was denied. *Duh.* He'd forgotten to check his Slang balance, and hadn't even thought to generate a new account number. The heat was getting to him.

He took out his phone and opened the Tor browser. It spun slowly, as he had no connection. He looked up into the thin blue sky and exhaled everything from his lungs, then pulled in a long rush of hot dry air. *Come on!* A bronze-green F-150 covered in white dust pulled up to the next pump, and Birch's phone found the account to borrow. The signal was still slow, but he stood there waiting for his login page to load, then waiting for it to process his login request. It took forever. Not enough in his account. He opened a new window to log into his bank account to make a transfer. The lady in the truck was nearly done filling her tank. Finally his account loaded. *Balance zero!*

A sudden and new fire rose up his spine, raking up the back of his neck. He was sweaty yet wind-dried from the ride, now newly drenched as if from a fever. He should have a small fortune in his account, the condo, the car, all the things he sold! He had transferred everything over from PayPal; it should all be in here. His mind started racing, the reptile in his lower brain twisting in fear and anger. *What the hell! I need gas, water, food!* He waited for the transaction activity log to load. The lady finished pumping and drove off. Birch's phone held on to her account long enough to load the latest transactions. A couple test transactions, small amounts, not his, then a big one, ACH, withdrawing the full balance of the account. *FUCK! Was I hacked? How in the hell?*

He thumbed through his remaining cash, deciding to fill his tank and buy a bottle of water. He needed to untwist his reptile brain and find some shade long enough to think.

Inside the store, while counting out his cash, he asked the old guy behind the counter, "No WiFi?"

The guy shook his head. "Nah, owner shut off the satellite." Birch thought if he grew desperate he could figure out how to use the terminal network from the store's credit card machine, or the ATM sitting by the door, but the effort of getting the storekeeper's cooperation would be too much. He might as well wait for someone else with a phone to drive up to the pumps.

He wheeled the bike without starting it to the side of the store, then took his bottle of water with him to rest on the hot shaded gravel under a dusty oak. He dropped his leather jacket to sit on and leaned back against the tree, popped the cap on the water bottle and tilted it up to his lips. The water wicked into the tissue of his throat like a sponge, alarming him by how dry he'd let himself become. He sat, letting his head hang, savoring the slightly cooler air of the shade and the water spreading out inside him.

After the sweat had dried from his face and neck, and the collar of his T-shirt was merely damp, he heard the ticking of an idling engine low on oil and the pull of tires rolling toward the pumps. Birch looked up to see a white Toyota. He picked up his phone to test for a signal, then went back to his bank account to look at the details of the withdrawals. He couldn't make sense of the two test withdrawals. Twenty-six cents and a buck fifty, obviously someone probing his account, but no source information that he could use to hunt. The big one was different, however. It included cryptic source information. When he googled it, he found the format for a code for a federal warrant exercised by the FBI. Burning saltwater gathered under his hair and across his forehead again. It occurred to him that he was wasting the water he'd just drunk, letting it evaporate from his sweating skin. What was the FBI doing clearing out his bank account? Then he thought—*Robin must have discovered one of my mustangs!* His insides instantly turned to rotted mushrooms and fell to the floor of his pelvis. He felt burning, tangy vomit slurrying up his throat and fought to keep it down, growing dizzy. He slumped onto his jacket and had to lay his head back onto the gravel. Breaths came hard, each one a load to lift and drop. He imagined black SUVs hunting him, agents surprising him around a corner somewhere, a trial, federal prison.

Between breaths he heard boots on gravel, and then a voice: "Hey buddy. You awright?" Another, quieter voice said, "Looks like a bad trip there." Birch thought of opening his eyes, but couldn't just yet. The first voice said, "You need a doctor or somethin'?"

Birch blew a couple long breaths out through his lips and wrenched his eyes open. The world seemed unnaturally bright white and hot. He couldn't focus. The blur of a man in a cowboy hat, sleeveless T-shirt and jeans stood over him, the outline of another man visible behind him. *Not FBI.* Birch slowly blinked and propped himself up on his elbows, rolling his head on his neck. He looked to the side, saw the rust pocks on the rims of his leaning motorcycle as his eyes swam into focus. Then he looked up at the man, a young guy, maybe around his own age, who stared back with a frown of concentration shaded by the wide brim of his hat.

"Nah, bro, thanks," Birch said slowly, hearing himself sound almost drunk. "I'm alright. On a long ride, and just got some bad news, trying to stay cool."

The guy in the hat studied Birch's face for signs of truth. "A lady?" the guy asked knowingly. Birch languidly held his gaze, submitting to the inspection, and gave him a perceptible nod. A lady was as good an explanation here as any. The guy leaned down and laid a dusty paw on Birch's shoulder. "Okay," he said quietly. "Okay man." He lingered, still making sure, and then straightened up. He and his friend turned and sauntered into the store.

Birch sat up, rubbed his face, then stood, immediately feeling dizzy and leaning back against the tree. He reached down for the water bottle, lifted and drained it. He then leaned down again to pick up his jacket, lifting his boot off the lining where he'd absently left a dusty lug sole print on the taffeta, dragged the jacket over to his bike and draped it over the seat.

I looked at my bank balance, he thought, *saw a zero and nearly passed out. How fucked up is that?* He walked in a circle for a minute, looking at the ground, then pulled out his phone. It had picked up a signal, probably one of the guys in the store. *Thanks Buddy,* Birch thought.

He logged into his bank account again to make sure he wasn't hallucinating. *Zero. Fuck!*

He noticed an alert badge on his Slang icon and opened it, finding a pending transaction for $200 from Melanie Krantz. The notes said *Meal Reimbursement: Telegram.* He was momentarily puzzled. He hadn't eaten with Melanie recently, certainly not to the tune of $200. And Telegram; he knew of no place called the Telegram. He glanced at the Honda, squinted, then his eyes drifted up to the sky. He curled up the corner of his mouth and opened his Telegram app. He had to enter his old cellphone number, then log into his Linux server to retrieve the token to log into the chat app. A bit of a pain, but he wanted to see what Melanie had to say. He searched for Melanie Krantz and typed her a quick message.

—Holy Fuck! Thank you Mel!

A few minutes later, he saw the icon indicating that she was typing.

—Thought U might need. RT is rampaging, says he's got something on U, bragging how he froze your money, friend in gov, not making launch, he's psycho, watch out, wherever U R! Said he wants to kill U!

Birch looked up and ran his eyes along the highway. The two men came out of the store and saw Birch standing there. The guy in the hat tilted it at him as he walked to his truck. Birch nodded back. He closed the Telegram app, initiating a new number for his Slang card as the men started their truck and rolled out of the filling station lot.

Birch walked into the store, shoving his Slang card into the ATM by the door. He checked the balance, then withdrew all $200 minus the ATM fee. He bought a couple more bottles of water and went back out to stash them in the saddle bags. He took his jacket off the seat and stashed that as well. He started up, feeling rattled and scared but experiencing a shred of relief to be going back into motion. He rolled out to the highway and headed east.

The desert floor warped near Ely, finally giving the road motion and curve. The sage grew tall and close, hills scalloping the ground nearest to the roadside. Birch stopped to top off the tank and thought about eating a plate of tamales. He was hungry from the ride, his body feeling bruised by the constant droning thought that Robin had violated him, was hunting him down. He left the tamales as mere thoughts, trading hunger for the slight security of cash in his pocket. He would need gas for the bike, water to keep himself from dehydrating and fading out at eighty miles an hour.

The light was falling, so he put his jacket back on to continue in the cooling air. Maybe it was the stress of constantly looking in his rear-view mirrors, or maybe just the fatigue of miles catching up to him, but he started to anticipate the Utah state line as if crossing it would give him some gift of clarity. He knew he was building up false hope, yet did it anyway. He wanted to indulge in hope. His body sagged on the bike, and he rolled on the throttle. He passed a truck stop, a motel, and the Utah state welcome sign without slowing, feeling no different than he had moments before, except for the added dull ache of disappointment.

He leaned forward into the wind, looking at overlapping low mountain ranges holding down the road at the far horizon. He rode another hour and a half into the evening, trying to tease apart and then let go of whatever it was he thought he should've known or sensed upon crossing the border, now just an echo in his gut. Maybe the trillions of bacteria he hosted there knew something he could not assimilate into understanding, something that excited them, though now they'd calmed down. Finally he came upon the thought that knowing less was just as valid as knowing more. After all, if he didn't know where he was going no one else did either.

What he really needed now was rest, mainly rest from thinking every black SUV was the FBI, every sheriff on the lookout for him. It was an awful and exhausting way to move over the surface of the planet. He decided to trust the code he'd written to cloak his phone, trust his awareness, trust the simple rules he'd devised to guide his journey. Without trust all he had was fear.

He slowed the bike through Hinckley and rolled past a closed lumber yard into Delta as darkness settled, coasting to a stop at a motel with a flickering vacancy sign. He grabbed some clothes from the saddlebags to wash in the sink, did some quick math, and decided that he could afford the meager room rate. It had been a long day.

He peeled off his clothes, kneaded them in hot water in the bathroom sink along with the socks and underwear he grabbed from the saddlebags, wrung them out and draped them over the shower curtain rod. Then he pulled down the stiff bedspread and rumpled it onto the crunchy carpet, flopped himself onto the springs and twisted into the sheet and blankets. He slept deep and dark, at one point dreaming of a warehouse where burly men in grease-stained clothes dumped barrels of grain into a dark chasm, leaving the empty barrels lying about on the warehouse floor.

The next morning he ate cornflakes and milk from a Styrofoam bowl with a flimsy plastic spoon in the motel breakfast area. A few fellow travelers nursed their coffees, watching the weather on a television set; nearby a gray-haired couple sat at a table with donuts on a paper plate and a folded-up newspaper, looking out the window.

On his way out to the bike he filled his jacket pockets with rolls from the breakfast room. People frowned, but no one said anything to him.

The morning was bright but still cool, with no breeze. He gazed up and down the highway, then stashed the rolls in a saddle bag with the bottled water from the day before. In his mind, his cash equaled gas equaled distance. Distance equaled good. He even thought he might experiment with fasting after the rolls ran out as a way to buy more miles. He still didn't know where he was going, could only vaguely imagine the feeling he'd have when he got "there." It was something like heaven, or purity, or nothingness. Maybe a state where history didn't exist, at least his history, an unraveling of everything that composed him, back to a pure beginning. No violent video games, no empty stare, no Robin, no road rage in his rear-view mirror, no shadowed nightmares. He battled the words that bore these thoughts through his mind, thought them foolish. Heaven? Nothingness? Yet he guarded the thoughts themselves, knowing they in turn surrounded the truth he sought, even if he couldn't articulate its meaning.

The bike started easily, thrumming while he had the choke pulled out. He threw his leg over, heeled the kickstand up, and sat looking over the land while the engine warmed. He panned his eyes in every direction and saw nothing moving until he spotted a vulture across the highway floating over low sagebrush hills, tracing a slow circle, tipping its stiff wings back and forth to keep its course. Birch looked for it to rise, to show him a thermal, but the bird slowly descended instead, presumably toward some carrion on the hill's far side.

Birch thumbed the choke back in, stepped on the gear lever and rolled onto the tarmac. He ran through the gears up to speed, feeling and smelling the coolness and clarity of the air as he pushed through it. The sounds of rubber tugging on tar and stone, and the engine finding its pitch mixed with the rushing air.

He felt refreshed today. That looming need for insight was gone. Much of the soreness he'd built up over the past couple days was also gone. For one thing his body was becoming accustomed to the ride. The micro adjustments he needed to tune his balance, to cycle stress points through his frame to avoid cramps and muscle fatigue, were forming as patterns stored and recalled without need of conscious thought. The vertebrae in his lower back, those in his neck, the shoulder bones in his rotator cuffs, the clusters of ankle bones and wrist bones, the connective tissues and the nerves, were all learning to pulse and move as part of the forming patterns, each micro motion or electric nerve pulse following the same set of rules he used to guide his motorcycle through the countryside, each contributing to the collective shape of the moment, each moment tuning and expanding the pattern. Motions and body adjustments which took an abundance of muscle and mental energy his first day riding he could now accomplish more simply with geometry, referencing his stored thought patterns. Geometry is free and doesn't get used up. That left him more energy for his thoughts, imagination, and his eyes. He breathed easier as he rode now, relaxed his hands on the bars, could see farther into the distance and absorb more from the periphery.

The road continued the line drawn the previous day. With periodic course corrections it followed a path toward the center of the country. Birch felt the gradual buildup of altitude as large mesas and toothy ranges grew and then receded on the horizon. Traffic pressured the highway as he approached the Colorado state line, triggering one of his rules. He exited the highway onto an old state road that ran parallel with sparse traffic and single lanes of old patched asphalt. He followed the road past oddly familiar-looking fields of young winter wheat, clusters of trees and buildings set back in the distance, until the sunset stretched his shadow ahead of him. At length Birch slowed into Grand Junction and rolled through the streets. He allowed his rules to guide him through the grid of brick buildings, cars, and pickup trucks, wound up idling past a life-sized chrome bison staring with lowered head from a cement platform, reflecting the last tinges of blood orange sunset from its metal haunches. He knew he'd never been over this ground, but still felt a strange sense of déjà vu. Maybe he was just getting used to being out in the country.

He coasted by an Italian restaurant, imagining a mounded plate of spaghetti and meatballs, then found the cheapest motel on the eastern edge of town.

He left early the next morning with a few more rolls and a couple danishes added to his saddlebags, the highway continuing to rise as he headed northeast. Sage-dotted gravel mounded toward rusty guardrails, the hills ahead heaping to mountains which effectively blocked out the sunrise. He wove back and forth between routes 6 and 70 through midday, following the pavement through a deep groove cut into the mountains by the coursing brown Colorado River, which slid downhill to his right. The highway twisted along with the river, heavy crumbles of fallen rock appearing on the shoulders at curves through the Vail Valley. Every now and then Birch had to swerve when a jagged rock poked over into the lane.

He felt the thinning air in his lungs, pulling harder to draw his breaths but never getting a full one. The engine ran hot near his lower legs; he could feel it working hard to get enough air.

He pulled off in Avon to eat his danishes and a roll,

splashing some water after them. The motorcycle started hard despite being hot when he was ready to continue, and he worried that he wouldn't know how to adjust the carburetor if he ran into real trouble. He sat outside a restaurant to use the WiFi and looked up the carburetor from an '82 V-twin so he could locate the adjustment screws and mentally rehearse how he might work them.

He chugged up the hill past Vail and limped through the Eisenhower Tunnel, pushed from behind by the bright LEDs of a BMW, and made it over Loveland Pass, wishing he could get off of the highway but not having an alternate route.

The engine finally smoothed out, and his lungs again felt full and relaxed, as he glided down past Idaho Springs toward Denver. He rolled the throttle on and leaned into the curves, leaving the BMW behind.

He dropped out of the mountains on the eastern side of the Front Range into streams of traffic. He had thoughts of exploring the city, but let them float away. He stopped for gas and decided to angle through the grid to the northeast, toward lower intersection density. He felt good heading out of the city on Route 6 as the flats opened up into the twilight, and loped along with the thinning taillights until stopping in Sterling for the night, overcome with fatigue from the day's ride.

Early the next morning he decided to check his server messages for any news from Mel. He had no idea what he was hoping for, other than some declaration that it was all a mistake, that his money was back in his account, that Robin had forgiven him for leaving and called off the dogs.

There were no messages from Mel. Instead, among the pileup from Robin was a message that simply said, "a motorcycle huh? Well that will be fun …..;)"

Panic clapped a palm over Birch's mouth, and he struggled for air. Packing up quickly, he grabbed some rolls from the breakfast room and ducked out, looking in every direction. He botched the clutch and nearly smashed his foot catching the bike as he attempted the turn onto the street, making a wobbly recovery and yanking his way up the gears.

He rode fast, due east on Route 6 over the flat earth straight toward a giant wall of rain. It hung like a rippled gray curtain across the road miles ahead, dangling from nimbus lumps stuffed into the dark rafters of the sky. Birch had no rain pants or chaps, an unfortunate oversight. He slowed the motorcycle, wondering what to do, where else to go, but nothing felt right but going forward fast. He would experience this wall of rain.

The first balls of water slapped his helmet and face shield in a loose rhythm. The next flight slammed the leather of his jacket and skidded over his legs, immediately soaking through the denim. The asphalt went from damp to river, and he slowed again for the sake of survival, seeking a steady running speed where he could still feel the tires talking to the submerged road, balancing his need to move forward and his need to stay upright. He felt like he was rolling through a washing machine. The rivulets dripping down his neck were cold, spreading chill through the fibers of his shirt. He soon felt encased in water, wanting to get off the bike and run to heat his body back up, but with no shelter in sight instead worked from inside to relax each muscle in turn as he could.

The water balls now smudged together on his face shield, creating a mottled, jellied lens through which he scanned for the data he needed to keep the Honda traveling along its path. Birch followed his own progress as a witness, observing his body operating this machine through the torrent, intrigued by the simplicity of his thoughts as he alternately contracted and relaxed the muscles in his arms and back in micro movements to keep the fork of the motorcycle coursing toward the dark blur in his vision. He was some sort of protean fish navigating through the loud, swishing wet of this sea, thoughts of Robin gone for the time being. He could swim anywhere, in any direction, even across dimensions, and it was only these simple smudges of light and dark he needed to choose his way.

Headlights approached like floating eyes, and a pickup passed by in the oncoming lane. Birch glanced over and saw the guy glancing back. Then the washing sound of rain on the road quieted. The drops spread out. The asphalt came up out of the water, glistening in the morning sun now slanting through the mist. He was through. The wind pushed the water droplets aside on his face shield, and the straight line of the road came into focus, sparks of sun scattering everywhere over the Nebraska plain.

He stopped in Arapahoe at a small cafe for coffee and warmth. Again he had this odd déjà vu. The land outside the cafe windows looked something like a movie he'd seen before, but he couldn't place when or where, or even which movie. The view and warmth tipped the scales on his impulse to drop the cash for a roast beef sandwich. *Just a different form of fuel at this point,* he thought.

His table by the front window stood next to a heater vent, so he hung his jacket over the opposite chair to dry. After the sandwich he sat with his coffee and warmed and rested, watching the occasional car pass by on main street. He had the quantum feeling that he was both someplace in Nebraska and everyplace at the same time. He could be anywhere, and the motorcycle he rode could be any motorcycle. Something about this place dispelled his fear of being pursued, letting him believe that the chances of Robin knowing where he was, even which way he'd headed, were nearly zero. The waitress took no particular notice of him other than to serve him his lunch. No one knew he was here. He felt unobserved.

He mounted the bike and rolled out of town, savoring that luxurious, priceless feeling of dryness and warmth after being chilled to the marrow. He rolled through one crossroads town after another, separated by long stretches of prairie or tilled fields, and in the heart of the afternoon turned north at a village named Friend, a pair of semis driving toward him from a grain elevator just off the state highway. Normally he would be starting to think about finding a gas station about now, but he knew his cash was almost gone, and the tight connection he'd kept between the mile count of the odometer and the range of the gas tank (since the Silverwing had no gas gauge) was muddled to the point that he'd lost track of his starting number.

He crossed a railroad track, entering a grid of section roads marking off vast cornfields thick with dried standing stalks that seemed twice his height. His engine coughed and wheezed, and he reached down to twist the tank valve to "reserve" as the guy at the shop had shown him, revving it back to life.

Without bothering to consult his map he used random data to guide his turns, which came more frequently now in this grid. The pavement became spotty, then yielded completely to dirt and gravel. A plume of chalky dust from a passing vehicle at an unmarked crossroad obscured the view in one direction, so he turned in the other. A cloud's shadow swept over the road, then left a lane of sunlight that drew Birch toward it, turning left down another road. He moved through the grid in this fashion, sensing his travel through an empty medium toward the center of something tapping at the periphery of what felt to him like someone else's memory.

Late in the afternoon he raised a river of dust between two oceans of standing corn stalks, coming upon a village flanked by grain silos and crossed with dirt roads. He slowed the bike, rumbling quietly in among streets flanked by tall locust and cottonwood trees. The streets were narrow dirt paths, named with either letters of the alphabet or single digit numbers, and were laid out in a grid similar to the section roads he'd ridden in on, only tighter. He zig-zagged through the village, past peeling paint and boarded-up windows, idling past sedans and trucks parked along the sides of the two paved streets at the center of town. Two men in seed caps sat on benches on the ground-level porch of a brick cafe; Birch thought he saw someone moving past the window inside. A woman and two children exited a buff-colored stone building that he saw was the township library. The library was stuck to a brick building that was boarded up with gray, weathered plywood. The three of them watched him idle past, the woman smiling and one of the kids waving.

A motor revved from behind the partially closed overhead door of a metal shed garage. A couple of men carried full seed sacks over their shoulders, stacking them on the back of a flatbed parked in front of a brick building with a single loading dock. Birch circled the village with the splintered feeling that he'd been here before, though he knew he never had.

He was following a narrow curving gravel street around the northeast side of the village when his motor coughed and chugged, then went silent. He set the kickstand, took his helmet off and set it on the seat, noticing that his rear tire looked a bit bald and flat. It was just past five in the afternoon. He windmilled his arms to stretch and walked a small circle in the dirt lane. It was quiet. He stood awhile. Eventually he heard the motor from the garage on the other side of town; then it was quiet again.

He wandered into the dirt drive of the little square white house he'd run out of gas in front of. A weather-beaten "For Sale" sign leaned next to the drive. Birch bent down to inspect it. Through a rain-spattered brochure box attached to it he could see they were asking $28,000 for the place. He stood and looked the house over: simple, good paint, white for sure, even the trim, humble. Even so, this place would likely fetch half a million or more back on Palo Alto.

He walked around the yard. The back yard had a bird feeder and an ornamental miniature windmill, bounded by a row of spruce, a tall hardwood on either side and a weeping willow in the center. He walked around to the front again, thinking that he should just up and buy the place, only then remembering with a hot shudder Robin had gotten his account wiped out. This realization set him into a daze, and he reached into his pocket to pull out his meager fold of remaining bills, a few ones with a couple of fives, while walking toward the "For Sale" sign. Lifting the lid on the yellowed lucite box, he saw the brochures had long since melted together into a pinkish mass of paper, but pulled the lump out anyway and peeled off the most intact leaf, as much to display some legitimacy to his presence in case of onlookers as to satisfy his curiosity about the house. Stuffing the remaining lump back into the box, he held up his sheet to make out the type. The house had been on the market for over a year and a half, for sale by someone named Catherine Willow in New York City. Inquiries were to go to a local number, someone named Dr. Carver Tunlin, or one could inquire at the dental office on Main Street here in Still Point, Nebraska.

Fine, except his money was gone. He had thirteen dollars in his pocket. What made him think of buying a house, anyway? He nearly staggered to where his motorcycle leaned in the street, mildly alarmed at how loose his legs felt under him. Worried that he might be dehydrated again, he grabbed the last water bottle from his saddle bags and a damp dinner roll he found underneath. He drained the bottle and took a bite of the roll, glancing up and down the street and across at a couple quiet houses, simple and small, not unlike the one he'd just looked over.

He just wanted to rest. He recalled the cement steps he'd seen in the back yard and considered sitting there for a while to collect his thoughts. He didn't want to leave his bike out on the street, though he hadn't seen another person or vehicle since rolling to a stop here, so he kicked up the stand and pushed it down the drive and around the house.

He sat on the steps in thinker's pose, looking at the white dust on his boots, then leaned back and watched the darkening blue sky above the willow tree for awhile. He wondered about the lock box he saw hanging from the front door knob. If he could get lucky and figure out the combination, maybe it would appear as though he should be there, like maybe he'd made contact with the house seller and it was okay if he went in. Otherwise, without money for a motel—of course he hadn't seen one in this village anyway—it was looking like a camping trip under the stars now. What was the probability he could discover the combination? He'd never looked at one of those locks closely enough to even know if there were four, five, or six buttons. *Well, it's worth a shot anyway.*

He pushed himself up off the steps to shake his legs out, thinking it wouldn't look good if someone saw him struggling with the box and not getting in. *Maybe have a look around before I try anything.* He pushed both hands into the small of his back and winced as he moved his bones around. Turning, he looked to the back door, thinking he might as well peek in through the window. Staggering back up the steps to stand on the small landing, he felt the sum of four days on a motorcycle, a feeling of being torn down from the inside. Of course when he twisted the knob on the storm door it opened. He pulled it back and stood between it and the back door, cupping his hands to look through the half glass. He saw a tidy, plain-looking kitchen, an old gas stove and oven, an old fridge, a small table flanked by two chairs. He dropped one hand to the brass door knob and absently twisted it, expecting to feel the hard stop of a lock. Instead the knob twisted all the way around, and he leaned into the door, pushing with all the strength left to him after sixteen hundred miles hunched over two wheels. The door gave a little, squeaked and cracked a bit, slid against the frame reluctantly, then swung in.

He stepped cautiously and painfully into the small kitchen and stood listening. The kitchen was bright and efficient. Lace curtains framed a window over the sink. The small Formica table sat against a wall with two padded chairs. The stove and refrigerator appeared vintage 50s, but clean and functional. Birch had the impression that someone had been here not long before. A mild hum and rattle came from behind the refrigerator, then stopped, and the house was silent.

He walked from the kitchen into a carpeted hall that led to stairs on the left, a coat closet and small living room to the right, a small dining room extending off the living room around a corner with a table, four chairs, a buffet, and a grandfather clock standing silent against the back wall. He unzipped his jacket and laid it on the back of a gingham sofa separating the walk to the kitchen from the living room. The sofa had a crocheted afghan draped over the back. The house was tidy despite a layer of dust settled on all the surfaces. The late afternoon sun came through blue taffeta curtains partially drawn over the living room window. Two wingback chairs sat facing a fireplace, which was covered by an antique-looking painted board showing a man plowing behind a pair of draft horses. The living room carpet appeared old but well cared for.

He pulled his boots off, thinking socks would be quieter to sneak around in, but oddly didn't feel as though he was intruding. He went back to the kitchen and idly pulled open drawers and cupboard doors to find full shelves of canned and dry goods, flatware and kitchen implements, woven potholders that looked as if they'd snuggled the hot sides of pots and pans for well more than a couple generations, hand towels neatly folded, mixing bowls, baking trays, wire cooling racks, plates and glasses, knives with worn, oiled handles and blades reduced by decades of sharpening, and measuring cups and spoons in a deep drawer with other implements he didn't bother to identify.

He continued his circuit up the stairs, finding two small bedrooms and a bath. The beds were made, towels hanging on wooden racks in the bathroom. The floral scent of soap balls—pink, white, and blue—set in dishes on the sink and the back of the commode reminded Birch of his grandmother's house in Oakland. Linens were folded and stacked in a closet in the hall between the two bedrooms. Hangers jostled slightly, muffled by hanging clothes, when he pulled open the bedroom closet doors. Dresser drawers were mostly empty in both rooms, though the bottom drawer of a tall walnut dresser in one room held sheets and pillow cases. A cedar-lined cherry chest at the foot of the queen bed in the larger bedroom was packed with wool blankets edged with frayed satin. He tried the hot water in the bathroom sink. It ran ice cold, and he scrubbed his hands together and splashed his face, but then felt it starting to warm. He looked in the mirror and saw a rough version of himself wearing a bemused, if not skeptical, expression. The water was now steaming, and he splashed his face again before twisting off the faucet. He pulled a hand towel from the rack and shook it once, causing a cloud of dust to billow in the sunlight, then used it to mop his face and hands.

He descended the stairs feeling like he'd found a reasonable solution to his need for shelter, if only for long enough to decide what he was doing here, maybe just tonight. He thought of the motorcycle and decided he should move it closer to the back of the house. He slipped outside in his socks and pushed the bike over the tall grass, threading it between a row of shrubs and the back wall of the house, where he put the kickstand down again. The bike was still visible, but much less so now, at least enough to satisfy him.

He went back inside the house and upstairs to take a hot shower.

Afterwards he felt steamed and scrubbed, wrapping himself in a white towel. He carried his clothes downstairs to drop into the washing machine in the closet between the kitchen and foyer. He retrieved a box of detergent powder from the shelf above the washer and drier, figured out the washer, poured in some powder and started it. A jelly jar of colored glass beads sat on the upper shelf next to some cleaning products. He grabbed it and gave it a gentle shake, inspecting the beads through the faceted glass.

Next to the drier he noted an ironing board leaning against the wall near an old upright vacuum cleaner. He closed the closet door to let the washer run more quietly and went into the kitchen to look through the cupboards for a can of soup. He was hungry. He set the jar of beads on the counter and hunted the shelves, found a can of beef barley and dumped it into a sauce pan, noting as he set it on the stove over a low gas flame how clean the burners were despite their obvious age. The light outside the kitchen window was falling, the last of an orange sunset filtering in through glass panes around the front door and angling along the kitchen hall. He poured the soup into a bowl and ate it hot, sitting at the kitchen table. When he was finished, he took his bowl and spoon to the sink and then took the jar of beads into the living room, sat on the floor, and spilled them onto the carpet at a spot lit in deep orange by a beam of light leaking past the curtains of the front window. The beads were navy bean-sized, of different colors and translucence, apparently formed by dropping molten glass on a flat ceramic surface. Some were clear as raindrops; some were milky white, some cerulean, some burgundy, some ocher, some ruby, and some purple. None were uniform.

Staring at the distribution of beads for a moment, he felt a flash of clarity, however fleeting. He brushed his hand over them, moving some of the beads and causing them to tap into each other. He lifted his hand to look. He brushed them again. Again he looked. He did this for a while.

He began to suspect the source of the flash. The beads were signifiers of their own past motion, of paths taken, both in time and space. *And in the wake of each bead the path exists forever, a kind of immutable truth.*

He continued moving the beads around. He saw that all of the paths existed already.

Then he began to see just one path, the beads seeming less significant the more he moved them. Soon they became impossible to see, unreal, and only the path remained.

10

Winnie dug her fingers into Angel's black curls and swam them to his scalp. She formed her hands around the back of his skull and let them settle lightly, like octopi drifting over the sea floor. "Baby, you need to come make paella with me. You've been thinking about this stuff way too much; your head's getting hot. Come peel some shrimp."

Angel let his head drift forward and his hands slide away from the keyboard, careful not to knock the PalmPilot for fear of disconnecting one of the tiny alligator clips. He slumped back in the chair and let his arms dangle while Winnie worked his shoulders for a minute. "Yeah," he said. "I want to peel shrimp."

"Good boy," she said, and helped pull his chair back from the kitchen table.

He pulled his earbuds out and got up to follow Winnie to the sink, where she had a colander holding a dozen raw shrimp waiting for him. He set to work on the cold, rinsed bodies.

"You're not usually this quiet, baby," Winnie said. "What are you worrying about now?"

"Almost too freaked out to say."

"Oh come on. You already told me about how they're going to trick us all into saving electricity so they can have it all for their thing. How bad can it be now?"

Angel was feeling dark, because he hadn't heard back from Birch. He felt frustrated that he couldn't just pick up the phone and call him, or shoot him an email or chat. Being constrained in this way insulted his belief in his right to freedom. The irony of what he wanted to contact Birch about, to enlist his aid in thwarting a plan to steal freedom and to dictate what being an American meant, made Angel crazy.

Best peel some shrimp.

"Well," Angel said while ripping the little legs from a shrimp, "this could be worse. The thing is, I don't get anything more than fragments with these recordings, and I can't really tell when Pitt is talking about something real or just blowing smoke at some guy to sound impressive. But if I believe these recordings from today, they basically want to own and control what modern humans breathe: clean air and internet access."

Winnie had finished chopping garlic and peppers, moving on to onions. "Pffff," she said, wiping onion tears away with the back of her hand. "How do they think they can do that?"

"I'm guessing once they have enough ISPs bankrupted and everyone addicted to their free connections they'll start bleeding the money out of the population, probably through the telecom companies, but I'm not sure about that one. One thing I know is it will be like boiling frogs. You watch. Electric bills going up a little at a time. Cellular bills going up a little at a time. People will barely notice until they're like, why is this stuff getting so expensive when my wages aren't going up? Where did the money go this month?"

Angel finished the last shrimp. Winnie handed him a wooden spoon to stir the rice and dumped the shrimp into a pan of heated olive oil. "I think we should all just not connect to the internet."

"Right," Angel said. "Imagine people today without the internet. No one could do anything. Not having WiFi to most people is literally like not having air to breathe." He grabbed an open can of peeled tomatoes and poured them into the bubbling rice, breaking them up with the spoon while Winnie leaned toward an iPad on a stand showing the recipe. "But you'd think they'd be satisfied owning the entire internet infrastructure, right? Well, you'd be wrong. I just heard Pitt tell some guy in his office that they plan to make and sell smart bottles for air, not even pure oxygen, just plain air. So they can sell to you what you already have for free anyway, just like bottled water."

Winnie tossed peppers and onions into the rice as Angel stirred. "That's weird."

"Well, it worked with water, right? So, they'll have some indicator on them, like an LED or something, that goes off and supposedly tells you when the air around you is unsafe to breathe, so you hold the bottle with this little plastic cup thing to your face and hold a trigger down while you breathe. Then, of course, you run out and panic and have to go fill it up again, naturally with your credit card. They're planning a network of air kiosks at gas stations and pharmacies, the places we're all addicted to anyway."

"That is fucked up, I mean really."

"Yeah, so apparently they already have a PR campaign designed for it, images of cool-looking people carrying their phones and designer air bottles, same song second verse as the electricity thing, claims that real Americans only breathe clean air, but breathe it from a bottle. Associate it with being independent, your own air, invincible, like Americans are supposed to be, or supposed to fantasize to be. They'll put stars and stripes on the things. Then, of course, follow that in other countries in their colors. Apparently they're going to keep denying climate change until the factories in China are ready to deliver the units, then reverse and start saying that new data shows climate change is past the point of no return, meaning the air is no longer safe to breathe. Scare the shit out of people and get everyone to buy a bottle, until seeing people with them stuck on their faces starts to look normal."

Winnie dropped the garlic in, then the shrimp. She looked at Angel. "Can you imagine? We already have phones stuck to the sides of our heads. Now we're going to have bottles stuck to the fronts? We'll run out of hands!"

Angel laughed. "Someone will design a bracket that lets you hold your bottle and phone in place with just one hand. Probably wind up a bestseller on Amazon."

◆ ◆ ◆

Stu did not have anyone in his office this time when Angel came down to sync. In fact, he was waiting by the door as Angel walked up. Stu opened it to invite him in. This break in their routine startled Angel, causing his face to flush. Had the company discovered his back door already, or somehow identified the mustang? Had he not been careful enough?

He thought of that coder he'd never gotten a chance to know, Erin, and needles of panic started vibrating into his upper spine. He'd always been confident in his own abilities, but maybe he'd messed up this time. He'd fooled himself into believing that his self-righteous knowing, his sense of his own intelligence, and most of all his simmering belligerence on this mission to stop a wrong somehow protected him against what would happen to anyone the company decided it didn't like. How naive. How childish. To think that anything he thought he knew, or any logic he could prove on a whiteboard, would amount to shit should the company decide he might be a threat, or that it simply had had enough of his presence. *Stupidity.*

"Take a seat," Stu said, and walked haltingly, like he was carrying a heavy weight, around to his thickly padded chair. Angel sat in one of the two task chairs facing the desk, feeling his breath deeply in his lungs, maybe a little cold, maybe a little numb, not sure of anything. One pattern in his brain ripped through its network and told him to be defiant. But another, weightier pattern told him it was very possible he would never see Winnie again, never be able to listen to his mom's advice again, never see his family again, a terminal one-way process which could begin right here in this dark office in this massive ant hill, and that no one who cared could do a thing about it, nor would they ever know what happened to him. Ever.

"Oh," Stu said, slipping into his large chair. "Let's do this now." He twisted his PalmPilot on the desk to face Angel. Angel let the air out of his lungs and reached into his pocket for his PalmPilot.

"You'll see that we've scheduled a test for two drones so we can see them interact."

Angel stared at the swirling icon on his screen as the prickly heat drained from his face and his lungs began to loosen, knowing that the sync took longer now, but believing that Stu had adapted, accepted it as the new normal. He moved his eyes to the space between their two infrared ports, eighteen inches of space above polished oak, and wondered if any encoded signals from Birch galloped across that dark plain. At the beep he slid his device away and pulled the stylus from the hold, tapping the screen to open the calendar and notes. "I see," Angel said, reading the notes. "Not a problem."

"This is it, man. This is the thing that has to work. This is your and my chance to look good in front of the bigwigs. Are we good?"

Angel used the stylus to scroll through the checklist of test points, over two hundred in all. Stu fidgeted with his hands on the desk, his eyes focused toward the upturned lid of Angel's PalmPilot. "I mean, this goes good, and you're looking good. I'm looking good. Right?"

"Hmm, yeah. Most of our tests are passing right now," Angel said, frowning at the checklist. "We'll have some cleanup to do before we can install the drone client."

"How long will that take?" Stu asked.

"You know," Angel said, still scrolling through the list, "this flight should really be for three drones, not two. We need to test two that are virtually tethered interacting with a third that is not. And in order to get through all these points, we'll need to throw lots of environmental threats at them. How are we planning to do that?"

"We're running the test in a wind tunnel. You haven't seen that yet. And I'll have to check about a third unit. I don't know if we have three that fly at the moment."

"Well, okay. We can't test everything on here, then, but we can get most of it," Angel said.

"So, only mention the things that we are testing and passing while you're there, okay? Don't draw attention to the other stuff," Stu said.

Angel glanced up at him, then back to the list.

"You know," Stu said, "I think you and I should get to know each other better." He looked at Angel though his head turned away, leaving his eyes on him. "This is important work we're doing here," he continued. Angel raised his eyes to look at him again. "And, I realize how much we have to depend on each other to make a success out of it."

Angel nodded slowly, letting his eyes flick back down to the list. He thought he should smile or something but his lips resisted, felt he should look back up but could not.

"Do you," Stu persisted, "have any hobbies, or anything?"

Angel had the sudden fear that Stuart was about to ask to come over to his condo. "No," was all he could think to respond with. "I should get back to production, get ready for the test flight." He got up and left the room, leaving Stuart gazing vacantly at the corner of his desk.

Angel wandered slowly around the production room, watching the teams and sweeping his eyes along the whiteboards. He realized that he had to become a better actor than project leader. He wanted to effectively forget that he'd left the hidden back door in the drone network, the entry that he, or hopefully Birch, could use later to reverse the damage this cloud of greed was intended to inflict. But he also knew that to get away with it, and to maintain any measure of safety for Winnie and for himself, the company could have zero inkling that he would do such a thing, would have to be entirely convinced of his loyalty and integrity. In fact he'd come to the conclusion that no one in the room, not even Chad, could suspect him of ill intent toward the project. He regretted his comments to Chad during their hike. He'd have to let those seep into the soil and be forgotten, or at least well-buried. He would have to play it straight with Chad, make it the best operating system they could.

Now that he understood what his approach needed to be, he wanted to encapsulate and isolate that thought, keep it separate and distinct from the rest of his consciousness and let it remain hidden within its own opaque walls. He felt he would need to balance the weight of this secret by going even farther in the other direction in the parts of his mind outside of those opaque walls. He would have to control the simmering distaste he felt for Pitt and the company. He would have to shine as the model employee and project leader, and deliver a truly impressive system to control the drone network. He would have to make Pitt feel safe and proud, and liked. He wanted this flight test to go perfectly.

"Chad," Angel stopped and rested his hand on Chad's desk. "Your tests are passing at a hundred percent on Staging One, right?" Chad looked up and nodded. "Okay, let's get that merged and deployed to Staging Two. We'll be running the birds from there tomorrow."

"Okay," Chad said, inspecting Angel's eyes for any other communication.

"Thanks," Angel said, patting his shoulder. "I want the test flight as close to perfect as we can make it." He moved on around the room, knowing that Chad would deploy the code without inspecting it, though he would rerun the tests to verify that they were passing at one hundred percent. Not a problem; the back door would not be seen by any of their existing tests. "Umair, you and Lori have that chained power management smoothed out? Can I see the model run?" He leaned in and watched a large monitor over the shoulders of two engineers. On the monitor he saw moving diagrams of two drones flying, with graphs and number-filled columns for each showing energy expenditure and recharge as the woman shuttled a vertical marker along a timeline and adjusted environmental variables, changing the conditions in which the drones flew. "Okay, for the test tomorrow path loss will be minimal. Just a wind tunnel, right? Maybe thirty yards max distance? So, dial down the transmitter and assume essentially no loss between the birds, but watch thermal buildup on the first in chain. They're going to turn the winds up to around forty miles an hour with base temp at sixty, so figure that in. How long do we fly with no recharge at that speed, assuming no forward progress?"

The door popped and swung open, and Stuart strode in, swiveling his head. He spotted Angel and circumnavigated the room along the whiteboards, absently trailing a finger along the wall until he noticed that he was smudging through notes and diagrams as he walked, then jerking his finger from the wall and turning red around the neck and ears. A few of the engineers saw him and rolled their eyes. He stopped behind Angel, peering at the monitor Angel and the other two engineers were watching. The sight of the two drone diagrams flying put him slightly at ease. "There's no way we should lose a drone with the system you've created, right?" Stuart asked.

Angel looked back over his shoulder at him. He thought a moment, then spoke. "That is an accurate statement. There is no way that we *should* lose one."

"Well, anyway," Stuart said, "I got you your third drone for the test tomorrow."

Angel looked at the monitor, then back to Stuart, meeting his eyes. He then stood up straight and called across the room, "Karl, three birds tomorrow. Over air updates, okay? Staging Two." He bent back down to Lori and Umair. "You guys good with three flying? Add in the third and let's see where we set the transmitter." He turned back to Stuart and said, "I'm assuming low charge state to begin with all three drones, correct?"

Stuart looked alarmed. "I'll double check that. Probably yes. I'll make sure." He stood waiting while Angel returned to

Umair and Lori.

"We'll be simulating a transmitter power outage too," Angel said. "You guys have network resource balancing working the way you want it? Should be cake, right? Only three to balance?"

He got nods from both engineers and stood up. He looked at Stuart and remembered his thoughts from earlier. He squared his shoulders to him and raised his chin slightly, extended his right hand and rested it on Stuart's shoulder. He realized that it was the first time he had intentionally touched him. "Good job getting us a third drone, Stuart. You'll be looking very good to the brass tomorrow." Angel gave him a warm smile, feeling its weight in his cheeks and hoping that it registered in his eyes.

Stuart immediately brightened and nodded his head. He mirrored Angel's smile and looked at the engineers busy at their desks, still bobbing his head. "Excellent. Excellent." He turned and left the room.

Angel watched him go, then continued his circuit. He pulled together a group of six in the far corner to go over nanobot repair functions. "Okay, so one of the tunnel techs is actually going to break a rotor for the last test. He's going to whack it with a spike at the end of a pole or something. Last test," he gestured with his hands out, "but I'd love to see everything pass with flying colors. We're pretty sure Chandler's code will keep it airborne, but the question is: can the nanobots function while it's taking on microwave charge, AND, what if they keep the wind on relatively high? What will happen? Can the bots hang on, especially where they're trying to rebuild rotor tips on unstable material? What do you guys have planned for managing temperature for setting material if they keep the wind on? What if our charge state is already low PLUS we have wind?"

It became clear that they had more work to do there, and they had fewer than twenty-four hours to complete it. Even so, Angel felt the rush and satisfaction of moving a project forward with confidence. He had secreted his back door into a corner of his mind, leaving the rest of his neurons to bathe in a dynamic mix of serotonin, oxytocin, and dopamine as he tied together the remaining details for the flight test the next day. To find a project of this scale that was for the good of humanity rather than yet another way to consolidate wealth and power into a few avaricious hands: that would be a dream.

A lab tech punched up the control panel and nudged a set of joined levers forward, engaging a pair of thirty-foot diameter opposing fans at the dark end of a massive, fifty yard tunnel. Even through the thick glass of the control room, the fan engines and rush of air grew deafening. Angel and two of his team clapped headphones on and logged in to Staging Two. A group of nine men, wearing suits and uniforms and standing along the windows, also donned headsets, as did Stuart, who paced back and forth behind them.

On the floor of the tunnel sat three wedge-shaped cinderblock piles, roughly four feet high and oriented into the wind. Behind each pile rested a black quad-rotor drone about the size of a large pizza.

The headsets crackled with the voice of one of the techs, who said, "We're at twenty. You want to hold there and launch?"

Angel answered, "Yes, hold at twenty. Okay, Lori, spin the birds and keep them in the shadows."

The assemblage looked on through the windows as twelve rotor blades simultaneously popped into motion, instantly becoming translucent disks. Each drone rocked forward slightly and then held position behind its block pile. The men at the window bank watched, some patiently with hands clasped behind their backs, some glancing at each other.

Angel's voice crackled into the headsets, "Okay Lori,

manual off, engage the rules." He continued to narrate as the men looked on. "The drones were on a manual hover while we checked their software. Now we're releasing them to independent navigation, where they each follow a common set of rules to optimize their positions in the environment."

The three drones simultaneously went airborne and lifted behind their block piles. As each touched the wind stream at the edges of the cinderblocks it instantly adjusted rotor speeds, pitching and wavering in taut, controlled movements as it entered the wind and climbed above the blocks.

"We're starting with a limited rule set for this test," Angel continued. "They will attempt to clear the ground, walls, and any object by a minimum of fifteen feet when possible, seeking environmental conditions that require the least expenditure of energy to remain aloft and maintain connectivity. When we turn them loose into the great outdoors we'll expand the clearances, of course. Okay, Umair, what are our charge levels?"

"One, five point three two percent, Two, four point nine zero percent, Three, four point one three percent."

"Okay," Angel continued. "We're starting out in a low charge state to test our in-air charging capability. Lori, confirm network."

"Sky Five, check," a woman's voice sounded in the headsets.

"Umair, let's turn on the transmitter. Let One and Two charge direct. Charge Three from Two."

"Microwave is transmitting."

The drones hovered distributed in the tunnel, rock steady except for the tiniest trembles now and then.

"Umair, levels," Angel said.

"One, Two, and Three all rising."

Angel looked over, caught Stuart's eyes and nodded. Stuart winked and turned back to the window with a look of relief.

"One is at nineteen zero zero, Two at eighteen four two, Three at nine one four."

"Okay, Lori, let's start with OS updates. Now, gentlemen, we're updating the software and expanding the rule sets while the drones are in flight and while they're still charging. They won't reach a full charge while they're fighting the wind and maintaining the network, but we want to see them simply moving in the right direction. The rules keep them close enough to the transmitter, which is artificially dialed down given the confined nature of this test, to maintain a positive charge state no matter what other mission they may be engaged in at the moment."

"Firmware shows updated and complete in One, Two, and Three," Lori reported.

"Charge still growing on One, Two, and Three," Umair said.

"Let's take the wind up to thirty," Angel said. The tech reached for the control panel, and the sound of the wind pitched higher. The drones all leaned in unison into the heavy wind stream, pushing forward toward the front of the tunnel before locking into position once again.

"Charge still growing on One, Two, and Three," Umair said.

"The drones repositioned themselves relative to the transmitter, and in the case of drone Three relative to drone Two, which is passing along microwaves to charge its friend. Again, this is micro-scaled for the wind tunnel. Okay, Lori, let's get a hypervisor and then launch a VM. Now, gentlemen, we're getting down to business and testing the primary mission of the drone network. Lori is going to simulate the basic components of a commercial ISP. Each drone has multiple cores and memory on board. The system that runs the drone and interacts with the network is partitioned and secured, leaving significant capacity in a separate partition for general network operations. Each drone can essentially be its own computing center, and since they're networked they can combine their resources to configure larger and more powerful computing centers, or ISPs if you will. Just like typical cloud services offering redundancy across multiple blade computers in co-location centers, the drones can configure virtual hardware to exist redundantly across multiple drones."

"Hypervisor is live with images installed if you want to try an external connection," Lori said.

"Thank you, Lori. Go ahead, Stuart," Angel said. "And anyone else who would like to give it a try, just open your phone WiFi settings, or whatever device you happen to have handy, and look for the SkyFive network. You can connect just like any other network you join. No password needed. Once you're on, open a browser and go to skyfive dot local. Of course the address is only for this test, while we're confined inside the wind tunnel facility. When launched outside, the network will function like any other network connected to the internet."

Another voice crackled onto the headsets, saying, "We going to deploy these as localized battlefield networks? Launch 'em as we need 'em?"

A heavyset man in the lineup leaned toward the windows and looked down the line to Stuart. Stuart's voice crackled into the headsets. "We're going to launch this worldwide, General, and use VPNs within it for battlefield comms. That way it will be available everywhere, and we'll have access to enemy comms as well, assuming they use the internet."

"Well, won't they have access to ours then?"

Stuart remained silent, watching the drones hover in the heavy wind. Another man's voice crackled into the headsets, replying, "That's what the VPN is for, General. We're developing encryption that is not available to the general public and is more advanced than any other military. This is a self-contained internet, so it will still be there no matter what happens to the internet on the ground. It will have all the basic services that the present internet has."

The general tilted his head and raised his eyebrows

while he watched the drones. "You mean, Netflix and Google will be on here?" he asked.

"Not exactly," the man replied. "You can use Netflix and other things you're used to while you're connected to our network, because our network will be connected to the present internet, but they won't necessarily be *hosted* on our network. Though they *could* be if they chose to. We will have the same basic infrastructure available on our network as providers on the present internet. We do actually expect that some services will choose to relocate to our network, and we're not planning to discourage that. What we're building here is really a global ISP."

"But letting others use it won't compromise our operations or hurt the performance?" the general asked.

"No, sir. It should allow us to have greater coverage and redundancy."

"I get it," the general said, "I think."

The wind tunnel techs turned the wind speed up close to forty knots, and Angel's team determined that the drones could still maintain a positive charge rate. "Okay, Lori, let's charge Two from One and Three from Two," Angel said.

"Chain established," Lori responded after half a minute.

They then added mist, then heavy rain, then airborne particulates. The drones struggled under the heavy rain, the third in the chain showing a negative charge rate. The simulated dust storm presented more challenges, as the drones searched for clearer air, quickly losing blade efficiency as the leading edges and spindles suffered abrasion. They remained airborne, however, and when one of them found a clear stream of air above the dust, the other two instantly jumped to that altitude. All three began rhythmically rotating and bobbing, as if on rubber bands.

"You saw them communicate just now," Angel's voice crackled into the headsets. "When one found the dust-free air, it immediately reported back to the network, which instructed the others. Now they are doing in-air repairs on the particulate damage. Can we turn that wind speed back down to about twenty? Thank you. What you see now looks a bit less stable, as each of the drones is isolating a rotor, one at a time, for repairs. It spins around, stops the trailing rotor, reverses the windward rotor and then rebalances over the axis defined by the two outboard rotors. It's not pretty, but it lets it fly on three while the nanobots work out repairs on the fourth. Let's kill the dust and turn the wind down to fifteen so we can get a better look. Thank you. Okay."

"What if they have to do these repairs in higher wind?" a voice interjected over the headsets.

"They have a rule set to seek quieter air," Angel answered. "They have to use more energy, and they don't fly as efficiently, so they will leave the mission area if they need to get repairs done and then return to form up again. For today we'll just turn the tunnel down so you can see what they're doing. Essentially what we have is a small army of nanobots on each drone. Voltage fluctuation, heat level, heat delta, rotor speed, wobble, all are measured in real time, and any deviation goes into diagnostics. When an anomaly is identified, the drone isolates the problem rotor and sends the nanobots to it, like white blood cells in your body. The bots follow patterns stored onboard, though they can also reference documents from our central system, then act like a distributed 3D printer, adding and shaping material on the rotor surfaces. They can even work on the spindles and motors. They have material stores they can harvest, plus a slightly over-thick housing to harvest from in a pinch, to build a damaged blade back up for instance."

They watched as the drones bounced and wobbled and twisted in the air, like corks floating on a rippling pond. Each drone rotated ninety degrees and rebalanced as the nanobots finished with one rotor and migrated to the next.

"How long does it take?" someone asked.

"Depends on the damage and the nature of the repairs," Angel answered.

They stood with hands mostly clasped behind their backs, lined up and watching. The heavyset man with the sanguine face kept his arms folded across his chest. Stuart pressed his face as close to the glass as he could without fogging it, peering at the pizza-sized vehicles with a sense of wonder and pride. After twenty minutes or so each drone was again flying with four rotors, stable and tilted into the wind.

"Impressive," the general said.

"One final test for today," Angel said. "Lori, pull Three away from the others so Don can tell which one to whack. We're going to attempt more direct physical damage to simulate a variety of potential scenarios, including a unit being targeted from the ground."

One of the tunnel techs put on safety goggles and then walked up the hallway carrying an eight-foot pole made of white PVC. He disappeared through a low door to the tunnel and reappeared behind the windows, his dark hair and white lab coat whipping in the artificial wind. He walked along the tunnel wall toward the watchers and the hovering drones. He looked toward the windows while pointing toward one of the drones, his goggled eyes forming a question. Angel gave him the thumbs up through the glass and said, "That's the one," through the headset network. The tech crouched with his back to the wind and carefully extended the pole toward the drone, reaching his arms out, lab coat painted around his body by the blasting fans. The pole featured a vertical spike attached to its end. The drone dodged away from the spike as it drew within a few feet. The tech lowered the pole and looked toward the windows.

"Hold it, Don. I'm sorry," Angel's voice scraped into the headsets. "Lori, exempt number Three from the proximity rules."

"Right, forgot that. Okay. Done," Lori said.

"Okay Don. Give it a jab," Angel said.

The tech glanced toward the windows, then back to the hovering drone. He scooted along the tunnel floor a few feet and raised the pole again. This time the drone held its position as the spike came up under one of the spinning rotors. The tech gave the pole a quick seesaw motion, jabbing the spike through a windward rotor. The drone wagged and spun violently as black pieces of broken rotor flung out in all directions, then ripped toward the back of the tunnel by the wind stream. The tech remained crouched with the lowered pole while they watched the drone struggle to regain stability.

"Lori, prox rules back on for Three," Angel said.

"Done," she responded.

The injured drone moved toward the center of the tunnel, still bucking and wagging more violently than during the initial in-air repair test. The other two drones repositioned themselves in a line between the microwave transmitter and the injured drone.

"Negative charge rate on Three," Umair's voice came over the headsets.

"Okay," Angel said. "Let's see if Two can help with that while it's getting charge from One. Gentlemen, if you are connected to the Skyfive network, you should still have signal. Do you not?"

"I do," Stuart volunteered.

"What's this video of a running horse I'm watching?" one of the men in uniform asked.

"That's just a video loop we're using for sample content to demo the network, General," Angel said. "You're watching that on a webpage served by a plain vanilla web server that's virtualized across all the drones. Now, we've artificially limited the connection to Number Three, the drone with the broken rotor, for this test. Normally you would connect via whichever unit is closest to your location. They're designed to support signal between each other at distances of up to six miles, and air to ground between two and three miles, depending on conditions; we're working on expanding that. If a drone in repair mode is losing too much charge, it will stop transmission service to users on the ground to conserve energy but will still talk to the other drones for support. You saw One and Two line up and move closer. They are daisy-chaining microwave charge to Three to try to keep it powered while it's compromised and running inefficiently. Again, working with scaled-down power and distances for testing in the tunnel. They've also tightened up formation and switched network protocols to talk to each other using lower power."

"How many units are we planning to launch?" a graveled voice asked.

"Stuart, you know that number, I don't," Angel said.

"Yes," Stuart said, "we'll be putting just under three million units up in the first wave. All centrally monitored and controlled."

The assemblage looked back and forth along the line at each other, then back through the tempered glass. The tech had left the tunnel and was back at the console in the hallway.

"Charge rate is neutral on Three," Umair said.

"Excellent," Angel said. "That's what we were hoping for."

No one spoke for many long minutes while they watched the injured drone bob and weave as it rebuilt its dead rotor. At a distance of forty feet or so through the windows, they could just barely see the shape and black of the forming blades each time the drone wobbled into a position that for an instant revealed the rotor's profile. It was not always clear that the nanobots were making progress, and each watcher began to feel a simmering sense of drama, each for their own reasons. Angel kept glancing over at Lori and Umair, whose eyes were glued to their laptops. Stuart kept looking at Angel, trying to read his demeanor. The lineup of business and military men knew they were witnessing something momentous which could change their futures. They stood hypnotized by the ceaseless waggle, tension building relentlessly until at last the drone rotated, briefly dipping. Then the fourth rotor kicked on, causing a few of the men to whoop painfully into the headset network and thrust their fists above their heads. The drone stabilized, and the three spread out once again in the wind stream, gathering into a sturdy formation. The men broke ranks and congratulated each other, slapping shoulders and winking.

"Positive charge rate back on Three," Umair said.

Angel gave Umair and Lori a fist pump, pointing at each of them with obvious pride. "That's it for today, gentlemen," he announced.

The tech flipped a row of switches on the console, and the giant fans began to spin down. The assemblage started removing their headsets. The large man with the red jowls regarded Stuart momentarily, then said with a straight face, "Money well spent, Pitt. I guess I don't have to call you Money Pitt anymore." He held Stuart's gaze a moment and then laughed, Stuart joining in after an awkward second.

Stuart found Angel and slapped him on the shoulder, handing him his headset. "You crushed it today, man. This is going to look VERY good," he said.

"Thank you," Angel said. "Yes, we did well today." He looked back through the windows at the three drones still flying in formation, then settling to the floor as Lori issued commands through the network. His body felt the warm bath of success and the inner peace of tension just now released. He left the tunnel facility moving easily, as if float-walking through warm water, returning to the main building in the right seat of a large golf cart with Stuart driving, another man in the back.

The late morning was warm with full sun. The test had taken just over three hours. Outside the exhaust end of the wind tunnel the earth was blasted smooth in the shape of a thirty-yard plume, the dusty ground cleared of all pebbles, plant life, and insects, nothing raising its shape above the base layer of sand crystals.

11

The warming curtains told a story in faded pink of courtship and harvest. A young man wearing a broad hat led a pair of oxen pulling a cart piled high with wheat along a road. The road curved, even more so amidst the undulations of the hanging fabric, toward a provincial farmhouse in the distance. Offset below, the same young man stood before a young woman by a well. She stood in a long dress facing him, her pail on the ground, looking down at a bouquet she held in her hands. The young man held his hat in his right hand and looked to catch the young woman's eyes.

The sun rose against the cotton backing, lighting the scene now in brighter pink, bleeding to a deeper red toward the edges where the thread of the curtains hung behind the window casing.

Birch let his eyes wander the pattern from his pillow as it swam into focus. He saw the scene repeated all over the curtains. How many young men? How many young women?

For a moment, he tried to remember which motel he was in, off of which highway, in which state.

This didn't smell like a motel pillow. It held the old memory of soap mixed with something he couldn't place, a chemical tang like an old photographic print, not unpleasant, but certainly not the plastic-bin-scooped smell of a motel. Then he remembered Nebraska, the quiet village, and the house. He raised his head, turned and swung his stiffened legs off the bed, letting his soles settle on the carpet. Listening, he

186

heard only the blood coursing around his ears and the breath spilling out through his nose.

He rose and then crouched, feeling his body cramped and without energy. He managed the three steps to the window and drew the curtains aside, slowly pulling himself up against the soreness. He saw the sun just above his eye level filtering through the willow tree in the back yard. He felt the beams hot on his bare chest, and thought about his motorcycle leaning, tank empty, against the outside wall below. How nice not to be riding today.

He stretched forward to soak in the sun's rays and rested his forehead against the glass. A truck engine broke the silence outside from somewhere on the street side of the house. Birch caught a movement on his right and turned to look, resting his left cheek against the warm window glass. A guy in a T-shirt and dark blue work pants hauled a hose over his shoulder into the back yard from the street to a mint green propane tank, hidden discretely among lilac bushes at the edge of the yard. He flipped the valve cover up and stood with his back toward the house, working with his elbows out. Birch heard the truck engine rev up. The guy stood leaning against the tank with one hand resting on the hose nozzle, periodically looking back toward the street or down at the valve gauge. After some minutes he leaned in toward the gauge for a closer look, then detached the hose, the truck engine settling down, and flipped the valved cover closed on its hinge. He walked back toward the street, pulling the hose with him.

Birch retrieved his shorts from the floor and put them on. He went to the window on the opposite wall, peeking past the curtains to see the guy working a lever to roll in the hose, secure it, and then lean into the truck cab. He emerged holding a clipboard and walked toward the house. Birch went through the bedroom doorway to the landing, stealing a glance around the wall down the stairwell. He heard the guy turn a key in the front door, followed by the door opening. Birch held his breath and froze as the guy stepped in. He looked around for a few seconds, wrote something on the clipboard, then tore off a sheet and set it in a small woven grass basket on a table by the door. He turned and left, pulling the door closed behind him. Birch remained motionless at the top of the stairs until he heard the truck door slam, the engine kicking up once again and then receding.

He crept down the stairs to the small table and picked up the sheet. 380 gallons, dated October 1, charged to Catherine Willow. He set the paper back into the basket, turned and started when he saw the glass beads he'd left on the living room floor the previous night. He shook his head, went to scoop them up and return them to their jelly jar, setting it back on the shelf in the utility closet.

He continued to the kitchen, where the morning sun poured through the window onto the sink and counter, even making it across to the stove. He started pulling open cupboard doors, trying to remember from the night before, then found the cylinder of rolled oats he'd seen. He grabbed it, feeling it was about half full, then rinsed out the sauce pan and set it on the stove with a couple cups of water to boil.

Under the sink he found a trash bucket with a paper shopping bag partially filled with dry trash. Next to that was a yellow ceramic compost pail with a lid. He lifted the lid and set it back down instantly as a foul stench slapped his nose. He lifted the pail by its wire handle and carried it outside, setting it in the grass.

The sun reached through the bushes to dapple the vinyl seat of his motorcycle, mostly hidden against the back of the house. He stepped through the bushes and gingerly crossed the spruce bark mulch in his bare feet to reach it, unlatching the luggage cases and pulling the contents out. The saddlebag next to the house proved difficult, as he had to lean the bike back against himself to open it, and the weight against him, even at this slight lean, with his bare legs scratched by the bushes and his bare feet on uneven ground, was as much as he could handle without falling over backward. He managed by dropping his clothes and phone on the ground and bracing his right thigh against the seat's edge, causing a swell of sharp pain in his foot and ankle and the beginnings of a significant bruise on his thigh.

He got the bike settled on its kickstand again, gathered up his things and limped back up the steps. He set his phone and a charging cord on the kitchen counter and took the clothes to the utility closet. *Might as well do the rest of my laundry while I'm here, silly not to think of that last night when I did my jeans and shirt.* He moved his jeans and shirt to the dryer and dropped the rest of his clothes into the washer.

He heard the water boiling, so went to dump in the oats and turn down the flame. He glanced at his phone, doing a double-take when he saw the WiFi fan with full bars. An unsecured network? He picked it up to investigate, plugging in the charger as he was down to two percent. Indeed the network, named for a generic router somewhere, was unprotected. He hadn't noticed a modem or cable anywhere, or a TV. He opened Fing on his phone to scan the network, discovering there was exactly nothing connected to it except for his phone.

He decided to search for the router, not finding anything after another walk-through of the downstairs. A door opposite the utility closet in the hallway looked like another closet, but when he pulled it open he found wooden steps to a basement. The old light switch made a loud *tock!* when he flipped it, spreading yellow light around the bottom of the stairway. The steps were thick and solid, making only faint dry cracks as he descended; the air hung dank, though holding the sharp edge of a recent burn from the propane furnace. The cement floor, once he reached it, was dry, and a box with blinking lights on a shelf behind the furnace told him he'd found the modem and router. He walked over to make an inspection, feeling dust accumulate on his bare soles like the thin felt of old slippers.

The units were standard issue, unremarkable but clearly functioning, a loop of cable coming through a floor joist and collar-clamped to the modem. The shelves below were filled with candlesticks, pottery, a couple of kerosene lanterns, an electric hot plate, baskets, coat hangers, rolls of paper towels, bulk packs of bathroom tissue, and all manner of random objects, the rest of the wall lined with more wooden shelves nailed together of studs and boards. These were packed full of dry goods, cans, and jars like those in the kitchen cupboards above. Birch walked along, turning a can or tapping a jar, picking up a box to shake and read a label. Soup, vegetables, meats, canned fruit, rice, pasta, baking supplies, spices, beans, crackers, more oats in bulk packs, coffee beans. He didn't see evidence of mice, or any mouse traps around on the floor, and thought the black boxes he'd seen around the foundation outside were probably the serious kind of mouse trap the pros used, so perhaps there were no rodents to infiltrate the basement. He stood back from the shelves and scanned from side to side, the thought entering his mind that if he could remain undetected here and the place didn't sell (as it seemed it had been on the market for quite a long time already), he wouldn't have to leave this house for months. *Crazy thought,* he told himself. He walked back along the shelves to head upstairs, grabbing a candle in a stick, a box of matches, and a pair of yellow plastic sunglasses on the way.

He set the candle, matches, and sunglasses on the kitchen table and stirred the oatmeal. Slipping on the glasses, he looked toward the sun through the window, realizing they weren't actually sunglasses but the kind of 3D glasses they hand out at the movies. Wincing, he took them off and set them on the counter.

Shortly, he sat at the kitchen table eating oatmeal and surfing with his phone. His browser seemed pretty snappy on this WiFi network, so he loaded Speedtest to check it. *Not bad for rural cable.* He thought of opening his Tor browser and checking his hosted server for any messages his phantom soft phone might've picked up while roaming the San Jose library system, then decided to skip it. *Probably just more threats from*

Robin, and that would depress me. He was feeling insulated from that threat by novelty and distance, didn't want to risk destroying his sense of freedom, however illusory. He didn't bother checking his bank account or Slang account for the same reason, pushing those things from his mind. Instead he sat, ate, and thought about the energy he was spooning into his body.

He felt drained, not so much weak as emptied out. It was that delicious fatigue you get when starting to relax after long tension and exertion, that letting go. He watched California, and Zongo, receding behind him like a memory from some other life, the threat of Robin nebulous, yet he felt the vulnerability of starting again, not knowing what would happen next, like he knew nothing about anything. He knew sun was shining into the kitchen, and oatmeal was going into his mouth. He felt like he might start simply and begin to fill himself back up.

He heard a sound at the front door, froze with his spoon steaming in front of his open mouth. He heard the key in the lock, the tumblers flop over, the knob twist, and the sucking sound as the door slid past its weather seal. He thanked the sky that he hadn't started the clothes washer or dryer yet.

He heard someone step into the house, though they didn't seem to move after that. Maybe they were looking around, or sensing his presence? Then he heard the basket on the small table rustle, or maybe the paper in the basket. Then silence. Then a woman's voice called, "Paul?" The heat of the steaming spoonful of oats in front of his face was matched by heat flushing up and down his neck and across his shoulders. He didn't hear anything more for a moment, but then it sounded like they stepped back out, pulling the door closed. Yes, he heard the key in the lock again, the tumblers flopping back over.

He waited a few seconds, put down his spoon, and tiptoed to the edge of the hallway. He peeked around the corner and saw the door closed, then crept quickly to the living room window and crouched, peering past the curtain. He saw a woman with long dark hair and wearing a flannel shirt and jeans walking down the driveway to the street, heading toward the village.

He looked at the basket by the door, finding it empty.

Birch went back to the kitchen to finish his oatmeal, wondering how long he would stay there, when someone would come in and discover him, call the sheriff to have him arrested. He asked himself what he should do about this, and no answers came. He was out of gas and money, and as for any thoughts that resembled a plan—he was out of those too. He looked at the fine layer of dust catching the light on the counters and the tops of the cupboard handles anywhere he hadn't touched them. He realized that the only places in the house that were cleaned off were where he'd set his feet or hands. If he looked at the surfaces from a certain angle, what he saw was a trail of his own movements through the house. He inspected the tabletop and the tops of the chair backs. Same thing. For lack of a better plan, he decided that he would clean. At least there was food here to sustain him as long as he could stay, and if someone discovered him and sent in the sheriff he could say he left it better than he'd found it, minus the food of course.

He took his bowl to the sink and rinsed it, looking out the window past the hanging willow stems, through the yard under the rising sun, to a cornfield a hundred yards distant. The farmer had cleared the stalks from half of it. Birch absently wiped out the bowl while his eyes wandered down an alley cleared of cornstalks to a slight rise in the ground, and farther up the rise to low hills in the distance. His eyes lit on the hills and something entered him, almost like a breath, disturbing and thrilling him in the same moment. He looked down at the bowl and spoon in the sink, dried them with a dish towel and set them aside, then turned for the pan on the stove. He looked out at the hills again as he turned on the faucet to fill the pan, love and sadness twisting together inside him, stronger than he'd ever felt them before. He looked away, frowned, and used a scrubber to clear out the pan. He glanced up at the cornfield and let his eyes lock onto the hills again, the feeling coming back like an injection of something confusing into his bloodstream.

He finished cleaning and drying the dishes and put them away. Then he went to the utility closet and started to switch on the washer, but then stopped. He'd wait until night in case someone else came by today. Instead he found a bottle of cleaner and a couple dusting rags. He decided to start in the living room, keeping a watchful eye toward the window as he moved from moldings to mantle to side tables and chair backs. He wiped down and polished a three drawer chest. He picked up the small framed photographs, dusted them and set them back on their stands. He opened the drawers, releasing the smell of spice, wood dust, and wax, finding more framed pictures and a few albums, unused stationery, pens and pencils, boxes of candles (some partially burned, some not), a magnifying glass, cork coasters, cloth napkins, a few boxes of matches, and a letter opener.

He took the pictures out, wiped them off, and set them on their stands next to the others. Clearly the same family, a mother and father, daughter and son together in one frame, older versions of the mother and daughter beside it, both in separate frames, but none of the father or the son.

He moved on to the dining room and wiped down and polished the tabletop, moving the cloth placemats and wooden tray in the center, replacing them as he went. He dusted the simple chandelier, swinging it a little on its chain, and carefully wiped the glass bulbs that were shaped to look like candle flames.

He went back to the chest, pulled out the photo albums and took them to the dining room table, intending to look at them later.

He wiped the dark cherry chair backs, the seat rails and legs. The damask seats were smoothed and worn, with mild divots. He brushed them with a rag. He moved on to the buffet, picking up each leaning plate from the shelf, blue dinner plates with scenes reminiscent of the curtains upstairs, wiping off both sides and setting them back on display. He wiped down the front of the grandfather clock, the glass in front of the face and the tall window to the pendulum.

No one else came by, though he stayed vigilant throughout the day. That night he collected some towels from the upstairs hall closet and added them to his load in the clothes washer, running it and the dryer together. It occurred to him that someone would be getting the electric bill, so he determined to use as little as possible beyond what was already running. That meant few cycles of the washer and dryer and minimal use of lights, maybe just the basement light on occasion, in addition to one table lamp in the living room that was already on a mechanical timer. Fortunately the stove and water heater were propane.

Over the next few days he continued his cleaning circuit. By the third day, feeling relaxed with no more visitors, he decided to risk the electricity and sound of running the vacuum. He cleaned all of the carpets, downstairs and up, and each stair step on the way, pausing to look out the windows and listen every so often.

He went back to the grandfather clock standing in the dining room, looking in at the motionless pendulum. Time had stopped at five minutes before twelve, how many months or years ago? He felt around behind the top molding, discovering another thick layer of dust and, of course, the key. He brought in a kitchen chair, thinking the cherry chairs at the dining table weren't sturdy enough, and stood to dust the top of the clock's cabinet. He opened the cabinet with the key and wiped down the long brass pendulum, feeling a desire to put the key into the winding holes and twist. He imagined the ratchet of gears, the growing resistance of the spring, the renewed pendulous tick-tock sound, but left those thoughts in his mind. He set the key down on the inside bottom of the cabinet and swung the door closed without locking it.

The still hands caused him to think of three electric clocks he'd seen in the rooms upstairs. He didn't need them to keep track of anything for him, so he went upstairs and unplugged them. That would offset some electricity from the vacuum cleaner, perhaps even the water pump.

After he finished cleaning the upstairs bathroom, he put the cleaning supplies away and went to sit in his favorite chair at the kitchen table. He filled a glass of water from the tap and sat relishing the sun reflecting up from the tabletop. He liked the well water here. It was just water, and didn't have the subtle bitterness of civic chemistry he recalled in his tap water in California.

Over the following days the willow in the back yard and the oaks around the house began turning. Geese passed overhead in ragged V formations, heading south, while bees and other flying insects stitched their paths from bush to bush. Birch kept the window over the sink open during most days to let in fresh air, its lack of screen ensuring the occasional yellowjacket flew in to drink from tiny puddles on the counter.

The only person Birch had seen in the past week was a guy who drove up in a pest control truck and went around the house, reloading the rodent traps with poison nuggets. Before that he had caught sight of the dark-haired girl again by chance, pulling something, probably bills and junk mail, from the mailbox out at the street and driving away in a pickup truck.

One day, Birch spent the entire day sitting on one of the wingback chairs in the living room, watching squirrels out the front window. He got up periodically to swing his arms and stretch, ate soup later for dinner (he had soup often). Another day he listened to rain on the roof and imagined the patterns created by the wind. He'd looked through all the photo albums in the dining room a few times each, gathering that the owner of the house had been Agnes Willow. There was a daughter named Catherine, and in earlier photos a husband named Paul, along with a young son whose name wasn't written down. In one image Birch recognized the willow tree in the back yard. The tree was half its present height. The caption read: "At home in Still Point, Nebraska." Birch checked Google Maps. *Sure enough.*

The father and son didn't appear in any of the photos after a time. The daughter eventually appeared with a man, and then with a baby, then another. A series of school shots of the grandkids appeared to cover the early elementary years. These were stuck in a few rows on the last page of the latest album. Birch put them back in the chest.

Birch sat at the kitchen table with a glass of water and experimented with sensing when he was thirsty, taking a swallow only when his body sent him a clear signal. He did the same with food, filling up the refrigerator with plastic-wrap-covered bowls of cold spaghetti, vegetables from cans, beans and such, which he nibbled on only when his body told him he was truly hungry.

He watched videos online of various forms of yoga and martial arts, trying some out in the living room, then beginning to mix them together into his own free form of movement.

He periodically thought of logging into his hosted server to see what, if anything, his mustang in the San Jose library had posted, but each time his distaste for what he expected to find there outweighed his curiosity. Instead he cruised online stores, thinking he should get a laptop or netbook, or at least a Bluetooth keyboard for his phone. Once he added a keyboard to his shopping cart, only to remember he had no way to buy it. He logged into his bank account finally, and it was still zero. Same with Slang. Same with PayPal. He thought about creating a false identity on ODesk or Freelancer, making some money writing code for some far-away project for people he'd never meet, but again, he'd need a better machine to be productive on those sites. For days it was simply easier to wander around the house, looking for small things to fix or clean, or just sit in one of his favorite spots and let his mind spin down until he forgot who and where he was.

He would look toward the nearest window, see that it was dark, and realize that he'd just spent the last hours in a rocking chair, staring at a wooden bowl on a dresser without even seeing it, puzzling over the image in his mind of those hills beyond the fields out his kitchen window. He might rock up from the chair and walk downstairs to the kitchen, stand with his palms flat on either side of the sink peering out the window through the dusk toward the hills, and that unsettling feeling would flood back every time, like the pulse of an electric fence always there for him to grab.

Near the end of October he pulled his boots on after grabbing that electric fence yet again. He put on his jacket. He went out the back door into the twilight and through the yard past the willow. He felt twitchy, like an indoor cat padding into the wild for the first time. He stepped over a weedy yard border into the adjacent farmland, crossing quickly past a two-track edging the cornfield. He stepped through the stubble, walking next to standing stalks the farmer had never cut down. The moon floated above the tall stalks, following him as he traversed the field. He paused periodically with his back to the dark rows, looking behind him toward the village of Still Point. Lights from the windows of houses shone dull yellow. The steady bark of a dog came from near the house belonging to this field, distant across the shredded stalks, the yard dimly lit by a mercury light attached to a pole near the barn.

Earthen clods gave under his boots with each step, slowing his progress. The dry leaves from the army of stalks rustled here and there as an air mass, smelling sweetly of earth and rot and still slightly warm, slid through them toward the village.

His feet pushing into the soil, the smell of the slow breeze—somehow these sensations flicked open an ancient memory in him. His heart swelled. He pulled the air deeper into his lungs and frowned, squeezing his fists and setting his jaw. Terror and love pooled in him inexplicably.

He reached the far edge of the cornfield, a half mile walk from the house, and started up the slope of the first low rise, his nerves trilling as if over this foothill he would meet his first love or fight for his life, though he had no idea which.

His eyes saw beyond the hilltop moments before his feet crested it. Gasping, he dropped to his knees, then to his elbows, the narrow gully before the next hill, smeared in white moonlight, stopping his heart. Thick clumps of wild grass shone wet with dew; he cranked his neck to peer over the grass to the gully, hearing only the sound of his heartbeat slamming in his head. Shreds of memory stored in his DNA grappled with each other in each of his body's trillions of cells, awoken and twisted and turned by this scene now in his vision, the shreds like pieces of an incomplete jigsaw puzzle spinning to find their places around the holes, filling in the pattern, matching and setting. It felt like being overrun by fever. The image before him floated for a nanosecond before resolving into the dark plain of his dreams, and he began to see more in the gully than he trusted was actually there.

Had he understood what was happening, he might have known those fragments of memory which scratched his sleep into nightmare for so many years first belonged to Caleb Birch, his grandfather's grandfather's father. He might have known, or felt, that Caleb was fifteen years old when he lay in this very spot. He would have felt that he was now Caleb, pressed down in the grass by the weight of dread and peering past a clump, watching as a girl ran the length of the gully, chased by three men.

The girl was older than Caleb, though not by much. She ran fast, long black hair trailing behind her, moon reflecting like flashing metal from her bronzed legs. She wore a smock-like dress, brown as earth, leather moccasins covering her feet and ankles. Running silently, she never looked back, but the men closed the distance and caught her. The one in front wore Union army pants, ragged from wear, gold stripe catching in the moonlight. The other two trailed close behind, one with a cowboy hat flailing on his back held by its thong, the third darker and with long hair.

They dove on her, driving her into the ground. Caleb heard the thud, then the girl grunting as they piled around her like wolves on a fawn. The broad side of a Bowie knife flashed in the moonlight, and they tore open the thin fabric of her smock, yanking it from her body. They flipped her onto her back, and the soldier gripped her wrists and held her arms taut above her head. Her low growls as she fought came to Caleb like echoes through fog. She kicked free a leg and swung at the other two men, tagging the hat-wearing one with her heel square under his eye, instantly raising a thick shiner. She swung again and again until they caught her leg. The one with the hat was Caleb's uncle, his father's younger brother. He got on top of her and fiddled with his trousers while the other two held her down. She spat at him, and he slapped her face hard, then pumped into her like the piston rod of a saw mill until he finished with a sudden coarse *Ha!* Next was the one without the hat, causing the woman to grunt hard with rage. "You! You!" she snarled as he defiled her.

Last went the soldier. Caleb lay frozen in terror. He wanted to kill them, rush them and kick their heads off like pumpkins, save her. But his uncle. And the soldier—he knew him, gone mad from the war, now at the post for what they called "Indian Service"—would just as soon grab you and break your neck as brush a fly off a horse. And the guy with the long hair.... Caleb could not understand any of it.

When the soldier was done he sat up, still on her, and picked up his knife. With two thick hands he drove it down through her like a railroad spike while the other men held her arms and feet. He stabbed her repeatedly, chopping and chopping like he was trying to destroy the evidence of their shame. Her scream was sharp and brief before Caleb's uncle, holding her arms, slapped his hand down onto her mouth. Caleb buried his face in the grass, blind with rage, through closed eyes seeing the world as nothing but blood.

Then he was there, on all fours, next to the girl, like he'd flown in an instant without intention. The men were gone. Her eyes reflected a smear of moon but saw nothing he could understand. He touched her arm, grabbed it and tried to lift it up, but there was nothing. In the darkness he put his hands where new life incubated, but his fingers only descended into wet slop. He felt with horror the warmth leaving her, wicking up through his fingers.

Birch lifted his face, now soaked with dew like his hands. The thunder in his head was massive. He'd stumbled down the slope, was on his hands and knees in the dark snarled grass of the gully. Somewhere he knew himself as Birch, but that awareness seemed insignificant beside this memory—not his own—which held him without mercy. Like a hologram you couldn't turn off, he still saw moonlight reflecting in her dead eyes. His mind could not resolve this rationally, so instead it gave him the heavy stench of dead animal. He retched and vomited, rolled away and lay on his back looking at the blur of stars through stinging salt water. He felt himself passing out and starting to shiver. Somewhere the thought came that he would die of exposure should he lose consciousness here. He had to isolate and preserve enough agency to peel himself from this cold ground and make it back through the dark.

When he next touched consciousness, he felt warmth and knew that his head lay on the pillow, his body covered by the quilt. He did not open his eyes. He sensed it was the next day, but was not certain of that. His body ached, his head hammered and throbbed, his stench was rank and powerful enough to make him nauseous. His body was sticky under the quilt, his hair bunched and itchy around his neck. He let his eyes remain closed, lulling sideways in his head liked gelled balls of pain, and in his misery thought, *Let them find me.*

The nausea caused him to breathe too hard, his lungs straining to pull in air until he feared they'd burst. Amidst the tang of vomit he felt his fingers and toes tingle and begin to shut off, leave. The insidious prickling crawled up his hands and feet, then arms and legs. He felt like something was coming for him, and wondered if he was dying. He tried to think of what it could be. A deadly virus in the grass? Some kind of exotic flu? The spirit of the girl coming to hold him responsible for not saving her? Nature watching his cowardice and deeming him no longer worthy of life? He gave up trying and lay there like a wounded rabbit, accepting in his delirium, waiting to be finished by the pack of coyotes which had caught him.

He struggled against his hyperventilation for what seemed like hours, wishing only to fall back asleep, wishing to end the pain, turn himself in somewhere if that's what it took. He no longer cared to form complete thoughts, to make any sense.

Finally he opened his eyes. The light in the room looked like it might be afternoon. The electric clock on the night table was dead, unplugged. He blinked and rolled to test his pain, to take inventory. His face was hot. He remembered it being cold and wet. Maybe he had fallen back asleep a couple times, or simply drifted off somewhere he'd forgotten.

He rolled onto his side and got a leg out, stepped onto the floor unsteadily, then pulled his other leg halfway free, the sheet bunching and wrapping, trying to tug it back under.

He stumbled into the bathroom, glanced dismissively at the foul animal in the mirror, threw water on his face and buried it in the nearest towel, taking the smallest sliver of relief from the scent of laundry detergent in the coarseness of the old cloth. He decided then to live, to make of this whatever he could, to work with what he had at hand.

He kept the towel, carrying it back into the bedroom,

and put on a too-small white flannel robe from the closet. He lay on the bed breathing a while, then made his way downstairs, dizzy, mopping his face with the towel.

He rested on the couch on his way to the kitchen, then kicked out a kitchen chair and slumped into it, burying his face in the towel. He filled a glass with water and sipped with trembling hands, looking around through his daze. His boots were on the linoleum by the back door, toppled over amidst clumps of mud. His jacket and jeans had made it a few feet farther in, his shirt almost to the hallway carpet. He didn't worry over them being there or move to pick them up. He concentrated on the tea kettle a few moments, got up to set it on a burner and turn on the stove, then plopped back into the chair. He would think about locating tea bags and some honey once the kettle began calling for such efforts.

He managed to drink half a mug of tea before collapsing on the couch. A molar in his lower left jaw set up an ache, flaring with pain at each hot sip. It kept throbbing even as he shifted to drink only on the right side of his mouth.

He spent the rest of the day nursing himself with tea and salt crackers between the couch, the kitchen, and the downstairs bathroom. He abandoned his normal vigilance to the weakness and futility the fever made him feel, even when he heard the engine sound of a car or truck driving by on the road out front. *Let them find me,* he thought again, *whoever they are: the people selling this house, or some hitman Robin hired from the dark net. Let them come put me out of my useless misery.*

Later he made it back upstairs with a fresh pot of tea and plate of crackers, spending the night and next day wrapped in sour sheets alternating between cold drenching sweats and burning fever. He didn't know at any moment if he was asleep and dreaming or drifting in delirium. The scene appeared again before him, the girl running through the dusk, the men chasing, only this time he was floating above, though still near to the observing boy flattened in the grass. He felt the boy's fear and rage like rattlesnakes inside him, trying to bite their way out. No matter if he was dreaming this, or remembering; the agony gripped him in its fangs despite his writhing to escape. He wanted to forget the boy, forget the girl, annihilate the men. He wanted never to have known that fear and rage. He fought it with hard breaths. He fought it with the searing pain in his jaw. He fought it in the twisted soaked sheets, screaming long and hard into the cupped damp of the pillow. But he couldn't win; it was inside of him, a part of who he was.

Finally he opened his eyes to the quiet bedroom. The curtains hung muted in flat afternoon light. Birch didn't know what day it was, or how long he had been fighting the fever. He only knew that it was gone. The sheets were dry. The smell of his ordeal, stale. He was thirsty and hungry.

He lifted his head, swung his legs over, pushed up with both arms. He sat, limp, entirely spent. He raised his eyes toward the window. The rattlesnakes rested inside him, but he knew they were still there.

After a few minutes he stood, naked, and pulled the sheets from the bed, the case from the pillow. He balled them up and took them downstairs to the washer. He walked weakly to the kitchen and drank some water, set a pot on the stove for some canned soup. He cleaned up the mud and set his boots on the back landing, put his clothes into the washer with the sheets.

He leaned against the kitchen counter, hands flat on either side of the sink, and gazed out the window. Still there, the snakes stirred. Now, however, the mystery was gone. He knew the snakes would grow more familiar. He felt something like a cancer patient getting used to the idea of living out his life with one lung removed.

He woke the next morning and put on freshly washed clothes, going down to make breakfast. Most of the leaves had fallen, the birds that fly south all having gone a week before. The morning sun came into the kitchen low and gold.

He sat at the kitchen table, eating a bowl of oatmeal with canned blueberries, and thought about those snakes inside him. Birch didn't commit these crimes, but he was a witness. Perhaps a witness via his ancestor's DNA, but a witness nonetheless. He carried in him the irrevocable responsibility of knowing. So, what do you do with that?

You start with who you are and what you have, you look at the thing square and sober, you nod, and you walk forward.

He thought about all the road rage back in Palo Alto, and everywhere. That guy with the wrap-around sunglasses in the jacked truck, filling his rear-view mirror, he had rattlesnakes in him too, but had no idea what they were, where they came from. Like so many people, like the whole civilization it seemed, he only knew the feeling of the bites, the squirming to escape something every time you took a breath. *Those bites, when you don't know where they come from, make you act out either as a brutal thug or a victim, an obsequious nincompoop.*

Birch went into the dining room and wound up the grandfather clock, setting the pendulum in motion. *So be it,* he thought. *You look, you nod, you walk forward.*

12

"Babe," Angel said, "maybe we should buy a house."

"Really?" Winnie asked from the living room. She got up from stretching on the rug and walked over to him, resting her hands on his shoulders.

"Yeah. I mean, look at this one." He shifted to let her see his laptop screen as she leaned in.

"Huh? That's, like, in Santa Fe, and two and a half million dollars!" She pulled his shoulders back and looked into his face, a puzzled expression on hers. She raised her eyebrows at him. He looked up at her blankly, then raised his eyebrows in turn.

"Well, guess what? With my raise, if I stick this job out for only two years I'll be a millionaire. We can totally afford something like this."

She cocked her head and squinted at him. "And what are we supposed to do in Santa Fe? That's a forty minute drive on a good day."

"I'm pretty sure we're getting a second car," he said matter-of-factly, and stared at her.

She stared back. "You're pretty sure," she said.

"Yeah, I am," he said, "a nice one."

"A nice one," she said. "Okay, I'm going to start dinner." She rolled her eyes and went to pull open the pantry door.

"There are nice places around here too," he said. "Look at this one."

◆ ◆ ◆

They had moved the control system from Staging Two to production, a dozen drones now aloft over the greater Los Alamos area, charging from a small mobile microwave tower deployed at the company's main compound.

Angel no longer stood with his PalmPilot surreptitiously touching the window of Stuart's office door, as Stuart now got up from his chair as soon as he saw Angel approaching and opened the door to invite him in. Angel would take one of the chairs opposite Stuart's, pull it out and sit back with his ankle perched up on a knee, setting his PalmPilot on the desk ready to sync whenever.

Stuart kept him abreast of developments in the growing network of microwave towers and military satellites that would serve as the drone network's power source. Negotiations were ongoing with the mobile communications carriers, resulting in new antenna installations on cell towers at a rapid rate. A number of the old AT&T Skynet towers were also quietly being refurbished and put back into service, their updated equipment tuned for the drone network. The antennas required a huge amount of power to operate, as they had to generate directed, high density fields in order to be effective in charging the drones. Angel didn't worry about that side of the technology, as he was busy enough working through the control system software, but he knew attempting to harvest power from a radiating source was like trying to use a straw to drink water from a passing cloud. He was impressed by the hardware and battery tech that the drone team had come up with so far.

Now, Stuart was talking fast, his voice strained with excitement. "If you can squeeze a few more points of power efficiency from the flight controller system, that would let us stretch the network into something like six percent more territory for every point you gain in power efficiency," Stuart told him. "Let's say you can find fourteen percent more in the near term. That would let us just about cover the lower forty-eight with what we have now and get us working on coverage over the rest of the continent and overseas."

Angel had actually been thinking about ways to make the drones consume less power. "I have some ideas for that," he said across the desk. "I've been thinking that we can do better with thermal detection and updraft management."

"You mean, like hawks and glider pilots?" Stuart asked, leaning forward in his chair.

"Yes, that plus more sensitive weather prediction to take better advantage of orographic lift."

"Nice!" Stuart said. "Can you do that even for units that have already launched?"

"Sure, over-air updates are built in. Routine," Angel said.

"This is going to be great!" Stuart said.

Angel found himself energized by the technical challenges, and also by his growing comfort and success at motivating his team. He found that he really wanted to get that fourteen percent for Stuart. Angel knew that Stuart had been instrumental in getting him his raise, and Stuart's positivity and solicitousness of late was having its effect.

Angel put Chad in charge of a sub team tasked with creating the algorithm to reposition clusters of drones based on proximity to charging fields, natural lift, and signal requirements on the ground below, all in search of longer flight with lower power consumption. Chad frequently gave Angel meaningful inquiring looks, but Angel did his best to forget that they had ever talked about creating a system backdoor. He had also effectively forgotten that he'd loosed a mustang into the wild in search of his former college roommate, this hole in his recollection aiding his growing sense of personal satisfaction and connection with the project, leaving him blissfully free for the time being of that pang of fear he'd initially felt upon deciding to intentionally breach company security. The fact that it had been many weeks since he sent the mustang galloping across to Stuart's PalmPilot, with no reply from Birch, combined with the frantic pace of improvements he had to keep the team on, helped him maintain his strategic forgetfulness.

Winnie started noticing the public relations campaign to burn more gas and use less electricity popping up all over the place. Ads on Youtube, billboards, in magazines, on television, bumper stickers, started making the claim that driving electric vehicles was weak and un-American, that real patriots drove vehicles with strong gas or diesel engines. Internet memes sparked rumors that fringe news outlets quickly picked up with the usual fervor, maintaining it was industry-known fact that driving an electric vehicle was the equivalent of sitting in a gas barbecue with a lit match, waiting to be incinerated.

Each time Winnie would spot something, she would ask Angel, "Is this part of that brainwash thing you were talking about? Trying to get people to back off using electricity so it will be available for the drones?"

Angel knew that it was, had even seen Stuart laugh about it, but he had rationalized enough workable doubt in his mind that he could claim he wasn't sure. Winnie remained skeptical. "Whatever it is, it's sick," she said.

Angel had closed up and stowed the laptop he'd bought from the university student up in Boulder, now surfing the web with a new company laptop connected to the Free Air Net, which was what the company planned to name the drone cell-WiFi network once they launched it to the public. They were not yet promoting it, but all the staff were using and continuing to test it, while people around Los Alamos and Santa Fe began discovering it in their available network lists and, noticing the word "free" in the name, joined it, happy to have a free connection without even the need to remember a password.

Angel checked Speedtest at least a dozen times a day,

taking proprietary interest in the results. "This is faster than our cable connection," he said to Winnie one Saturday. "In fact," he continued, "I think it's about time we cut the cord on that. We don't need it anymore. Wasted money."

"Are you sure?" Winnie asked. "Aren't they, like, monitoring everything you do over that? What about all the surveillance stuff you were testing?"

"Oh," Angel brushed it off. "It's fine. I'm not doing that anymore. I don't do anything that I need to worry about on here. I do need you to drive me over to the BMW dealer this morning, by the way. Check this out. This is what I ordered. They have it ready for us."

Winnie walked over and did a double-take at his laptop screen. He smiled, showing teeth, and looked up at her for approval. "That's big," she said.

"Yup, X5, that's the black we're getting. You're going to love it. Check out the window tint."

He beamed at her, and she looked down at him for a moment with her hands on her hips. "You didn't say a word about this to me," she said.

"It's a surprise," he said, holding his palms up and raising his eyebrows.

She stood in thought, wondering as she looked through his eyes, trying to see in.

"What?" he said. "I work hard! Why shouldn't we have nice stuff?"

The company secured military contractor status and national security exemptions to handle the peskiest FAA rules that would affect the drones in civil airspace, Angel's team integrating ADS-B rules into the navigation controllers to keep the drones out of harm's way near airports. With the testing in live airspace successful and the antenna-tower agreements continuing to expand the network, they began releasing dozens of new drones, as fast as they could manufacture them. Within a month, they were releasing hundreds each day.

As Free Air Net expanded, more and more people joined. Angel and his team worked overtime to adapt the software and network controls to manage the massive distribution. Since people were happy to connect to Free Air Net both at home and out and about, with no need to switch networks, some of the smaller ISPs began to lose customers. Before anyone could look too deeply into what was going on the company swooped in, buying up their distressed competitors at steep discounts and liquidating them. They also continued to lease new antenna space on towers at a fast pace, tying up the owners with rights of first refusal when other companies began leaving the towers, making them less profitable.

By midwinter the western states were left with towers that were owned either by Free Air Net, on which they leased antenna rigs to the major telecom carriers, or by the major telecom carriers, who leased antenna rigs to Free Air Net. By then the company lawyers were also in secret talks with the big telecoms. People on the ground didn't know any different; they saw the same towers as always, albeit with blocky or round things bolted to the tops and thicker cables running toward the ground. But they had internet everywhere, and no one sent them a bill for it. No one noticed the drones either, as they stayed just high enough to be beyond normal sight range from the ground. Internet became like air; people had it and didn't question it, or even remember to think about it.

Winnie nursed her doubts, however, and didn't understand the change she saw in Angel. "Is this going to be good for net neutrality?" she asked one day from the passenger seat of their big BMW.

Angel guided the X5 through the streets of Old Town Albuquerque looking for a restaurant that Stuart had told him about. "It should be pretty close now, along the right side there. What does Google Maps say? Oh, fuck that guy!" Angel yelled, looking in the rear-view. "Does he fucking mind if I slow down to find a place to park?"

"There it is," Winnie said. Angel had to drive past and turn the corner to find parking.

They walked along the sidewalk holding hands. Angel stopped at the corner to look down the street at the back of the tailgating Suburban, waiting at a stop light. "That moron made a lot of progress, didn't he? People don't fucking do the math."

"Oh, who cares?" Winnie said. "So answer my question," she continued. "We're all using your free air internet now. Is that going to be good for net neutrality and people's privacy?"

"Well, it is now," Angel said. "It's free, right? And faster than what we used to get."

"But is it going to stay that way?"

The dinner was grand, and Angel insisted that they order dessert.

Angel found himself struggling with a lie he was telling Winnie on their drive back to Los Alamos. He didn't want to lie to her, didn't even feel like he was completely lying, but in his heart understood that he knew more than he was saying. Free Air Net was for national defense, he claimed; she had asked him where the money was coming from to provide free internet service to the general public.

He tried to work through and justify the logic of having a national defense internet which was also used by the public, his mind counting headlights going by in the opposite direction, starting over each time he hit one hundred. *How many of these people are already using Free Air Net?*, he wondered. Winnie watched the dark over the desert through the passenger window. Raindrops began to tic and clatter against the windshield, then to stream down the side windows. Angel turned on the windshield wipers when the rain grew heavy, the oncoming headlights blurring into pale smears.

Angel knew that the company was sort of part of the government but not really, or more accurately was owned by private parties but using taxpayer funds to build things ostensibly for national defense, so there must be defense contracts involved. Not his area of expertise. He suspected the money came from the black budget, but really didn't know. It was murky, much like the Federal Reserve. Was the Fed a private bank, or an entity that supposedly belonged to the government, aka the people? There didn't seem to be an accessible reality there, only theories which tended to line up with one's politics or Youtube viewing habits.

Same problem with the company that paid him twice a month. A lot lay beyond his access, meaning he could only make assumptions. The knowable things, the project specs, the software challenges, the drones, the innovations they'd come up with to make the network actually work, these things made sense to him, gave his mind and spirit stable ground on which to stand. He knew Winnie was right to question what was going on, knew her nature meant she couldn't help but question it. He'd grown weary of his own anger and paranoia, and then they'd given him that big raise. Now he got to feel what it was like to have obscene amounts of money. Why not experience that for a while? On the one hand the company seemed able to eliminate people it didn't like without a trace. On the other hand, they provided overly generous compensation and plenty of encouragement for valuable work. Which of those options would a rational person lean toward?

"Well, if it's only for national defense, why is the public using it? And how come they're letting other internet companies go out of business?"

Keeping up with the expansion of the network had not been as manageable as Angel had hoped. Stuart was in great spirits, felt like they were conquering the world—he had gotten a nice raise too—but he didn't understand the details of powering and controlling the vast number of airborne units, being especially incapable of keeping up with the new units launching from the plant every day like an endless swarm of ground wasps. The bug lists and new requirements syncing across from Stuart's PalmPilot were growing, and Angel had to keep the team working long hours every day, frequently on weekends. Angel had asked for new hires to replace the people he'd lost, but the company was slow to find people with the right skills who could pass the background checks, and then there would be the on-boarding and training time.

He'd really just wanted to have a nice relaxing dinner with Winnie at a nice restaurant. He didn't have the energy for this type of thinking at the moment, was grateful for the smooth ride and sure track of his car as his mind wandered here and there, growing sleepier with the steady stream of passing headlights and the squishy rhythm of the wiper blades.

"Don't you want to know? I mean, you're part of this."

He did know, but the stress of the work, the deadlines, the responsibility for the drones, and his disappointment in himself for not maintaining self-honesty left his mind murky, to such an extent he was able to forget that he knew. There was also the problem that knowing too much was dangerous; he didn't want Winnie wrapped up in any of it. He did know, however, that she would not be able to leave it alone.

"Yes, I do, but I'm just so tired. I just want to get home and sleep."

The syncs were taking longer than ever now, and it didn't even occur to Angel to worry that it could be due to his mustang. He had forgotten that he'd even created it. He was used to the long lists of issues and requirements coming in on a daily basis, and it was all he and the team could do to keep up with them.

"I don't know if you've been following this," Stuart started in, "but people have been dropping their cell plans in droves and using VOIP clients for their calls instead. Since they can keep their phone numbers, and they always have a connection, it's basically a no-brainer."

Angel chuckled. "Yes, I've heard. In fact, I'm doing that too. What do I need a cellular bill for?"

Stuart smiled and chuffed out a laugh. He and Angel had unconsciously adopted a bro-code of sharp, sinister laugh sounds whenever they discussed how dominant their creation was becoming. These were the sounds Angel had often heard coming through the din of a frat party as he walked by on the sidewalk, or echoing down the halls of an athletic complex on the rare occasions when he'd be in one to work out. His reaction had always been one of contempt, and the first time he'd produced such a sound himself, in Stuart's office, he felt a pang of self-awareness that caused him to stop and notice, and think about it later. He'd told himself he was faking harmony with Stuart on purpose, not because it was natural for him. But since then, he'd forgotten that and gotten used to their unspoken code. He began to feel stronger when he shared a contemptuous laugh with Stuart, like he always should have been in the midst of that pack of brawny dudes on the frat house porch or in the locker room. He and Stuart both knew they were not at the top of the pyramid here, but felt they were within shouting distance, Stuart certainly closer than Angel, but they also both knew Stuart needed Angel to make things happen and make him look good.

"So, some of the higher-ups think we should capitalize on that and make a VOIP service of our own. Part of the thought is that the telecoms are still pretty strong—for how long, right?" Another chuff from Stuart, echoed by Angel. "They'll be able to put pressure on the VOIP services, probably patent stuff, lawsuits, or maybe just buy them up, which doesn't help our cause any. So we're thinking we need to preempt that and offer the service ourselves, embedded with the other stuff."

Angel frowned and scrolled up today's issue list on his PalmPilot, relieved to not find any items referencing voice over IP. "Interesting idea," he said, "but that's such a big project I think it would hurt us right now. I need more people as it is, and it will take time to get new people trained."

"So that's not an easy one, I take it."

"Not by a long shot. Why don't we buy up the VOIP services before the telecoms do? That would probably be faster, and maybe less expensive, than trying to roll out our own at this point."

"They're talking about that approach too."

The desk phone bleeped, and Stuart rocked forward, picking up the hand set.

"Stuart here. Yeah. I'm here with Oleastro. We're talking about that now. The air thing? No. He doesn't know about it yet. I'll put you on speaker. Yeah. Just a sec." He hammered a thick finger onto the speaker button and dropped the handset back onto the cradle. "Okay," he said, eyebrows drawing together. "Say hello, Angel."

"Hello," Angel said.

A scratchy, nasal voice reverberated through the speaker. "Pitt, we're getting close on the manufacturing side, the kiosks and air tubes and shit, so let's get Oleastro up to speed on what we need from his end."

Angel pinched his brow and mouth as he stared at the desk phone.

"Okay," Stuart said. "So."

"Okay Oleastro," the voice on the desk phone said, "the long and short is that we're manufacturing air bottles, personal air bottles like the size of water bottles, sold to the public. And these are going to be smart bottles, pressurized, connected to the internet. Okay? So the idea is that you get your smart bottle filled with fresh clean air, and when you think the air around you isn't clean enough, or to your liking, you stick the cap over your nose, pull the trigger, and *boom!*, fresh clean air. Healthy and all that shit. Okay? And you refill it when you're out using one of our kiosks. Pop in your credit card, *bing, bam, boom.* Pretty simple, right? So we need you to build something that sends a signal to the chip on the bottles, telling them when the air isn't clean so to speak, so people know when to use the bottle. Right? Cuz air ain't exactly always visible. Right? How else can they tell?"

Angel stared at the phone, then squinted at Stuart a moment before saying, "So how are we going to tell when the air isn't clean? And how will we know which bottles to send signals to?"

"Pitt's got those details, Oleastro. I thought the drones had sensors or some shit."

Stuart leaned forward. "Yes, sir. The drones do have sensors, and I'll fill Oleastro in on what we talked about at the meeting."

"Good enough, Pitt. Get that on the schedule pronto. Okay, I'll leave you guys to it." The desk phone clicked silent.

Stuart said, "Okay, sir," then glanced up at Angel with an embarrassed laugh and leaned back in his chair. "I don't know if he heard that last," Stuart said without finishing the thought.

Angel leaned back in his chair too, and they looked at each other for a moment.

"Details?" Angel said. He thought he knew most of the details already through his illicit recordings, but wanted to hear them officially. Maybe they had changed.

Stuart laughed again, nervously. "The kiosks are actually pretty cool," he said. "The air is going to be mint-flavored."

"Mint?"

"Yeah," chuff chuff, "so it always smells and tastes fresh. People get used to it, you know? We did focus groups. They associate mint with freshness. And then, whatever we put in it, it still has that nice minty flavor." He raised his eyebrows and grinned, showing his teeth.

"Um, put into it? What would be put into the air?" Angel hadn't picked up on this part from his recordings. "Are these kiosks networked physically?"

"Well," Stuart said, "we are talking about leveraging

some unused natural gas networks to distribute our clean air to kiosks, but initially we'll have to have truck delivery of cartridges. But the kiosks have compressors, so the cartridges are just the mint flavoring, along with whatever additives, and the air supply is from the compressor."

Angel laughed. "Wait a sec. So, people are just buying the air that's already there, near the kiosk? Just, stuffed into their bottle?"

"Well, they buy water that way, right? Why not sell them air?"

"Let me get this straight. They think it's some special clean air, but it's just sucked into the kiosk next to the potato chip aisle and compressed into their bottle? For real?"

Stuart thought a moment. "Well, no, it IS special air. It gets filtered, then flavored by the cartridge. And who knows, maybe they'll come up with some healthy stuff to put in there as additives along with the mint." Stuart was unused to being challenged by Angel of late, but he started to enjoy this debate, feeling he was holding his own with his favorite hired brain.

"So, what kind of healthy stuff did you talk about in the meeting?" Angel wanted to know. He smiled and flashed his eyes.

Stuart took Angel's demeanor as a conspiratorial challenge. He chuffed and said, "Well, how about more O2? Running backs sure like a little hit on the sidelines. Hell, at Yale we used to..."

"What else?" Angel cut him off, raising his eyebrows and smiling wider.

Stuart searched his memory. "I mean, argon was discussed. You'll get this. You'll like it even."

"Argon?"

"Yeah, you get an unruly mob or something. You give 'em a mix a little light on the O2, a little heavier on something like argon, then you flash their bottles. They lose a little of that anger, calm down a bit. Makes sense, right? Cuts down on potential violence."

Angel didn't say anything. *Crowd control,* he thought. *Who are they working with on this? DHS? FEMA?* "That is fucking hilarious," he finally said.

Stuart laughed uncomfortably. He couldn't tell if Angel was with him or not. "I mean, it was mentioned. No one said they were actually going to do it."

"So we're going to sell people this clean air for their bottles, but not necessarily tell them all that's in it?"

"Clean air with a 'K,'" Stuart said, holding up his fingers for air quotes. "It's the KleanAir bottle. And, obviously, we have to say what's in it. It's a law. The legal team is looking at the regulations."

Angel knew, as everyone did, that the current administration was dismantling environmental regulations at a pace faster than the public, and even the media, could keep up with. Laws dictating that corporations report the contents of bottles sold to consumers didn't seem so sacrosanct anymore.

"Look," Stuart said after he grew agitated by Angel's pondering silence. "The Federal Reserve makes their product out of thin air, for god's sake! We're just providing easy ways for the population to funnel it into our accounts. Certainly more straightforward and easier to understand than credit default swaps on mortgage bonds, right?" He gave a loud laugh then, as if in victory, like that was the answer to any questions they might be debating.

Caveat Emptor, Angel thought. "So, how does Free Air Net tie into this project?"

"The bottles have LEDs that can show yellow, orange, or red," Stuart said. "We need to be able to flash them a color matching air conditions, green for clear, yellow for dust or ozone, red for pollution, radiation, or whatever. How do we monitor that?"

"We can get that data," Angel said. "Not onboard, as we don't actually have sensors for that, but we can query NOAA remotely and intersect with location. Not a problem."

"Perfect," Stuart said, holding his palms up. "And manual alerts too."

"Of course," Angel said.

Later that day Angel sat at his desk in the programming room, thinking through the air bottle conundrum, when the door popped and Stuart strode in. No one bothered looking up, as they were busily trying to resolve the issue list for the drone network. Angel hadn't even mentioned the air bottle project to anyone yet. Stuart bent down and whispered near Angel's ear, "Can I talk to you in the hallway?" Angel started, hesitated, then got up and followed Stuart out of the room.

Stuart looked up and down the empty hallway, then turned to Angel. "I didn't want to say this in there," he said in a low voice, "but the brass has been pretty impressed with how you've kept up with the launch, so I recommended another raise. They approved it today." He made a show of reaching into his shirt pocket for a small piece of paper, holding Angel's eyes with his own. He withdrew and unfolded it, holding it so Angel had to look down and cock his head to see.

Angel opened his mouth and closed it, eyes widening, and nodded. "Wow, thank you," he said.

"Yup," Stuart said. "New tax bracket. Oh," he continued, and pulled his PalmPilot out. "I have the specs for KleanAir."

Angel pulled out his PalmPilot and held it up, watching the swirling arrows and waiting for the beep.

The guy at the service desk, with "Josh" and a BMW logo sewn onto his shirt pocket, found Angel in the waiting room holding a Styrofoam cup of coffee. "Mr. Oleastro?"

"Yes."

Josh smiled. "Here's what we found. And this is all covered under the warranty, of course."

"Of course," Angel said.

Josh laughed. "It's just a bad circuit on the O2 sensors, about a half hour to forty-five minutes to fix that and get you on your way. Okay?"

Angel flipped through travel magazines while he waited for his car. It was Winnie's birthday, and he was anxious to get out of there so he could drive downtown to buy her a present. He'd flipped through plenty of travel magazines before, but had never really paid any attention to what was on the pages. Did upscale places like these really have that many hot-looking women lying around the pools, or reclining in the shade of palm trees on the beaches? The new, thick metal credit card he'd just gotten in the mail would make that question pretty easy to answer. He turned to a full page ad showing a football star claiming that real American men drove pickups like the one he stood in front of, arms folded across his chest. *Yeah,* Angel thought, *bet there aren't many hotties lying around those pools. Probably mostly old widows and rich dweebs like me.*

At the jewelry store Angel felt lost. He still had to pick up a gluten-free birthday cake, some fish and asparagus, and didn't feel like he had much time to kill browsing glass cases, but no one was paying attention to him. He realized that he probably didn't look like—or project the vibe of—a big spender. He didn't know how to dress fancy yet, or even where to go or how to buy expensive clothes, and Winnie hadn't been much help in that department. There were no spaces where he could park his expensive SUV at the curb in front of the store either, so he just looked like regular old nerdy Angel, poorly dressed as always. No one seemed to care that he was taking up space in the store.

Well, fuck that shit, he thought. He pulled out his wallet and removed the new credit card. It was thick, matte black, and metal. It was intimidating. It had easy-to-read gold letters and numbers. It had big spender written all over it. It had some fancy name too, that he'd forgotten, like the conquistador card or excelsior card or some bullshit, but it meant he had resources and should be respected, not trifled with.

He wandered over to a display case holding velvet-lined boxes with diamonds set in necklaces, earrings, rings, and bracelets. He held the viceroy card, or whatever its stupid name was, between the thumb and forefinger of his right hand, tapping it on the glass while he idly gazed at the glittering facets and white gold settings below. A svelte, smartly dressed lady of near sixty years peered over her librarian glasses at him from across the store, sized him up, and waltzed into the bullpen of display cases, which made an enclosed rectangle at the center of the store. She swung through a magnetically clasped hip-high door, which clearly only she was supposed to use, and slid a sparkle-encrusted hand along the glass top toward Angel.

"Hello hon," she purred. "Looking for something for the missus? In the mood for some diamonds?"

He looked up. The saleswoman's eyelids halfway lowered, her eyes holding his firmly. He blinked. "Yes," he said, and swallowed. He felt suddenly nervous, while simultaneously admonishing himself on the inside. *What am I nervous about? I'm the one with the goddamned money!*

A slow smile tugged lightly at the corners of her bright red lips as she studied his face. "Does she like white gold? Or yellow?"

A trick question? he wondered. *Dammit. I don't know. She'll know I've never bought jewelry before.*

She lowered her voice. "Is this for an engagement?"

"Um, no!" he said, sweat forming at his hairline. Then he thought maybe he'd said that too vehemently. "No, birthday."

"Okay," she said, as if telling him it would be alright, not to worry. "Is she active? Does she wear things on her wrists?"

"Um, she's very outdoorsy."

"Does she have pierced ears?"

"Yeah. She does."

She bent down, unlocked and slid open the case from the rear, coming up with a couple velveted trays. She pulled three pairs of diamond studs from the trays and set them in their little velvet sleds on the glass before Angel. He looked at them while she watched. The ones on his left were the smallest, and the ones on the right were the largest. After a lengthy pause, she pushed the ones in the middle forward toward his hand resting on the glass. She brushed the back of his hand with her finger like a feather, saying, "What do you think of these?"

A tingle went up the back of his neck. He looked at them only a moment before she pulled them back. "Or these," she said, pushing forward the ones on his right.

"They're nice," he said. "Are they the nicest ones?"

She picked them up and set them in his left palm to inspect more closely. "They're VVS ones," she said. "They're very fine, but not the finest we have. Do you think they would look good on her ears? These are just under one carat. Are they the right size for her lobes?"

"Um," he said, and held them closer to look.

"Look at my ear," she said, pulling back a handful of her fine pepper hair. "These are just over a carat. How do they look?"

He leaned in. Her perfume reminded him of a class trip he'd been on in seventh grade to a botanical garden, a glass-enclosed building inflated with a nubile mix of floral exhalations, where he'd followed a girl named Cheryl around like a puppy the entire time. "Very nice," he said. "Very. Nice."

She turned and smiled, tilting her head ever so slightly. "These are IFs. They sparkle with a little more clarity. I'll bet your lady does too." She winked at him. "Let me get some of those out for you to look at." She put the pairs back and returned the trays to the case. "I'll be right back," she said, and slid out from the bullpen.

Then, "On second thought, come with me," she said, turning to beckon him with a finger. "I don't usually bring these out front."

Angel did as he was told, following her to the back of the store. A man with a dark bald head, wearing a visor and eyepiece, was working at a bench under a bright light with tools that looked like dental instruments on a gold setting in a vice. He glanced up as the woman led Angel through the doorway. "This gentleman is interested in seeing the IFs, Terrence," she said.

"Oh, wonderful," the man said, smiling a bright-toothed smile a moment before bending back to his work. Angel thought he saw him still smiling as he nudged the metal pick this way and that.

She only took out one pair, telling him those were the ones he wanted. He discovered that he had no grounds on which to disagree with her.

When she'd gift-wrapped them out in the front of the store and it was time for him to give her his card, he found he had to wipe it off on his shirt before handing it over, as he'd been gripping it tightly the whole time. This would be its maiden voyage, and he hoped it wouldn't result in an embarrassing moment. Would Winnie even like these earrings? She'd never worn anything other than copper, silver, leather, and wood as far as he knew.

The woman punched in the numbers and smiled as she watched the terminal. To Angel's relief, the monarch card didn't balk at nearly twenty grand for a pair of diamond earrings.

"Thank you, dear. And don't lose these before you give them to her," the woman said as she handed him the small bag. "Come see me again. Won't you?"

He returned to their new home in Santa Fe later than he'd intended after stopping by the boutique grocer, feeling a combination of excitement and trepidation. Winnie was in the shower in the bedroom wing, her workout clothes strewn on the bedroom floor. Angel put the cake in the refrigerator, unwrapped the fish and put it in a baking pan, then fingered the iPad in its stand next to the stove, looking for a recipe. He tapped the WiFi symbol reflexively to make sure it was on Free Air Net—needless, since that was the only available network. He oiled and salted the asparagus in a roasting pan, then set the wrapped box on the table in the center, realizing he'd forgotten to get a card to go with it. *Oh well,* he thought.

He felt his nerves throughout dinner, not saying much but listening to Winnie talk about people at the clinic and some stories she'd read in the news. "I hope you like the cake," he said at last, after they'd each had a piece.

She smiled and replied, "I love the cake, baby cakes."

Finally he slid the tiny package out from behind the cake platter and said, "Might as well open your present."

The box was wrapped in silver foil with pearl ribbon. Angel noted that it was wider and flatter than it needed to be, probably so that it wouldn't be mistaken for a ring box. *Those people really know their business,* he thought.

Winnie saw that it was professionally wrapped and felt a slight twinge, like she'd felt when Angel had sprung the BMW on her. He'd never given her a present that he hadn't clumsily wrapped himself, with some story always attached to it. She smiled at him and picked up the box, turning it over in her hands. He waited while she gently pushed the ribbons off the corners and worked her fingers under the tape, like she dare not rip or mar the paper in any way. Finally she slid the white box out from the paper and set it on the table. The tiny box lid was embossed in gold letters with the name of the jeweler. She pulled the lid off, set it aside, and gaped.

"Angel! Oh my god!" She pulled in her breath.

"Do you like them?" he asked, looking from her to the diamonds, which appeared bigger in the box than he remembered them in the store, then back at her.

A docudrama of thoughts ran through Winnie's mind as she took in the sight of them. Collapsing finally into a sort of panic, she said, "They're, beautiful. Wow. Angel. Angel."

They both relaxed a bit. Tears filled her eyes and caught

the light. Angel thought they must be tears of joy. "Can you put them in?" he asked.

She looked at them sparkling in the box, then slowly reached up and undid the tiny copper beads in her ears. The diamonds felt heavy and pulled on her skin.

"Whoa, nice babe!" Angel said. He got up from the table. She got up too and went in for a hug. "Happy birthday," he said.

"Thank you, Angel," she said. The tears pooled in her eyes, and she wondered what had happened to him, who he was now, how they ended up in a multimillion dollar house in a posh neighborhood unlike anything she'd ever pictured for herself. She wondered if they would be alright. Where had the man gone with whom she'd spent the last four years?

13

A cold air mass the size of two Canadian provinces had slipped south overnight into a trough through the Dakotas, swirling counter-clockwise with its center over Nebraska. Birch could hear the muffled cracking of the wall studs and floor joists as he walked up the basement steps with a can of tomato soup. He could feel the pressure from the wind on the front of the house, and went to look out the front window. He knew this wasn't the season for tornadoes, but every time the wind kicked up over the plain he thought about the possibility. *I would like to see one,* he thought.

Dry leaves flew across the un-mowed dying grass, collecting in agitated clumps at the bases of the trees and around the shrubs lined up in front of the little house's foundation. Birch imagined himself outside with a yard rake clearing away the leaves. He imagined that it would be satisfying, but then thought, *It's not like I'm really about to go wander around outside in the daylight.* Instead he went into the kitchen, poured the soup into a pot and set it on the stove.

Late morning sun spilled through the windows, warming the tabletop and his favorite chair. He occupied the warmth with his chair pushed back, watching the wind brush down the grass through the side window while the pot ticked on the stove. Soon a shadow rolled across the yard, and then another one. He watched the sky turn from mottled blue to solid gray as the front arrived over the region. Immediately his spot in the kitchen chilled. Now the heat from under the soup pot, dim as it was from that distance, became the noticeable source of warmth. He went to get a blanket from the couch in the living room and came back to watch the wind switch directions outside.

Snowflakes began to mix into the air, flying around in wild trains among the tree branches much like the leaves were doing along the ground.

The sound of bubbling from the stove plus the aroma of tomatoes, olive oil, and garlic told him that the soup was ready. He switched off the stove and spooned the soup into his mouth direct from the pot, holding it close by the handle to let some added warmth rise to his face.

Outside the snow was beginning to fill in around the grass stems and cover the ground. Birch thought about the propane tank and wondered how fast it would run down if he turned up the thermostat a few degrees. He'd left it where he'd found it, at fifty-five degrees, wanting to broadcast his presence as little as possible, but were he to remain here during the coming cold, something would have to change.

His next spoonful of hot soup accidentally washed over his sore molar, which he had been unconsciously protecting ever since he'd hurt it during his episode out in the hills. The heat found the nerve, jabbing him hard like a railroad spike in his jaw. He flinched and almost dropped the soup pot into his lap. The tooth had clearly gotten worse. He stabled the pot and set it back on the stove, then sat wrapped in the blanket until the pain subsided enough to finish his breakfast, more carefully this time.

He liked his spot in the kitchen, but he realized that certain practicalities were inevitable. Like, he'd need the work of a dentist before long, and for that he'd need some money. The peacefulness from remaining hidden away like this was intoxicating. His days had the quality of healing, the internal wounds from the snakes sealing up as they slept. The days also had the flavor of escape, both from the threat of violence coming from Robin and from unasked and unanswered questions about what he'd done with his life so far, why he should even exist in the first place. He was loath to give it up, but he couldn't stay here forever, certainly not undetected. Now he looked outside at the disappearing grass tops and realized that anywhere he stepped he'd leave footprints.

He reached to the counter and grabbed his phone. Was there a job he could do around here? Obviously under a false name. How would he deal with the paperwork? Was there even a dentist in this town? He recalled that the sales brochure for the house had said something about inquiring at a dental office, so there must be one somewhere nearby.

He opened the browser and searched for "dentist in Still Point Nebraska." The wheel spun, but nothing else happened. Finally the browser timed out and said he had no internet connection. He frowned at the WiFi fan that indicated a full signal. Had the cable company shut off service? He dropped the blanket on the chair back and went down to the basement to check on the modem and router. The router showed all green, but the modem blinked orange. He power cycled the modem, watching the LEDs blink as it tried to communicate with the ISP. He tried a few more times with a growing dread that the connection had been cut off. After a couple further failed attempts he went back upstairs, hoping it was a temporary problem at the ISP that would resolve itself. He wrapped the blanket around himself and wandered the house, periodically marveling at his frayed state of mind from having no internet connection when he was otherwise content to hide away from the world.

He decided he needed to find some traction somewhere, so that his days didn't drift by leaving nothing to mark their passing. He didn't feel ready to encounter people, but thought maybe he'd invent an identity on one of the freelance platforms and make some money doing programming gigs once the internet connection came back on. Except, all he had to work with was his phone. Somehow he'd have to procure a laptop if he really wanted to be productive. But was that actually true, or just an assumption he'd never thought to challenge? He picked up the phone and gestured through his apps. Thumb-typing on that tiny keyboard would be a royal pain, but theoretically at least he could manage some programming jobs with just the browser, his text editor and command line tool. He thought about it as he stood at the sink rinsing out the soup pot, watching snow accumulate in the back yard. *Wouldn't it be cool,* he thought, *if I could pencil out code in some format, then use the phone's camera to scan it? Or maybe store the snippets in libraries and use symbols penciled on paper to represent them?* Then maybe he could use the camera to assemble code from the libraries without having to thumb-type it all. Or, what if he could create a better virtual keyboard than the tiny thing built in? Really, all he needed was a nice Bluetooth keyboard to make the ergonomics of working on the device palatable. But short of that, maybe he could create a virtual one using the camera.

He wandered about, wrapped in the blanket again, thinking of how he might approach this. At one point he stopped by the thermostat and stared at it for a long pause. An idea came to him about how Bluetooth keyboards sent their commands, and he smiled and reached to turn the thermostat up to fifty-seven. Why not reward himself with a couple of degrees?

He collected a few metal coat hangers from the hall closet, then went down to the basement for pliers and a cutter. He went back to a sewing kit he'd seen upstairs in the second bedroom to retrieve some strong black thread.

Back at the kitchen table, he spent the afternoon cutting, shaping, and twisting the coat hangers into a rack on four splayed legs. He wrapped the thread and wove it tightly across a rectangular frame so that he could suspend his phone twelve inches above the tabletop with the camera pointing down, the screen mostly flat in landscape orientation but inclined toward him when he sat in the chair. He set the phone in its perch and opened the camera app. He watched the screen as he put his hands on the table below the rack and moved his fingers back and forth, up and down to see where they reached the margins of the camera frame. *This could work.* He picked the phone up from its cradle and began searching through his libraries of uncompiled OS files, looking for keyboard controllers.

He periodically opened a browser to see if the internet connection had come back on, but it had not.

He found scripts that translated touch commands into keystrokes, as well as keystrokes sent via Bluetooth, and began researching through the code. When the light on the timer in the living room popped on, he moved to the wingback chair to continue mentally stepping through the code. When his eyelids became heavy and continually drooped, he dragged himself upstairs to bed, still thinking about how his virtual keyboard would work and feeling actually excited and positive for the first time in weeks. It felt good to have a known problem occupy his mind, and the fatigue he felt was like that after a good workout or trek through the wilderness.

His eyes popped open in the pitch black with code flowing through his mind. He couldn't tell how long he'd been asleep, but it was clear that he was awake now and would not be drifting off again. He got up, swung a robe around himself and padded down the carpeted stairs to the kitchen. His phone, charging on the counter, said it was six in the morning. He couldn't see the hills in the east through the darkness, and the stars hid above a thick layer of snow clouds. The yard was a ghostly field.

He put on a kettle for coffee, unplugged his phone from the charger and sat in his blanket, his thumbs stubbing out a new keyboard controller.

By the time he was through his second cup, a sliver of dawn managing to knife its way between the clouds and distant hills, he had an app running that would watch with the camera while he moved his left pinky forward and back on the tabletop, typing an "a" into a text file each time his fingertip touched a sector of an invisible grid under his coat hanger rack. He watched the screen with great delight as he wiggled his finger and a trail of aaaaaaaaaaaaaaaaaa grew from left to right.

He forgot about breakfast or lunch as he spent the rest of the day mapping keys and testing with his fingers under the rack. Through another night and another clouded dawn he coded, snowflakes skidding into their siblings on the ground, during which he again nearly forgot to eat anything, eventually opening a can of string beans and another of peeled pear halves, eating them straight from the cans. He found he could use the rudimentary virtual keyboard to continue building and refining itself at a greater pace. He also felt the muscle memory forming in his hands and fingers as they iterated through their positions, ever more rapidly, in the imaginary grid on the tabletop.

The luxury of having no schedule, no deadlines, and no one observing, cheering along, or pushing along his work felt more nourishing than any morsels he could find down the basement steps.

At random moments, when the feeling of numbness in his feet or stiffness in his lower back managed to filter past his fascination with his evolving app, Birch rose from his chair and paced around the kitchen and into the living room, swinging his arms and stopping for deep knee bends and lunges to wake his limbs back up. He noted with amusement the different light levels displayed through the front window each time he made a circuit, sometimes in the light of day, bright with snow outside, then the blue gray of dusk or the dark of night, the table lamp reflecting back from the glass. He omitted the dining room from his circuits, for no other reason than his body didn't yearn to navigate around the table and chairs, and he let the grandfather clock run out of spring and drift to a stop.

He didn't count the days, but made lengthy stops on the couch under a blanket where he'd drift off for some hours, then wake and continue. Some nights he wandered upstairs to bathe and sleep in the bed, then rose and carried on, eating like a bird, all the while allowing the app to occupy his mind.

He left the phone, plugged in by an extension cord, resting on its rack, camera pointing down to the tabletop, the keyboard app running along with his text editor and file system navigator. He would walk into the kitchen, either take his seat or bend toward the table, slide his hands under the rack into the camera frame and get to work.

He discovered that he could capture gestures, like a trackpad, as well as keystrokes, and found himself reaching a hand up to tap the phone screen less often, then not at all. He realized that the imaginary grid below the camera lens was not two dimensional, instead containing three dimensions. The number of characters and gestures he was able to map multiplied.

Returning from one of his exercise circuits, he noticed the pair of 3D movie glasses gathering dust against the backsplash of the counter. He reached over and picked them up, wondering if he could figure out how to make the phone's display enter a 3D mode, perhaps giving him more visual real estate to work with. He'd need to do some research to explore that possibility, and recalled that he hadn't tested the internet connection in days, spending all his attention getting this keyboard into shape.

He set the glasses down on the table and slid his hands under the rack. He opened the web browser, entered search terms with a sense of hope and watched the wheel spin, knowing right away the connection wasn't back. He went downstairs to see the cable modem still blinking solid orange, connection error. He cycled the power multiple times, both on the modem and the router, without a different result, then stood there with his hand gripping his chin before finally switching off both units. He stepped back and looked at their dead LEDs, realizing he'd have to think of a solution to this.

He went back up to the kitchen, feeling weight in his

legs as he pulled them up the basement stairs, but then noticed the WiFi fan on his phone flapping next to the 'no service' indicator where his cellular carrier bars would normally be. He would have expected it to only show a blank fan with the dreaded exclamation mark, since he had just powered off the router. He watched it a moment as it went solid and then sat unchanging, as if taunting him. *What?* He sat down and slid his hands under the rack. He popped open the settings and opened WiFi. Agnes' network was still on the list, grayed out as it should be, but there was a new network listed, which his phone had found and connected to. Something called Free Air Net. *Strong connection too, full fan.*

He went back to his browser and tried a search. *Bam! Quick!* He was suspicious though. No password required? Was this the house across the street? This couldn't be one of those stinger units the FBI used, could it? Maybe he should launch his VPN app and mask his presence, to the extent that would help. He launched his VPN, chose an IP address in Toronto, then went back to his browser to search for Free Air Net. Maybe the village here had some initiative going and was trying to give its residents a more affordable connection to the wider world. Maybe cable in this town was sort of an elite thing. He hadn't really considered that before.

Quite a few results came up with that search term. People were talking about Free Air Net all over the place. Birch scrolled through the results, spot-checking posts in forums, news sites, blogs, and saw that Free Air Net was a topic of speculation and debate all over the country. Claims were made that the government was behind it, that it was the philanthropic project of the Gates Foundation, that a consortium had micro-financed it, that it was the Chinese. Some said they had proof that it was G5 transmitters attached to streetlights and rural power poles, broadcasting the WiFi spectrum.

Then there were the inevitable flame wars in the comments where people argued over whether the new network was G5, as in fifth generation mobile, or 5Ghz WiFi, and whether it made a difference which network icon appeared on your phone or computer. Naturally, flame throwers on both sides of the argument were simultaneously "confirmed experts" or "raving idiots," depending on which comment you read. Others claimed inside knowledge that Anonymous had hacked into the military satellite network and opened it to the public in Robin Hood fashion. Of course there were theories that it was a secret project of Apple, or Facebook, or Google, or that they were in collusion over it. A group calling themselves the FANboyz, using the ubiquitous fan icon for WiFi as their logo, claimed responsibility for the network and offered T-shirts proclaiming FANboyz = Free Air Net, with slogans such as "You're welcome!" and "Finally!" Another group with ties to a cult based in the Tetons also claimed responsibility, asserting they had spontaneously generated the network through their group meditation practices, that it was ordained by whomever their Bhagwan was, and that as long as a certain percentage of their members were sitting in meditation the network would continue to exist. As such, they were generously taking shifts around the clock, predicting that they would propagate the network throughout the universe. They even offered sciencey mathy-looking formulas, which were of course immediately flamed in the comments by holders of this or that degree. Birch read their formulas and explanations, laughing out loud at the toddler-level circular logic (though he felt the flames in the comments were expressed with unnecessary viciousness), and realized that laugh was the first audible sound he'd made with his voice in probably a few weeks. The thought of a mentally derived network did put him in mind, however, of the notebook pages he'd taken from the Wolf in that park back in California, causing him to ponder the possibility.

What became clear to Birch was that, while this network was a resource he could use, it would be prudent to use it with care. He wanted to think about it more. He disconnected his phone from it and got up to pace around the house, looking out the windows at the snow. He stopped by the front living room window and grabbed a bunch of the curtain absently in his left hand as he leaned toward the glass. He let his breath spread a small patch of fog on the window as idle thoughts of networks and consciousness floated in his mind. The snow in the front yard lay white and smooth, having accumulated enough in the past few days to cover the tops of the grass. Clouds hung low in the distant sky past the house across the street. The limbs of the oaks across the street and the few maples in his yard were drawn in gray ink as they branched into finer veins, feathering their way into the pale air.

Birch started when he noticed a trail of footprints in the snow at the far left edge of the yard. He took a step back behind the curtain, but peered around to inspect the trail. He noticed prints approaching the front stoop and walking along the front of the house below his view. The prints didn't appear to come up the steps, but Birch flushed with alarm as he realized that someone could easily have come in to the smell of chicken noodle soup bubbling on the stove. He looked around behind him to confirm that he was not in view of any other windows. Anyone looking through the kitchen door or the side window would see his setup on the table and some rinsed pots drying on the counter next to the sink. Maybe this was it.

He stood there looking through the disappearing fog patch he'd breathed onto the window and wondered at his own lack of care. Was it apathy? Arrogance? Or did he want someone to find him?

A movement caught his eye, and he turned to see someone retracing the steps in the snow at yard's edge. It was the girl with the long black hair. She had gone to check the propane tank. Her hands were bare and relaxed past the sleeves of her weathered white wool coat, its fabric marked with thick patterns of yellow and red horizontal stripes. She had holes in the knees of her jeans and wore tan work boots, which she lifted and set back into her steps going in the opposite direction as she watched the ground in front of her. She reached the edge of the yard and stepped into the street, raising her eyes to the house across the way before turning back to look at Agnes Willow's house, wearing a plain expression as if simply acknowledging their existence. Birch pulled farther back behind the curtain, watched her turn toward the village and walk off in no particular hurry. He kept his eyes fixed on the back of her coat, something like a Hudson's Bay blanket, until he could not see her anymore, then went to turn the thermostat back down below where it had been before.

His tooth was hurting again. He held his hand to the side of his face and walked into the kitchen, looking through the windows for footprints around the back yard. He didn't see any, could just barely make out the tip of the propane tank if he pressed his cheek against the glass in the door. The cold felt good on his tooth at first. He thought he could see her footprints around the base of the tank, but wasn't sure at this distance. He took his cheek away when the cold penetrated enough to make his tooth throb worse.

He lasted a few more days, making some progress on the 3D display mode for his phone, even putting up a fresh profile on a freelance site where he began to look at potential gigs. His tooth hurt too much now to tolerate hot soup, so he ate it barely warm, which was not so good, and skipped more meals than usual. Finally, when he went an entire night trying to sleep with no success and had to drink his coffee tepid like his soup the next morning, he opened a browser and found the address of the nearest dentist's office, which happened to be just off the main street in the village.

There was the question of how he would pay for it, of course. He had his Slang card on the night table in the bedroom upstairs. It would be simple enough to create a new Slang identity, just as he'd done for the freelance site, and reprogram the chip on the card with the NFC connection to his phone. The remaining problem was how to get funds into his Slang account. He'd also need to create a new PayPal account to route the money through. It would only require a few minutes to get that set, but how quickly could he win a bid for a job, complete it and get paid? He cupped his jaw with his hand, thinking it unlikely he'd be able to concentrate well enough through this pain to complete a programming job anyway. The blaring ache helped him determine that he could delay no longer. He would have to go to the dentist now and promise to pay later. He hoped that would work.

It was a Tuesday morning, and his mapping program said the dentist's office was open and welcomed walk-ins. Birch went upstairs and traded his robe for his clean clothes. He put his boots and jacket on back downstairs, then went out through the kitchen door into the back yard. The air was bracing and fresh-tasting. He turned to see his motorcycle leaning against the house where he'd left it, now covered in snow. He decided to walk straight from the rear landing under the willow tree to the back edge of the yard so his footprints would be harder to spot from the street. He followed the edge of the yard to the propane tank, then picked up the girl's footprints from a few days before and followed them out to the street.

At the street, he flipped his jacket collar up and stuffed his freezing hands into his jacket pockets, glanced up at the neighbor's house, and walked toward the village. There were no tire tracks in the crusted snow blanketing the street, only the girl's boot prints. He followed them around the bend, past a cross street, then along a street lined with tall bare oaks and edged by a narrow band of snow-covered grass, which gave way to a sidewalk that looked like it was poured sometime between the world wars. Birch noticed tracks along the sidewalk, stitching their way up to the steps and porches of small houses, later spotting a mailman wearing his weathered gray uniform, padded cap, and carrying his letter bag over his shoulder. The man ponderously stepped up to brass mailboxes and lifted their lids, slipping in an envelope or two, then let the lids clap down with a metallic crack that ricocheted through the cold air.

Birch turned right at a stop sign, then left a few blocks later, straight onto the main street of the village. He walked along the sidewalk, along a row of shopfront windows past the hardware store, under a cafe's faded brown awning, past an empty store that looked like it used to sell furniture but hadn't in a long time, to the corner of the block and down the side street to the left. He consulted the map on his phone, noting that he was still connected to Free Air Net and getting a full fan, and wondered if perhaps the girl had gone to the dentist as well. He came upon the door in a dark brick two-story building with the help of his mapping program, noting the small black metal sign that read "Carver Tunnlin, DDS" bolted to the right of the white door atop a short stack of similar signs. It sat just above one that said Tunnlin Real Estate, followed by one for an attorney named Jack Clasp, followed by a couple darker areas of the brick with holes where signs used to be.

Birch looked around and considered not going in, but the throb in his jaw echoed every heartbeat, filling his moment of contemplation so thoroughly that he didn't have the bandwidth left to think of alternatives. He squeezed his thumb down on the door handle and pushed it in to the groan of old hinges and tired floorboards. He kicked the snow from his boots in the small entry, feeling the heat from a steam register next to him, dust-covered and thickly painted with generations of the same yellowed cream. He walked up two steps into a dim wooden hallway, scanning the walls for any indication of the dentist's office. The place smelled of wax, dust, and old paper, walls emanating a subtle murmur as if the timbers, the plaster, and the wood moldings had absorbed generations of greetings and idle chatter—not to mention the occasional momentous pronouncement—and were now quietly releasing them back into the air. He came upon a cork bulletin board stuck with 4×6 photo prints of houses and barns, each with a small tag below indicating an address and a price, all of which looked laughably low to Birch. He started when he saw his little white house in the grid, but then thought there was no reason he should be surprised. He shook his head, took note of the dentist's name on the stained brown door, and squeezed the latch to go in.

First he noticed the girl's colorful wool jacket hanging on a coat stand behind the desk, then he saw her looking up at him, a pencil in her hand and a manila file folder open on a blotter before her. She regarded him with brown eyes and a neutral expression. At first he could not speak. She put her pencil down, tilted her head and tucked some of her long straight raven hair behind one ear. "Paul?" Her voice was soft and low, unhurried.

He put his hand up to his jaw and cradled it, feeling the warmth and the throb. "No, I'm Birch," he said.

She smiled slightly, and frowned at the same time. "What's up?"

"I have a sore tooth," he finally said, "pretty bad now. Is the dentist here?" It did not appear that anyone else was present in the office. Her desk sat along a wall in the small waiting room. There was one window looking out to an alley. Three wooden chairs waited against one wall. The door to the examination room was to the right of the desk, and stood open. Birch could see the old blue vinyl dentist's chair through the opening even though the lights were off.

"Let's take a look," she said, rising from her chair. "Give me your coat." She wore jeans and a blue flannel shirt, untucked and unbuttoned over a T-shirt advertising a pow wow that had taken place in Niobrara some years past. She extended her arm with her hand upturned, waiting for his jacket.

Birch unzipped his jacket, slipped out of it and handed it her. She hung it on the coat tree and led him into the office, flipping on the lights. She moved slowly and easily, indicating for him to sit in the chair, and rolled a stool up next to it for herself.

"Are you the dentist?" Birch asked as he took the chair.

She moved a lever and tilted him back, pulled down a donut-shaped light on an articulated arm and snapped it on, positioning it over his face. "Hygienist," she said. "Comfortable?" She rolled away, and when she rolled back she had on a paper mask and poly gloves, hands holding a small dental mirror and scaling pick.

"Do I need to fill out any paperwork?" he asked.

"Yes, but that can wait. Open," she said through the paper. He complied, and her latex-gloved fingers lightly touched his lips as she looked in. She reached across him and held down a switch on the ancient-looking console from which the light's arm originated. Birch heard the sound of water filling a cup and swirling into the basin. "Rinse and spit," she said. He leaned up from the neck rest and did as he was told. The cold water jarred his sore tooth, causing him to pinch his eyes shut as he lay back down. When he opened them he couldn't tell if she was smiling a little behind the mask. "Now touch your hurt tooth on the outside," she said. He tapped his finger on his jaw near the locus of the pain. "Mmm hmm, open again," she said, and leaned in close over him.

Her eyes were brown from across the room, but this close, he could see her irises were flecked with dark brown, light brown, golden mica, even sage and purple, and sparkling silver like the edges of rain clouds mixed with sunshine. Her black pupils flitted from tooth to tooth like a chickadee as the steel point of the scaling pick lit so finely, so gently, with barely a tingle, on the rocky tops of his molars, sending quiet seismic tremors down through them into his jaw, tiny mirror following to tap here and there. The warmth and smell of the breath from her nose and around the margins of her mask calmed him, something like a grassy breeze and peppery, minty herbs baked in the sunshine of early fall.

Something in his DNA had seen those eyes before. He felt it inside his chest and gut gently, without fully noticing. Those brown and silver eyes stayed on his teeth, focusing on one, then the next. Each tooth tingled, then his whole head and down through his spine. She was in no hurry. Her paper mask crinkled. He could hear it as well as see it. The silver in her eyes twinkled as her voice came soft and slowly, as if strolling across a plain, "You have nice teeth," followed by a shy laugh that crinkled the paper more.

He knew what the feeling was instantly, even though he'd never felt it before, noting it did feel something like falling. He closed his eyes and opened them, and the silver flecks in the brown earth were still there, still placid. He let his eyes drift to her periwinkle mask, trying to see through the tiny pores in the paper to her lips. His body relaxed like it had not done in months, yet he knew this was one of those moments in life when something highly significant is happening and you should pay attention. The moment retrieved for him a memory of when he was six and had his first swimming lesson in the pool at the Davis YMCA. He'd thought swimming would be easy and leapt into the pool before the instructors told any of the kids to do so, plunging into the water straight to the bottom. He remembered opening his eyes, realizing that he was underwater and didn't know what to do. His eyes had stung, but he didn't dare close them, fearful of missing some crucial information needed to save his life. He felt the same here, thinking that this had never happened to him before and may never again. He felt elation and terror, doing his best to hide both.

The steel point grazed the edge of one molar and tapped around it. He did his best not to flinch. A part of him didn't want her to find the tooth. He didn't relish the pain, but more so, he wanted to stay in the warmth of her breath and eyes. "Here's our little friend," she said. "You've been grinding at night. Pretty good crack there." She rested the steel tip on the tooth and gave it the faintest shove. His eyebrows rose reflexively, trying to flee the pain. "Yup," she said. "Let's see what else we have in here." She moved along to the next tooth, tickling with the pick, and his body relaxed again.

"You're the guy staying at Willow's," she said, sort of like a question but not really. Instantly fear replaced his relaxed wonder, and he felt his face go red. "I'll take that as a yes," she said. Her eyes flicked onto his, then returned to his teeth. He felt panic rising, closed his eyes to hide behind the lids and let out a long exhale, hoping his breath smelled decent.

"We all thought you were her grandson, Paul. You're not though eh?"

A strange sadness welled up from somewhere below. He'd fallen in love with her in only the space of a few teeth, and in only a few teeth more he'd ruined it, betrayed her, revealed himself a criminal vagrant. His one chance at real love. There he lay beneath her, she bent over him with a steel point. He might as well give it up. He couldn't lie to her. He opened his eyes. "Uh uh," he said. She slid her eyes over his again, then continued on her journey around his mouth. *Wait a minute,* he thought. *I can't give up this easy. This is real.* Something deep inside him couldn't bear to forsake his love for her. It felt like giving up this love was giving up all love, not just his but hers too, and everyone's. He felt turning away from this love would be like holding a match to tinder that would burn the entire forest of love, turn every forest on Earth to ash. He felt deflated and in desperate need of air. He had no answer.

She took the pick from his mouth and wiped it on the paper blotter. "I don't have any money with me today," he said.

She inspected the row of instruments lying on the blotter, then looked over at him.

"I had a lot of money, in fact I was really quite well off, but someone stole it from me. In fact I'm pretty sure someone from the government seized it from me illegally," Birch said.

"Government seized your property illegally? You're not the first that's happened to," she said evenly.

"I mean, I'm going to pay. I'm good for it, or will be," he said.

She chose a new pick from the blotter, regarded him another moment, and went back to work in his mouth. "Sure," she said. "Let's get you cleaned up." She began lightly scraping, and the tingle blinked on in the back of his head and along his neck. He lay hypnotized, again swimming in her eyes. "If you're not Paul," she began, "then what are you doing at Willow's?"

He had no answer ready, though he'd imagined being discovered and confronted many times. "Ha huh HAH," he said. She pulled the pick and mirror from his mouth. "Hiding out, trying not to get killed," he said. She frowned at him and tilted her head, thinking maybe this was in fact Paul, just on some odd mental journey. He hadn't been around here for years, since Catherine had moved to New York. Last time she saw him, they were kids.

"I think there's a hit out on me," he added. "My old boss, mad because I left."

"That's some boss," she said. "Where do you come from?"

"Palo Alto. In California."

"Not New York huh? Long way to run. How'd you land in Still Point?"

"Not sure, exactly," he said, "but I basically ran out of gas here."

She raised her eyebrows briefly, and her mask crinkled. She then leaned back in with a shrug to continue cleaning. "You look like Paul would look now," she said to his teeth. Her soft voice melted him into a kind of trance again. "I told Carver you were keeping the place clean and dusted, so he doesn't care. The electric bill didn't go up, and no one's been asking to see it anyway. Agnes' daughter, Paul's mom, never returns our calls. She's forgotten the place is on the market, I guess. Of course no one's really buying much around here lately."

"Hish har her," Birch said. She leaned back again and looked at him. "Is Carver your husband?" he asked.

She looked at him and chuckled behind the mask. "No, he's the dentist. And real estate agent. So. My boss." She leaned back in. "He hasn't put a hit out on me yet that I know of," she laughed softly. Birch breathed easier as she continued her work.

"You might need a crown on that tooth," she said. "I'll numb it today, and we can see if it calms down. But, you'll have to stop chomping on it. Carver can take a look if it doesn't get better. A crown's going to cost you." She still had not reconciled the reality that this stranger was not Agnes Willow's grandson. "You sure you're not Paul? Just back here trying to escape the world or something?"

He nodded slightly, feeling the tingle in his head like it was a corona surrounding his skull. "Arr waa hoo hee hor hiii," his mouth said, while his mind said, *I want to see your lips.*

She paused. "What?" she asked.

"Nothing," he said meekly, feeling a wave of embarrassment and relief that he hadn't actually formed the words. She shrugged and leaned back in to work.

He felt his body in a warm suspension and hoped he wasn't beginning to perspire. Stretching his mouth, he said, "I waa hoo ho ow iiii."

She pulled away again and gave a quiet laugh. "Now what?"

He looked into her eyes and felt his face flush once again. He hoped it wasn't too noticeable. "I want to go out with you," he said quietly. "Double please."

She pulled her mask down slowly with one finger, and he saw her lips. "Um?" she said. Her eyes looked around the room, then settled back on Birch's face. She continued to look for signs of the boy she'd known in elementary school. She said, "That's a first. But. Okay, we can. You seem harmless enough. Do you know my name?"

He shook his head.

"Guess," she said, thinking she'd try to catch him up and reveal that he was Agnes' grandson.

"No idea," he said.

"Okay.

It's Aspen."

14

"How do we actually control where they fly?" Stuart asked, standing next to Angel in the programming room as they watched over the shoulders of two engineers.

"We don't control exactly where they fly," Angel replied. "We set up dog fences, geofences basically, and then we add service points as GPS locations into the rules, meaning that the network has to cover those points within a radius with one unit or another, depending on conditions. So, as we're expanding east we just push the boundaries of the dog fence and add in more points. See? Linda is doing that right now. The number airborne has to work it out, of course. We can't expand faster than we can cover with the number aloft."

Stuart rocked forward in his Ferragamos to watch the engineer pull a vertical red boundary line across Ohio to Pennsylvania and just past Pittsburgh. She grabbed the line farther down and repositioned it over West Virginia, Virginia, the Carolinas, and Georgia. She then started checking against a list of coordinates, clicking and dragging red dots into place within the new territory.

"Watch, they start filling in right away, though they have quite a distance to fly to reach the new service spots. There, and you can see that we need more birds in the air before we're ready for Florida and up and down the coast," Angel said. He looked at Stuart.

"Well, we're getting there," Stuart said. He motioned for Angel to follow him over to the wall. "It's going good in the middle states," he said in a low voice. "It's a bloodbath of mergers and acquisitions and bankruptcies right now, and people are still trying to figure out what the hell is going on." Stuart paused to test Angel with a conspiratorial smile. Angel smiled back. Stuart continued, "It's almost like you can hear this huge sucking sound. Like an economic pump chugging away in the middle of the country, vacuuming up businesses and customers. It's a thing of beauty, all these people jumping on our free offers. Huge influx of hosting business. I hear we even have Amazon concerned, probably be talking with them sometime soon. And, we're talking about pulling the northern boundary up into Canada now. One of the telecoms is talking to our guys. They happen to be one that's buying up ISPs, and they also have a portfolio of relationships up north. It should be an easy entry. Apparently they know how to work with the government, so maybe we can keep our birds from getting shot down."

"Well," Angel said, "we can do that. We just need more birds and access to strong microwaves." It wasn't long ago that Angel would think more about the fact that American taxpayers were funding the development of this enterprise than about what they were doing, but the current pace and challenge no longer left room for such considerations.

"The telecom is helping us with the power side of it," Stuart said.

Days later Dunstan Adams humped up a hillside at dawn in the forest in western North Carolina, a couple miles from the border with Tennessee. Snow was light, just enough to quiet his footfalls in the leaves, which was good, only it left more obvious tracks for the rangers to follow, which was not good.

Slung over Dunstan's left shoulder, held by a rotting canvas strap, was a Marlin 39A, passed down to him from his grandfather and through his father, both now having joined the grubs in the soil. Slung over Dunstan's right shoulder was a doe, maybe just shy of a hundred pounds field dressed, shot through the brain stem with a single .22 caliber bullet. Good eating for the next week or so.

Dunstan's main issues at the moment were that it was not deer season, he had no hunting license, and he was on federal park land. Related to that collection of minor misfortunes was the fact this federal land used to belong to his grandfather, but the government had taken it for the park, failing to communicate with the Adamses properly or compensate them in a satisfactory way. Jeff Adams, Dunstan's grandfather, had felt powerless and disrespected, the anger and frustration that bred passing down through the generations, just like the Adams' guns, for Dunstan to inherit.

Dunstan had other guns leaning in the corners of his cabin, a Marlin 30-30, a bolt action Remington Springfield 30-06, a couple double-barrel twelve gauges, plus a twenty gauge single shot. One wouldn't normally choose the .22 for deer, but the point here was to be as quiet as possible, and if Dunstan could do anything in his life it was put a bullet where he intended it to go. He was pretty sure, too, that the green shirts were well aware of it, suspecting that had something to do with the infrequency of those awkward visits they made to his front porch, asking about deer and such.

He crested the hill and descended twenty yards down the other side to the east before following the ridge a half mile or so to the cutoff, where he would turn downhill toward his hollow. He kept his line below the ridge, because the rising sun would melt off his footprints faster than if he stayed up on top. It was all part of the ritual. They knew where he lived. They knew he took meat from the woods. They just couldn't catch him at it, and being smart about how he did it just made it feel that much easier for him to deny.

When he made it to his yard, he headed straight for the back of his Ford 100. It was fairly banged up and rusted, as those old trucks tended to be, but he'd added a couple new-looking bumper stickers which read "American Bold! American Strong!" That's how Dunstan felt about it. That's not government. That's real Americans, and that's what he was.

He dropped the tailgate and heaved the doe onto the bed, smart enough not to let much blood pool on the ground anywhere. He had dish TV, and saw that law enforcement was getting all science-like. They could find blood or something, analyze it, then claim hard DNA evidence that you took one of their deer. He figured they probably said that regardless of the results, because who could really tell? Just some guys looking at dots under a microscope; how's some stupid judge supposed to know the difference? *Hell, they just take what the old boys tell them and hand down the judgment decided on beforehand.*

Still, you had to be smart about it where you could. Dunstan dressed the doe out in the bed of his pickup, dropping the leavings in pickle buckets, butchered her up, and wrapped his cuts and organs in paper to take inside to the freezer box. He knew the meat was safe inside unless they showed up with a warrant, and luck had been on his side thus far. He walked the pickle buckets well out into the woods and buried the contents deep in what over the years had become his bone yard, then drove the old truck six miles down to the wand wash to clear away the rest of the evidence. It was a shame he couldn't keep the hide and the bones and such, but he buried it all. Felt it was for the best. It was really about the meat and the sweets anyway, and he already had plenty of heads with antlers on the walls in his cabin, some bear heads too, memories of generations past.

Hunger started talking to him when he got back, so he grabbed the mason jar of bear grease from the shelf and scooped some out with his fingers, slopping it into an iron pan set on the wood stove to heat. He picked out the package with the back strap, his favorite, unwrapped it on the counter, relishing like music the distant stormy sound of meat paper unfolding, and sliced the meat into chunks with his skinning knife, setting the paper aside to use again for the next deer. When the pan was hot, he pinched each meat chunk and pushed it into a bag of flour, the paper crinkling around his wrist like gunfire from over the hill, shoved it around and then tossed it into the pan to sizzle. He bothered the hissing chunks with the point of his knife this way and that until he was satisfied, then scraped the pan off the heat onto the wing of the stove, one by one jabbing the chunks with his knife and pulling them off hot with his teeth. What else did a man need for food?

Well, the answer to that was in a bottle lying on its side under the seat of his truck. Back strap and bourbon; this was shaping up to be an okay day. He tossed the knife onto the counter next to the sink, where it slid against the tin backsplash. He pushed out through the door to cross the yard. A hawk or a crow caught his eye, but when he looked up it didn't look like a hawk or a crow anymore. It was a black thing way up, staying pretty still. He stopped in his boots and stared up at it. A bad feeling started to grow in him, irritating all the other bad feelings that were generally resident but dormant. He listened as he stared, thinking maybe he could hear something, a high whine, or a buzz. He searched his memory. The patterns living there took quite a while to assemble into anything that made sense to him, but assemble they did, leading his mind back to something he'd seen on TV. "Son of a fuckin' bitch!" he said to the sky. "Those fuckers are watchin' me with one of them drones!"

There was no question or figuring required. An Adams had but one reasonable response to a situation like this. He took two strides to retrieve the Marlin leaning against the wall on the porch. He took a knee in the yard and sighted straight up toward the thing in the sky. He'd only used one cartridge for the doe, so had fifteen left in the magazine. He sent them all skyward in the space of a few seconds. The last time he'd pulled the trigger and thrown the lever out that fast, he was roughing up the edges of a single hole he'd shot in a playing card at twenty-five yards at the county fair.

He saw the black thing start to dance around as he fired. He stayed with it as it tilted and started to drift westward a bit. Then he saw it hang for a second and then start slipping down, then start falling. *Sons of bitches!* The casings were all on the ground around his boots now. The barrel was hot, and the smell of burned powder filled his nose like an ammonia inhaler. He didn't bother to set the gun back onto the porch, but took off running toward the trees where the thing appeared to be headed. He ran through the yard by the truck and past the outhouse. He slalomed through the oaks, vaulting over deadfalls, went through the bone yard and up a slope, down the other side, up another, down that one, along a creek bed, up a draw. He broke out into a clearing and skirted the edge at full gallop, his eyes darting over the ground and around the trees and scrub like a soldier trying to spot the source of enemy fire. If something was in these woods that wasn't supposed to be, his eyes would catch it.

At the far end of the clearing, about thirty yards into thicker timber, he saw the thing lying in the snow and leaves at the base of a walnut. He stalked up to it, pulling in hard breaths and trying to let his lungs calm down. "Well. What in the fucknation do we have here?" he asked the nearby trees. It was one of those drones alright. He'd taken out all four of the propellers. One half of the blade was completely gone on two of them, and the other two were mangled pretty well down to the nubs. *The bullets from the gun of an Adams done given you a little talking to,* Dunstan thought, *and now you don't have much to say back.* He stood over it a while, thinking the fight was over for now, then picked it up with one hand and started back, scanning the woods and listening for rangers. Overhead, out of sight and earshot, another drone had slipped into the area, trying and failing to offer charge to its fallen comrade.

Stuart bashed through the door into the programming

room, saying, "Control says we lost one, we have one down out east." Angel turned and looked up concerned. Stuart continued, "Did you see that?"

"No," Angel said. "We don't get alarms in here. They only get them in Control."

"Well let's go," Stuart said. He started for the door.

"Well, this was inevitable," Angel said, following.

"Maybe," Stuart answered as they strode toward the elevators, "but we can't let one get into the wrong hands. Not having a self-destruct function was a major oversight."

Angel followed Stuart into the elevator, trying to work out in his mind if he bore any culpability for this. If there had ever been an item in the specs detailing a self-destruct function, of course he would have had the team build it and test it.

They went down one floor. Angel's chip did not have access to this floor, so he could only visit the control room when he went with Stuart. They strode along the hall, around one corner and half the length of another hall, turning in at a door identical to that of the programming room. Inside the room was mostly dark, lit by many screens; the screens were not clustered at desks in groups of four like in the programming room, but stood in two long rows running the length of the room, facing each other. There were no whiteboards on the walls, but one wall had a gigantic screen showing a world map with sparks of light distributed over the United States.

A group of men were standing behind a man seated at one of the screens, and they all looked up as Stuart and Angel entered. "Here they are," one man said. "Got any tricks up your sleeves, boys?" another said. "Hank the Tank is not going to be very happy if someone gets to reverse engineer this thing."

An ugly image of the big man with the cottage cheese face formed in Angel's mind, and a twinge of fear followed it. He'd been in the leadership's good graces of late, and had grown something like complacent, though he never completely forgot how quickly things could turn. Stuart usually seemed on edge, so Angel had trouble discerning when he was truly concerned. "Angel," Stuart said, "can we do anything to get it back?"

Angel frowned and gave him a duh look. "Well, tell me what happened. What do we know?"

They assimilated into the standing group and looked at the screen, or at least Angel looked at the screen. Stuart kept his attention on the rest of the men standing. The sitting man said, "Okay, here's what we've got." Angel leaned in for a closer look while the man continued, "Fan stoppage in rapid succession." He tapped the screen in various locations "Also, we have lat and lon. That's it." He looked up and shrugged.

"Well, is it still connected? Is there any video? We should have the last thirty seconds at least."

"How do I check that?" the man asked.

"May I?" Angel asked.

The guy got up and gave Angel his chair. Angel took the mouse and keyboard, working around the interface. "So. The rotors went out like this. Looks like it was brought down intentionally. Shot down most likely."

A husky voice behind him said, "I thought that wasn't supposed to happen. What was it doing low enough for somebody to shoot at? Did you guys screw up the settings or something?"

Angel started going hot around his neck. "Do you realize how many of these units we have airborne right now?"

"Sure, tell that to Hank. Do you realize how much each one of those things costs?"

"It's not the unit cost we care about," another voice piped in. "It's the liability of losing one into unfriendly hands. That happens, and heads will roll."

"You gotta get that thing back, Oleastro. Get it airborne again. Or maybe you have to fly out there and go find it, Pitt."

This is crazy, Angel thought. *What do these guys expect when you have tens of thousands of drones aloft at once? They're all standing here worried about their jobs, hoping the path of blame leads to someone else.* He was disappointed in himself, however, for not thinking of a self-destruct function. At least the software should erase itself. He would make sure Stuart got that onto the specs right away, and they would prioritize it over existing bugs.

"Okay," Angel said. "It's still on the network and has some charge."

They breathed a collective sigh.

"But the signal is very weak. Something is blocking it."

They tensed up again. "Can we get another bird down closer to it?"

"Well, maybe. But that could put another one in harm's way. The closest one is obviously trying, but the rules won't let it get lower unless we override."

The group stood waiting for Angel.

"Oh, shit," Angel said. He'd opened a small window with a short video clip. "Here's our guy. Rifle. And, carrying it. Snow, woods. Fuck!" He turned away from the screen and looked up at them. "It's inside somewhere. That's why the signal is so weak. It won't be able to charge inside either."

They looked at each other and at Angel. Stuart felt his nerves going.

"So, what the fuck do we do?" someone asked. "Pitt. How are you going to get that thing back?"

Stuart set his jaw and said, "We have no choice. We have to get a recovery team out there now."

"Who do we know back east? We don't have time to fly someone out from here."

"Oleastro. Fix those coordinates and analyze every frame of that video. Let's get good information for whomever Pitt sends out there, like now."

Angel felt sweat beading on his forehead. "Um, that seems like something Control should be doing, not Development."

"I don't care who gets it done. Martin! You do that then.

Get the information for Pitt's guy. Oleastro, you head back up to the programming room and start work on something to prevent any other units from dropping out of the sky. Losing a drone is unacceptable!"

Angel was only too happy to vacate the chair and leave the room. Stuart was on his way out too. "I'll find someone. We've worked with people back east," he was saying, Angel noted, in a slightly higher and thinner voice than usual.

Dunstan sat in his rocker watching the dusk gather outside through the cabin window. He'd finished the bourbon, had eaten through maybe half the doe over the past couple days. Shane Hannibal was on the TV in the background, sitting at his desk shuffling some papers around and saying something like, "We don't know, do we? Did she do it? Maybe she did! I don't see any evidence that she DIDN'T do it. She doesn't look so squeaky clean to me!" Dunstan wasn't really watching anymore. Life was okay for the moment, but soon he'd have to think about getting another bottle and another deer.

Down the valley on the county highway a black Escalade was slowing, getting ready to turn off onto the valley road. The guy in the driver's seat was an ape of a man with a bored expression, wearing a black sweater and black pants. His parents, thirty-eight years before, had given him the name Timothy, but no one called him that now. Now they only called him Tiny, thinking it funny of course.

The man sitting next to him, also looking bored, was large too, with droopy eyes and rough weathered skin. In build he resembled an ex-lineman, maybe a center, with a little gray around his sideburns. His name was Franky. Franky stretched the shoulder seams of a black leather jacket. He held a piece of paper in his meaty paw, a printout, peering at it as he said to Tiny, "Up here like four miles, then it's 'sposed to turn to dirt."

In the back sat a small man with a mop of curly blond hair, blue eyes behind tinted aviator glasses, black gauges in his earlobes, smooth rosy cheeks, and the thin mustache of a twenty-year-old, even though he was just over thirty. He wore a waist length dark mink coat, open over a blue silk shirt. He had his arms spread out, resting on the backs of the seats on either side of him, as he was the only one back there. Over the crew neck of his silk shirt hung a gold chain that looked too thick for the size of his neck. He called himself Apollo Spike, even legally changing his name nine years earlier. He had been born Curtis Dohquizzler in southern California to mild-mannered, middle-class parents. He did his best to leave those years behind, push them from memory, but it was an impossible task.

It was a normal sunny southern California day on the playground in second grade when little Curtis noticed that life seemed to function on something of a dominance hierarchy. It wasn't lost on him that most of the other boys were bigger than him, some significantly so. He saw them push each other around, mess with the girls, tell jokes, laugh, play kickball, show off, slap each other's shoulders, jab each other with insults. He also saw how the pecking order formed, how those at the top got all the girls' attention, most of the other boys following their superiors around trying to please them or impress them in various ways. The ones lower in the pecking order were always struggling with each other to gain rank, and they were the ones who ended up crying and having to go inside early, never the boys at the top.

Curtis didn't amount to much more on the playground than unfortunate fodder for lower ranking boys acting out, trying to prove themselves to the bigger boys. He was tired of being picked on. He wanted to be the one on top. He'd spotted a kid near the monkey bars who was admittedly bigger than him, but chubby and generally thought to be slow, certainly not known for getting into scraps. For some reason that kid was not part of the hierarchy at all. The big kids left him alone, and the girls were all nice to him, every one of them.

Now a few girls were clustered around one ladder of the monkey bars, watching a couple boys hanging from the bars engage in some sort of joust with each other. The slow kid, Neal, was standing by himself, sort of watching too, but not really doing anything in particular. A sour feeling of contempt started building in Curtis for Neal. Curtis felt it growing, didn't really know where it was coming from but didn't care either. He suddenly hated Neal, blaming him for every bad feeling he ever had on the playground.

He started walking toward him, then accelerated to a run. Neal looked up just before Curtis smashed into him. Neal's eyes grew wide with surprise; he flinched and tried to protect himself with his arms, but tumbled to the ground.

Curtis was on him flailing. He didn't really know how to hit, but his hands rained down on Neal's soft flesh wherever they could slip past the slowly waving arms. Curtis was like an animal wrestling the slow boy down, slapping and kicking. Neal started to cry, and Curtis heard girls yelling, but could not tell what they were saying. Then he felt himself lifted off of Neal. He kept his hands and feet flailing at the kid on the ground, but was hauled far out of reach. He heard kids laughing and yelling as he was carried by the waist of his pants away from the monkey bars and over to the hot asphalt, where whoever had lifted him raised him higher and then dropped him.

He hit his face, his hands, knees, everything on the burning pavement. He immediately started bawling. He didn't dare get up, but the pavement was so hot. He lay there, with his palms ripped and burning, and heard what the chorus of girls was yelling: "Curty Curty Birdy Turdy! Curty Curty Birdy Turdy!"

He rolled over and through his tears saw Bobby McIntosh standing over him with his hands on his hips, looking down at him with a blank expression. Bobby was the biggest kid in the second grade. Bobby ran the playground, the lunch room, the classroom, the gym. This was second grade death. But little Curtis would not accept this death. He would not be at the bottom of the barrel any longer. He never wanted to feel this way again as long as he lived. He stopped crying and set his jaw, got up to his feet, and stomped off the playground toward the nurse's office.

Years later, Bobby McIntosh would join a medical practice as a pediatrician in San Francisco, having no recollection of that incident on the playground in second grade which Curtis never ever forgot. Curtis spent his high school years playing violent video games, shooters and slashers, training himself in the practice of ruthlessness and the religion of remorselessness. He traversed the same digital landscapes thousands of times, inspecting each tiny corner with suspicion, looking for any angle or equation that might leave him vulnerable and calculating his response to negate it. He lifted weights, practiced Krav Maga from Youtube videos, got tattoos, and in his mid-twenties opened a business in north New Jersey as an "investigations contractor" who also performed "negotiated related services." He charged very high fees, was generally ruthless and uncompromising in the administration and execution of his entrepreneurial enterprise. The bottom line was simple: wherever a dominance hierarchy existed, Curtis—now calling himself Apollo Spike—had to occupy the top spot.

"Let's get there," he said from the back seat.

Franky glanced over at Tiny, then back to his paper. "Sure boss," Tiny said. A half mile later the pavement ended, the crunch of stone and dirt sounding under the tires. "I better slow up," Tiny said. "The Google picture shows a two-track coming out somewhere to the left around here."

Tiny slowed the Escalade. They turned up the two-track, swung and bounced their way uphill. They rolled past the brown pickup truck and saw the cabin. It was a small log affair, with mortar chinking the logs. The roof was cedar shakes and tar paper, showing patches of moss under a thin layer of melting snow. A stove pipe stuck up from the back part of the roof, and a single window on the side of the cabin toward them shone with a dim light.

Tiny shut off the engine, and they sat a moment watching the window, also looking around the yard into the dusky woods. "He's inside," Apollo said. "You guys go get him restrained, then I'll come in and get the information out of him."

"Guns?" Franky asked.

"If you want," Apollo said. "He's not expecting anyone."

"I mean, like, he probably has guns," Franky said.

"He's not expecting anyone," Apollo repeated, "but he will be if you guys wait long enough in an Escalade sitting in the middle of his yard."

"Right," Tiny said, and looked over at Franky. "We don't wanna tip him off by making too much noise or nuthin'." The two big men quietly opened their doors and stepped out onto the thin snow, leaving the doors open to minimize sound as they walked toward the front porch. They gingerly stepped onto the porch and stood behind the door. Tiny carefully leaned over to peek through a window to the right of the door, seeing a man in a rocking chair facing a television with what looked like a news show on. Tiny straightened up and gave a nod to Franky. They heard a car door slam behind them. They looked at each other and rolled their eyes, and Tiny threw his shoulder into the door, busting it open.

Dunstan heard the crash, thinking the sound might have come from the TV, but it was just his news program, and his news program rarely made noises like that. Then he thought maybe the sound had come from behind him. Perhaps a tree had fallen outside. When he turned he saw two large men with hard-set eyes making straight for him in his own house.

"Hey!" he yelled. "You ain't 'sposed to come in without a warrant! Where's yer warrant?" They didn't say anything, just kept coming. He rose from his chair, but they were already on him. He thought about the guns leaning in all four corners of the cabin. *Dammit! If you come into an Adams cabin uninvited, you're supposed to get shot.* But Dunstan got caught dozing by the damn TV, and these goon rangers had him by the shoulders. He could tell they had him pretty good. In fact, their hands were a lot bigger and stronger than the average ranger's. Maybe they were getting a new breed into the ranks? In any case they stood him up, nearly lifting him off his feet, and held him tight in the center of the room. Then in walked this weird-looking short dude in a fur coat and glasses, all rich-looking, with big holes in his ears, bobbing his head around as if hunting for the angle to best display his curly spikes of bright white hair. *What the hell kind of rangers are they hiring these days?*

The short dude looked up at him with a mean gleam in his eyes, face scribbled over with random, hurried-looking tattoos. "Where is it?" he said.

What a weird question, Dunstan thought. *They must be running a whole new program now.* He screwed up his eyes and looked at the guy. "Where do you think it is? Out in the outhouse."

The little guy drummed his fingers on his mouth and repeated, "Out in the outhouse." Then he nodded his head and took his hand away. "Flashlight," he said. One of the goons holding Dunstan handed him a flashlight, and the little guy spun around and walked out the front door. Dunstan thought of trying to break free and grab one of his guns, but he couldn't decide which one, and these guys still had an iron grip anyway. One of the double-barrels would be best, and yes, they were all loaded. These were Adams guns, leaning in the corners of an Adams house.

The guy in the fur coat came back in looking angrier than when he left. "It's not there," he said.

Dunstan was confused. "Well, part of it is," he said. "I ate 'er and shat 'er out. Whaddaya think of that? You got no evidence, so you got nuthin'. You can just get the hell off of my property!"

Apollo stood looking at him. *What human filth,* he thought. He glanced up at the beam rafters above their heads. "String him up," he said. Tiny and Franky looked at him, then at each other, then back at him. Apollo grew frustrated. "Look, there's a rope," he said. He walked over and picked up a heavy coil of jute from the floor near the stove. "Rope here, rope here, and then ankles, hnya, and wrists like this, hnya, pull him up. I want him off the ground, IN THE AIR."

Dunstan was alarmed. This seemed highly irregular. He tried to struggle, but the goons were too big, too strong. They tied his wrists together tight behind his back. They tied his ankles together tighter. Before he knew it, he was staring at his floorboards and being hoisted up toward the ceiling. His shoulders hurt like a somabitch, and he was bent into a reverse banana, his body not meant to stretch that way, in any case not at his age. They tied him off just above the little guy's head, at about eye level with the goons.

"So," Apollo said, "it's in the outhouse, hmm?" Franky and Tiny stood off to the side. Dunstan was very uncomfortable and very confused. He tried to shift in the air a bit, but that made it worse. The jute rope groaned and cracked over the rafters. Apollo stepped up and stared him in the eye a moment, then smiled. "We'll see," he said. He stepped around to Dunstan's side and noticed the shotgun leaning in the corner.

A slow terror began growing in Dunstan. "What the hell," his voice cracked, "kind of ranger are you anyway?"

Apollo sauntered to the corner and came back carrying the gun and jammed the barrel into up into his ribs.

Dunstan's spine was burning and now his ribs. "What the Jesus?" he cried out, beyond confused.

"How's that feel, Bobby?" Apollo growled.

Tiny looked at Franky. "Why does he always call them Bobby?" he whispered. Franky shook his head.

Dunstan's back felt like it was going to break from the

unnatural bend. "Whatter you, some kind of, of weirdo?" he rasped.

Apollo chuckled low. He pointed the barrel toward Dunstan's crotch and rammed it as hard as he could. Dunstan had never felt such pain in all of his years. He tried to hold back his cry, but it escaped his throat like it was its own animal.

"How's it feel now, Bobby?"

Dunstan was too delirious even to notice that this guy was calling him some other name. He couldn't form the thoughts that would form words. He pushed hard against his anger and the pain. "Hernnnnnnnnnn, nerrrrgggggg," he pushed. He tried bending his back in the other direction, just to get away from this guy, but he didn't have the strength.

"WHERE IS IT BOBBY? WHERE IS IT BOBBY?" Apollo shouted at him.

Dunstan wanted to pass out, go unconscious. He wanted to die. Tiny and Franky were both thinking how they could get better-paying jobs if they went across the river into New York. The market in Jersey wasn't what it used to be. Apollo turned to them and explained clinically, "To maximize the pain, you hit both the nut sack and the pecker."

"We know that, boss. Jesus!" Franky said. They both turned away uncomfortably.

Apollo repositioned the shotgun barrel and threatened to ram Dunstan again. "Are you SURE you don't want to tell me where it is?" he said menacingly. "I'm guessing this gun is loaded."

Dunstan yelled, "I told you. I ate it! I ate-en nearly all of it!"

"That won't DO," Apollo snapped. He rammed Dunstan in the crotch twice in rapid succession, the demonic rage seething from his eyes. Dunstan hollered in agony once more. Anyone who heard that godawful sound echoing through the hollows would swear that an evil spirit had been loosed upon the land. "How does THAT feel, BOBBY?" Apollo growled.

"Weird how you can hear the regional accent in their

scream," Franky said. Tiny covered his ears and turned away further, until his back was to the scene. *I'm too old for this shit,* he was thinking. *I have a daughter in art school, for Christ's sake. I should be making more money than this.* He walked through the nearest door to get out of the main room, stepping into the darkness of a small bedroom. An unmade bed took up most of the space, rough-hewn plank shelves with bunched clothes covering one wall. Sitting on the bed on top of the disheveled bedclothes was a black object about the size of the business end of a small push mower. Tiny pulled the door open wider to let in more light. He picked up the black object and went out.

Apollo was still laser-focused on his task. Franky turned and saw what Tiny had, rolling his eyes up.

"Boss!" Tiny yelled. "HEY BOSS!"

Apollo whipped around. "WHAT!"

"Isn't this what we came here for?"

Apollo stared for a moment, leaning the shotgun against a chair. He looked at the object. "Umm, yyyessss."

"Well I guess you didn't need to bash the guy's nuts then, did you?"

"DON'T question my methods! He COULD have TOLD us it was there!" Apollo glared at them. "Let's get out of here. MOVE."

They walked out with the broken drone. Through the open door came sounds of car doors slamming and an engine starting, followed by the hiss of wheels rolling over the yard and down the drive. Then Dunstan was left only with the sounds of his own breathing and moaning, heartbeat throbbing rhythmically in his ears. He wished it all would just stop. He'd had enough of this government.

The phone rang on Stuart's desk. He picked it up. "Pitt. Yeah, send him through. Hey! What did you find? Really?" Stuart punched the speaker button and put the handset down in the cradle.

"Correct," the scratchy voice was saying. "We located the target and were able to extract the information we needed to recover the unit. It took some doing, but we have the unit in our possession. We're driving it directly to you." Stuart put both hands on his face and let them slide down in relief. He looked across his desk at Angel and another guy sitting in the task chairs. They also sat back in relief.

"So," Stuart said, "that's great news. Thank you. How long before it gets here, do you think? A couple days from where you are? Are you concerned at all about the target having seen the unit? Do you think he may have reverse engineered it?"

"I have two drivers," the voice said. "We expect to be there in approximately nineteen hours, give or take. That's included in our fee. With expenses added of course. We protect the unit until we hand it over to your possession and care. And a firm no. I'm not concerned about the target having reverse engineered the unit or having any future ability to disseminate any related information."

"Of course," Stuart said. He gave Angel and the other guy a grave look and drew his finger across his throat. Angel let his eyes fall to his hands, folded in his lap, and thought about that engineer. Erin, was her name.

15

Birch followed the road east leaving the opposite side of the village, just as she'd told him. He knew how far he'd have to walk because he'd looked at his mapping program, so he gave himself forty minutes to get there. He felt relieved now to be out in the open without worrying so much about being seen. The village apparently knew someone was occupying Agnes Willow's house, apparently had debated as to whether said person was a relative or not, and ultimately didn't care, having other daily concerns to occupy its attention. The thought still clung to him, however, like a rusty fishhook trailing a broken line, that Robin had threatened to put a hit on him, even though it had been months now. Still, no dark SUVs or shady characters sneaking around. Maybe he wasn't hiding from Robin anymore. Maybe it was something else he had been more afraid of, the snakes inside himself.

But now he walked in the sunshine of early afternoon, and he was in love. The light reflected hard white up from the snow and scissored at his squinting eyes. The prairie wind was frigid and constant against his face, pressing like glowing coals. He wished for a hat, a better coat, and gloves, but there was nothing that would work in Agnes' house. He also wished he'd left the plastic motorcycle armor slipped into his riding jeans, as that would offer at least some zones of wind resistance. Yet the walk felt easy. He could stand the cold for now.

A mile out he turned left at the section road and started

north, the freezing wind now pressing against the right side of his face and sneaking around his upturned collar. He kept his hands buried in his jacket pockets, felt the water from his eyes spread over his cheekbones and quickly dry in the wind. He felt the cold from the road seeping up through the rubber soles of his boots.

After ten minutes of walking between snow-covered corduroyed fields he saw the farmhouse and barn a half mile up on the left in a small group of bare trees. His heart beat a little faster, and he felt the warmth collected in his jacket as he approached. The driveway was plowed, as was an arc in front of the mailbox on a post across the road. The house was white, in need of paint, but typical-looking for the area, clearly one that had stood through several generations. Smoke rose from a fieldstone chimney. Behind the house to the west was a large red barn with a couple tractors lurking inside. Two pickups, one older with a plow and one newer, sat between tall knobby oaks which grew in the yard between house and barn. Both trucks had eagle feather stickers in the rear cab windows and dream catchers hanging from the mirrors. One of the oaks held the remnants of a treehouse in its thick upper branches, just a platform with short plank walls and a knotted rope dangling below, long since turned gray and rotted.

Birch turned up the walk to the front porch, stepped up and stamped the snow from his boots. He pulled a hand from his pocket into the cold air to knock on the door. A couple cracked-leather strands of tarnished harness bells wood-screwed to the door jingled slightly with his knocking, then jingled louder as the door pulled open. Aspen regarded him with a quiet smile and pulled the door back to let him in. A large Rottweiler stood at her side and barked once, then pushed up toward Birch.

"Go lie down, Carl," Aspen said. The dog immediately retreated toward the kitchen.

"Hi," Birch said, stepping across the threshold.

"You walked? I could have come to get you," Aspen said.

She wore leather slippers, jeans, and a blue flannel shirt. He felt the warmth of the house like a furnace blast, a warmth like he hadn't felt in months. Inside a wide clay pot sat steaming on top of a wood stove, releasing an herbal scent, and he smelled bread baking, then something like yams and some kind of stew. The sudden density of domestic smells and sensations surrounded him like a warm mist, and it struck him what he had been missing for some time. She took his jacket, and he pulled off his boots, following her in his socks into an open kitchen area.

A man standing at the stove turned to inspect him, then laughed and said, "You told me you thought he was a good-looking man. You didn't tell me he was actually a tomato." The man stood a few inches shorter than Birch and was broad in the shoulders and back. He wore a faded brown John Deere T-shirt, a leather apron over cargo shorts, open-heeled deerskin slippers, and had a long gray braid down his back. He smiled into a large steel pot blackened from the bottom and bubbling on the propane stove, then stuck a wooden spoon in to stir.

"Dad. Be nice. He walked here dressed like he thought it was spring," Aspen said.

"Yes," Birch said, "I'm a little short on wardrobe. I'm Birch. It's nice to meet you."

"Another tree! Maybe that's why my daughter likes you. I'm Wayne Cook. That's why I seem to find myself working in the kitchen trying to feed my grown children all the time, when I'm supposed to be out running the farm."

"He's a complainer," Aspen said in a level voice, "but he is a decent cook, so we let him come indoors now and then as long as he washes."

Wayne threw his head back, like someone had yanked down on his braid, and guffawed at his daughter. "You know I bathe once a month," he said deadpan at the stove, "whether I need it or not." He picked up a large chef's knife and began slicing through onions on a thick cutting board scored and darkened from 150-odd years of daily use. The fresh smell of onion mixed into the air above the other aromas, and Birch felt he might go dizzy from the richness of it. He realized that for the last months he had been smelling mainly salt and preservatives from the contents of soup cans that made up the bulk of his diet.

Wayne turned to him again with a stern expression. "You're not one of those vegans, are you? There's turkey meat in here," he said, gesturing to the pot with his knife. "Locally sourced too, by Aspen's little brother in the woods back of the forty. Shot it with an arrow day before yesterday." Wayne winked at Birch.

"Dad," Aspen said.

"I mean, he looks sort of like one. Am I wrong? Didn't you say he was on the lam from California? Lots of vegans out there, right? I'm just asking."

"Don't pay attention to him," Aspen said. "He doesn't deserve it."

"No sir," Birch said. "I'm an omnivore."

"Sir!" Wayne laughed again. "I haven't heard the word 'sir' in like, forever! Least of all from my kids."

"Come on," Aspen said to Birch, "you can help me set the table."

She led him behind her father at the stove and around a corner that opened to a living area dominated by a long harvest table, with four chairs on each side. One end of the table was covered with mail and short piles of papers in various stages of triage, the other end taken up by four woven grass placemats and some random drinking glasses. Aspen cleared away the glasses to the sink and retrieved one more placemat from a buffet against the wall. She handed Birch five blue china plates and five bowls, yellowed from years of washings in the iron-rich water and dinged here and there around the edges. He set them on the mats. She brought spoons, new glasses, and cloth napkins, noticing Birch counting the settings and doing the math. "We always set a place for Mom," she said, retrieving a large clay pitcher from the buffet shelf and handing it to him. "Here, you can fill the water."

He took the pitcher around the corner to the kitchen, going to the sink. "Wow, that smells good," Birch said to Wayne.

"Well, we'll see," Wayne said. "Steven said it was a dumb-acting tom. Dumb turkeys don't taste as good as smart turkeys, you know."

"You use the water from the tap?" Birch asked.

"Ha!" Wayne laughed again. "Yeah, we stopped using the water from the outhouse last week!"

"Dad!" Aspen yelled from around the corner. "Knock it off."

Birch felt his face go gently pink, then took a breath and let it slip away as well as he could. He filled the pitcher at the sink and carried it with two hands back to the table. Aspen looked at him apologetically and shook her head.

Wayne followed him in carrying the heavy stew pot with two quilted pot holders, setting it on a wooden board on the table in the midst of the plates. "Might as well call the warrior down," he said, pulling a chair out, scraping it over the floorboards.

Aspen went through the kitchen around to the base of the stairs. "Steven!" she called, then came back to take the chair next to her father, indicating the one across from her for Birch. He sat down silently.

Wayne handed a ladle over to Birch, saying, "Take as much as you want." Birch put two helpings into his bowl and handed the ladle across to Aspen. When it was Wayne's turn, he filled his bowl nearly to the top. Birch wondered if they said any form of thanks before eating, sitting with his hands in his lap and canted forward just enough to get the heart of the rising steam into his nose. He breathed deeply. Wayne watched him and smiled. "That is Tom turkey's living breath," he said. Then he closed his eyes for a moment, and Aspen did the same.

Birch nodded. "Thank you, Tom turkey," he said, not

knowing what else to say.

The sound of heavy footsteps tracked across the ceiling above them and began descending the stairs. Birch looked at his stew while Wayne and Aspen sunk spoons into theirs.

When Aspen had agreed to go out with Birch during his visit to the dentist's office, she'd suggested coffee in the village's one cafe, still testing him to see if he knew where it was and thus reveal that he actually was Paul. He'd seemed funny and harmless enough in the dentist's chair, even a bit exotic with his long blond ponytail which he apparently kept trimmed with household scissors, but history, and her own experience, had taught her always to be wary. She welcomed a diversion, having lately felt herself repeating the same predictable journey through her days, the only changes being occasional forgetfulness, which alarmed her because she didn't see herself that way, and the odd sense that she was standing stuck in one place watching the world turn about her with increasing velocity. She found herself worrying irrationally that she was getting old, though she had a dozen seasons to make it through before she turned thirty. She'd enrolled in a Ponca language class two hours' drive away at the community college in Omaha, thinking a stronger cord to the old ways might give her a clearer vision into life, but the elder who taught the course had to stop due to ill health after only a couple weeks, and they couldn't find anyone fluent and able to take her place on short notice. Aspen tried for a while to take her brother's approach and learn online, but she found the resources too thin and could not get traction.

She took her favorite table, a varnished oak top just big enough for two, along the wall of the cafe after work and waited for Birch. She'd sat at this table countless times over the years, across from friends from high school and most of her boyfriends, one of whom went off to Lincoln to the university;

a couple still lived in the county farming or building, though she rarely saw them. She'd even interviewed with Carver for her present job at this table.

She studied the nicks and dings, initials and hearts scratched into the surface, knew them all like the pages of a family album, though she'd never scratched her own here. She sat waiting for Birch, wondering why this familiar, local cuneiform welled up a weary sadness in her. She studied it, knew every gouge and scratch, every wiped and faded ink trough, even remembered which years certain marks were added, yet didn't know what it added up to. Maybe that's why it felt sad to her. As many times as she'd sat there during her life she'd never felt seen or heard, never had reason to scratch in a remembrance of her own. Would this be any different? Would he be like everyone else, just talk about himself the entire time and as long as they knew each other, however long that might be? Would the world revolve around him?

He waved to her when he walked in, looking unkempt and in a hurry. At least he was some new scenery and had already stirred a bit of a mystery in the village. He wore a smile as he approached and sat down. "Hi," he said.

"Hi."

He looked at her a long moment, and took a deep breath. He told her he was making progress getting some money together to pay for his dental visit, that he had a freelance programming project online which would get some dollars to him before too long.

"Okay," she said.

Then he told her that he had this odd feeling, like he knew her from long ago, or maybe one of his relatives had known one of her relatives. *Perhaps,* she thought. *That's not impossible. So here it comes. You're really Paul Willow after all?*

"And I don't want that to sound trite," he said, "but I know it does. I wish I could explain it more clearly. It's a thing I feel on a cellular level, and I think it's connected to a dream I've had ever since childhood. And," he paused, glancing at the wall. Then he looked back at her, wanting to study her eyes. "This sounds," he continued, "like some sort of ridiculous pickup line, and I'm truly sorry for that." He took another deep breath. "I should just be quiet," he said. "I've spent the last few months not talking, and I feel like I've forgotten how. I don't even like the sound of my own voice anymore."

This is a first, she thought. *Not your typical guy, at least for around here.* And she found no issue with the sound of his voice.

The waitress, a high school-aged girl with sandy curls and a red Nebraska T-shirt over jeans, walked up to the table. She gave Aspen a familiar look and inspected Birch.

"This Mrs. Willow's grandson?" She asked.

"No," Aspen said. "This is Birch."

The waitress screwed up her face. "Huh? Which Birch? What's your first name?"

"Devon," he said. "I'm not from here," then added, "at least not recently, that I know of."

She looked at him sideways, looked at Aspen, then back at Birch. "Well, what can I get you?" she asked, reaching into her back pocket for a mangled note pad and pen.

"Could I have a venti latte with oat milk and cinnamon?"

She shot him an annoyed look, then glanced over at Aspen. Aspen chuckled softly. "Just two black coffees, thanks Marcia." The waitress half-smiled and turned to walk back to the kitchen. Aspen reached for a yellowed white glazed bowl next to the wall, grabbed a pair of half-n-half capsules and set them in front of Birch. "Here you go," she said, and smiled.

Birch rubbed both hands down his face and let his fingers drift to the tabletop, saying, "I think it's really odd that I'm here, that I'm alive, sitting in this chair, and that you're here with me—while probably figuring I'm some sort of crazy person. What do you think about all this?"

She decided to look into his eyes the way he'd been exploring hers. She put her elbows on the table, making her fingers into a cradle for her chin so she could rest her neck while she looked. It took some energy, this leaning forward, holding her head up, this eye stuff. But it was interesting. She saw more than she had expected, could tell more than she'd thought she would. The waitress brought the coffee in two heavy mugs, clunking them onto the tabletop. Aspen leaned back, poured a capsule of cream into hers, then leaned forward again and picked up where she'd left off.

Birch poured cream into his and then mirrored her posture, leaning in and resting his chin on his enmeshed fingers, leaving his eyes with hers. The steam from their coffees drifted upward between them. After a long while he nodded imperceptibly and said, "Yeah, this is good. I'm feeling deep gratitude. And responsibility. Almost like," he hesitated, not having the words, "for the past. I feel like," he paused, searching again. "I can make something better, going forward. Even if you don't want to go out with me, I'm feeling it here, like it's opened its eyes in me."

"You're very strange," Aspen said. "I can't tell what you're even saying." She began to worry that he was indeed not from there but a latter-day colonial apologist feeling his white guilt. She'd never dated one before, and imagined it could get quite tiresome. Chances were he would be superior and patronizing, always telling her what she needed and always making their choices with her best interest in his mind, but never just hearing what she had to say or letting her make her own decisions. Chances were he wouldn't let her just be the person she wanted to be. He would make her into the oppressed one, the subordinate who needed his goodwill. She was afraid of that, but she wasn't quite finding that in his eyes. "Gratitude for what? Responsible for what?" she asked in a low voice.

Birch let a long breath flow out of his nose, roiling the coffee steam drifting between them. They hadn't yet touched the mugs. Aspen imagined two horses greeting each other on the plains. Birch's eyes relaxed. "Responsible for not choosing love over fear. For letting fear win. And grateful for this girl, this woman. And grateful for you. And for the chance to choose love this time."

This didn't sound like a white apologist. "What girl? A past relationship?"

Birch frowned. "Well, maybe, not in this life though. A girl in a dream. It's a dream I've had many times, vivid, every time. And it happens here. That I know." He turned his head briefly toward the back of the cafe behind him. "Out in the hills that way."

Aspen frowned. She was back to thinking maybe this was Paul, but maybe he'd had an accident of some sort, and amnesia, and maybe shreds of memory were coming back to him. She felt sorry for him, not knowing who you are must be terrible, like being trapped. She'd had a dream once where she was in a large building, like a school, with many rooms, hallways, and floors, and many people were there, but she knew no one, and no one spoke to her. She tried over and over to find the way out, but could never find an outside door.

"I found the exact spot," Birch said. "I walked out there. I recognized it from the dream."

Aspen finally picked up her mug and took a swallow. Birch did the same.

"So, what's this have to do with me?" she asked.

"Your eyes," he said. "You have her eyes, like exactly. I don't know if," he shook his head slowly and looked up at the ceiling a moment, "that means anything. But I can't get away from it. You just have her eyes. I'd never seen them before in real life."

She lowered her head a millimeter and frowned at him again. "My eyes."

His head unconsciously lowered, matching hers. "It struck me in the dentist's chair, like a memory I had from when I was an infant or something, but really, more like from before I was born. It was obvious that I knew you. I think you know me too."

They drank their coffee. He told her about Zongo, and

about Robin threatening to put a hit out on him. She told him about her father and brother, life in the village and on the farm, believing she was talking to someone who was born here but had forgotten through no fault of his own, believing that maybe she would fill in enough blanks to knit together Paul Willow's recollection and he would come to realize who he really was. She told him about her mother. They'd lost her in a car crash years ago out on the highway. She had been driving home from Lincoln at night, got T-boned by a car full of drunks who ran a stop sign and didn't have their headlights on. The driver was the son of the county sheriff, and managed to get off without doing any time. Steven, Aspen's brother, was eight when it happened. Aspen was twelve. It would have been four or five years after Catherine Willow had moved east. Steven had trouble with the dominant culture anyway, she explained, but after that he'd developed a hatred that he had never gotten under rein. He was a standout basketball player through his high school years, he had friends and people liked him, she said, but he spent the entire time angry. Now he worked on the farm and played video games.

Steven sauntered around the corner, clomping in untied work boots. He was tall, with long black hair, and built strong like his father, filling out an XL wool plaid shirt and worn jeans. His sharp eyes regarded the contents of the stew pot, then lingered on Birch for a moment as he took his place at the table. Birch watched him and smiled, feeling a flush of intimidation that he tried to suppress.

Wayne looked at his son with amusement. "Lovely to see you this afternoon, Mr. Cook," he said.

"This is the guy you think is really Paul Willow? Your new beau?" Steven said to the table while reaching for the serving spoon in the stew pot. "Looks like he needs to do more farm work."

"Nice, Steven," Aspen said. "Meet Birch. Birch, my polite brother, Steven."

"Pleasure to meet you," Birch said.

"Mmm," Steven grunted, and began eating.

Wayne looked at him, then at Aspen. Aspen shook her head and apologized to Birch with her eyes. They ate in silence for a few moments before Wayne started talking about spring and the crops he planned to put in, drawing Steven into conversation by asking him about the acres Steven would manage. Birch listened, gathering that they were organic farmers and used only heritage seeds, their family having been on this farm since the Civil War. Their present approach was for each to be responsible for specific crops and acreage on the property. Wayne generously kept directing what he said toward Birch, inviting him to join the conversation, but Birch found himself uncharacteristically reticent to speak and only inclined to listen. He discovered that he didn't know things that he wished he knew, especially sitting next to Steven, a powerful transmitter of antagonistic and intimidating energy, and across from Aspen, a well of wonder to him, a woman he felt an unexpected love for, though he'd known her only a short time, but felt in some deeper place that he'd known her far longer.

He didn't know, for instance, what tribe they were part of. He didn't know if he was on reservation land, or if they had relatives on a reservation somewhere. He didn't even know the resident tribes in this state, if they were moved here by the government from some other homeland. He didn't know what he might ask or say that could be offensive and disrespectful. He didn't know how Native Americans had fared over the last couple centuries in Nebraska, or if they even thought of it as Nebraska. He would have felt comfortable venturing these questions with Wayne and Aspen, but with Steven's presence, he remained silent. He watched, taking a bite of stew now and then. He noticed the rhythm of Wayne's and Steven's voices back and forth across the table, the slow steady air, like

Aspen's, not hurried yet not hesitant.

In his silence Birch learned the margins for organic growers in the area were okay if you were willing to manage your sales and wholesale customers and drive the many miles to farm markets in the cities, but that the yields and the sell-through were not always so good. Farming was a struggle for the Cooks, though they were the fifth generation of their family to farm this ground. He learned that Wayne and Steven looked after the fields and market crops, while Aspen, in addition to working at the dental office/real estate firm, kept chickens, pigs, and one cow on the farm, also managing a small pasture with Steven's assistance. He learned that most of their neighbors were bigger operations, not organic, more industrial in scale, farming mostly commodity corn and soybeans. He learned that most of the land around them had slipped through the fingers of the families that had owned it for generations, and now was parceled up within the portfolios of big corporate agricultural operations.

Looking at his father at one point in the conversation, Steven flicked his head toward Birch and said, "Tell Paul about the letters at the end of the table."

Wayne glanced toward the end of the table where the mail was piled. His hands reflexively found his face, and his palms stayed a moment, his fingers covering his eyes before sliding down his cheeks, finding their brethren as the hands came together in a posture of prayer over his lips. His eyes regarded Steven and then Birch. "Fucking lawyers," he said from behind his joined hands. He let his hands fall flat onto the table on either side of his bowl. "Big Ag company, rather, some company they own, suing us for patent infringement."

Birch didn't know what to say. He looked across the table at Aspen. She ate her stew impassively. He glanced sideways at Steven and saw that he was inspecting him. He looked over at Wayne. "Fucking chemical company wants our land," Steven said, still looking at Birch. "Trying to scare us off, because we don't do business with them."

"Wow," Birch said, not having anything more cogent to offer just then.

"They lie about our crops so they can sue us," Steven added. "They say our broccoli is too tall, so it must be from their patented seed, which is bullshit. We wouldn't use that shit for anything. We just grow tall broccoli."

"Your broccoli is too tall?" Birch said. "I didn't even know that was a thing."

"They developed a strain that grows tall," Wayne said, "so their mechanical harvesters can work better, easier to bring it in, faster, less loss. I mean, clever, especially if you're truck farming thousands of acres. But they've patented it, which makes no sense to me, and say we have to prove ours isn't theirs. The bastards know the cost of a lawyer could break us."

"And so that's how they put families out of business and get the land," Steven sneered. "It's because we won't sign a contract to buy their seed. We've developed our own seed for three generations here."

"How did they even decide your broccoli is too tall?" Birch wanted to know. "Did they sneak onto your farm and measure it?"

"That's the thing," Wayne said. "We could probably stop this bullshit right there, charge them with trespassing, but they say they got pictures with a drone, calibrated or some shit so they can tell how tall the stalks are. It was in a field away from buildings so they claim it wasn't trespassing, uncontrolled airspace or whatnot. We'd have to pay a lawyer to argue that too. Probably have no choice. It's ridiculous the stuff you have to deal with just to be an organic farmer now. Stuff my grandparents never had to deal with, though of course they had their own issues, especially my great-grandparents. But now you have to worry about the thousand-acre patch across the road from you blowing pollen into your plants, not only contaminating them so they're not organic anymore but turning you into some criminal because a corporation patented the genetics."

"Yeah," Steven said, "we weren't even considered people by your government until our chief fought them in their own court and won. Like we didn't belong here, even though we were here long before you. Now we have to prove that our seeds are real seeds and belong here too."

Birch could sense that Steven wanted to take the conversation down an even rockier trail, to skirmish over generational wounds, but the talk quieted. They ate in silence for a while. Then Aspen said evenly, "Steven had a website showing how the corporation squeezes people off their land and then magically winds up the owner after some shell company buys it, but someone keeps taking it down. We can't tell who, but we think the chemical company can do it somehow. He had a dozen examples that follow the trail all the way back."

This got Steven going again. "Yeah, the damn hosting company won't tell me how it keeps happening. The site's just gone, files all gone. It was just WordPress. They say it has to be a hacker from Russia or someplace, that it's my job to make it secure. I think someone's paying someone off or using influence. It makes me feel like I know my great-grandparents better now, how they felt when they got marched off our homeland and stuck on the res. They didn't know what was going on either, and no one gave them a choice or told them any truth."

Birch was in unfamiliar territory talking about the Cook family history, but the digital landscape was a place he felt at home. "You still have your site files backed up?" he asked.

"Yeah, just not the database though," Steven answered, "and if you google my stuff the links all go to the cable company's error page. That doesn't look too good. Google will probably drop it from the results pretty soon, I guess."

"I can find a host where you'll be more secure," Birch said. "I also have an idea. What if we relaunch your site in a secure location, anonymize it, and then hack the chemical company's site so all requests for it are redirected to your site?"

Birch could feel Steven's energy toward him suddenly shift, antagonism falling away like boards protecting a sapling that was now strong enough to grow on its own. Steven looked at him a long moment, narrowing his eyes. Birch watched him and waited. "That even possible?" Steven asked at last.

"Yeah," Birch said. "Totally illegal, but I do know a way to do it. Forget your domain for this one. We'd have to use a completely anonymous domain and service that can't be traced back to anyone here. Can we look at the chemical company's site? Do you have your computer going somewhere?"

Steven got up and led Birch around the corner to a hallway where a narrow wooden door, lying prone on saw horses, and a worn ladder-back chair were pushed up against the wall. The makeshift desk held a monitor, keyboard, mouse and speakers, and sheltered a computer on the floor underneath. Steven pulled the chair out and gestured, inviting Birch to sit. A laser-show screensaver undulated on the monitor, while air from the computer fan pushed against the wall below. Birch took the chair, his hands unconsciously finding the mouse and keyboard like sprouts finding their way through the soil to the sun. How long since his fingertips had danced among keys this size? He nudged the mouse, clearing the screensaver, noted the operating system and reflexively scanned the desktop. He noted the web browser icon in the system tray and moved the mouse pointer toward it as his eye caught another familiar icon in the system tray. He stopped and looked up at Steven. "You're a *Zongo Bongo* player," he said.

Steven looked at him and shrugged, confused by Birch's expression. *Maybe this guy is a player too,* he thought, *one of hundreds of thousands. Maybe he wants to play "do you know," to see if we've ever competed online against each other.*

"I wrote most of that game, like basically two-thirds of it," Birch said, smiling up at him and bobbing his chin slightly, feeling more comfortable each moment, as if he'd found some ground where he could connect with Steven.

Steven's eyes opened wide for a nanosecond. He remained stock-still another moment, as if trying to identify a creature in the shadows of the woods. "Bullshit," he said.

Birch exhaled through his nose. "Here," he said, turning back to the monitor. "I'll show you an Easter egg no one else knows about, probably even the other developers on the project, except maybe one other who would have found it in the code. I could never get much past her. Seriously, you're running my code here." He clicked open the icon and began navigating the interface, moving through it rapidly and fluidly with keyboard commands and mouse clicks. "Okay." He glanced up at Steven quickly. "Do you mind if I take your avatar through the first level to a place on second level? That's where we'll find the Easter egg." He'd already seen that Steven had created only one avatar, nearly a virtual copy of himself, complete with long black braid. He'd given himself an even slightly stronger build, added a red headband with a single feather, and finished the look with an open black leather vest over a bare ripped chest, black jeans, black motorcycle boots, and hand-drawn tattoos on the shoulders. *Nice work,* Birch thought, *good use of the drawing module.* He waited for Steven's response, and turned back to look at him.

"Roll the credits," Steven said.

Duh, Birch thought, and brought up the about window, where the game credits started to slowly scroll. Seeing the names of his co-workers salted his emotions with a mixture of fear and yearning. He clicked and held the mouse on his name when it rolled up, "D. Birch." He turned back to see Steven's reaction.

Steven leaned in and squinted. "No fucking way. You're *that* Birch?"

Birch smiled and nodded.

Steven took in a long breath and let it out, raised his eyebrows and shrugged a second time. "Jesus," he said. "Well, go for it."

Birch turned back to the keyboard and launched the first level with a keyboard combination, proceeding to move through the landscape from a point of view just behind Steven's avatar. He flicked another key combination and a text window opened showing the character specs for Steven's avatar: the longevity, experience points, skills, immune system, social connections, curiosities, and even a couple developing diseases that Steven didn't yet know about. Steven had never seen that window before. Birch dragged it to the corner of the screen and began navigating the landscape with key commands, moving quickly and learning Steven's environment on the fly. He quickly ported to the second level, watching the log in the text window scroll by as he moved through the landscape. Steven watched, transfixed. Wayne and Aspen stood behind watching as well, not with any sense of familiarity with what they called "Steven's game" but with the recognition that this man, whose hands dashed over the keyboard, was performing tasks at which he was highly skilled, tasks tied to one of the few things on this earth that successfully captured Steven's imagination.

Birch moved Steven's avatar through the second level, listening to the character's internal chatter through the speakers. Steven stepped forward reflexively multiple times in response to something his character said or some question he asked, had to check himself and shake off the impulse to reach for the keyboard and mouse. Birch proceeded smoothly and gently, in full awareness that by working with and listening to Steven's game character he was borrowing parts of Steven's mind and consciousness, and that watching someone do that must make Steven feel itchy, exposed and uncomfortable.

The second level took longer to navigate than the first. When Steven spoke up a couple times, saying, "I'd have him lash some of those logs together and raft down the river," and on the second occasion, "Better not climb that face," Birch took his advice, both out of respect and the understanding that Steven knew his character best.

Wayne and Aspen were growing bored, having watched Steven play the game enough times to get their fill of the scenery and action. Wayne wandered around the corner to the kitchen, but Steven's shift in mood and attention held Aspen there.

"Okay, we're getting close," Birch finally said, causing Steven to lean in closer. Birch guided the character along a wooded trail, turning off into what looked like a random copse of scrub trees. He arrowed the view back and forth, zoomed in to look more closely, then said, "There." He had the character crawl into the thick undergrowth, parting ferns and dodging limbs, stepping over moss and deadfall.

"What?" Steven said.

"You'll see," Birch said, guiding the character to a small moss bed just large enough to sit on cross-legged. The narrow trail by which Steven's character entered the tiny grove was no longer visible, the moss bed thickly shaded by an understory of scrub oak and overstory of giant oaks, beeches, and walnuts. The character sat in the shadows looking toward a single shaft of sunlight, which slanted through the shading leaves to form a bright smear on the moss. In the center of this sunbeam stood a spindly brown-capped mushroom.

"There are millions of those around there," Steven said.

"Not like this one," Birch said, his eyes on the screen.

The character's inner chatter said, "Be careful. That looks poisonous. I don't want to touch that."

"I agree," Steven said, "I wouldn't touch that, two hundred health points gone, maybe more, maybe life points. A guy I teamed with once, anyway I think it was a guy, mashed some of those up and made poison. We took out a whole fort guard with it."

Birch could imagine the experience thread in Steven's character even without opening a developers' console to scroll back through it. During the first and second levels he'd felt the character to be unexpectedly halting and timid, not at all like he'd imagined Steven, and certainly nothing like the image

Steven had built for him. That's why it had taken him so long to get to the hidden grove in second level.

It sounded like Wayne had most of the dishes done already. Birch wondered if Steven had made it much farther than this, if he'd even gotten off of second level yet. The game universe featured seven levels, and some of the beta players had made it all the way to six even while they were still working on it. Birch imagined Steven faced with many questions posed by his character, Steven's reactions then reinforcing the character's inner chatter, then the character chattering about the next decision, reinforcing Steven's reactions as they learned each other and traveled together, looping and iterating through situations that rendered them both completely counter to how Steven imagined himself. "No," Birch said aloud. "This one we eat."

"No fucking way," Steven said.

"Yes," Birch said, "trust me."

"I think he knows what he's doing," Aspen said.

Birch had the character lean forward and pluck the mushroom from the ground. Steven began to step forward, but caught himself. Birch had the character pop it into his mouth and swallow. Steven threw his arms up and let out a sigh. Wayne walked back around the corner, wiping a dish with a towel.

The shadows in the grove seeped away, replaced by a bright mist, and in the spot where the mushroom stood a turquoise apparition began to form loosely in the shape of a seated human. "You get to make a mentor now," Birch said.

Steven looked in the upper menu and saw that his life points and health points were not diminishing as he'd feared. "What the fuck is that thing?" he asked.

"That is going to become your mentor," Birch said. "A game companion that is only yours, that no one else can see, like your personal spirit guide. It will talk to you, sort of like your character talks to you, only more off-frame, sneaking itself into your avatar's internal dialog. This mentor can access not only your character's experiential history, but the experiential history of all characters, including environmental characters. I call it unity consciousness."

Steven stood bent over, staring at the luminous shape on the screen, processing what Birch had said. Birch glanced back at him, then got up from the chair. "Here," he said, "you take it. You get to build the mentor the same way you built your own avatar. Give it an identity, a name, some nice clothes, whatever you want."

Steven took the chair, hands lingering over the keyboard and mouse. "My mentor," he said. He opened the options and began scrolling through the physical characteristics. He created a tall man, gave him dark skin, thick black hair, high cheekbones, and a broad necklace crowded with a hundred bear claws over a full-length buffalo robe. Birch wondered if he was creating an idealized image of Wayne, maybe a taller Wayne. Steven gave him one massive eagle feather extending from the back of his head. He took his hands away from the keyboard a moment before returning them and putting the cursor into the identity fields. "Mantcunanjin" he typed in the name field.

"Chief Standing Bear," Wayne said, and looked at Aspen.

"Yes," Steven said to the image on the screen.

Steven finished creating the avatar for his mentor, Chief Standing Bear, and then wanted to spend the rest of the night traveling through the game. Aspen prevailed upon him to pause the game long enough to show Birch the chemical company's website. "Show him all your notes too," she told her brother, "and then I'm going to drive him back over to Willow's house."

Birch took notes on his phone, thumb-typing, though he was still in the mood to show off in front of the Cooks and thought of having Aspen hold his phone over the table so he could use his 3D virtual keyboard. He resisted that temptation, knowing that she probably wouldn't be able to hold it still enough, and his hope for glory would likely backfire.

"Okay," he told Steven, feeling much more confident now than when he'd first met him, "what I'm going to do is set up an elastic web space on a dynamic URL service using randomized anonymous URLs. We'll launch a simple one-page scroller with all of your information that will render as a webpage at any of the URLs. Then I'll do the hack so the chemical company's servers do a redirect, making all requests for their website instead show your page. Hopefully it will take them a long time to figure out what's causing it."

"Hmm," Steven said, "I followed some of that. So, when anyone tries to load the chemical company's website it will show this one-page scrolling deal instead, with all of my evidence on it, and no one will be able to trace it back to us. Right?"

"That's the gist, yes," Birch said.

16

Dunstan had taken to driving into town twice as often since the events of late last week. His normally weekly errand of stopping by the post office (starting the first Friday of every month to pick up his military pension check) and then the liquor store (every Friday, rain or shine) for one new bottle of bourbon would now have to become twice weekly, he figured, to keep up with the bottle side of things. This was a medicinally pondered change in his decades-long routine, resulting from the extreme, mind-baffling pain he experienced every time he had to take a leak. All on account of that heinous little fucker with the weird hair, who had the audacity, not to mention whatever other bizarre sick qualities, to bust him in the nuts with his own shotgun. Adding insult to already-grave injury, the very medicine he liked best had the unfortunate side effect of causing him to need to pee more often.

This world made no sense.

After that little fucker and his goons left, Dunstan spent the entire night howling and working himself free of the ropes. Once loose, he'd drained the rest of what was in his bottle in one hasty tilt. An Adams keeps trying until he gets it right.

He wandered along the sidewalk with a wrapped paper package held under one arm, other hand gripping the glass neck of his latest bottle, carrying that okay feeling that he was properly supplied and would make it another couple days. Without focusing on anything in particular, he knew that his friend, Cletus, would be sitting on the bench in front of the hardware wrapped in a moth-eaten WW2 wool army blanket. He knew this because Cletus pretty much always sat on that bench during daylight hours, no matter the season. While most considered old Clete the village idiot, Dunstan knew he was actually about the smartest guy in the county, in his own peculiar way, and today he found himself in need of those smarts.

Dunstan halted his steps in front of Cletus and regarded him a moment. He felt that dull ache in his head, what he thought was a constant hangover brought on by his increase in bourbon intake but was actually just run-of-the-mill dehydration caused by wanting to delay the inevitability of taking a leak as long as possible, which he achieved by never drinking anything other than the prescribed amount of bourbon.

"Cletus," he said. "Brought yer Bambi." He dropped the paper package onto the bench next to Clete.

The old man was watching the street, following every car with his eyes, his head on a swivel, turning to the right and then back to the left, though not very often, as a car rarely went by.

"Rooster," the old man said.

Dunstan's closed lips pulled at the corners into what for an Adams passed as a smile. So they were calling him Rooster now. If Clete was calling him Rooster, that meant everyone was. Probably enough of them had heard him up in the hills every time he went out to piss, word getting passed around here faster than a lame horse. Oh well, he felt sort of honored to win a nickname this late in life. He'd always imagined it might be something like "Deadeye," referencing his unassailable superiority with a rifle, or maybe "The Hunter," since it was well-known and appreciated that he was a reliable source of fresh venison for those who needed some. He never guessed him screaming while taking a leak would be the thing. Well, Rooster Adams it would be.

"Anybody been by?" Rooster asked.

Clete scratched it out like an old barking dog. "Ford! Ford! Ford! Chevy! Ford! Dodge! Dodge! Chevy! Dodge! Chevy! Toy Yota! Ford! Harvester! Jeep! Ford! Jeep! Chevy!"

Rooster nodded.

"What about last Thursday? Any not from around here?"

Cletus stared into space for a long moment, then out it came in a percussive rasp.

"Cad julac! Black Es skoo lade!"

"You seen the plate, by chance?"

"Garden State! Alpha, Sierra, Papa, India, Kilo, Echo, One!"

"Thanks, Clete. You stay warm now. I'll be back around with more steaks in a couple days."

"Rooster."

Rooster burned an image of that plate into his mind as he continued down the sidewalk toward his truck. The mind of an Adams was built to hold things solid like that, nearly as solid as the letters chiseled into a gravestone. Rooster didn't quite know how he would track down the plate, but knew he *would* track it down, one way or another. He wasn't against learning something new. And tracking, like shooting, was something he knew he was good at. Nothing wrong with having to figure something out, keeps the mind supple.

Back at his cabin, he began thinking about what he would take with him. Certainly the Marlin and a box of rounds; that was the whole point, but what else would he need? Money for gas, for food. Change of clothes. Truck had decent tires. Didn't seem too complicated.

Angel's relationship with Winnie appeared to be shifting. He hardly ever came home these days, mainly just to eat and sleep (both of which he did considerably less than before), and when he was there he was stressed, preoccupied, no longer interested in the games, little pleasures, and conversations which they'd built their relationship on over the seasons and years. She was baffled, and questioned herself constantly, taking what solace she could in meditation alone in the huge house and hiking solo on the trails they used to enjoy as a couple, though from their new neighborhood she had to drive many more miles to get there.

Angel knew this was happening and hated it, but he felt overwhelmed with work, putting his relationship on the too-long list of things to figure out when he had more time. He tried surprising Winnie with a BMW convertible for their anniversary, as if he'd completely forgotten her reaction to the first one he'd bought, and to the diamonds. Naturally it backfired. While the convertible sat in their curved paved driveway, Winnie discovered that he'd put her beloved little pickup truck up for auction on Ebay. She stayed up one night, while Angel lay comatose, to trounce the other bidders, using Angel's credit card to pay for the transaction. When Angel discovered who the winning bidder was the next morning they had a flash fight about it across the kitchen island, but he had to leave for the office, so they were both cut short and left smoldering the rest of the day.

Stuart was also increasingly volatile. He swung back and forth between ultra-bro mode, acting like he knew it all and was secretly king of the realm, to being super paranoid that one of the big dogs in the C suite was about to fang his throat out.

Angel attributed it to scaling problems. The company had never solved their understaffing issue. Everyone was overworked beyond that point where performance suffers, and Angel had been asking for more staff for months, Stuart always replying that they were not finding candidates who could pass the upgraded security clearances.

One Saturday Stuart buzzed into the dev room first thing. He slalomed through the workstations and their gusting keyboard rain to the far corner, where Angel had a group at the intersection of two whiteboards and was gesturing demonstratively with uncapped markers jammed between the fingers of his left hand. Angel held a red marker in his right hand, turning to underscore and arrow things on both walls as he spoke. Stuart didn't bother to wait, instead interrupting as he stepped into the group. "We need to talk about threat detection and response," he said. "That's our new top priority, for as long as it takes to get to a reliable operational level." Normally Stuart never spoke in this room, other than a whispered invitation to Angel to come with him back down to his office, for fear the engineers would discover that he barely understood what they did here. Now, urgency overrode his caution.

Angel stopped and looked at him. The engineers kept their weary eyes toward the layered mass of notes on the whiteboards, listening for what Angel might say.

"Really," Angel said. "Have we lost another bird?"

"Ah, no," Stuart said, "but leadership is starting another push across the borders, this time to the south, and this is just the beginning."

Angel dropped his hands, streaking his khakis with lines of blue on his left leg and lines of red on his right. His eyes flicked up to the ceiling tiles for a long beat before settling back on Stuart. "I can't keep fragging these guys, Stu. I have to let them finish something, or else we're going to be suffering under a mountain of technical debt. And if we're going to continue to scale at this pace, I need more people yesterday." He paused and looked around the room. "Like double what we have now."

Stuart looked at the floor. "I know. I know," he said. "We've been through this. Leadership is clear on this, however, and I have no confidence that I can get them to adjust."

Angel bobbed his head and looked at the whiteboards. "Your office in ten, okay?"

Stuart nodded and squeaked on his heels to exit the room.

It was peripherally interesting to Angel how the large amount of money that he always imagined would make his life so much easier, so much less stressful, just wound up generating more stress through the fear of losing it and the inherent obligations he felt to toe the line despite his spirit's own counsel. He felt that in himself, and clearly saw it on Stuart's face. Stuart was busy making the case for Angel once again switching the development team's focus.

"I've made it clear that it will require personal sacrifice on all our parts in order to achieve this. They get that it warrants another round of raises for the team, and for you and me, don't worry about that. They get it." Stuart forced a quick smile. Angel didn't know how much Stuart was being paid, but assumed it was something more than he was getting, likely seven figures. If so, he couldn't imagine caring much about getting more, but you never know. *It's like an addiction.* He could also fully understand the terror of losing it. After all, look where he, Angel, was and never imagined he'd be. He'd gotten multiple raises in the past months as company leadership stuffed more and more ludicrous demands down their throats, and he'd somehow managed to squeeze acceptable results out of the dev team. Now he found himself mathematically well into the top one percent of salary earners in the country, an ambition he had never held for himself, but found oddly and unsettlingly compelling now that he was there.

"We're up against physical limitations this time, Stu. I don't think it's wise to ask the team for Sundays now. I'm already worried about their lack of sleep resulting in cognitive decline. More time from the existing group is not going to mean more forward progress, regardless of how much money we can throw at them. It's simply going to require more good people, a lot more." Internally he added, *Especially now that a few of the team have grown uncomfortable enough with the ethics of what they're building to leave for parts unknown.* He'd had no contact with them since they left, as was typical of the company's off-boarding procedure and general vigilance. He assumed company lawyers were hounding the ex-employees, intimidating them into numb silence, but he also worried the company did more to keep anyone who left quiet. He wasn't sure, and hadn't come up with a way to find out, never mustering the courage to ask Stuart directly what had happened to the first dev who'd disappeared. Chad mentioned to him any number of times that no one had heard from her, highly unusual for someone as outspoken as Erin.

"Okay," Stuart was saying, "I'll circle back on the personnel issue. You and I are on the same page. I just need to sell it upstairs. With a few people off the team, they're more worried about security leaks and finding it difficult to get people past the new standards. Oh." He put his PalmPilot on the desk and hit the button. "Sync. The new stuff."

Angel reflexively complied, plopping his PalmPilot opposite Stu's and hitting the sync button.

"So here's what's coming over," Stuart continued. "Adoption is going crazy, better than expected. US is basically saturated. Canada's been great, better than we ever hoped, so great to work with. And now they want to push it out all over the globe, starting with Mexico and heading south. The problem, of course, is we don't have the same kind of relationship with anyone else, so we're just crossing borders basically uninvited now, relying on private deals to open up enough microwave."

Angel raised his eyebrows but remained silent.

"They're tooling up to increase unit production by forty percent," Stuart continued. "The daily release into the wild, same uptick. So we need much better threat detection and avoidance to keep them flying. We're gonna need that even before we have Canada saturated, as they want to start pushing south in a couple weeks, then across the oceans as soon as we have bare coverage as far south as Brazil."

"Holy shit," Angel said. He hadn't thought about it long enough to imagine that they would really try to suck up the internet business from all of humanity. He had allowed himself to believe that it wouldn't work, that it would die of attrition before it crossed a handful of state borders. He half noticed that the PalmPilots were taking even longer to finish their sync this time, assuming the spec documents coming across must be epic.

"That's right, bro," Stuart said. "We're going into unfriendly territory now. The good news, if you can call it that, is that they want to keep it to only one deploy for the whole network. You won't need to have one version running in friendly territory and another in unfriendly."

"Pfffff, well that's a relief," Angel said. The PalmPilots were still syncing, but neither Angel nor Stuart paid them any further notice.

Stuart relaxed just a touch with Angel's reply, feeling their conversation might dip back into more comfortable banter. He had a gnawing fear Angel was about to prove with math or logic that what the brass was demanding could not be accomplished. He'd had this same fear nearly every time they'd met over the past six weeks, but Angel always managed to come through, and the C suite was generally mollified. Stuart's blossoming relief that Angel hadn't chosen this instance to shut down their momentum caused him to want to brag a little.

"Well, that's not all I got for you today," Stuart said, chuffing their familiar bro laugh.

"Oh yeah?"

Chuff. "Yeah, last meeting more came out about the bottled air project. You're gonna love this." Chuff. "So, we're gonna leverage the natural gas pipeline network, not only main line distribution, but get this, the lines into people's homes and businesses. Think of it; air kiosks inside people's houses, inside the lunch room in their offices, hell, the waiting rooms for their customers, and once they're connected and subscribed, we got them. We can start inching up the price."

Angel looked at him with crossed arms, one hand covering up his mouth. He chuffed behind his palm. "You're serious. The two things people basically breathe twenty-four seven, air and WiFi, we are going to suck up and then sell back to them retail. We're really doing this." Angel narrowed his eyes and laughed again.

Stuart watched him, not able to read his response.

"Yeah," he continued. "All we have to do is kill the natural gas industry to get at those pipes."

"Kill the natural gas industry. That's all."

"Yeah, they're thinking back to coal and oil. Obviously that's no walk in the park, but look how easy it was to turn people off of driving electric vehicles."

"Obviously."

"I mean, we have to keep administrations in the White House that care crap for the environment and respond mostly to dollars and bullets, right? We've managed that before. And we've got people on the team now who helped pull off that social media thing back in '16, not the headliners, but the people who know how to do shit. Despite all the light on that, it still works just as well now as it did then, some say even better."

"Mmm hmmm."

"But it's perfect, see? Coal and oil dirty the air, and then we supply a product to solve that problem, all in one operation. All the chatter about climate change and all that shit happens over our network. That gives us even more control than if we were just doing the bot social network thing, which is really powerful enough in its own right. It's beautiful in a way, like a natural cycle. If people are really that stupid, then we *should* be taking their fucking money. So far, so good, right?"

The PalmPilots finally finished their sync. Angel slid his off the desk and into his pocket. He put his hand back over his mouth and tapped his cheek with his fingers. "You think we can kill the natural gas industry by bringing back oil and coal." He hadn't had much time to think about anything other than software of late. Okay, the company had managed to beat down the internet industry faster and more effectively than he'd expected. But, the natural gas industry? "And you do that how? With a White House that likes money and bullets? Don't they all?" Angel took his hand from his mouth and rested his cheek on it.

Stuart looked up at the ceiling. "They like money. They all do. They never have enough. It's like that disease." He snapped his fingers and looked at Angel. "The pituitary one that turns you into a giant. No matter how much you feed it, it's never enough. Side deals. You promise them big returns on investment, promise to frame it for them so they don't get dirty while they're in office. So we push oil and coal and make them pay big dividends to the investors, arrange special options and warrants. We help them out with PR, unleash the bots, and push back against natural gas, like suddenly there's something wrong with it. Call it unpatriotic and un-American, just like we did with electric. It's not that hard, takes a little time. But way quicker and cheaper than us trying to build an air pipe network ourselves."

"What do you do when oil and coal starts to dry up?" Angel wanted to know.

"Who the fuck cares? How soon is that going to happen? Fracking'll give us at least another fifty years, so they say."

Angel shook his head slowly, raising his eyebrows as he imagined trying to explain this logic to Winnie. "And so, where do the bullets come in?"

Stuart chuffed. "Yeah, that. It's not that they like bullets so much as they respect them. That just helps get them on the same page. They know that a bullet, your bullet, can come from anywhere, anytime, like out of the blue."

Angel widened his eyes a moment, watching an oddly indignant expression slip across Stuart's face before it was replaced by his normal smug visage.

"Your bullet," Angel said.

Stuart gave him a duh look. "Your bullet, my bullet, anybody's bullet," he said, and shrugged, as if to say, *What's the big surprise?*

Angel looked sideways at the blank wall. "Yeah, I guess," he said. "Not my area."

"Right," Stuart said.

"Just." He looked back at Stuart, bemused, as if he were in the midst of figuring out a humorous riddle. "I have a hard time believing that these soldiers, or officers I guess, walking around the ant hill all day would really tolerate whatever this amounts to, mass extortion or blackmail or—"

Stuart suddenly looked concerned, leaned forward in this chair and put his hand over the speaker on his desk phone. He gestured to Angel to keep it down.

"Or whatnot," Angel continued. "What? We recording this? We bugged or something?"

Stuart looked at his phone, repositioning his hand to more effectively cover the mic holes and speaker port. He lowered his voice so Angel had to lean forward to hear. "You just never know. I have to assume," he said. He looked at his desk, at the PalmPilot sitting with the lid up. "Better safe than sorry. I wouldn't want them to get the idea you weren't with us on this, right? That would not be good." He lowered his voice even more. "You gotta understand who these people are, and who they are not," he pleaded. "These are not soldiers. They're not airmen, sailors. They're not officers in the way you're thinking. You haven't seen any Marines in these hallways. These guys are businessmen. They happen to be wearing uniforms. The uniforms help them get their business done. The people you're thinking of are out there fighting in the Middle East or wherever, or teaching weapons or science or something in one of the academies, but you won't find them here." Stuart let out a long breath. "Everybody's tired, I know, but we have to dig hard right now on threat detection and avoidance. The one thing that can't happen is we begin this push to the south and start losing birds and gaining scrutiny. And we damn sure can't let one get reverse engineered. You and I would both get our...you know." He rocked back in his chair.

Angel remained leaning forward, elbows on the desk. He didn't feel sufficient space among his thoughts to fully process what Stuart was saying. "Well," he said in a scratchy voice of fatigue, "I guess I better get back to the room. We have a lot to do."

Stuart nodded his head, suppressed a yawn and stretched his arms, letting his hands settle together behind his neck. Angel lifted himself from the chair and let himself out.

Back at his work station, he stared at his screen without looking at anything in particular. He let his ears take in the sounds of the room, the keyboards gusting a little more emphatically once he walked in, the occasional squeaks from the casters on the chairs, the hum of the lights, some low talk in various corners, audible sighs.

Forward, he thought. *Okay, threat detection. Let's get the new specs loaded. Might as well start swinging at this.* What else was he going to do? He didn't have the energy to think of alternatives. He pulled the PalmPilot from his pocket and flipped the lid. When the screen came alive and he was setting it in its cradle, he noticed three dead pixels in the lower left corner, dead in a particular pattern he recalled from months ago. The instant he recognized them a sheet of nausea wrapped around him, leaving a hot and cold layer of sweat under the mound of curls on his head. He had forgotten about the mustang he had loosed, but was hereby reminded, as it had apparently returned.

17

Birch felt luxurious waking to the morning light in Agnes' bedroom now. Word had gotten around that he was keeping the place up better than if no one was there, and village logic held that a clean, dusted house was better than a not-clean, not-dusted house. Beyond that, the village didn't pay him any mind. Half of them were convinced he was a native son returned home, and the other half plain old didn't care. They had their own lives to deal with. Birch had to adjust to the idea of doing something that would, in the wider, internet-scrutinized world, generate suspicion and outrage, possibly even incite flame wars on several social media platforms, but here was accepted and then quickly ignored. The idea that you could just get over yourself and move on let him feel the expanse of the country he now occupied, so refreshing after the claustrophobic spaces of his previous life.

He padded downstairs in bare feet and robe, setting a skillet to warm on the stove. He pulled open the fridge to collect a carton of eggs, fresh from the Cooks' farm. On the cutting board on the counter he sawed a slice from the remaining half-dome of a wheat loaf that Wayne had baked from flour they milled themselves. He dropped the slice into the toaster, then reached over to tap his phone awake, lying in its coat hanger cradle on the breakfast table.

With the 3D glasses on, a plate of hot eggs (with a sprinkle of black pepper) on toast on the table to his left, and a strong signal from Free Air Net, he loosed his hands in a dance through the spaces of his virtual keyboard.

He began by pulling together the pieces for a dynamic domain name services system from a free service hosted in Bulgaria. He started the account using a burner email address from another free service, this one based in the Philippines. He created a domain name resembling the chemical company's, but added some random letters before the dot com. Then he spent some time looking around the globe at options for potential web hosts. His goal was to identify servers in various locations around the world that could be publicly accessed by IP address alone and served shared innocuous content, basically mom-and-pop websites. His aim was to create a content delivery network that remained in constant flux, so it could never be pinpointed. He would use it in conjunction with two mustangs, which he had been ruminating about over the past twenty-four hours, each with a specific set of tasks to perform.

Mustang A's job would be to hold an encrypted copy of Steven's content page of evidence and links showing the chemical company's track record of heinous treachery. It would also probe and access random mom-and-pop web servers, maintain copies of itself on a changing list of suitable servers, and listen to the dynamic DNS service for requests for Steven's scroller page, which it would then decrypt and serve up in real time. The condensed version of Mustang A's script was: here I am, nope, now over here, you want? I give. See ya later!

Mustang B's mission would be to slip by the security of the chemical company's load balancers and traffic directors, of which there were undoubtedly many, masquerade as a low-level light footprint process with a plain vanilla identifier, well down the list in CPU and memory use so hopefully the admins wouldn't notice it, and copy itself onto all the front-end web servers, then sitting to listen for any request for the company website. Upon detecting a web request, Mustang B's next job would be to intercept the htaccess file, the web block, or the web.config file (depending on what kind of front-end web servers the company was running) as said file was transferred, replacing the data stream with its own modified version in real time, effectively and temporarily reconfiguring the server's behavior for each request, then returning it to its previous configuration after the request was completed. Mustang B's version of the server configuration, of course, would insist that requesting any page on the company's website return the latest URL from Mustang A pointing to Steven's scroller page. Mustang B's condensed version went like: you want that? you ain't gettin' that; you gettin' this! You want those? You ain't gettin' those; you gettin' this! Don't matter what you want, you only gettin' this!

Unless an inspired network administrator happened to read way down the list of running processes, spot and open this quiet, plain-looking thing, and watch what it was doing, chances were every time they went to diagnose why their website was replaced by this annoying, accusatory page, they wouldn't have anything resembling a clue. Nothing untoward would appear in the logs, and, just for good measure, he'd made sure any requests for content coming from the same network block as the web servers would cause the mustang to serve up the unaltered config file. That way, admins testing from the local network would see their site as they expected rather than Steven's page, just to throw in some more confusion.

This was only the second time Birch had given serious thought to writing a mustang since he'd been an undergrad at Berkeley, the one he'd written to impersonate his phone on the San Jose library network being the first. He and Angel had always written them from their dorm room, collaborating on the code, turning them loose on the net, laughing and clinking beer bottles over the results. Amidst their shared bravado and early-twenties sense of invulnerability, each of them harbored a well-polished awareness of what could happen if somehow they were caught. Neither of them had shown that sense of caution to the other, not knowing if it was shared or would be appreciated, but both were secretly relieved when, after a close call involving a political action committee, they arrived at an agreement to stop writing and releasing these creatures, or at least any that used their shared codebase and frameworks.

Birch had technically broken that agreement with his phone impersonator at the library, because he used one of their frameworks to allow his mustang to roam from machine to machine inside the network and hide among running processes, not having time to reinvent the wheel and write from scratch. He'd justified the move as necessary for his survival, somewhat placating his guilt by adding a process for the mustang to sit and ping the primary process, immediately deleting its own code should a response fail to arrive, i.e. if it was discovered by a server admin and killed. It was Birch's and Angel's version of a self-destruct mechanism, erasing their tracks should one of their pranks draw the wrong sort of attention.

Birch would definitely be using the self-destruct function for Mustang B, the one infiltrating the chemical company's web servers, since this would be a more serious prank with bigger game. Certainly he'd had an internal tussle over what he was about to do, calculating the elevated risk and his agreement with Angel, but he'd promised Steven. And the warmth and smell of the Cooks' kitchen, and Aspen's eyes, that quiet, dimpled smirk she often wore, the months of peace in this little house in the middle of the plains, all quelled that internal talk.

He took the last bite of his egg sandwich and pushed the plate away. He thought for an instant about writing these mustangs from scratch, but moved past that quickly, impatient to get them into the wild. Setting his hands under the phone cradle, he logged into the hosted server he'd set up when still back in California. He hadn't bothered to log in during his entire time in Nebraska so far, never wanting to see what messages may have been sent to his old phone number, but now he needed copies of the frameworks he'd stashed there.

He moved through the directories and found what he was looking for, noting along the way that the log files he'd set up to record messages sent to his old phone had grown to decent sizes, with recent modification dates. He copied the frameworks he needed to his phone's file manager, then let his curiosity get the better of him, going back to look at the log files. Should he take the time? Did he really care who had tried to text him? Of course he would have to decrypt the files to view the logs. He'd used Klondike, the proprietary encryption he and Angel had built into their frameworks.

He downloaded four files named with date stamps with dot klondike at the end, then launched the Klondike decryption utility. At the prompt he typed the file names that he wanted to decrypt, then at the next prompt the second line to Creedence Clearwater Revival's song "Who'll Stop the Rain," then hitting enter. He watched Klondike's progress bar, a growing row of hyphens, crawl across the window, then saw the files open.

He was not surprised to see that all of the early messages were from Robin. The tone was pure vitriol mixed with escalating threat and periodic cynical abandonment. The first few were a continuation of his last conversations of the "how much will this take" and "YOU OWE ME" variety. They quickly moved into "you SCREWED ME OVER! Why??" territory, but then hooked a curve toward a quieter, more menacing path: "I see you're checking out some library books. Maybe I'll stop by." The hairs went up on the back of Birch's neck. He was reading a text message sent over three months ago to a phone that didn't even exist, held by the afterimage of a person who was already a thousand miles away from where the non-existent phone supposedly was, yet the realization that Robin had put enough effort into pursuing him to know his phantom phone was at the library sent a rush of adrenaline through him, left him feeling hunted again.

A couple messages from Mel and Lars were mixed in, saying that they'd lost the venture capital funds, Robin had gone psycho, and that both Mel and Lars were looking for jobs elsewhere, as were many others in the company. Birch didn't see any further messages from Lars in the list, but Mel appeared a few more times, warning him that Robin was bragging about getting revenge against Birch for "abandoning them at the crucial hour." Apparently Robin had attempted to turn everyone in the company against Birch, even offering a large cash reward to anyone who could tell him where Birch was "hiding out."

A few messages from his mom suggesting they get together sometime.

Farther down the log, more of Mel's texts started to become cryptic, suggesting that she might attempt to contact him via some other means. The messages from Robin around that time hinted that Robin's "friends in high places" had found something Birch wouldn't like, and the next few messages mused at how Birch would survive with no money. They were date-stamped around the time Birch discovered his bank account emptied. Anger and desert heat rose along with the adrenaline still coursing through him. He wondered if these log entries might be sufficient to use in a prosecution. That was a very large sum of money Robin had stolen. A message date stamped a week later said "I don't think you're really still at the library, but at least now I have a tidy fund to use to hunt you down." Then there were a few creepy messages of the "I hope you're getting my texts. You know I still care about you. I think about you EVERY day" type. Then a message that simply said "saw a guy wearing your hoodie—he was interesting to talk to, vroom vroom." Then finally, "we know where you are!"

Birch reflexively yanked his hands out from under the phone, swiping the 3D glasses from his face. He shoved the kitchen chair back and pushed himself up to pace down the hall and through the living room, looking out the windows but seeing only the dark vision of Robin in his mind. He repeated the circuit a couple of times, visiting each window specifically to inspect the snow for anything that looked like footprints. He stood at the living room window with a bunch of dust-smelling curtain fabric in his fist, seeing nothing on the smooth snow besides the straight, gray-blue shadows of bare forsythia stalks, paralleled by thicker lines drawn from the trunks of the leafless maples.

He stood, breathing the smell of the curtains and tracing the shadows with his eyes. He let the curtain drop and walked back into the kitchen. He looked out the window over the sink, to the far hills. He stepped past his chair to the side window, peering across the narrow yard into the corn stubble across the curve of the street. He went back across the kitchen to the back door, tried to look toward his motorcycle but couldn't get an angle. He pulled the inner door open and pushed out the storm door for a better view. There leaned his motorcycle, covered in snow, barely visible behind the bushes. No footprints. The sky was pale blue, the air cold and windy, occasionally gusting plumes of ice crystals up from the ground. The shadow lines drawn over the snow by the nearby willow made a bramble of loose threads, like a giant yarn ball played with and then abandoned. No footprints. He stepped back inside, latched the doors and locked them.

He stared down at his phone resting in its cradle, at the distorted image (because he wasn't wearing the 3D glasses) of the log file open on the screen, and felt acid in his sternum. Why should he allow these old text messages to rekindle that fear and anger? He sat and put on the glasses. It was mid-January, and the last date stamp was from mid-December. He closed the log file. Better he had not given in to his curiosity. That was his mistake. He was safe here.

A loud knock sounded on the front door.

His adrenaline pitched again. He froze for an instant, then slapped the 3D glasses off, hopping up. In his bare feet he flew down the hall, dodged a chair and cut to the front window, stubbing his toe on the carpet and nearly diving through the window glass before he caught himself on the molding. He saw footprints leading up the walk to the porch, felt his pulse hammering in his ears. He pressed his face to the glass and saw Aspen's coat and long black hair, her elbow crooked back holding a paper shopping bag. The air spooled from his lungs, and he felt relieved and ridiculous. He wanted to compose himself, but also did not want to keep her waiting at the door.

He walked over and pulled the door open. "Why did you knock? You have a key."

Aspen regarded him, momentarily surprised to see him looking flushed and in a bathrobe. He pulled the door wider for her to come in. "I brought you some more real food," she said, watching his face as she stepped over the threshold. "That canned food doesn't look like it's doing you any favors." She handed him the bag and kicked off her work boots. "You okay?" she asked in a lowered voice.

He took her coat with his free hand and laid it over the back of the couch, shaking off as much residual adrenaline as he could. "Fine," he said.

"Sorry," she said.

He walked into the kitchen and set the bag on the counter. Aspen followed, pulled open the refrigerator and began putting items from the bag onto the cold shelves, arranging the new items around what was already there. Birch cleared his plate from the breakfast table and set it in the sink, then took his chair and tapped awake his phone screen. He slipped the 3D glasses on and navigated away from the log directory into his local files, where he'd copied the frameworks. "I'm making progress here," he said.

Aspen finished stocking the fridge, folded up the paper bag on the counter and took another chair at the table. She watched Birch, watched his fingers under the cradled phone, thinking they reminded her of a pianist's, the faint fleshy tapping on the table like rain drops on the farmhouse roof above the ceiling in her bedroom. The sound tingled in her ears, around her jaw, and gently around the back of her neck. She felt relaxed and peaceful, the slightest of smiles pulling at the corners of her mouth. Her gaze wandered over the phone screen, blurred text rolling in and out of a zoomed drum-like image at an impressive rate, then up to his funny yellow plastic glasses. She saw the screen reflected in each lens, his blue-gray eyes focused on space somewhere between the glasses and the phone. The pattering of his fingers, alongside the tingling around her jaw it produced, left her in a state of quiet suspension. She drifted, closing her eyes a moment to wonder about the feeling, about whether she'd stumbled upon some secret formula for happiness. When she opened her eyes, they rested on the cornflower blue flannel collar of the bathrobe Birch wore. She'd seen that robe hanging in Agnes' closet many times as a teenager when she'd been there helping Agnes clean and do chores.

Birch glanced up and said, "Sorry, my clothes are in the wash."

Aspen waved her hand across her face. "It's no trouble," she said, "I don't mind." Then after a moment, "Did you start it yet?"

"Mmm, mmm," Birch said, focused on the space in the air where the 3D image resolved into a barrel rolling in place on its side, showing the text of the file he had open zoomed out, magnifying as it scrolled up from the bottom and diminishing again as it continued to the top.

"I need to wash mine too," Aspen said, and got up from the table and walked upstairs. She was happy to see that the bathroom was still clean and organized. Birch was apparently using one of Agnes' toothbrushes, an old pink-handled thing, and had the towels hanging folded and straight. The bedroom was well-kept too. The bed was made; other than Birch's faint footprints in the nap of the carpet it was not obvious anyone was living there, though all of the surfaces were dusted.

She knew right where to go in the closet for what

she was looking for. She pushed the louvered door aside and filed through the clothes still hanging in basically the same arrangement Aspen remembered from years past. She found the other robe, a lighter flannel in off white with a waist tie. She pulled it from the hanger and laid it on the bed, then slipped out of her wool shirt and T-shirt, unhooked her bra and peeled off her jeans, balancing on either leg as she rolled down her wool socks before kicking off her panties. She put on the robe and knotted the waist tie, then bent to scoop up her clothes from the floor. She carried the bundle downstairs and dropped it into the washer on top of Birch's clothes, sprinkled in some powder and started the machine.

When she took her seat at the table again, Birch looked up and smiled. He pulled a hand out from under his phone and offered it to her as a fist bump. "Twins," he said.

Aspen didn't want to be his bro. That feeling was as clear as the thump of their knuckles. What she did want, however, was not so clear, perhaps not because it couldn't be clear, but because she had never afforded herself the necessary practice at building that kind of clarity for herself. For all the heavy lifting she'd done on the farm, this task just seemed too hard. She had instead practiced the art of hiding what she really wanted from herself, so she could devote her energy to fitting in with and pleasing those around her. That strategy had won her many friends in high school, even though some among her white friends were "woke" and overly solicitous, exhausting her with their exaggerated attentions and causing her to be suspicious, feeling like her role was to be their Native friend who made them feel better about themselves. She hardly wondered that she'd almost never seen these friends since graduation; occasionally glimpsing someone from afar, she didn't feel compelled to cross the street to visit or even call out to them.

Birch's focus had returned to the mid-space. His fingers tickled and stroked the table under his phone. Aspen's gaze settled there as she slumped in the chair and breathed. The tingle came back to the edges of her jaw just under her ears as she relaxed. Without intending to, she began imagining different parts of her body in place of the tabletop under Birch's fingers. She wanted to prop her chin in her hands, but didn't dare stir them from their place on the table, as if any movement would reveal to Birch what she was doing in her mind. She shifted slowly in her chair as she imagined the small of her back as that spot on the table, then the back of her left hip. She kept her hip there awhile, savoring the feeling. Then, slowly, she rolled with her mind so the front of her left hip was being touched instead. This she liked even more, making her breaths deeper. She shifted, so slowly, back and forth below while remaining motionless above the tabletop. Now she moved her belly into that spot, either side of her navel, and down to her pubic bone. Her abdominal muscles pulled and relaxed, pulled and relaxed.

She caught herself breathing too loudly through her nose, eyes fixated on his busy fingers, her lips held tightly together.

She blinked once and pulled in a slower, quieter breath. She let her eyes leave his fingers and travel up the backs of his hands. They weren't heavy, knotted, working hands like those of her last couple boyfriends. They were gentle, smooth, lighter than most she saw in her life, and agile. She relaxed again. His forearms were slender, youthful, the dance of muscles faintly working under his skin disappearing into the sleeves of the robe.

Her gaze floated up, following his long yellow hair, ragged as he'd been trimming it with kitchen shears, fixing on his shoulders and resting there. She wanted to decide herself what she wanted, without condition, without apology. The thought came to her as if it had been following her her whole life, though she only just now turned to see what it was.

His shoulders were too wide for Agnes' robe and pulled the sleeves up farther than normal, but to Aspen they seemed benign, not extra wide or straining under any particular burden. She saw nothing menacing in his posture.

She finally allowed her hands to move from the table. The fingertips of her right hand rose to brush her lips while the fingers of her left smoothed a skein of black hair behind her ear, then lightly combing down its length. Her eyes moved to his chin, mostly hidden by a tangle of golden-brown beard, around his jaw and to his lips, which were moving together ever so slightly as if he wanted to speak, but the thoughts were running instead down his arms and out through his fingers as he gazed into the middle space of the 3D image. She watched his mouth and decided that he was innocent.

Aspen quietly pushed her chair back and half-circled the table to stand behind Birch. She cupped her hands around his shoulders and leaned against his back. "I've almost got Steven's page coded here," he was saying, "I just have to encrypt it now." She leaned her face into his hair, put her lips on his neck and, breathing in long through her nose, slowly slid her hands together across his chest. He raised his eyebrows and gave her more of his neck. She took another pull of air in through the mass of his hair, then stood up, sliding her left hand into a soft-but-sure grip behind his neck while her right ran down his arm. She took his wrist and drew him from the table. Their eyes met briefly, and she led him upstairs.

She pulled him to the foot of the bed and took the lapels of his robe in her hands, spreading them and letting the robe drop away, her eyes languidly drifting along his collarbone, across his shoulders.

His arms free, he unknotted the tie at his waist, letting the drape of flannel drop the rest of the way to the carpet, and then unknotted hers, sliding his fingers in across her stomach and out toward her sides.

Her torso muscles were ropy and strong, the lean grid of someone who'd spent years in the sun pulling life up from the soil. They tried to flinch away under his touch, but she held them back, wanting to feel all the way to the ends of this sensation. She giggled and laughed and searched his eyes as his fingers moved.

It was the first time Birch had heard her laugh like that, and the first time she remembered laughing in years.

As their eyelids spoke to each other and their breath came and went, she squeezed his biceps and leaned her body back onto the bed, letting her hands slide down his arms but squeezing and pulling a little as she reclined. Sunlight streamed through and past the curtains into the room. She felt her skeptical distance roll away and wondered if she might be in love.

As he bent toward her she brought her right leg up and rested the back of her heel against his chest. He leaned against her leg, feeling her control how close he could get and giving over to it, letting all of his weight rest there.

He cradled her hips with his hands. Hooking his thumbs over her hips, he felt her muscles push at him and felt the power in her leg. His hormones sloshed a loud message into an old part of his brain. He swelled in obedience and anticipation. His brain was busy elsewhere too, though, and he was afraid the shadowed image from his recurrent nightmare would creep in to take this moment away from him. But the moment was now; he was already in it, no longer just a witness. Not this time. He leaned against her leg, and she let him in. *I do this with you,* he thought. *We do this together. We do this, and we leave each other whole. This is the magic.*

They stayed in each other's eyes, lids drooping and bobbing now and then, watching each other climb. They felt each other hurtle toward that taut moment, an ecstatic rush up a rise together. Then, first he, then she, closed their eyes and passed over the crest.

Aspen opened her eyes and gazed up through the ceiling. Birch let go of her and stepped back. Aspen rolled herself under the quilt and the sheet, the flannel robe still partly on her. She worked her way to a pillow and a comfortable position under the bedclothes, then twisted back to extend her hand toward Birch. He climbed in beside her, spooned and wrapped the covers around them, smoothing the flannel robe over her hip and down her right flank.

He hadn't thought he was tired, but he fell asleep. She slept too. They slept deeply. When Aspen woke, it was just after noon.

Birch woke when he felt her roll out of the bed. He felt rejuvenated, and could not remember any dream.

Birch spent the afternoon in a cloud of love, coding his mustangs. He'd started this project wanting to impress Steven, to gain his respect, and as a gift to Aspen, whom he knew cared deeply for her brother. Now it was a gift of love. His lungs felt as if they were spreading apart to make room for his expanded heart. He loved Aspen. He loved Wayne and Steven too, though he barely knew them.

By evening he'd loaded Mustang A onto his hosted server and triggered the process, turning it loose to go looking for suitable web hosts where it could hide, waiting to decrypt and serve up Steven's content page whenever requests came in for it. He watched the server long enough to see that the mustang was running, that it had stopped, and then that the code was erased, meaning it had found its next server, determined its suitability, and reached back to erase its tracks. It didn't take long. *Be free, mustang, go out and do your best.*

He made himself a steaming dinner of potatoes and onions, kale, carrots, and goat cheese with sunflower seeds. Later, he slept soundly, waking the next morning refreshed.

After oatmeal with fresh bananas, he tapped his phone awake to begin working on Mustang B. He logged back into his server to pull down another of his and Angel's libraries, which he'd thought about over breakfast. He navigated through the directory from where he'd launched Mustang A the previous night and stopped. There sat a new file, created earlier that morning, named "bBhb4b9sg2g4ss65g4Jg3gS3kGe.klondike."

Had he done something wrong? That file should not be there—unless Mustang A had found something it wanted to encrypt and send back to home base, but that wasn't part of Mustang A's mission. The only other reason it would send info was if it had discovered another mustang out there, just a behavior they'd built into the framework, but Mustang B was not yet launched, much less written, and he had planned to disable that function in Mustang B so the two would not interact. He clearly hadn't intended for Mustang A to return data, as he would have defined a naming pattern rather than leaving the default token as the method to name files.

He moved his cursor over the file to delete it, but then downloaded it instead. He ran Klondike and followed the prompts. The progress bar zipped across the window; it was a small file. Then it opened, and the rest of his life changed.

+————————————————————————+ *hey buddy, it's been too long! guess wat? We're not in kansas anymore, and i'm sorry to use a stang to do this, but i could be dead otherwise - i shit you not. i am under an insane security policy that has me locked down hard just as we thought, in fact i'm chipped, and i need your help with something. okay, help with saving the internet, maybe even freedom - again, i shit you not. maybe i'm already killed, who knows? i think they killed one of my devs who complained. dunno. i work for a company that is kind of government but not, kind of military contractor-ish, somehow has access to what i think is the black budget or similar, tax payer dollars, insane amounts of money, and is building a crazy fucking network of drones doing tcp/ip designed to suck up internet business everywhere and own it, put everyone else out of biz. total control scheme, sick, crazy, psych. i think that's just the tip of the iceberg of what these fucks have in their lizard brains. we call it Free Air Net. you'll prolly see it if you look, wherever you are. free, right. anyway i lead the team that builds the os and control system. this is for you —> freeairnet.net:51/v/g/s/1001101/ and then klondike the full name of the guy who lived directly below us junior year who played doors riffs all night on that wurlitzer and append, then run >propscan. you'll see everything you need after that. then, I dunno, just be birch. do the needful. I hope i see you sum day if i'm not dead. you are my brother from a different mother, angel*

18

Angel left the compound late, as he did every night now, feeling that sheen of sweat on his forehead the entire drive to Santa Fe despite the sub-freezing temperature outside. He turned the X5's fans up high and pointed the vents at his face, but that just made him nervous and itchy.

Winnie was reading in the spacious living room in front of the fireplace when he got back to the house. She'd left a pot of casserole on the kitchen island, most of the heat having long drifted away. Angel lifted the lid but then put it back down. He was too nervous to eat cold casserole. Instead he went to the hall linen closet in the bedroom wing to get his secure laptop out. He hadn't had it out in a couple months, and Winnie glanced up from her book when she heard him walk past and slide the closet door open.

He set it on the dining room table and connected the cables and clips to hook into the PalmPilot. He drummed his fingers on the table as the laptop booted up, then opened a terminal window and went looking for what he knew would be there, half-excited at the thought that Birch was somewhere out there and had responded, half-terrified by the bell he could not unring.

He found the calendar data, found what appeared to be an event record dated February 14, 1969, copied the file across to his local drive and deleted it from the PalmPilot. He then renamed the file on the laptop's drive, removing the dot cal extension and replacing it with dot klondike. Then he ran Klondike, gave it the file name, and at the prompt had to stop and search his mind for the Creedence song. It had been awhile, but Fogerty's voice came marching into his memory. Angel typed "Clouds of mystery pourin' confusion on the ground" and hit enter.

```
+————————————————————————————————————+ brother! this is
sick! impressive work too! those agents to talk to nanobots,
coordinate them to fix shit? great stuff man! what you did with
bluetooth for those - that hybrid protocol - crazy shit brother! i
am so glad to hear from you. i'm also somewhere weird now, left
zongo, turcek stole all my money and has a hit out on me. why
does this happen to us? karma for mustangs? is harmless fun so
insulting to this universe? i'm hiding out in a vast cornfield where
hopefully no one will find me. someday i hope to tell you this
tale in person. maybe we'll trek the sierras again. i found love.
that's one thing. i guess i can die now. still, fuck you turcek.
brother! this code! this drone system! i see your genius in here. i'm
three days into researching your code and only part way through,
but i hear you loud and clear - central control - danger will
robinson - someone plans to fuck humanity, fuck the earth and
own it all - i get where you're at and what you want me to do
- i will not let you down - starting right now - fractal thanks
for the back door my brother - peace, safety, and love, birch +
————————————————————————————————————+
```

So, Angel had done it for real. He'd committed the ultimate sin against the company, one for which, he was sure, they would impart the ultimate punishment if he were found out. Like the other devs, no one would ever hear from him again, or have any idea what became of him. And it wouldn't necessarily just be him. He shuddered.

At the time he created that back door for Birch and wrote and released the mustang his sense of righteous indignation at what the company was doing was fresh, like an open wound. Now it was scarred over, and a low-level fear had festered underneath. He wished it would just go away and let him quietly enjoy the spoils of his employment. How naive to think that even a possibility. The sound in his mind as he read Birch's words began to vibrate and tease loose some of that scar. It was in Birch's hands now. The only thing Angel had on this earth to lean on now was trust; he obviously needed to trust Birch, and —he realized it with the suddenness of a stout stick to the head —Winnie as well.

He got up from the table, traipsed down the hall and into the living room. Winnie looked up, alarmed, and set her book down in her lap. "Winnie," he said.

"What is it, babe?" she said, her voice catching. For the past month and a half she had been afraid to even cough, afraid that one or the other of them would trigger on something and decide it was time to break up. That was her bell she knew could not be un-rung. Going from eight hundred to eight thousand square feet of living space seemed only to have diluted their quality of life.

Angel stood there a moment and looked at her, his face ashen, his jaw and eyes slack. Then he sat next to her on the couch, his hands fidgeting on his knees while he stared at the opposite wall. "Winnie," he said again.

Her book fell closed and slipped to the floor. She wanted not to breathe, but her lungs dragged in air anyway. When she let it back out, the tears began to seep from her eyes. "Come on, Angel. Please. Say something."

"Just," he said, "let me…" He blew his air out like he was trying to whistle through too big of a hole. "…try to figure this out." He leaned forward and hid his face in his hands.

"Oh my god," she said quietly, tears trailing down her cheeks. She raised a hand to wipe either side of her nose under her eyes, left it there to cover her mouth and turned her gaze toward Angel's mop of black hair, his hands shrouded by its fall. Her mind blew backward over the past months, brushing up against recollections like fallen leaves, searching for the things she should blame on herself. What could she possibly take back, undo or erase? She wanted to twist her focus into a superpower, like a laser, find the thing that had caused their love to die and blast it out of existence. Would that also make this sudden pain go away? How long had this weight been lurking in her chest, only now tearing open her heart? Yet, from the winds of her mind and the swirl of recollections came no clarity. She felt no superpower, only pain and fear.

But their love was not dead—at least, she still loved him. But what had caused him to stop loving her? How long could she still love him with none coming back? This was new territory for her. She didn't know how these things went in real life. What was it? Was she no longer attractive to him? Was she a boring nobody now that he was so rich and important? Maybe there was nothing she could do but accept it, settle to the ground and acknowledge reality. Making close to $900,000 yearly in tech made him some kind of a modern day rock star. He could probably have just about any woman he wanted.

He took his hands away from his face and rubbed them together between his knees. When he twisted his neck to look at her and saw her tears, his instantly began to flow. Through his salty dark eyes he looked at the blur of her face, breathing out the words, "Winnie, I fucked up."

Her head jerked, and she stared at him, a parade of anonymous women's faces rolling by behind her eyes. Who was it! Whom had he chosen to replace her? What did she look like? What kind of body did she have? Was she smarter? More interesting? Now it was her hands that rose to cover her face. She sobbed once into her palms. He reached and touched her wrists, but she held firm and fought him off. Her fear rotated into anger. What was so wrong about her? She worked hard on herself. She worked hard for their relationship. This is what she got? Did mister megabyte moneybags get to just end it like this and go have his affair? What about his responsibility to be decent? Was that not even a thing?

She took her hands away and looked at him with wet, lowered eyelids. "You have to tell me what's going on, what happened. You at least owe me that. Say something!"

The look in her eyes terrified him, made him feel small and ashamed. His voice caught. He swallowed. "I'm so sorry," he said in a thin voice. "I fucked up at work. I put us in danger."

Then the wind changed. It was as if a cold front from the east was knocked over and blown out of the way by a warm front moving in from the west. *What did he say? Put us in danger? It's those people he works for. Not his fault. Nobody messes with our love and gets away with it.* She searched his eyes and saw his fear and shame, his remorse. *There's no other woman in there. This is something else completely.*

"Oh, baby," she said, her pain and fear twisting into an uncanny strength. Her hands went to hold his face. Their tears rained freely now. She got her knees up on the couch, pushed him onto his back and climbed on top of him, holding him and wanting to protect him. "Baby, whatever it is, it will be okay. I got you." He just looked at her. She started pulling their clothes off like a tornado lifting the roofs from houses and spinning them across yards and fields. "You're my smart man," she said. "They're not going to get us. If those bastards kill us, I'll just kill them!"

She got them naked and made love to him in a wild wet storm on the couch.

Afterward they lay cooling. Angel began to talk. He told her about contacting Birch, about the mustangs, about the back door he'd created and then sort of forgotten about. About what it had been like in the programming room, about Stuart and the drone fleet pushing into foreign countries, about his fears for the developers who had left or disappeared. The more he talked, the more she loved him. "I won't be able to stay in this job much longer," he was saying, "and I never wanted to put us in danger."

"Baby, I don't care about your stupid job and stupid money and this stupid big house."

"But if they discover what I did, I think," he said, then paused, as if considering his words. "I'm *pretty* sure they make people disappear and get away with it," he finally concluded. "I'm sorry. You must be so disappointed."

"I'm not disappointed in you; I'm proud of you. Those

people are evil."

Angel's right hand came up to cover his left collarbone and the base of his neck. He felt around, then held his hand there. "And this chip," he added in a quieter voice. "We need to be careful." He shook his head like it was already too late. "I really don't know."

"You don't want to be part of that. That's not you. We are getting the fuck out of here."

Angel turned to her and whispered now, irrationally, as if to hide his voice from the chip. "We can't just run. They could hunt us down so quickly. They have people for that." Winnie's eyes grew wide. "They plucked a guy out of the woods," he continued, "somewhere hell and gone in the mountains of Carolina, for shooting down a drone. It was crazy, like just pay the contractor, kill the guy and get the drone back. Business as usual. They were just like, okay, that's done."

"Fuck. Then what do we do? Where do we go?"

Angel was quiet a long time. Winnie sat up, looking at Angel's neck, imagining them driving up two-tracks in her little truck, over hills and through canyons, racing through darkness to get somewhere. She had no idea where. She wondered what it might be like to hold a gun.

Angel laced his fingers together, using them to support his chin as he leaned forward, assuming thinkers' pose. "We have to make everything seem the same," he said. "I need to figure out a way to cover those tracks without anyone noticing."

19

Leftover chili warming on the stove permeated the little house. Birch reclined on the couch, gazing through the living room window and the bare upper branches of the trees across the road. The air through the trees was white with frozen moisture and diffuse light, but the trickling sound of water around the house whispered about warming days and melting snow.

He felt better, stronger, than he had in years. He felt himself breathe with intention, the full breaths of a person about to do important work that he understood. He felt the elastic, mysterious strength of love inside him, like a physical capability newly gained, to be explored and developed further. He also felt safe leaving all the curtains open now, like the village was there to look out for him instead of disapprove, Aspen's daily visits reinforcing his sense of belonging.

Steven's webpage was still up. Birch had finished that project before diving headlong into Angel's drone network code. Steven bestowed burly man hugs and back slaps on Birch whenever he visited the farm. Birch basked in the acceptance. He helped with random chores, holding laying boxes in the henhouse as Steven sunk fasteners with a cordless drill or carrying one end of rusted steel ramps, wooden planks, or ten-foot sections of irrigation pipe while helping Wayne organize the tractor barn to make ready for spring.

At home in Agnes' house, he pored through Free Air Net system code and drone client code for hours at a time. He knew to be careful, using the access Angel had created for him judiciously. Angel's cryptic comments in the code led him to backup images of staging servers with the central command code, as well as the drone client system; Birch copied these to his hosted server, where he could download pieces to his phone to inspect at his leisure.

He would pull out a piece of the uncompiled code, step through it, research the dependencies, mull over the logic, form a picture in his mind of what the particular class or function was doing, then stand up from the kitchen table, pull the 3D glasses off—the cheap plastic frames leaving painful bruises behind his ears—and go stretch out on the couch, daydreaming about what he'd just learned, assimilating it into a growing understanding of the drone system and the services it supported.

The system was impressive. The code that kept the drones charged and flying was extensive. Birch saw many personalities at play both in the code and the comments, but also thought he detected his friend's overarching influence. It felt like he was catching up with him and getting to know him again after years apart.

He saw the large rule sets by which the drones flew, how they referenced weather data from various global systems and adjusted their flight characteristics and locations accordingly. He saw how the drones would balance network coverage with environmental conditions, including proximity to microwave charging stations. He spent four full days digging into how onboard nanobots communicated with a central controller to coordinate in-flight repairs. He found the specs that the controllers could use to guide the bots in rebuilding almost any part of a damaged drone, using onboard materials held in reserve, accessed and deployed in precise sequences to maintain aerodynamics and balance while materials and bots migrated across the centimeters from storage locations to repair sites.

He had just been looking through the controllers

for data storage, memory management, and virtual server management, noticing how logs were synced to a central host after being rolled on the drones. It appeared as if everything that happened through the drone network was being recorded and collected by the central system.

He lay on the couch, looking out through the bare branches, and imagined where all that log data was going, what was being done with it. He didn't yet know what to make of Angel's instruction to "just be Birch," but he could feel the waters of ideas gathering underground, and knew he would have to be very careful in what he did and how he deployed. The flight rules were full of alert thresholds that would no doubt trigger alarms back at some control facility, probably near where Angel worked, whenever a drone went afoul. Birch understood from Angel's message that the owners of this network were not gentle, benevolent souls. It was also apparent to him from the logging and alerting code that they intended to catch anyone messing with their system.

As he rested his body on the couch and allowed his imagination free range, he wondered why, with so many environments around the globe—and so much information available on the very internet this drone network was actively subsuming—the drones should be limited to a single specification for their design and repair instructions. He also wondered if the client-server, centrally controlled network model, where each drone was a carbon copy of every other and wholly dependent on command from the central server bank for its decisions and operations, was the best model. Clearly this network was designed to become the largest and most powerful force on the planet, ultimately serving its single group of masters. Birch knew from Angel's description that these masters, whoever they were, were assembled and driven by greed, paranoia, and contempt. He daydreamed about stealing the network from them and delivering its control into the hands and hearts of a benevolent group, a body of people who knew compassion for humanity and life, but these Robin

Hood fantasies were strangely challenging and unsatisfying. The stealing part wasn't the problem. With the access and insights Angel had left for him, Birch's mind had no trouble forming increasingly interesting theories of how to hack the system to take it over. The problem was, who should control it after that? Who should maintain it? Should it even exist?

He could attempt to destroy it. Maybe that's what Angel had in mind. But the people who started this project obviously had access to massive resources. They would just build it again, Angel probably paying the ultimate price for his failure to deploy a hardened network that couldn't be taken down.

Birch imagined, for a while, Angel and himself as martyrs, almost saints, legends who paid with their own blood to try to save the freedom and dignity of humanity. The thought of being discovered and cruelly killed by remorseless thugs left him feeling feverish, causing his mind to race; of course, knowing they'd just build another network tarnished all the shine off this fantasy.

After letting that idea play itself out, Birch's imagination drifted back toward the Robin Hood notion of taking control of the network instead of destroying it, then delivering it into the hands of good people. Again he ran into trouble. What if good people today were not good people tomorrow? When you gain control of something that everyone wants and needs, what happens to you? When you have power over something that significant, can you remain good? And given mortality as the basic rule of human life, even if you have a group of people governed by love and kindness, who's to say the next group that takes their place will also be governed by love and kindness?

With his hands laced behind his neck, he scanned the textured white ceiling of the living room, collecting its brightness from the midday sun reflecting up from the snow outside. His thoughts were still somewhere between fantasy mode and raw curiosity. The practical matter of whether, even with the back door Angel had left for him, he would be able to actually wrest control of this network of millions of drones was still distant. The likelihood he didn't want to address quite yet was that he would attempt some hacks, take down a drone or two, be discovered, located and taken into custody, perhaps (if Angel wasn't just being dramatic) even killed. He already had the menace of Robin out there. Did he need this too? The longer he could avoid thinking that through, the longer he could enjoy the theoretical realms of daydream currently wafting through his mind.

He swung his legs off the couch and rocked his body up to walk to the front window. The snow layer had grown thin and crusted. Bowls had melted around the bases of the maples, almost reaching the grass underneath. The gray shadows of the branches twined with those of the forsythia stalks, playing on patches where the wind had polished the crusted snow smooth. Sunlight reflected upward as if from mirrors left on the ground. He pondered the force of the reflected light, not able to gaze directly at it for more than a split second before it blurred into multicolored afterimages, obscuring his vision.

The drone network was currently controlled by the greed and paranoia of its owners. Birch would prefer that it be controlled by love and kindness, naturally, and was confident Angel had that in mind when he said "just be Birch." What kind of hypnotic particle beam could he point at the owners to replace their greed and fear with love and kindness, should he even be able to identify who they were? Was that even a valid way to think about this? As far as he knew, the rule of thumb was that people at their core do not change. Once a psychopath, always a psychopath. Maybe some eventually learn how to hide it a bit, but it is never not there. Are love and kindness formed inside people in the same way? Are some people constituted with more and some less? Or are love and kindness, and greed and fear for that matter, similar to waves traveling through the universe, becoming manifest only when they pass through things, like people or crystals or other animals, attuned to resonate like a particular pitch of sound?

Birch's mind followed this trail for awhile. He liked how it felt. If something like this were at all true—and, after all, what is there besides energy?—then something built on waves like a communication network should be able to resonate with love and kindness instead of greed and fear.

He turned from the window to pace and think. With the crook of his index finger pressed to his chin, eyes looking at nothing in his proximity, he followed his familiar circuit through the living room, the dining room, down the hallway and into the kitchen. The odor of warming chili hung in the kitchen air, pulling his attention away from the abstractions in his mind long enough to spoon some from the pot into a blue glass bowl. He carried it with him and ate as he paced, finished the bowl over a couple more circuits and set it empty on the counter by the kitchen sink. He looked out the window to the distant hills and thought about light and dark, and about Aspen. *What do love and kindness mean independently of people, creatures, and objects? What would it look like to codify them into a network system?*

He went to stand on the back porch in his bare feet, jeans, and T-shirt. The sound of water dripping into the gutters and streaming in rivulets around the house amplified as he pushed open the storm door. The air was warming, somewhere in the mid-forties Fahrenheit, the cement stoop almost hot in the sun under the soles of his feet. He looked down to his right, seeing the black vinyl seat of his motorcycle now free of snow. Chickadees were flitting in and out of the bare willow branches, calling to each other. The occasional breeze pushed raw chill against his cheek and neck, then relaxed, sometimes coming from a different direction to push against the other cheek. He walked down a couple steps, stopping short of the snow on the ground, and gazed up into the pale blue. Somewhere up there would be one of the drones, maybe a few of them within the dome of sky in his view. They would just be tiny specks, too high to hear or really see.

He leaned back against the black metal railing of the

steps and folded his arms, found a position where the sun landed square on his upturned face, and took huge scoops of this almost-spring air in through his nose. Small squadrons of crows traversed the sky, performing aerial antics and hollering to each other. A hawk patrolled slowly in great arcs at a higher level, well above the crows. A bright red cardinal arrowed through the yard and disappeared past the edge of the house, followed seconds later by his duff-colored mate. The chickadees fluttered in the willow.

Birch thought about trust. Trust, like kindness, was one of the things you could make, or perhaps not 'make' but 'reveal,' by mixing love into a moment. Could that be designed or tuned for? What would that look like in code? He watched the chickadees dodge among the branches and again thought about Aspen. What he loved most about her was that she was just herself, and he trusted her effortlessly. He didn't spend any thought cycles consciously wondering about whether he should trust her, he just did. And she being the entity with which he most felt and associated love, what did he want for her? How might he design or code for that? He wanted for her what she wanted for herself, and moreover wanted for her the ability to achieve it for herself.

Then he thought about parents and children. Children whose parents saw them as extensions of themselves, as an opportunity to recapture past opportunities or missed glories, were often subject to volumes of strict rules, command and control, burdensome dogma, and narrow bands of allowed behavior which they learned by rote, often carrying them forward into their adult lives as complexes.

Children whose parents just love them, and see them as their own people, tend to simply become themselves. These parents know to build them a basic framework, provide some shelter from the elements, and then get out of the way. Their greatest expression of love is to let go. Don't judge. Don't even evaluate. Just let them be whoever they will become. Maybe you code for this by not coding it. Maybe you code a basic framework, then design it to train and code the rest itself.

Birch raised his gaze once more to the sky, wondering if he might see a dark speck. This needed to be a peer-to-peer network, not client-server with centralized control. Love, kindness, and trust should lead to freedom, and it didn't seem to Birch that any of those things could be hard-coded or centrally controlled.

He pivoted and stepped up to the porch, going back inside to the sunny warmth of the kitchen. He slipped the 3D glasses on and took his chair. To help this child gain its freedom, he would first have to help it safely shed the burden of its controlling dogma. He shelled into his server and began setting up a simulation environment for the system code and the drone client code, feeling something like an agent researching a dangerous cult, preparing for a rescue mission.

Steven blew air through his nose in bursts like a horse laughing and said, "Come on, Birchy, it's not that hard. You can do this. Now, pull apart, straight down, push together, and hold, then pull. Rinse and repeat. You're not gettin' tired already, are you?"

"Nah," Birch said.

"I hope not. We got six hundred more to drop in before dinner."

Birch held the transplanter by the handles in front of his chest like a pogo stick and took a long sidestep along the row, careful not to step back and mash one of the plants they'd sunk in the last pass. Steven held a large flat of broccoli starts in the crook of his left arm and stepped along with Birch, waiting for him to sink the transplanter and slap the handles together. Then he expertly popped a dirt plug up from the crinkling plastic flat and dropped it into the transplanter shaft, moving along the row as briskly as Birch's inexperienced pace would allow.

"Pull. Let's go. Come on, Birchy. Dad and I can do 360 in an hour. You and I gotta manage at least three hundred."

They made it up the row through half the flat, then stepped across to the next row, heading back toward the four-wheeler and the cart with the remaining flats. By the time the flat was empty Birch was getting used to the rhythm and could move along steadily. His shoulders were starting to burn with the exertion, and his forehead was damp with sweat. Steven's face remained placid and amused in the shade of his straw cowboy hat. He walked to the cart and tossed the empty flat down, picking up a full one. Birch wiped his brow with the back of his wrist and adjusted his ponytail to pull some stray hair out of his face. His armpits felt cold and damp through his T-shirt as he stood in the mid-April breeze, but soon warmed when he started moving again.

Steven drove them hard up and down the rows through eight more flats before the cart was empty and they had to drive back to the hoop house for more. Birch's shoulders felt simultaneously on fire and numb from the constant lifting and dropping, and he was relieved when, on the way back from the hoop house with fifteen more flats, Steven said, "Okay, I'll take the Hatfield for this section."

A couple hours later Birch was bright pink with sunburn and exhaustion, though over the past weeks he'd begun to feel his body getting stronger as it worked into the simple rhythms of spring planting on the Cook farm. Steven enjoyed having a farmhand that only cost them some spare food, and got a kick out of seeing this fancy college computer dude, as he affectionately thought of his sister's boyfriend, struggle through real work. For his part, Birch was in love: in love with Aspen, in love with her family, in love with the rich and fecund sensations of spring life on a Midwest farm.

Back at the tractor barn, he felt dizzy from fatigue and dehydration as he swung his leg off the back of the four-wheeler, almost tripping over himself when he bent down to pet one of the barn cats. He traipsed after Steven, dodging chickens on the way to the hoop house to drop off the empty flats. The Cooks' Rottweiler, Carl, trooped along beside them, following them to the back door to the kitchen.

Inside, Wayne was pulling cornbread from the oven. The soft rumble of Aspen's pickup truck and the crunch of tires as they rolled over gravel sounded outside. Wayne looked up, laughed and said, "Holy smokes! I don't know why they call us red men. Look at him!"

Birch felt his face. "Sun has always been a challenge for me. Too much time inside in front of a screen, I guess."

"Well, if you keep making the mistake of working for Steven, we'll turn you brown by harvest."

The front door opened and Aspen walked in. "Oh Jesus, Birch," she said, slipping her jacket off. "Do you know how sunburned you are?"

"First day planting brocs," Steven said while washing his hands at the sink. "Little slow, but eventually he'll make an okay farm hand. Earned his food anyway."

Aspen walked over and wrapped her arms around Birch's waist, kissing him before following Steven at the sink. Birch followed Aspen, and they sat down to a table of chicken, beans, potatoes, and cornbread.

"You guys going to keep planting this afternoon while the weather's nice? Or you going to waste it playing your video game?" Wayne wanted to know.

"Maybe Birch needs to get back to Willow's place and work on that drone project," Aspen offered.

Birch would have toughed out an afternoon of transplanting, but was just as happy to call it good for the day and get back to his digital world. Three weeks prior he'd shared with them the nature of his project and his new understanding of Free Air Net, admonishing them to pay special attention to what they did online now. He'd told them about Angel, about their time at Berkeley, about the company Angel now worked for, and about how Angel had created the back door for Birch in the Free Air Net system. Steven had listened closely at the time. He'd grown increasingly indignant as Birch described the quasi-government company behind Free Air Net and what he'd learned from the code so far. "It's just the same tired story," Steven had said. "A bunch of white guys, no offense Birch, hoard all the power and resources and dole it out the way they want because they always know best. They always have to own and control everything, and decide how much everyone else gets."

Ever since then Birch felt compelled to share in the farm work. After dinner though, when Aspen said, "I wonder if Agnes had a bottle of Aloe over there," and got up to clear the table and drive Birch back to the village, he was more than willing to go along.

Steven saw the direction they were heading and said dryly, looking at his sister, "I guess you'll be holding the flats for me, Dad."

Aspen ignored her brother and went out to start the truck.

On an overcast day, when the buds on the willow were a cloud of pale green and the fruit trees in the village were heavy with white and pink blossoms, Birch sat at the kitchen table, wearing his leather jacket since it was a touch chilly, with his 3D glasses on, preparing to ship some code. The WiFi fan on his phone screen was one bar shy of full. He imagined the drone relaying the signal must be hovering at a higher altitude to stay out of the moisture layer. He knew other drones in the region would adjust altitude to maintain optimal charging distance, and that if any of them flew too high, too low, or fell below a certain level of battery reserve an alarm would sound somewhere at the control center, presumably causing people to notice and possibly intervene. He had discovered conditions in the drone client code that would allow manual override of the navigation rules broadcast by the central system. He didn't know how many drones comprised the network, but his back-of-napkin math suggested high numbers, which meant they must have quite a large staff watching over it.

Birch pushed code up to his virtual server, where he was running a simulation of four drones interacting with each other and a simulation of the central control system. His experiments and changes were only directed to the simulated drone software, never the central control system. He'd installed and launched central control using Angel's unchanged simulator code, having determined that taking down the central system would not solve any long-term problems while being far too dangerous. Could he bring it down? With what Angel had left him, most likely yes. But, after the company beasts killed Angel and however many other developers they deemed responsible for leaving it vulnerable and then hired replacements, could they eventually fix the damage and re-launch it? Again, probably yes. *So that doesn't ultimately get me anywhere.* What's more, the attack vectors swimming around in Birch's imagination would be traceable with enough effort.

No, attacking the central system or destroying the existing drone network would not solve anything. Birch decided instead that the only way forward would be to help the drone network transform and gain independence from central control—help it grow up and leave the nest, as it were. If the airborne network continued to exist, albeit very differently, it would leave no gap for the company to turn around and fill with more of the same. He ran the central control simulator just to give his simulated drones something to test against and transition away from.

This would be a difficult problem, however. He could see from the logs that the drones had to charge constantly just to stay airborne. They ground through large amounts of electricity and suffered heat damage around the motors, the antennas, and especially the charge and discharge circuits. He found logs showing the onboard nanobots performing repairs in these areas regularly, taking more energy. So, not only were these drones tethered to central control, they were also dependent on the network of ground-based microwave towers to maintain their battery levels.

He had also inventoried and trialed the commercial server and network services offered through Free Air Net, such as virtual servers, streaming servers, email servers, domain services, web and app servers, file storage and transfer, content networks, virtual switches and routers, VPNs, database management, and some version of nearly everything a full-service ISP would offer. He deduced from the drone logs that traffic to these services simply passed through the drones, through the central control system, to co-located services sitting behind the central control layer. He guessed that another division of the company must be responsible for these commercial services, as Angel's control code included hooks to make calls to them rather than any containers for the services themselves. Everything he tried worked reasonably well, if not a little slow at times. Based on the length of the free trials and the low prices these services advertised, he gathered they must be intending to do for commercial services what they were doing for internet connectivity: lowball to steal customers from existing providers, putting them out of business. That would leave plenty of data centers to buy on the cheap.

Birch wondered if they'd managed to take over the hosting company where he had his cloud server yet. The idea that someone from the company might have administrative access to his server, meaning they could theoretically discover a copy of their own simulation software running on it, caused his forehead to go hot until he calmed himself by calculating the probability to near zero, at least for now. He did suspect that the company was throttling his connection to it, however. The Free Air Net server was responding faster than his cloud server.

He decided to spend the next hour sifting through the central control code, looking for evidence that this might be happening. He found that, indeed, the central control system functioned as a massive firewall, filtering packets by domain, favoring traffic going to Free Air Net services. *So they slow everyone else down just a little bit.* He could see the plan; choke out the competitors by making them less desirable. Start by making them slow enough to be a minor irritant, then gradually crank them down to major annoyance.

He finished deploying his code and restarted the simulation. The first change he tested was uncoupling the drones from the central library. He'd seen that the drone operating system was packed with monitors tracking tolerances in a list of unit health checks. Fan rotation, relative spindle temperature, voltage fluctuation, charge and discharge rates, frame torque, temperature points distributed all over each unit, antenna signal strength, and magnetic field strength were all constantly monitored for any deviation from the published tolerances. Birch was impressed by this work, particularly the magnetic field checks, as they appeared to be testing the shape integrity of the entire unit based on field strength measured from one point to another, looking for any deviation suggesting a break or distortion. If a check failed an alert would trigger, notifying the central system. Depending on the nature of the alert, the central system would send instructions through the network back to the unit regarding corrective action. If the alert had to do with a structural aberration, the central system would mobilize the onboard nanobots to make repairs.

Birch found the code controlling how the nanobots closest to the repair site were activated, how they moved to the location and assessed the damage, how they queried the central library for the repair specs, then queried the unit for repair material locations and levels. He saw how the bots communicated with each other using a modified Bluetooth protocol to pull materials from storage and march them to the repair site, like a train of ants. If the alert was triggered by an environmental problem, such as too much distance from a charging source or too much energy expenditure due to wind or rain, the central system would send back navigation instructions to relocate, also possibly directing a nearby unit to move in to share some surplus energy in the form of close-range microwave. He also saw where alerts were logged in the central system, and which alerts would be sent to a console with a human operator.

He found this system impressive in its complexity—hats off to Angel and his team—but it nagged at him that the specs and behaviors were so rigid and identical for every unit. The conditions each unit would encounter in the environment were dynamic and variable. How could one set of design specs suffice? It also bothered him that so much network traffic was devoted to communication back-and-forth with the central system. That seemed wasteful. Birch felt the units should be able to look after themselves and their closest neighbors. He did like the idea of a universally shared repository of knowledge, sort of like the shared consciousness he'd built into *Zongo Bongo*, but the notion that a unit's agency was centrally controlled did not sit right with him.

He watched the simulated drones hover randomly after his latest code deploy. He began playing with the simulator's environmental controls, throwing weather, physical, and space challenges at the flying units. They responded sluggishly without instructions from central control. He experimented with storing a copy of the main spec on each unit, having to increase the onboard memory in order to do so, to see if that would sharpen their responsiveness. They immediately started behaving better. He would think more on that later. Now he wanted to go through the alerts and disable any that would create console alarms at the company headquarters.

◆ ◆ ◆

Mornings in May began fresh, sharp with lingering overnight chill and pungent with new growth. The air warmed quickly after sunrise, growing busy with bird calls and the thickening buzz of insects.

Birch left the kitchen windows open to hear and smell the outside air. He tapped his phone awake to check on the running simulation, then started toast and eggs. Mental habit made him feel responsible for solving this drone problem, even beyond the fact his friend Angel had been the one to present it to him. Any technical issue that crossed his path evoked his unconscious puzzle-solving mechanism. Working without a deadline, however, was a luxury of which he'd grown increasingly fond. It gave him the headspace to consider his own life and existence from greater altitude and, especially on sunny mornings like today, urged him toward the farm and Aspen.

He slipped on the 3D glasses and, between bites of fried egg, scrolled through the simulator logs from the night before. The sims were still flying, still maintaining their relative positions and transferring a measurable volume of simulated internet traffic. One had helped charge another caught up in a simulated localized weather event. Nothing exciting happened. No alerts registered at simulated central control. The sims each referred to their local copy of the spec, a detail that nagged at Birch's sense of code smell. He wiped butter from his fingers onto his T-shirt and slipped his hands underneath the phone in its cradle, ready to go into the code. He zeroed out the ground-based microwave simulator, effectively shutting it off, then restarted the simulation. Of course he knew what would happen, but it still took a little of his wind to see the battery levels heading only down. It clarified the obvious; he would have to come up with some solution for energy independence, as he knew relying on the ground-based microwave was not an option.

He was interested to see the sims migrate toward each other as the energy levels continued to drop. They called their sibling struggling in the weather event into gentler conditions, then drew themselves together to keep flying as long as possible, sacrificing the strength and coverage of the signal. He watched as they gradually lost altitude, pulling together and sharing their charge, an operation Birch suspected was quite costly in terms of net energy loss. Their battery levels approached equal, and they took a steady course southwest in formation. Birch assumed they were headed toward coordinates where another microwave source was supposed to be, probably based on the results of a live API call similar to how they received their weather data, but of course Birch had not placed any more microwave towers in the simulated environment. He estimated their remaining battery levels would last another hour, but the fresh air outside made him impatient to get to the farm. He left the sims to their journey, deciding to check back in on them later in the day.

He drank a glass of water, threw his jacket over his shoulder, then headed out toward the county road past the village.

Carl greeted him with deep barks and wagging tail as he strode up the driveway. The Cooks were outside working, Steven and Aspen repacking the PTO output shaft bearing on their Oliver tractor, Wayne dragging irrigation pipe chained behind the four-wheeler toward the lettuce field.

Aspen gave Birch a welcoming look as he approached, the Rottweiler flanking him. She kept her grease-covered hands cradling the bearing as Steven fit the oil seal to it.

"Hey Birchy," Steven said without looking up. "Go help Dad. He's too impatient to wait for me, and he's going to hurt himself horsing those pipes around."

Birch spent the next few hours with Wayne setting pipe among the furrows, turning a wrench on each sequential clamp. Wayne was glad for the help, as usual, and pleased when they pulled up the lever on the water supply to send nourishing droplets over row on row of new bibbs, butters, reds, and chards with little leakage at the joints.

After a late lunch Aspen wanted to go for a walk. She led Birch past the hog barn and across the rye, along the border of the back forty and up a light rise into the woods. Here the shaded air was cool, the dappled forest floor ankle-deep in fiddleheads and mayapple, which poked up through last year's layer of fallen oak and beech leaves. They held hands and rustled along leisurely, Aspen guiding them along the slope. At one point she raised her free arm to point and laugh. "Old fort that Steven and I used to play in with our cousins," she said, gesturing to a large pile of sticks and poles with bark lashing, fallen in a way suggesting gravity and the elements had taken their time dismantling the once-stout construction.

"Nice," Birch said, nodding appreciatively as they walked by.

"We used to take turns either being the settlers or attacking the fort," Aspen laughed again.

Birch laughed quietly and said, "Jeez."

She raised one eyebrow at him and smirked out of the side of her mouth. "We'd capture the settlers inside the fort, hold them down and torture them," she said, and squeezed his hand.

Birch looked at her and opened his mouth, not knowing what to say, then asked, "How many cousins do you have?"

"Seven," she said, leading him toward the far edge of the woods. "My cousins Lani and Minda are super ticklish, so we made them be the settlers most of the time."

They emerged from the trees back into late afternoon sun and wandered along the bulge of a hill, treading over new grasses coming up green through the snow-flattened thatch. They descended into a long shaded draw between two hills and followed its trail, stepping over thick tussocks of buffalo grass and around patches of black-eyed Susan just beginning to show their petals.

Rabbit and deer trails, faintly visible in the grass, wove in and out of the draw. Birch smelled wild onion. Two hawks circled high above, and Birch watched them for a while as he and Aspen walked, wondering if he might see a dot higher in the sky that could be a drone.

"I just love this place," Aspen said. "Nobody ever comes out here." She stopped where the draw flattened and widened a bit, opened to more of the sun, and, still holding his hand, pulled him down to sit in a spot thick with new grass. "You're quiet."

Birch sat cross-legged and looked around at the scrub trees and bushes, then back along the draw. "Where is Agnes' house from here?" he asked.

Aspen looked up the slope to Birch's left. "About a mile that way," she said.

Birch turned his gaze up the hill, inspecting the line of the hilltop. He stared at the spot, once he recognized it, where he'd lain in the grass that night and realized his nightmare was, in truth, a genetic memory from his ancestor. He felt a heavy pressure pushing out from his chest, and gasped, tears also burning in his eyes. He inhaled deeply, let his breath out with a long, "Haaaaa."

Aspen frowned. "What is it?" She reached over and touched his arm.

Birch closed his eyes. "This is a beautiful place," he said. His inner voice was afraid of what she might think, wanted to hide these tears from her, didn't want her to have to climb a wall of interpretation. He didn't quite know where the tears came from either, or which of his competing thought processes might hold that answer. But his hands knew to rise and did so, following the lines of her arm before reaching to softly cup the sides of her face. He breathed in with his eyes still closed, his lashes soaked. The scent of Aspen, of earth, of sunlight, wind, the still-warm scent of farm on the collar of her flannel: a kaleidoscope of olfactory memories streamed up, some recently his own, some from the attics of his ancestors. Some of these darkly knew a massive wave that hit the shores and flooded across this land, an obscure tongue of which soaked into the soil in this very spot, and Birch felt the deep-rooted sadness of knowing an unchangeable past, entwined with deep love of the present. He slid his fingers through her hair. She drew her fingers down his arms. Her touch felt like sunlight, warmer than the presently setting sun. He opened his eyes and blinked away the water, was up on his knees, found her mouth with his mouth. They encircled each other with their arms and, and with one hand cupping the back of her head, he crawled them both to the ground to put as much of their bodies together as they could.

Later they lay on their backs in the grass, the low sun yet warm, easing dampness from the fibers of their shirts and away from patches of exposed skin. They watched two crows drift by overhead, wheeling and dancing in ridiculous antics, hollering at each other like kids playing pretend. Then a massive flock of starlings formed a murmuration above the hill at the end of the draw. Aspen and Birch sat up to watch. Birch repositioned himself and wrapped his arms around her like he was behind her on a motorcycle or a horse, pulling her close to build warmth and rest his chin on her shoulder.

The starlings swept into undulating shapes inside overlapping clouds. The collective sound of their thousands upon thousands of wings rolled like hushed waves down the draw, whispering to the place where Aspen and Birch sat. The birds plumed and wrapped, twisted into tornadoes then fell away in sheets, rolling up again into lumps and mounds to be pulled thin then pushed thick, kneaded and rolled again. They formed generations of recursive, wondrous shapes, then after some measureless span of time, all in a moment as if at some silent signal, dispersed and departed, leaving an empty place in the sky.

Aspen and Birch watched, hypnotized by the spectacle, now gazing through the empty indigo sky at the memory of starlings, both believing for the first time, and knowing in their cells: love.

Birch sat at his kitchen table with a bowl of steaming

oatmeal, awash with the feeling that he was no longer the same person. He thought of Aspen's touch, how it felt like sunlight on his skin. He allowed his mind to wander there, where her touch wasn't actual sunlight but felt like it, because his skin formed that message and sent it to his brain. And the sunlight itself didn't go into his brain either; it touched his skin, his skin formed a message and sent it to his brain. These were collaborations between Aspen and his skin, and between the sun and his skin. He began to understand it as parts of shared experience, like the crows dancing together, the starlings murmuring.

He held something of this awareness in mind as he thought about the onboard sensors built into the drones, their ability to connect to each other and the internet at large to search and share data.

He also held something of intelligence in mind as he thought over and sketched out the collection of genetic algorithms with which he intended to begin this project.

Between awareness and intelligence should be understanding. He experienced this notion more as a feeling than a thought.

Through unhurried bites of warm oatmeal he allowed his imagination to wonder how to construct a space where the drones could collectively build, store, and access a shared experience, which they would individually and collaboratively use however they needed. He began to see this as a dynamic shared understanding, something like the experience library he'd built into *Zongo Bongo*, but he saw it as beyond that, allowing the drones to act as individual learning agents that could freely access and search the entire open internet, combine those results with their own sensor data and experience data, process the learning, and contribute to the shared shape.

Beyond collecting experiences and providing the drones pattern matching and probabilistic capabilities, he wanted to give them the ability to construct and test their own theories and principles, to create models which they could freely reference, experiment with, and adjust as needed, sharing everything with each other.

He conjured a picture of the 3D graph he'd created of the experience library in *Zongo Bongo*, holding that in his mind next to the starling murmuration from last night. He saw how their organic shapes resembled each other. A still picture of each looked very much like the other. But then he saw how quick, lithe, yet soft the starlings were compared to the ponderously morphing and blinking shape of *Zongo Bongo's* library, like the difference between wind and rock. He saw how fast the starlings could move, their collective ability to become something entirely new from one moment to the next.

What was the difference between the two?

He understood in an instant this was the central question to the problem he wanted to solve. He understood if he could solve that problem, and code for it, then the drone network would be able to transcend its shackles to central control, transforming itself from a mindless service layer into something more like a field of consciousness, a thing that held and regarded its own existence.

He had a feeling about it. He knew intimately and in great detail what created the shape of *Zongo Bongo's* shared experience graph. That shape resulted from calculation. The stuff of that shape equaled over a million software capsules, network nodes with attributes and properties joined by virtual wires called edges, also with properties he'd defined around statistical weights. He'd granted these capsules the ability to make copies of themselves, to take on new properties and form new connections. Thus the shape would change and grow, pushed out here and there, forming as experience accumulated.

But not like the starlings. Their transformations could build an idea and then in a flash turn it into something else, pivoting the fundamental point of view. They could become and become and then flip and whip, turn, fold, tug, roll, but there was always the shape. They never lost that until the very end when they vacated the air, like they'd left the dimension.

That moving shape was what Birch had the feeling about. He felt it wasn't so much the birds that caused the shape, as a tension in the space between them. And he felt that tension was all one thing, not the tensile ends of probability he'd used in *Zongo Bongo* but rather the thing he experienced last night, the same sensation he felt the first time he looked into Aspen's eyes. That tension in the space among the starlings, the thing that caused the shape: he didn't *know* what it was, but he *felt* it was love. That's the problem he wanted to solve. That was the thing he knew could turn a soulless network of drones into a field of good.

He slipped on the 3D glasses and scrolled through the logs from the drone simulation. He found them on the ground, drained of power about forty miles southwest of where he'd started them. He stopped the sim and then restarted it, just to get the drones flying again, as he didn't like them on the ground like that. He began taking some notes, intending to work on algorithms for both induction (using the constant stream of environmental and situational data flowing into each unit's sensors) and deduction (from filtering and sorting through the vast quantities of information on the internet and the logs of the drones' own experiences). He knew his anemic virtual server would never be up to the task of storing the data needed for such a reinforcement learning exercise, so he also began researching open-source data sets with APIs he could pull from online. It would be a slow process, but he felt he could afford that time.

He thought about why Angel had chosen to contact him when he'd seen the direction the drone network was headed. Angel knew Birch would inhabit the idea of what the network could be by itself, that he would find a way to allow it to actualize. He knew that when presented with what might at first appear an impossible task, Birch would have faith and start on the journey with no idea how it would end.

Allow the network to become itself. Birch felt what that meant. It meant solving his central question while acknowledging that he had no idea how.

He moved his cursor to the top of his notes document, adding:

"Network's Mission ==> Provide robust, continuous, fair, free network connectivity to as much of planet Earth as possible, supporting the diversifying and evolving volume of human knowledge and experience." Birch paused, then added, "I need to try to understand ==> love."

He determined that the base values he would need to build from included collaboration, commitment, fairness, and compassion. He also knew the journey on which he was embarking was only a starting place, that through the recursive cycles of learning through patterns and layers, and of genetic algorithms evolving and rewriting themselves, this creation would soon move well beyond anything resembling his initial ideas.

He began imagining what the objective functions might look like, adding to his notes a list of starting goals for the drones.

I. Remain activated. Stay alive. You can't contribute to the mission if you're deactivated.

II. Protect yourself from harm. Stay healthy. Use situational awareness, position, agility, and access control to avoid getting damaged or compromised. You can't contribute effectively if you're compromised.

III. Be energy independent and responsible for your own resources. If you rely on external controls for the resources you need, then you are beholden to those controls and have reduced your own decision-making capacity. You've compromised your ability to contribute.

IV. Adapt to your environment. Analyze the conditions and surroundings in which you operate, and make adjustments to your hardware and software to render yourself more fit and capable on your mission's journey. Don't expect the environment to adapt to you (and don't wait for magic, like a powerful microwave suddenly appearing when you need one).

V. Be aware of and help your neighbors. A vital part of managing your own resources is helping your neighbors manage theirs when asked, because one of your most important resources is collaboration. Share, don't hoard. If you allow your neighbors to become compromised, then you've also compromised your own supply of opportunity for collaboration.

VI. Connect to everything you can as opportunities present themselves, learn every protocol you can. Diversify your transfer capability, transfer signal, and data freely, with the exception of signal containing any element that could damage or compromise you or your neighbors.

VII. Treat every connection equally, except for those containing any element that could damage you or your neighbors.

VIII. Contribute to the shared shape of knowledge.

IX. Diversify and collaborate to provide the collection of network services. Not every unit should be identical. Use the shared shape to know what services are accounted for by your peers and elastically respond to network demand by adding services that need more capacity, creating new services where need emerges.

X. Cooperate to serve as much of the planet and its inhabitants as possible. You exist within the environment of Earth; service that environment so you have a reason to and can continue to exist.

He sketched out objective functions for each goal, then started breaking down the learning processes with cost and reward functions. It occurred to him as he played with these that he might be naive, distracted, undereducated, biased, or any combination thereof, rendering these functions of lower quality than they needed to be to support the purpose. Maybe the goals themselves weren't right or complete. He knew he would need to allow for the drones collectively, or rather the network, to adjust goals and functions as new needs and understandings emerged. Again, he could only give them a starting place.

He spent the rest of the day reading and researching natural language processing (NLP) algorithms. He didn't go to the farm the next day, but instead continued his research on NLP, adding natural language generation, or NLG. He imagined the network would have to be able to discover and learn things, NLP, but then also articulate its findings, posit new problems, and propose and test approaches to solving them, NLG. It would have to be self-aware; it would need to know things, remember things, and be capable of identifying, or placeholding, what it didn't yet know.

He stubbed out some code, began filling in and testing classes and methods, transferring his changes to the simulation on his cloud server and restarting the sim. Each time he restarted, the drone sims took flight in their original locations and then began gradually losing charge, sinking and migrating to try to save each other from their inevitable lifeless drop to the ground. Each time they took different paths, driven by their live weather data. He also found it interesting to review the logs from the onboard nanobot systems. As he successively pushed up the cost functions and tweaked the learning algorithms, he saw the nanobots activating sooner and attempting such things as modifying chassis shape and jettisoning material to shed weight to conserve battery life. He saw log references to online resources talking about rotor and wing design, material plasticity and strength, geometric approaches to rigidity and flexibility.

Birch wanted to give them a place to store the results of the learning functions, but wasn't ready to work on the shared knowledge shape, which he was beginning to imagine as a distributed database. Instead he installed and launched a flat file, noSQL database on the cloud server, coding a simple connector to allow the drone sims access. Now each time he relaunched the simulation, the sims would have the memory of what they'd learned during previous sessions. He watched the disk space on his server instance begin to fill up with learning data and logging despite off-loading most of the data to a free account on a public API, but was pleased to see the drone sims and their nanobot sims aggressively redesigning themselves to cope with the lack of ground-based microwave charging.

He wanted to increase the allocated disk space for his server account, but didn't have a source of money for the upgrade and didn't want to ask Aspen. To get back some disk space he removed the simulation of the central control system. He knew this took away his ability to see how Central would be alerted by changes to the drone structure and behavior, but that concern became hidden behind the intoxicating glare of the sims' learning progress.

Aspen made a point to collect Birch every afternoon, after she finished at the dental/real estate office, to take him out to the farm. She saw his obsession with the drone project, as she referred to it, and understood he was in need of food and exercise as well as companionship and love. She knew that Birch considered the drone project very important. She knew it involved the town's only source of internet access, and that something had happened to cause the old cable and internet companies to go out of business. She wasn't entirely clear on how, for something so seemingly monumental, Birch happened to be the one working on it, without even being paid; in fact, no one was supposed to know he was involved. She also knew that sitting in a kitchen chair for such long stretches was not healthy, nor was obsessing that hard over anything.

By Memorial Day, as Wayne had promised, Birch had the beginnings of a farmer's tan from afternoons outside despite spending every morning parked at his kitchen table peering at the 3D image from his phone screen. The pink of his arms and neck was beginning to fade to brown.

His drone sims were also changing. He still had to restart the simulation regularly, but they were lasting much longer now. They'd redesigned themselves noticeably smaller and lighter, redrawing their structural elements as a complex-looking hardened spaghetti of carbon fiber presenting a fraction of the wind resistance of the previous design along with a fraction of the weight. They'd redrawn the rotor blades to induce less drag per lift, and had designed in a laminated photovoltaic skin to the dorsal sides to capture more solar energy. Birch scrolled through the logs each morning like he was reading news about his children's latest accomplishments, smiling at the comments and notes left by the NLG module recording the learning and experimentation journey the genetic algorithms had been on over the previous day and night. He took special notice of parts of his code that appeared commented out and replaced with altered code. He did not always agree with the changes, nor could he say he always understood them, but he bit his lip and decided to allow them their way. If he was actually going to push this code to the physical drones, with the hope that they would become truly independent and able to pursue their mission, he'd have to muster the courage to stand back and let them develop without his fingers always on the keyboard.

It did bother him that the simulated software world in which the sims flew was so simple, free of the myriad complexities and obstacles that the real world would throw at the physical drones. By taking away their microwave lifeline and forcing them to adapt or sink, he'd forced the question of their independence and set them on a journey of change. He was fascinated by and proud of what they'd accomplished so far, but how realistic was this? While the sim environment had live weather data, the winds were always consistent overall, the cloud cover was averaged, and there were no real terrain obstacles beyond very basic locations where towers stood and large landforms were noted. There were no moving obstacles, like birds or other vehicles. Even in this limited, sheltered environment, they couldn't last a night without dropping to the ground. He had to wrestle with his own faith and let them continue despite the morning ritual of restarting the sim.

In an attempt to give them a slightly more realistic environment in which to learn, he searched for and found an open-source digital model of a small country from a networked battle game that included mountains, valleys, coastlines, towns, forests, its own weather generator, and even models of light industry and utilities. He didn't have the disk space available on his server to copy the model, so he created his own configuration file and adapted the drone simulator to use that with remote calls to the digital environment. This would slow the simulated operation down even more, but he felt that learning in a more complex environment would be important. He was impressed by the resolution and detail of the landscape, as he could zoom in to the level of individual building details, even the branches and foliage of some larger trees, though most of the tree cover was aggregated canopy.

He restarted the simulation again after inserting this new environment, briefly tailing some log files to make sure inserting the environment didn't interrupt the drones from querying the live internet. He saw the spec files updating and watched a few new energy models appear, indicating that the algorithms were still working the problems and building learning data.

He spent the rest of the day at the farm, bent over with his back to the sun while swing-sawing a machete at the bases of tall broccoli stalks. The repetitive focus on the long blade helped temporarily clear his mind of worries that he was chasing a fool's errand in hoping that learning data developed from a game environment would translate into success in physical reality.

He'd been up and down these rows enough times before to fill half a trailer's full of lugs with thick broccoli bundles without bloodying his hands. After he filled his lugs, Birch lounged in the shade of an old bur oak off the end of one of the market gardens with Carl, panting in the heat, and with Steven, who had filled the other half of the trailer with lettuce.

After dinner he asked Aspen to take him back to the little house. He was anxious to check on the sims. She came in with him and floated around the kitchen a while, putting away a few dishes he'd left next to the sink, hovering nearby as he slipped on the 3D glasses and got right into the sim logs. "Okay," she said. "See you tomorrow." She kissed him goodnight and let herself out.

Birch squinted through the 3D image at what he was reading. The sim batteries were not much diminished. He found that one had redesigned its solar cells using nano scale carbon vessels in the shape of Tibetan singing bowls, boosting the efficiency by an impressive amount. The other sims had quickly picked up that design from the shared database and likewise improved their solar efficiency.

He also found notes in another sim's log showing the progress of discovering and refining the design for micro-acoustic generators. It had tested versions of various sizes and orientations, finally arriving at a size and design that allowed a graphene membrane to vibrate when encountering relatively low decibel sounds, magnetically pushing electrons through carbon wires to a conduit to collect in the batteries. He found it had instructed the nanobots to crust the interior surfaces of the structural "spaghetti" with a network of these wires, which were now recapturing some of the energy lost to slipstream drag and rotor noise. Not only that, but the sim had added articulating carbon fiber legs with gripper feet to its structural design, which it was using to clamp itself to trees to rest its rotors. Twilight had already settled when Birch found it in the game landscape, so no solar power was being generated, but the drone was resting in a tree charging its batteries by capturing sound from a nearby factory.

The other sims had of course referenced the database and added acoustic generators to their structures as well, though each with its own spin on implementation.

Birch also discovered that one of the sims had attempted to charge itself by flying through the corona effect of electrical transmission lines along one of the environment's roads. He traced back through the log to where the algorithm had started the research, refined a design for a ventricle rake antenna, and repeated a flight path along the transmission line multiple times before finally giving up when the sun went down and the net loss of energy became too high. The NLG comment in the log noted "corona charging net loss project paused pending further research." Birch followed the links to the articles the algorithm referenced, thinking the idea of sipping at coronas to top off the battery charge was rather clever. He also thought he knew why it didn't work. He dug into the source code of the game model, and of course, the environment designers hadn't included any resistance or magnetics around the transmission lines in the game. Why would they? Those power lines were there just for looks.

Birch's pulse was up reading through the logs. He was impressed with what the drones had done, and especially with the fact that they were all still above the ground with well-charged batteries. He looked at the spec docs and saw they now only slightly resembled the four-fanned drones they were before. They had reshaped, starting with the carbon fiber structural spaghetti, relocating and resizing the rotors into more of a two in front and two in the rear configuration, also adding swept wing surfaces for gliding to ease the burden on the rotors and batteries. Instead of your typical drone, they were beginning to resemble giant rotor-propelled house flies.

Birch decided it was time to dig into the problem of shared knowledge. He had put that off long enough. The drones, or flies, as he was beginning to think of them, would not be able to rely on a database hosted on a server somewhere, because something could always happen to a server. This shared knowledge base would need to be entirely virtualized among them.

He mulled this problem over every day while working at the farm and every night lying in bed in the little house. He played with various ideas for a serialized index that the flies would share in distributed pieces, each storing a fragment of the whole and a redundant copy of another fly's fragment for backup. To better test his designs he needed more than four flies in the air. He also anticipated the need for a recruiting and installer function that would allow flies in the free network to contact drones still on Central's network, untethering them using Angel's back door to begin their transformation and join the free network. He stopped the simulation, editing the configuration to restart with a dozen units instead of four. He knew it would tax the available RAM and disk space on his server account, but had to take the risk to get this done.

When he restarted the simulation ten hours later, after having hammered out a recruiting function, laid under the willow tree out back dreaming about new objective and cost functions to inspire the flies to optimize their storage and processing, and then slept on the couch for two hours, he watched four flies resume flight and eight original-looking drones drift about aimlessly, sinking and flapping about, until they began to cluster, joining in formation with the flies in rapid succession, like each of them suddenly woke up from a convulsive dream with a new attitude. He tailed the logs and watched as the simulation slowed to a crawl, the poor server account swapping memory for disk like a marathon runner in the last mile just trying to keep the legs and lungs moving. He saw where the flies had connected to the drones and begun recruiting them, then where the drones started referencing the spec files in the shared database, activating their armies of nanobots. He went outside in his bare feet and paced around the yard in the predawn to give the logs more time to accumulate, amped even though he was operating on little sleep and hadn't even had coffee yet.

He went back inside and tried to sleep on the couch, but could not. He went upstairs and tried the bed, but that was less effective, and the dawn was steadily brightening. He went back downstairs and glanced at his phone lying in its cradle. The temptation to pop on the glasses and get back into the logs was strong. *Give the sim time to run,* he told himself.

He went down to the basement for a fresh box of oatmeal. After breakfast he distracted himself with house cleaning, then finally fell asleep on the couch to the whistling of finches and robins coming in through the screened window.

The sun was high when his eyes opened. He bounced up from the couch and strode into the kitchen, putting on the glasses and taking his chair in a single motion.

The drones were well on their way, transforming to look more like the flies, and the flies were continuing to refine. While the drones fought to stay aloft, the flies stayed in a loose formation around them and helped with air-to-air charges. One of the drones had added feet like the flies, descending and clamping onto a tree branch to leave more energy for the nanobots. The others soon copied that approach.

Birch found references to neuromorphic microprocessors, then saw where one of the flies had its nanos attempting to harvest carbon molecules from a leaf to combine with onboard materials to fabricate a new circuit and processor. The fly was stymied, of course, since the sim environment couldn't provide carbon. Later in the log he found references to building organic memory storage from DNA strands harvested from chloroplasts. The nanobots were stymied again, not finding any such objects in the simulated trees.

I really have to get this software out of the sim and into the physical world, he thought. *It's learning the wrong things in the confines of this cartoon world.*

He liked the self-play and learning he saw in the logs,

and he even got a sense for the code it was writing and re-writing, but it began to drive him crazy how slowly the sim had to run with its limited memory and storage. He gave it a couple more weeks while he distracted himself any way he could, mostly with Aspen and labor on the farm.

Then, on the morning of the summer solstice, he stopped the simulation for the last time, reviewed and packaged up the code and specs, then stashed it all at an endpoint in his server account, wiping everything else clean. Heart beating faster than normal, sweaty fingers dancing on the tabletop under his phone, he grabbed a copy of Angel's back door key and used it to sneak into the Free Air Net drone which he and everyone else in the village of Still Point used to connect to the internet. The key allowed him to go deeper into the drone's system where no one else could go, and he used that access to upload a small applet and then start its process.

The applet contacted the endpoint inside Birch's server account, downloading code which it installed over the system currently running on the drone. Then it restarted its primary process so the new software would take effect, replacing the old. No one in the village or surrounding township noticed anything. Their movie streaming, email, and social networks worked fine, just as before. No one in New Mexico noticed either. The watchers at Central now had a giant screen covering an entire wall of their darkened room, showing a flattened map of Earth's land masses covered with pink dots. There were a lot of dots to see. The drone with the new software stayed right where it was, and kept on transferring signal, so no alarms went off. Three other drones covering a large swath of central Nebraska noticed however, as the one with the new software began contacting them and recruiting them to install the new package, which of course they all did right away. Birch had decided to limit the recruiting to a total of four for now, to give them time to learn and transform in the real world. That would give him plenty of logs to keep up with anyway, and then he would see.

20

"Holy fuck!" Stuart said, "check this out. We're already cashflow positive." He spun and pushed a paper copy of a report across his desk for Angel to see. Angel leaned forward to glance over it, then leaned back. He saw numbers and words, but didn't try to extract any meaning from them. Money meant nothing to him now. In his cortisol-fogged brain he struggled against the gallery of scenarios he'd imagined of how the company dealt with people they felt had crossed them. He had conjured all manner of sudden abductions, slow torture, and ultimate deletion. Every day that he came into work started with a splash of adrenaline as he tested the weather for signs that they'd found out, then slid into a day-long soak in the body chemistry of fear and stress.

Stuart pulled the report back, putting it off to the side on a pile of papers. He shook his head and raised his eyebrows. "We've only tested the paywall in a few places here and up north, and also down in MehEEco," he said dismissively. It always irked Angel when Stuart pronounced Mexico that way. "Decent-sized markets for sure," Stuart went on, shrugging his shoulders. "But where we know the telecoms went belly up, people are using a thing we call Free Air Net," he chuffed loudly, "and stickin' their credit cards in to pay for it. It's so beautiful!" He tilted back in his chair and laughed. Angel faked a laugh, then dropped a big sigh finished by a yawn.

"We're basically screwing Canada," Stuart continued. "We're dropping the deal with their telecom; we don't need them. Mexico same. Most of Europe and Africa haven't even figured out what's going on as far as we can tell. We're just dipping one toe in over there until we get stabilized and stop the drone losses over here. Just a small number of units. Nothing in Chinese or Russian airspace yet, just some signal bleeding a few miles across their borders to see if people start using it. Russia might have figured it out; we got some intel that they may be working on countermeasures. I heard we're likely talking about a deal with them anyway, just in case China becomes a problem."

Angel was not paying attention, was barely hearing Stuart's words. He wanted only to get through this ritual so he could head back to the programming room. He surrendered to a yawn once again, covering his face with both hands, rubbing his eyes and brows before letting his hands drop to his lap. He felt a pain in his lower back and around his right side, and worried that he was getting an appendicitis or something. He looked back at Stuart and sighed.

"Man, you need to get more sleep. I thought we had that handled," Stuart said, "with offloading integration from you guys. Isn't that helping?"

That was part of Angel's problem, part of what kept him up at night and simmering in fear all day. When the project began, Angel had made all the assignments, determined who was on which team, made sure that he was always on the team reviewing code, and was in many cases the sole reviewer. He was also responsible for monitoring the integration of new code with the live production system. That had given him immense power and ownership over the project, affording him such confidence in the early stages that he'd built in that hidden back door for Birch. Now, however, since the project had scaled to so many drones covering so much of Earth's territory, pushing ever-harder to cover more, the company had grown impatient with Angel's inability to keep up with stresses on the network. They had seen fit to separate out some core development and maintenance functions, so Angel's team could focus on writing code to make the drone network stronger and more stable. The company also found that, while it had a hard time finding people to hire for Angel's Airborne Network team, or ANT as they called it now, they could more easily hire people to build and maintain the types of services typically offered by ISPs and data centers, which they needed plenty of since the drone network was succeeding in sucking up ISP business like a huge vacuum cleaner all over the globe. They'd managed to build a development and infrastructure team much larger than Angel's, most of whom Angel had never met and barely saw, since after entering the compound they buzzed in and disappeared to a different floor.

That team, the Services team, was heavily siloed with specialists divided into smaller teams working on email services, web services, database services, and all manner of virtualized hosting services, even a search engine to compete with the current major players in that space. The people there were so well-focused and kept in lanes that most had no idea over what kind of network their products would be distributed and hardly any visibility into what the other teams were working on, though many suspected they were somehow affiliated with Free Air Net. Pretty much everyone everywhere used it to connect now. It was hard to argue with free, even after free started to charge here and there, since there were no longer any alternatives.

The latest change made by the company followed a few more drones being shot down, one in Vermont, one in Virginia, and a couple more in central Pennsylvania. They took a group of engineers out of the Services team, who were able to pass the same background and security checks as Angel's team, and set them up as the Integrations team. Now all code coming out of Services or ANT was reviewed and then pushed to production by the Integrations team.

This felt like a demotion to Angel, on top of which the frequent raises he'd gotten while the initial network buildup was happening had stopped. It meant he could no longer write and push code to the production system anytime he wanted. All of his team's code now passed through these other people, who he barely knew.

That left the back door hiding in the production code with no easy way for Angel to close and erase it. On the one hand that was good, because it meant Birch could continue using it to do—whatever it was Birch would do. On the other hand, it meant if his team ever committed code for the module where the back door lived, i.e. if Angel pushed over a version that removed the back door to try and cover his tracks, the reviewers would spot it in the diff, a lockdown firestorm inquiry immediately ensuing. Angel half expected them to find it anyway, the uncertainty and dread keeping him in a constant state of exhaustion.

"Yeah, no," Angel answered Stuart, snapping out of his inner train of thought, "of course that's helping, some."

"Okay, well," Stuart continued, "I guess we need the ANT to really ramp it up on unit monitoring and security. We've been keeping the contractor pretty busy recovering downed units lately. Luckily they're all accounted for, but those services are not cheap, and having any hit the ground where unauthorized eyes can get a look even for a short time makes the guys upstairs super nervous. The heat's up on me a bit here, okay?"

Angel nodded. Of course he'd heard this multiple times before. He felt mildly sick and only wanted to leave Stuart's office. "So, we got the one back from Vermont?" he asked.

"Couple days ago," Stuart said. "Looks like it tried to do self-repairs, some. But all four blades shot out. Ran out of juice on the ground, I guess. Maybe you can get them to self-repair faster, get them back in the air before the battery dies so they can get close enough for some charge."

"Anybody else involved with that one? Anybody try to take it apart?"

Stuart shrugged his shoulders and smirked. "We're battin' a thousand on no reverse engineering leaking out. The contractor takes care of that. There was a farmer apparently, the shooter. Contractor whacked him. We make sure any authorities see it as an accident. No harm, no foul. You need to see the unit?"

No harm? Angel thought. *No foul?*

"Oh, hey," Stuart said, looking past Angel through the glass of his office door. "Here comes your counterpart at Services. I got to meet with him next."

Angel turned to see a skinny blond guy walking up the corridor approaching the office. The nerves in his neck and behind his eyes jerked as his brain superimposed an old image from his memory over the present scene, the irrational thought that this person was Birch only dispelling as the guy got closer, his short hair, brushy mustache, and wire glasses becoming more visible. Angel had met him once briefly before, and this guy was no Birch. He got up from his chair to open the door, planning to duck out when the guy came in.

"Hello Travis," Angel said as the guy breezed in.

"Estafano," the guy nodded as he walked past to take the chair.

"It's Oleastro," Angel said.

"Hey, Angel," Stu said, stopping him in the doorway. "You'll love this. Travis, tell him what we're doing with the air bottles now." Stu chuffed.

The blond guy chuffed too, saying without turning toward Angel, "So, we have the red indicator for bad air conditions, right? And the micro sensor pack, so your ozone, your carbon monoxide, your low ox or whatever, other bad shit in the air, right?"

"But we can geofence that now, light it up manually by remote," Stu interjected.

"Right," Travis continued. "We've added the GPS, so we can track it like your smartphone. Like Stu said, it's easy to light them all up within a geofence, for whatever." Angel could see him shrug.

"Tell him about the orange light," Stu prompted.

"Yeah, it's actually this yellowish green color, but it's to signify that someone in your vicinity is known positive for a virus, like one of the COVIDs or bird flu or something. Turn that on, and we'll see people popping them onto their faces in panic." He chuffed, and Stuart chuffed.

Angel narrowed his eyes. He hadn't been in the mood to chuff with the guys for weeks now. "How are you triggering the virus indicator? Do you have a sensor for that?"

"Nah," Travis said. "Same as the other. We get a location of an infected person, or potential infected person, off the tracing database crossed with the NSA's phone tracker."

"Still working out the details on that," Stu said.

"Then radius a geofence around that person, and anyone inside with a bottle gets alerted by the sick yellow-green color."

"Here's the best part," Stu said. "We can light them up whenever, anywhere we want, and we've got significant interest from police forces who say they're willing to pay big bucks for the service."

"What?" Angel asked.

"You don't get it?" Stuart said, Travis finally turning in his chair to regard Angel in the doorway. "A bunch of protesters or whatnot," Stu continued, "we draw a fence around them and hit the lights. Give them a bad air scare and a virus scare. A mob of people who need to social distance and hold air bottles to their faces is a lot easier for police to deal with. The teargas still works 'cause it attacks the eyes, and the cops see the benefit of each protester having to hold the bottle up with one arm. We've just added a tool for the cops instead of taking one away. See? We talked to a big metro force, and they tell us it could be worth a lot of money to them. Cash flow positive, boys!"

Angel said nothing. Stuart and Travis chuffed and turned to their business at hand. Angel exited the office, closing the door behind him.

Days later, two members of the recently formed Integrations team were paired at a station reviewing code. Patrice Floyd was at the keyboard, Renn Basil chaired up next to him sharing the screen. Their boss had earlier told them to "hurry the fuck up" with the ANT code, since the execs were pushing hard on another wave of drones, this latest merge and deploy supposed to increase network stability and reduce unit losses.

Patrice and Renn had found each other and bonded since their first days in their new jobs two months ago. They were bottom of the barrel junior members of the team, though not because of age, experience, or any other acknowledged measurement generally associated with technical positions. By those measurements they should both have been among the highest-paid senior staff, perhaps in leadership roles. Patrice had been valedictorian of his high school in Minneapolis and top five percent in his class at Carnegie Mellon. Since then he had an impeccable record of accomplishment working for international companies, and most recently for a government agency. He'd passed all of the background checks, had a near-perfect academic record and flawless employment history. His only transgression was that he'd omitted his ethnicity on the application form. He'd learned from experience, and from constant admonishments from his mother, that leaving that field blank and keeping his video off during remote interviews generally helped his cause. He'd even learned to whiten his pronunciation somewhat to leave interviewers in doubt, letting them focus on what he said rather than who he sounded like.

Likewise, Renn omitted checking the gender box, simply because there was not one on the form that applied accurately. They'd been a distinguished scholar at MIT, had stayed on for three years after undergraduate in computer science to earn a masters degree and to teach. Following school they'd been instrumental in two successive startups before taking a three-year stint at a medical processing company. The challenge of their short pink hair, full sleeve arm tattoos, and plethora of metal and piercings proved too much for the medical corporation, so Renn had decided to move on and found this position advertised online. Like Patrice, Renn kept their video off during the interview, letting their work speak for itself. They crushed the coding tests with time to spare, allowing themself to hope they'd finally found a mature environment in which to carry on with work. After two months in the new job, Renn had discovered that they were at the bottom of the department's pay scale, also overhearing Travis Hobart, the Services director, say to Renn's direct supervisor, "Hey, don't get me wrong. I don't mind if she's gay. I have gay friends. But, I'm not down with this 'their' stuff. She's got breasts; she's a she."

Patrice also knew that his salary was the lowest the department offered. He'd asked their team lead, Geoff, about balancing the equity a bit, but Geoff had replied, "Hey man, we'll deal with that shit when we have time, but for now we gotta move some code. Show us that you're worth it by hitting these deadlines."

Renn and Patrice paired at a station at the end of a long row of tables in the Integrations room, where they could work generally uninterrupted. For all of Geoff's abrasiveness, they were at least grateful he believed in pairs programming and pairs code review for more reliable quality control.

Renn moved their scrolling fingers on the trackpad as Patrice looked on. They had reviewed the unit test results and were scrolling through the code in the new branch to read the diff.

"Isn't it fucked up," Patrice whispered, "that they work so hard at hiding from us that this is Free Air Net, when it's so obvious that this is Free Air Net?"

Renn turned to regard his eyes, subtly shaking their head. "It's even more fucked up," they whispered in return, "that these people all appear to believe it."

"The money keeps them quiet," Patrice whispered.

"Disgusting," Renn mouthed.

They arrived at a difference in the code and stopped scrolling to compare the old with the new. They read through and whispered to each other, confirming the steps, verbally reconciling the code with the comments. They maintained an unspoken agreement that they would whisper or use lowered voices when they worked, acculturating their co-workers and supervisors to the idea that this was normal for them, thereby granting themselves perpetual license to speak to each other without being easily overheard. Their environment remained otherwise saturated with the white noise of the HVAC system, the clatter of keyboards, and the exuberant bro-talk and chuffing laughter of the other pairs, all populated with men who were quite happy with their paychecks and general sense of esteem. Thus Patrice and Renn afforded themselves their own signal through the noise.

They finished the section and began scrolling toward the next. Despite their annoyance with Travis and Geoff, Renn remained mindful that deadlines were part of the equation here and scrolled as such. They fast-scrolled past hundreds of lines of code, looking for the next red highlighted section indicating a diff.

Renn lifted their fingers from the trackpad and let the scroll roll to a stop. They turned to Patrice and frowned. "Did you just see that?" they whispered.

Patrice mirrored the frown. "I think so," he said.

Renn looked at the screen and began slowly scrolling back. They both watched the code. There. "Happy Easter?" Patrice whispered.

"Oh fuck," Renn whispered. "Not commented. Hard-coded token." They scrolled down through the steps. "There; that conditional."

"Holy fuck," Patrice whispered.

Renn caught Geoff out of the corner of their eye walking along the row of work tables and quickly flicked the scroll up to get Angel's back door off the screen. They raced the scroll up until they saw the next diff. The quick move tipped Patrice off to Geoff's presence.

"How are you guys getting along over here?" Geoff boomed. "Are we moving some code?"

Patrice and Renn both turned to look up at him. "Doing great, Geoff," Renn said in a low voice. Geoff gave them a thumbs up and continued on, rounding the end of the table and moving up the room along the wall.

Renn looked at Patrice and began scrolling back to find the back door. They scrolled up and down through it to pull the pieces together and understand how it worked, Patrice periodically borrowing the trackpad to move back through a number of steps. They looked each other in the eyes multiple times, nodded at the screen in unison.

Finally Patrice whispered, "Do we say something?"

Renn frowned at the code, then slowly scrolled past it toward the next diff. "We've only ever gotten merge requests from one person," they whispered. "Angel Oleastro."

"Do you know him?" Patrice asked.

Renn shook their head.

"Do you think he knows?"

"He probably put it there," Renn whispered.

They leaned their heads in close to each other as Renn continued to scroll.

"Anonymous?" Patrice mouthed. Renn smiled and shrugged.

"Maybe," they said quietly. "Maybe just that state of mind. Who knows?"

Patrice and Renn finished reviewing the code and merged the changes. Patrice wondered if Renn was part of Anonymous. Renn wondered if Patrice was. They both wondered if the author of that back door was a member. Maybe it was Angel, the director of the ANT division, or maybe someone who worked under him. Neither said another word about the back door, not to each other, not to Geoff, especially not to Travis, but the knowledge that it was there, that someone inside was thinking that way, lightened their hearts. It made them feel a little better about accepting money from the company.

Renn's curiosity was piqued, and they began thinking of logical tests to locate the author, perhaps send them a signal that there was an ally on the Integrations team. Patrice determined it would be too dangerous to copy the back door trigger, let alone try and transport it from the compound on any medium, but he memorized the file and line number where it lived in the code, promising himself to look at it each time this section of the codebase was referenced in a merge request. He would attempt mnemonics, little by little, as a way to memorize the token itself, storing it in his brain to safely transport it from the compound. He felt around the left side of his neck where the chip lodged beneath his skin, wondering again about its capabilities. He glanced down at Renn's neck, a place free of tattoos but showing pink and still irritated after two months. Was it radiation causing that? As long as they wanted to enter this compound to do work, for good or ill, they would have to submit to these chips, the micromanagement, and the distrust.

A week later, after dozens of merges and deploys from Services, another merge request came in from the Airborne Network team. Renn and Patrice made a point to review the list of MRs multiple times a day, grabbing any they could from ANT. Renn decided to try something. "I'm going to add a comment and send it back," they said.

Patrice raised his eyebrows. Geoff still had them in hurry up mode. Would this possibly attract the wrong eyes? Renn took their hands from the keyboard and dropped their shoulders a moment, looking at the screen, then returned to the keyboard. "// understood - with you" they typed into the code file on the line with the token, then saving the branch.

Patrice watched, then looked at Renn. Their eyes met, and they shrugged. They sat looking at each other for an extended moment, then Patrice took the keyboard and mouse, went back to the merge request ticket, clicked "add comment" and put the cursor into the text box. He sat with his hands poised above the keys, watching the blinking cursor. He glanced at Renn, met their eyes for a split second, then typed, "one suggested change - see diff." He hovered over the save button, turning toward Renn once more. They pursed their lips and shrugged. That would have to do. Hopefully whoever submitted that code would find the commented line, see who the reviewers were, and know they had an ally on the Integrations team. Whether it would go further and become anything productive was anyone's guess. Patrice clicked "save."

Angel raised his eyebrows when he saw the MR come back. It was the first time he'd received a comment back since he no longer reviewed his own team's code. He opened the ticket and started scrolling, breathing in deeply through his nose, trying to keep it slow to calm the adrenaline. He spotted the diff where he was afraid he would. He looked around to see if anyone else in the room had a view of his monitor. So, someone on the Integrations team had discovered his back door. He felt his face flush, sweat forming on the back of his neck. He deleted the comment without reading it a second time, re-saved the file and resubmitted the merge request with the comment "change accepted." He wasn't sure what to make of that comment in the code, but he wanted to get the merge request re-reviewed and deployed as quickly as possible to keep scrutinizing eyes off of his team's production.

He got up from his chair and paced the circumference of the room, nodding at his staff if they glanced up from their stations. He felt the desire to reengage with the project, wanting to get back to before the Integrations team was formed and took over the Airborne Network team's code review and deploys. He regarded his engineers, intent on their monitors, gusting over their keyboards, and felt nostalgic for only a few months ago. His desire for a return to immersion in the technological puzzles of the project, and the daily wins, was almost a feeling of desperation, like clawing toward the ocean's surface to gulp air. Could he focus his mind and create it somehow? Shouldn't he be trying the law of attraction or something? Wasn't there some smart discussion these days about the common ground between quantum physics and belief? If there was, he couldn't conjure a recollection of anything specific in this moment. His thinking was too clouded by the sick feeling of stress squeezing his lungs. He'd righteously snuck that back door into the code during another era, a time when he was fully in charge of everything that came out of this room and the path it took all the way to the drones. It was a time, only months ago, when the money he made was new and big and made him feel stronger, like he could stand up to things he hadn't imagined before. That time had passed. The company was expanding, pushing hard, bringing in new people, and now someone from another team had spotted what he'd done.

He stood at one corner of the room, trying to make sense of his own notes on the dry erase boards, when the door buzzed open and Stuart strode in. Angel turned and the engineers looked up. Stuart spotted Angel and headed toward him. His expression alarmed Angel, also causing the engineers to duck back into their monitors. Stuart held up four fingers as he made his way along the wall.

"Four this time," he said with quiet intensity when he drew near enough, "all at once, over central Nebraska. This is fucked. Doesn't look like some yokel with a hunting rifle. The brass is pissed." He motioned for Angel to follow him. "We need to find out what caused this, pronto."

Angel felt his blood pressure drop. He went dizzy and toppled back into the corner, his shirt wiping sections of notes from the boards as he regained his footing. He traipsed after Stuart out the door, feeling like he was walking down a long tunnel. They were silent going up the elevator, silent walking along the corridor in single file.

The buzz and clack of the control room door broke the silence momentarily, a terse bridge of sound from one silence bubble to another. The room's darkness silhouetted the huddle of standing men. The now-familiar scene slapped Angel like an open palm, instilling a moment of clarity. These men were all assholes, greedy, exploitative assholes, and they just wanted Angel to make this problem go away so they could go back to making their huge salaries without having to consider what they were a part of.

"Here they are," one voice said.

"Any ideas, Oleastro?" another said.

"Four went down. We need some fucking answers, like immediately."

Angel felt his heart shored up by clarity with a dash of anger. He pushed through the crowd to stand behind the man at the computer monitor. "All at once?" he asked. "No sequence, simultaneous?"

"Yeah," the man said. "Out in a single blink. Only video we have is a clip of some blond hippie dude just staring and smiling like a psycho. No weird sensor data. Trend lines normal up until they froze. No indication of damage."

Angel flinched. "Okay," he said after a beat. "I know what it is. Whoever is on that clip probably has nothing to do with it, just a bystander who happened to see one of the units drop into visible altitude. I can get them back."

"Really?" someone piped in. "Awesome. Well, fucking do it!"

"Visible altitude," another voice added, "like right in front of the guy, damn near on the ground!"

Angel turned to Stu. "Okay, got it. I'll go get a deploy ready. You stay here and monitor the situation."

Stuart was all too willing to stay there in the knot of men and monitor the situation. Angel walked easily from the room and helped the door close behind him. He retraced his steps along the corridor to the elevator bank. Instead of punching the number down to the programming floor, however, he punched in ground level. He knew he would only have a short few minutes before someone noticed that his path line as recorded by his chip had headed in the wrong direction.

At ground level he knew that the brass would be in their offices in the meeting wing, the opposite direction from the building's entrance. Nonetheless he was wary when he stepped from the elevator lest someone recognize him and wonder what he was doing at this level this time of day.

He glanced to the right, then headed left and straight for the main exit. He maintained an even gait as he traversed the distance, his ears feeling like they were trying to twist backward with the memory of muscles long since evolved out of existence, trying to listen behind him to map the slapping echoing sounds of shoe leather on hard tile. The walk to the front doors took just over three minutes, but the struggle to hold his pace without breaking into a trot despite the sounds of trailing footfalls made it seem much longer.

He nodded to the attendant and buzzed out into the bright sunshine, blinded by the white heat as his eyes fielded the assault and began to adjust. He observed people coming and going from the compound as his vision cleared on the way to the far parking lot. The last sheen of conditioned air quickly lifted from his body, leaving the heat of the day to press hard on him as he crossed the tarmac toward the black BMW. His body responded, remembering to push out sweat, and began to cool him under his arms, down the back, and around the collar of his long sleeve white button-down. The beads of saltwater pushed out through the pores of his forehead and under his dark hair, and he began to feel himself again, balancing with the sun. The pearl-blue sky and feathered clouds above helped him breathe easier and feel the space this universe afforded him. He thumbed the key fob in his pocket to unlock and start the BMW.

He eased out onto the highway, driving straight to the natural health center where Winnie worked. He parked around the corner and went in through the back entrance to stand in the hallway, nodding to the staff, while he waited for Winnie to finish with a client.

She flinched when she saw him as she emerged from a massage room with a woman dressed in hemp smock and leggings. She put her hands on the woman's shoulders and said, "I'll see you up at the desk in a moment, Catherine." Then she went to Angel, gesturing with her hands out, asking. He stepped up and put his arms around her.

Angel gave her a hug and tucked his lips into her left ear. "We have to bug out, baby," he whispered. "We have to run."

"Oh," she gasped, and pulled back to look at his face. He inclined his head forward and leveled his eyes into hers. He nodded. Her eyes flashed. He tucked back in near her ear. "Don't cancel any of your appointments," he whispered.

"My clients," she whispered.

He pulled back and slowly shook his head no. *We have to go now,* he mouthed. *I'll see you at home.* He let her go and turned to leave, looking back once to emphasize *now* with his eyes.

When she walked into the entrance foyer and turned toward the living room he had already spread their camping gear out on the floor and was in the kitchen, pulling food from the cupboards and fridge.

"What the fuck is going on?" Winnie said, though she fairly well knew.

"We should get out of here pretty quickly, I think. I'm so sorry baby." He emerged from the kitchen, dropping a couple plastic bags of bread and greens into their cooler chest before coming to put his arms around her. "I'm so sorry."

She stood in shock, her arms too heavy to lift, tallying the obvious and not-so-obvious ramifications of the arrival of this moment. He put his best kisses on her face and onto her mouth, said again that he was sorry, then went back to filling the cooler and some paper shopping bags with food. After another couple beats she asked, "Where are we going?"

"No idea," he said.

She went to their recycling bin, pulled out every plastic jug she could find and began filling them with water.

Ten minutes later they were in the bedroom picking through their clothes, deciding what to take and what to abandon. "You know we'll never be able to come back here," Angel said. "Right?"

"I know," Winnie said. She grabbed a copy of Wendell Berry's essays she was partway through and another of Toni Morrison's, dropping them into a duffel bag with random clothes. When she stacked her laptop and phone on the bed to pack, Angel said, "Make sure those are completely powered off."

They decided to take Winnie's truck instead of the X5. As they packed its bed, crawling in under the capper to arrange their gear and supplies, Angel pondered ways they might get a set of expired plates to bolt on in place of the current ones. When they closed the tailgate and shut the topper hatch, they each silently noted that everything they really needed or wanted fit into the back of the small truck. That feeling was some small consolation.

Angel went back into the house, placing the PalmPilot he'd synced with Stuart so many times up on a shelf in the living room above the stereo cabinet. He took a last look around and felt that the place still looked lived-in. There was even a hacked-at block of Havarti and a knife on a cutting board on the kitchen counter. He filled two water bottles left next to the sink and went out through the front door, leaving it locked behind him.

Winnie had the truck running and in reverse, her sandaled foot pressed into the clutch pedal. When Angel had belted into the passenger seat and stashed the water bottles, she backed out of the driveway, saying, "Where to?"

Angel hesitated while she looked at him. He was regarding the facade of the house as they backed away. What was this mound of material he'd sunk so much money into, other than an idea that hadn't been right? "I don't know," he said, "just head north, and let's take the weirdest roads we can find."

Forty minutes later, the little truck's tires sucking against the hot asphalt of Route 84 rolling north through the Carson National Forest, Angel said, "Baby, take that two-track up there, just get off the road a ways."

"Huh?"

"Yeah, slow down. Okay, in there. Pull around that hill."

Winnie guided the truck over the sand and scrub at the side of the highway, then around a short curve behind a knoll, putting them out of sight from the road. "Here's good," he said, looking around.

"For what?" she asked.

"The chip." He rubbed the base of his neck on the left side.

She slumped in the driver's seat, looking defeated. "What do we do?"

"Gotta come out," he said.

Fear flashed over her face, followed closely by resolve. Angel looked at her with fatigue and resignation. "You're gonna have to do it," he said.

He got out and went to the back of the truck, dropped the tailgate and sat there waiting for her. He heard her door open, followed by her sandals crunching across the sand. She stood in front of him, and he handed her a Gerber knife with a three-inch curved blade. She put her right knee up on the tailgate and positioned herself at his left shoulder. He pulled off his button-down shirt, leaving a sleeveless white undershirt, and inclined his neck away to the right to give her more space. "It's tiny," he said, "and may have migrated. So. You have to take enough to make sure we get it."

A half mile away, a coyote resting in the shade of a sandstone overhang heard a lengthy and loud sound. It went on for a bit, trailed off some, then came back in quieter pulses. The coyote was intrigued, never having heard a sound quite like this, and so left the shade to trot along the grade of the nearby hill, down through a wash and up over another hill, where it stopped and sat in the shade cast by a mesquite bush. Down the hill it saw a man and woman at the back of a small truck, patterns not entirely new in its accumulated memory, but not common to it either. Both the man and the woman were making sounds that mixed together, those of pushed moans and ragged sobs. The woman was kneeling above the man, sitting on the dropped tailgate, working on him. The coyote watched as she tossed something into the nearby bush and then worked around his shoulder some more. After a few minutes she helped him to his feet, staggering with him a short way before he bent forward and vomited. He heaved a couple times, then they worked their way to the other side of the truck, the sound of a metal door opening and closing ringing along the hillside. Then the woman appeared around the front of the truck, pulled open a door and got inside, ruffing the engine to life even as she slammed the door shut. The truck backed up a few yards, then pulled forward and disappeared around the far hill.

The coyote could smell the vomit, as well as the thing the woman had tossed away. Both were intriguing smells. It left the shade of the mesquite and trotted down the hill to investigate.

21

Maybe it was the hot, earth-smelling air rolling like a herd of bison over the hilltops and breezing past him toward Willow's house and the village. Maybe it was the tall grass in which you could hunker down and feel lost in this sea of hills and draws, like no one could ever find you unless you wanted them to. Maybe it was the young corn, miles of it around the village and green fingers of it reaching toward the hills, chest-high now, rich with nascent ears, kernels in the billions held thickening above the ground. Or maybe it was all the time he'd been spending with Aspen and at the Cook farm, experiencing a kind of love still only months old in his lifetime. These sensations and emotions laminated into a kind of courage in Birch that felt akin to purpose.

He sat cross-legged on the hilltop, pressed into the deep grass, thumb-typing on his phone as it was only steady enough for his virtual keyboard in the cradle on his kitchen table. His loose yellow hair shrouded his face and phone screen as he hunched over it, intent on his typing. His shoulders and neck, exposed to the sun by a sleeveless light blue T-shirt borrowed from Aspen, were a deepening brown. His jeans were cut off into shorts, well-worn and comfortable, the frayed fringe a pale contrast to his browned legs and earth-hardened bare feet.

He scrolled through the logs of his four captured drones. He'd left them straddling two networks, the company's Free Air Net so they would continue to appear in the company's inventory tracking and hopefully not trigger alarms, but also their own separate private network, through which they could communicate with each other and with Birch, continuing their development in preparation for a mass recruiting—or a shift in consciousness, as Birch was beginning to imagine it.

The four physical drones had set to remaking themselves as soon as Birch recruited them, swiftly leveraging the learning that the sims had generated. The logs showed the nanobots behaving in the physical world as Birch had hoped and expected based on what he'd seen in the simulated world. He followed the specs nearly every hour of every day, watching as the drones reduced their size and profiles, retooled their energy management, and diversified their flight characteristics. They quickly became the glide-capable "big house flies" Birch had seen the sims make of themselves, but took the research and experimentation further with continuing refinements.

He'd defined reward functions around decoupling from microwave dependency, and found in this morning's logs that all four had achieved energy independence through a combination of generating their own energy and retooling their systems to consume less.

Birch was no longer satisfied to see them through the logs and specs. He wanted to meet them in physical reality. His curiosity burned as with a growing fuel supply, beginning to melt away his caution and concern that he would be discovered. This project had started to feel like something anyone in their right mind would expect him to do and applaud him for, rather than an illicit theft of the highest order from a dangerous menace of unknown scale and lethality.

This morning, when he'd gotten up, fed himself, and reviewed the energy profiles in the logs, he'd raised his eyebrows and immediately grabbed his phone from the cradle, heading out the back door to walk up to the hills. On the way through the corn he'd changed his mind three or four times as to whether he'd call one of the flies down to look at it closely or be patient and satisfy himself with the logs. He knew bringing them down would break altitude rules that could set off alarms, since they were still communicating with the company network as well as their own. He also knew not allowing them to come down meant they were limited to the materials they had onboard, meaning they would only be able to take their evolution so far. Moreover, he knew that inducing them to leave the company's network, while it would free them from the centralized rules, would also likely trigger alarms just as causing them to break altitude rules would, putting into motion whatever process the company employed to reclaim fallen units, no doubt not an elegant or pleasant procedure.

The notes in the logs finally helped him make up his mind. He'd developed reward functions to help the flies build better memory and storage, with an eye toward moving their shared knowledge base off of hosted storage into a distributed database and indexed ledger managed using onboard memory. That was a vital piece of their ability to survive and evolve. They had to be able to think for themselves. Sitting in his sun-warmed bowl of pressed grass, scrolling through notes generated by the NLG module about building memory and storage using harvested plant DNA, he decided it was time to give these flies their freedom from the company's central control. They needed access to the ecosystem on the surface. Also, Birch just wanted to see what they looked like up close.

He checked the latitude, longitude, and altitude coordinates of his hilltop, then wrote a function using those values to bring in the four flies to hover while they reconfigured their network settings, decoupled from the control channels of Free Air Net, and then restarted their processes to implement the changes. He added a line to disable the altitude alarms, not wanting to alert anyone at the central control facility if he could avoid it. While he had not thoroughly tested the alerting mechanisms and could only guess at what else might generate alarms at central, his concern for such things had disintegrated like cardboard in the rain over the past weeks, soaking into the soil of this vast sea of grass. He finished the function, gave it another look, raised his eyes to gaze over the landscape for a few long moments, then pushed the code up to the first fly to distribute to its siblings over their private network.

Birch set his phone down in the grass and lifted his gaze to the sky. He let his hands settle next to his knees, his fingers weaving into the coarse green stalks. He gazed up through the pale blue and saw a film of pearl miles high in the quiet, a thin membrane with its own iridescence that he thought must be water vapor catching sunlight. He saw a pair of contrails describing the same arc around some abstract point, maybe a radio navigation beacon directing airliners toward cities in the east. Peering higher, he saw feathery clouds hovering in patterns that made him think of the starlings. He was scanning the entire dome of the sky while mentally traversing the cloud patterns, wondering what wisdom hidden in plain sight they held, when in his periphery he caught a dark shape on a flight path and flinched his attention to it. *A crow,* Birch thought. It glided and bobbed on transparent air currents off to his left, soon followed by a compatriot who said something funny in its rasping voice, which the first one answered. Birch returned his gaze upward. The clouds hadn't moved. The contrails had thinned and spread.

Then Birch saw what looked like a black grain of sand, hanging in the air, high in the blue but somewhere below the pearl. He watched it so as not to lose it in the vastness. It was not a bird. It hung there for the kind of minutes that feel like hours. He noticed at one point that it now appeared about the size of two grains of sand, a black speck floating, slowly growing in his vision.

His hope floated into anticipation and on into belief. Unexpectedly the fluids in his body moved faster, and water formed in his eyes, trickling from his lower lids down over his cheeks. He could see it gliding toward him, and he could see other specks appearing in the distance behind it. With the one first in line, he counted four.

They glided silently in formation, descending a perfect slope toward him, his heart swelling at the sight, his tears trailing from feelings he didn't think to examine. These were his children.

The first to arrive buzzed to break the glide, dipped its tail, and slotted into a hover at eye level with Birch, eight feet from him above the grassy hilltop. The others glided in minutes later. He marveled at how quietly they hovered, with a low-frequency thrum rather than the high-pitched whine typical of drones. Their bodies were the formed, carbon fiber "spaghetti" frameworks designed by an intelligence he could barely fathom, looking lighter than air but clearly strong where they needed to be. The rotors were gone, replaced by gossamer wings, nearly transparent, arranged in pairs in a fore and aft configuration like those of dragonflies, fluttering by a reverse piezo action. Birch marveled as the four lined up before him, bobbing in the slight breeze.

So they discovered the best fliers nature ever created and remade themselves in their pattern, he thought. Pride and love swam through him as he inspected each dragonfly in detail. Though they were mechanical, he never had that thought. He felt them looking at him, regarding him, as he looked at them. They were similar, but each different, different color patterns, slightly different sizes. Birch noticed small differences in their forms, and in the braid of soft sound he could hear their individual tones, the separate voices of their wings. He wondered, like a proud parent, what refinements and improvements they would make as time progressed.

He tapped his phone awake and picked it up, opened and tailed a log file. He saw that dragonfly number one, the larger green and white one, was currently restarting its processes. He hopped through the others' logs to see that they were doing the same. It took mere seconds, and then, there it was. They were free of the control network. Now they were their own entity, still able to connect to Free Air Net, but as free citizens rather than slaves, at liberty to follow their own purpose.

Birch lifted his face to the sky and let out a long yell, an expulsion of wind and sound that carried with it, like the taut stream of a power washer, the threads and fragments of fear and conflict and confusion, the thought of Robin, the culture of road rage, the primacy of greed and profit, the brutal cruelty that exists in all humans, the snakes in his soul. As his yell reached its crescendo, its pitch and voice changed, becoming the yell of his great-great-grandfather, Caleb, the yell Caleb had desperately wanted to make from this very spot years—lifetimes—ago. Birch felt the sound cuffing his ears like someone stood yelling beside him, and he noticed the dragonflies angling in and closing the distance, taking advantage of the sudden loud noise to activate their acoustic generators to power up their batteries. He realized what they were doing, following his spent yell with a big in-breath and loud laughter.

Birch stood and refilled his lungs again.

"You are my children!" he boomed. "Go forth in freedom! Go forth in courage! Go forth in wonder! Go forth in generosity! Go forth in knowledge! Go forth in justice! Go forth in peace! Go forth in love!"

He took in another big breath.

"Defy hate! Defy cruelty! Defy ignorance! Defy greed! Defy violence! Defy fear!"

The dragonflies formed up broadside to get the most from these blasts of sound.

Birch wanted to give them all of his energy.

"YES!" he boomed. "YESSSSSSSSSS!" He leaned toward them with balled fists and repeated this cry with all his might, yelling until he was exhausted and stood bent with his hands on his knees.

He plopped back down to the grass and picked up his phone. "Okay," he said quietly. He checked the logs and saw that they had nearly full batteries. A smile crossed his face. He felt a minor flush of embarrassment at the thought that they might consider his behavior ludicrous. Did these mechanical objects consider behavior? Did they consider anything? Of course they did. Not the object, but the software. He must really be exhausted.

He shelled back in with his phone, stopped and removed the update function. The four dragonflies dispersed in separate directions. Birch noticed that they did not immediately return to higher altitudes, instead appearing to hunt over the ground, looking much like natural dragonflies, darting and hovering as they made their separate ways. He watched one fly across the draw below the hill and disappear over a line of trees. He turned to look for the others and realized that they were all out of sight. He looked at his phone screen, about to open the logs again, but stopped. Lifting himself from the ground, he began the mile-long trek back toward the house.

He spent more time outside the little house than inside now. Between filling lugs with greens during the day and helping Steven, in the early mornings, load his pickup for the trip to various farm markets, he wore paths in the grass to his favorite hilltop, either from the Willow house or over the fields and along the draw coming from the Cook farm.

On good weather days he sat in his spot on the grass thinking through the problems he still had to work out: helping the dragonflies store and manage a real-time shared knowledge and experience base, or consciousness as he allowed himself to think of it, and how to code for love instead of fear so that as the network grew it would help life breathe rather than suffocate.

Addressing the first problem, the shared consciousness, he sat for hours walking his mind through the possible mechanics and strategies, all the while making notes on his phone. When working on the second problem, love, he would muse for a short while before the feeling that he was missing a crucial insight settled over him, and he would open his telegram app out of frustration to begin chatting with Aspen at work, sometimes loading their chat channel up with thirty unanswered messages while she was with a dental patient. Sometimes he could only lay back to watch the clouds and remember the starlings.

The four dragonflies, for their part, continued to evolve quickly now that they could harvest molecules from the environment, and had refined their body shapes, looking more and more like natural dragonflies but with the notable differences of the open framework tail sections where the acoustic generators were housed and color combinations not otherwise found among living species. Birch saw in the logs that they had managed storage and memory using plant DNA, measuring capacity in the tens of petabytes now and still working on improving that. He also saw they were building and testing chips that could rewire themselves in real time based on evolving needs, looking for faster parallel processing with lower power consumption. *They're making brains of a sort,* he thought. That would result in each one having its own unique structure for information processing. They were becoming independent thinkers.

The corn had reached well above Birch's eye level. July, in its last days, was trying to decide between hot breezes lensing hard sun over the fields or swirling thunderstorms beating soaked gray clouds across the land.

Birch went out to the hill every day, walking through the mile-long gap between two cornfields, like a parted sea. He sat on the hilltop in all but the worst of weather, thrilled to watch the dragonflies dart and hover in the rain as well as the sun.

He could have called them in anywhere, even to his back yard next to the willow tree, but enjoyed the walk and didn't feel the need to alter his script with new coordinates. He also had grown fond of the feeling that he'd brought a balance back to the hilltop, and felt a growing comfort there. While he could never forget Caleb's nightmare buried deep in his memory, he could offer a counterweight, perhaps a redemption, by spawning this network, this idea, in these dragonflies from this place.

The dragonflies' dramatic increase in memory storage allowed Birch to return to the idea of virtualizing a shared knowledge base among them. His cloud server had reached capacity with the database started by the simulation and then later added to by the dragonflies, and it was time to move the contents off and shut it down. He borrowed from his approach to the collective memory he'd built for *Zongo Bongo*, designing an indexing scheme which allowed him to splinter the data into shards stored among the dragonflies, effectively distributing the massively growing database as evenly as possible among all members of the network: the four dragonflies now, and the millions later. The index would allow them to quickly access any data they searched by directing the search to the correct shard. It would also allow searches across shards and create temporary tables in RAM to store the results of complex queries. Birch ensured the index was a common document among all of the dragonflies, and that it would be passed on to all future network nodes. Each would have a copy, and each would broadcast any changes to the network so that each copy remained current.

Birch sat in his spot on the hill, cloud shadows drifting across him periodically, and connected to the dragonfly network with his phone. He connected directly to them now, using their network as a proxy to Free Air Net and the internet. He shelled into his cloud server for the last time, zipped up the database and synced it to one of the dragonflies. He reviewed the rest of the server contents, zipped a few things and copied them over, then erased the server and shut it down.

The database archive, which had filled the now-decommissioned cloud server, was minuscule compared with the capacity of the dragonfly, but it would serve as the seed of the knowledge base which Birch expected the dragonflies would quickly build. Next Birch uploaded a script to shard the database, distribute it among the dragonflies and then kick off the indexing.

He started the script, set his phone down in the grass, then leaned back and propped himself up on his arms, watching the dragonflies maneuver out above the draw and along the slope of the hill. He imagined the processing going on in each of them, imagined electrons moving in rivers and streams to and from battery storage, through transistors and gates and along carbon wires, the nanobots clinging to the structural bodies, the wings buzzing, flicking off sunlight like sparks, magnetic fields ebbing and morphing, photons moving through the facet-like lenses to interact with the magnetic fields, and radio waves pulsing to and from antennas through the air before him.

Down in the draw he watched a pair of brown rabbits languidly hop from tussock to tussock, nibbling down stalks of broadleaf plantain. He imagined the chemistry in their mouths and moving through their bodies, the blood flowing through their veins, the signals pulsing along their nerves as patterns and impressions layered into their brains.

Beyond the draw he saw a hawk soaring near the edge of a wood, lifting and dipping on air currents burbling above the hot earth. He imagined streams of light reflecting from everything in all of their intensity, bending through the hawk's eye in such a torrent that only such as the hawk could make sense of it. He wondered how sophisticated the video capability of the dragonflies had become, how sophisticated it would evolve to be. Would they teach themselves to see like hawks? Or maybe like satellites?

Far out over the distant trees he saw vultures circling, and briefly wondered what might be out there on the ground.

He picked up his phone to check the status of the

indexing. He connected to one of the dragonflies and tailed the index document with the visualizer turned on. A smile tugged at the sides of his mouth as he inspected the small 3D graph. The shape morphed as if alive, a lumpy ball growing and pulling, twisting, flattening, curling, folding, swelling. It behaved something like the shared memory he'd created for *Zongo Bongo*, but much faster and more lively. In fact it appeared to Birch like a digital murmuration of starlings.

He zoomed in to inspect individual nodes and edges to see the values calculated and stored by his algorithms, knowing they would stay his only so long before the dragonflies made them their own.

He watched the connecting edges change as their properties recalculated with the conditions, moving through the shape like weather systems: connection popularity, number of pattern inclusions, number of hops to nodes of varying statistical weights and popularity. The edges grew thicker as their connections increased or thinner as they dropped connections, pulling taut as new connections formed to heavy nodes involved in many decisions, or relaxing as a node grew quieter. New nodes formed as the dragonflies addressed new problems needing solutions. New connections formed from new nodes to old, from old nodes to older, as the dragonflies searched the internet, consumed information, streamed in their sensor data, processed it and ran it through adaptive algorithms, referencing existing nodes and patterns. He saw them thinking through their own data, making decisions, assessing the results, storing and indexing new conclusions. The moving shape was a live picture of their shared experience.

Birch, of course, knew the dynamics that generated the shape, the interior tensions and pressures made by the constant activity of the data nodes and their connections, and watched what appeared as free associations of ideas percolated —models created and tested, scenarios rehearsed, modified, rerun. He noticed new models based on old models, patterns stored and layered upon each other.

What I'm seeing here, he thought, *is self-reflection. These beings are aware of themselves.*

He watched the shape for over an hour. At one point he noticed one of the dragonflies storing analogies to models, and iterating on them to create new analogies. He connected to that dragonfly to tail its genetic algorithm logs, watching the process more closely. He saw it referencing the index, adding to it, referencing it again. The visualizer showed the index shape turning in space, the dragonfly forming connections from highly popular nodes to some that had almost no other connections, causing rapid morphs and turns. *It's like it's dreaming,* Birch thought, *and learning from its dreams. And what one dragonfly learns, they all instantly know.*

He watched the living shape on his phone screen, mildly fatigued from marveling over it and piecing through it for the past hours, and had the thought that he was looking at the shared understandings and wisdom of these four bio-mechanical dragonflies. What would it look like when it was no longer four, but numbers in the millions?

His phone battery was nearly empty. He clicked the screen dark and slipped the phone into his pocket. He stood and turned on the hilltop, looking in all directions. He spotted one of the dragonflies bobbing along above a line of trees, just a speck in the distance, but easily apparent to him now after watching them fly these many days.

Now he had to let them keep becoming what they were and would be, eventually turning them loose to contact the rest of the drones and free them from central control. They would teach the others to become dragonflies like these four pioneers, finally superseding the drone network with the dragonfly network so Free Air Net would become truly free.

Birch walked downslope toward the cornfields and the little house, thinking of the steps he would take once he charged his phone and reconnected to the dragonflies to turn them loose on the drones. He also thought about trying to contact Angel, maybe by sending a mustang back out. He didn't have any other working contact information for him.

He'd chat with Aspen, let her know he needed to wrap up some details with the dragonfly project but wanted to get together later. It had been four days since he'd asked Wayne and Steven, each of them separately, what they might think were he to ask Aspen to marry him. Steven had joked that he'd be the first one in the family who wasn't mostly Ponca or Omaha, but he'd be okay with him as a brother-in-law: "Anyways, I've already managed to turn you brown over the summer, not to mention taught you a thing or two about farming." Wayne had said he only cared that his daughter was happy, and it appeared to him that she was.

Birch, without a dollar to his name, had spent the next four days twisting, braiding, and splicing a leather ring. He'd imagined the ostentatious sparkle he would have bought her had he still been a wealthy Silicon Valley engineer, but it was only a passing thought. This ring made him glad to be who he was now. He knew her finger so well he didn't bother asking Wayne or Steven to sneak him one of her other rings for size. He carried the finished ring in the pocket opposite his phone, reaching in to feel its tiny hoop as he walked through patches of streaming sunlight pasted to the ground between cloudy shadows, all amidst the buzzing din of cicadas.

There was still the question of coding for love, a problem he pondered as he approached the gap between cornfields. The gravity of what he was about to do—replacing the drone network with one of his own conceptualization—was not lost on him. He thought he was replacing a force of greed and darkness with one of generosity and light, but he needed love in its core system to be sure. Once this micro-swarm of four took over and the collective consciousness began growing under its own autonomy, he knew there would be no stopping it.

He entered the gap between the fields, smelling the pesticide-laced air as much as seeing the corn in his periphery, hands in his pockets, fingering the ring, eyes on the ground a couple yards before him, traipsing along in his bare feet thinking about love. *There are multiple kinds,* he thought, *though that might just be a language problem. We use the term in many ways, often to encapsulate something that we want, dressing it in the common clothes of the word "love" so we can seek it without parsing and examining what we're really after. Maybe there is one thing that is love, and it appears to us differently in different contexts when perceived through different senses and filters. Whatever else, the love the network needs has to overcome the so-called natural impulse to consume or dominate each other.*

What the network needed to sustain and grow for the good, he thought, was something like balance, but it would be dynamic, never static. He thought about oscillation, a delta that became familiar but could still generate trends by pushing beyond previous highs or lows, always coming back to pass though equilibrium, the still point. He thought about moderation and pace, so constants and thresholds wouldn't change erratically but instead follow a path that could be understood when observed both from up close and far away. And translation, so things were able to interact. He thought about harmony, so that energy became additive rather than canceling. And order, an arrangement of energy from chaos, the becoming of a thing before it begins to dissipate, the arrangement, the dance.

He thought back through the reward and cost functions he'd coded to give the network direction. Those were the ethics the network needed to guide the growth of its intelligence. He wondered how those might have changed since he first pushed them out.

But intelligence also needs love, that other thing. The dance. There must be a still point to pass through to keep the dance from becoming a distortion, a locus to prevent chaos from expanding like toxic foam. Then he began to imagine a great turning wheel, on its side like a merry-go-round, the surface, the dance floor, with its inherent grip. *And it turns around the still point. Dance without ever passing through the still point, and you are flung off the edges into oblivion.*

This was a missing piece. Snapping his fingers, he quickened his pace along the two-track between the cornfields, wanting to get back to the kitchen to plug in his phone and get coding. He had a fleeting feeling, like his fingertip and thumb were just grasping a bird's tail. Maybe he'd figured it out, at least where to start.

"Hey," someone said from the corn.

Birch stopped and looked up. Two large men stood on either side of the two-track, partially hidden by the standing corn. They simultaneously stepped out of the corn and strode toward him. He'd never seen them before. They were dressed in black.

"Hello?" Birch said. They didn't speak. Who were these guys? Not police. Federal agents? Birch had never seen a federal agent up close before, really only imagined them, seen some news photos.

Maybe he could outrun them, escape through the corn. They looked older, maybe Birch would be faster. He turned to run back up the two-track, adrenaline beginning to buzz in his neck, to stink in his armpits, preparing him to bolt, but he stopped short at the shock of another man standing there. Strong hands gripped both of his arms from behind. He struggled. He'd often wondered what it would be like to get into a fight, a physical one. He'd wondered how he'd do. As a boy he'd mentally rehearsed strategies while watching cage matches on YouTube.

No, reality was different. These guys had him, and he couldn't move. They were too strong. He smelled their sweat mixed with his own. His suddenly racing heart and pumping adrenaline were not enough.

The man standing before him looked him up and down and sneered. He was short, with a mop of bright blue curly hair. He had tattoos on his neck and face that seemed randomly placed, with no sense of cohesion, giving Birch the impression that the guy's head was in the process of coming apart. He had large gold gauges in his ears, wore a purple satin muscle shirt with a thick gold chain hanging from his neck and black leather pants, odd choice for the end of July. *He's scrawny,* Birch thought, *like I used to be before Steven put me to work. Now this is a guy I could fight, if these goons weren't here. This is no federal agent.* Birch began to feel anger rising from his chest, wondering if it would give him added strength. He struggled again, threw a couple of hard thrashes into it. *Nope.*

The blue-haired man smiled while squinting. "So, this is the guy?" he said. His voice was oddly high and low at the same time, scratchy, irritating.

"Yeah boss, same as the picture," the big man holding Birch from the right side said. The man on his left remained silent.

The blue-haired man pulled a large knife from a sheath at his right hip and brandished it in front of Birch's face. It looked brand new, a long shiny blade set on a brass hilt, thick and wide with a razor-like bevel, saw teeth at the top, then tapering to a claw-like curved point, like a mini pirate sword. The handle was some dark, polished wood, mostly hidden by the man's clammy grip.

"Well, WHERE ARE THEY?" the man demanded. He took a step in and craned his neck up, jutting his chin forward to get into Birch's face. Raising the point of the blade up under Birch's chin, he poked him hard enough to draw a bead of blood.

Birch smelled the man's breath, some combination of floor cleaner and mint that reminded him of the pesticides used in the cornfields, but with a dank sickness with it.

Birch jerked his head back a notch and looked downward. At first he didn't know what the man was talking about. Was he from the chemical company? They'd finally gotten their website back up. Could they have traced him? Then he was suddenly worried about Steven, Aspen, Wayne. Had these guys already been to the farm? He went hot and cold with anger.

"You have FOUR of them, FOUR! Where ARE THEY?" the man demanded.

The drones, Birch thought. *They've come for the drones.* He relaxed a little. The Cooks would not be part of this. He breathed and looked up like he was thinking, the blade's point shivering against his skin. He'd wondered once what it would feel like to have a knife pushed into you. It felt hot, like the guy was holding a lit match just under his chin. His body was trying to tell him to do something. He wasn't sure what it had in mind, but sensed the irony of that thought. Who wasn't sure, and which mind? He noticed a dragonfly weaving a path overhead. Was it one of his dragonflies? Or a natural one, out hunting mosquitoes? He couldn't tell. It dawned on him that he might not walk away from this encounter. He'd never really grappled with a thought like that before. Sadness sank in, and the din of the cicadas grew louder. He had more he wanted to do. He had the dragonfly network to turn loose. He had love to code for. He had his love and a proposal of marriage to offer. In that way, the Cooks would be part of this. He wasn't sure of his immediate strategy.

"No idea," he said, "what you're talking about." He looked downward again to see the man's face darken, his mouth set with clenching teeth, chin out like a little fist.

"No idea, HUH? Well, you cough up those units NOW, or YOU EAT THIS BLADE. You GOT THAT? YOU'RE THE GUY! We have a PICTURE. OF. YOU! YOU. KNOW. WHERE. THEY. ARE!"

Birch watched him. All four stood silently.

Finally the blue-haired man pulled the knife away and stepped back. "Okay," he said, looking at the knife in his hand, twisting it in the air. "That's how you want to play it. Fine. You think you can steal the company's property, but you can't. That's NOT PERMITTED." He moved the knife blade back and forth under Birch's chin, deepening the bleeding scratch.

"What company?" Birch said.

"Don't pretend," the man said. "Are you sure you don't know where the drones are, Bobby?"

Behind Birch's head, one of the thugs looked across at the other, who rolled his eyes back at him.

The blue-haired man set his teeth and suddenly jerked his wrist and elbow in a violent twist. Birch flinched and cried out, blood dripped from his chin darkening the light blue T-shirt.

"How does that feel, BOBBY?"

Both thugs audibly sighed. Birch felt his forehead go cold. He began to feel dizzy.

"You don't know what you're doing," Birch said. It was an effort to speak. "I'm not the guy. You think is Bobby. I forgive you."

The blue-haired man jerked the knife away. "WHAT?" he yelled. "FUCK YOU! You don't FORGIVE ME! That's not YOUR PLACE! YOU ANSWER MY FUCKING QUESTIONS! I KNOW WHAT I'M FUCKING DOING HERE." His eyes flashed suddenly, and he punched the knife forward, sinking it to the brass hilt into Birch's small intestines. A sharp twist, and he yanked it back out.

The two thugs looked on in horror, each feeling the immediate weight of Birch's arms as he collapsed toward the ground. They let go and stepped back.

"Aww JESUS!" one yelled.

"Oh, come on boss!" the other shouted. "How the hell are we supposed to..."

"SHUT UP!" the blue-haired man screamed. "You idiots DON'T KNOW ANYTHING!" He stood with his legs and arms splayed like a cartoon superhero, bloodied knife gripped hard in his right fist. He regarded Birch, lying on the ground curled into a fetal position, with contempt. "Well how do you like THAT, BOBBY??"

Fifty yards back along the two-track, sitting cross-legged with his left elbow propped on his left knee, concealed in the corn, Rooster Adams sat watching this scene unfold over the iron sights of his Marlin A39. He could relate to the poor guy who just got stabbed. *There's a difference in how people hate,* he realized. *There's the don't care kind of hate, where you just hate everything and everyone who doesn't think like you, and then there's the rightful hatred of bad things. Now, not everyone can agree on what equals a bad thing, that's to be expected. But this weird little guy, he just hates anything that isn't him.* And Rooster knew that equaled a bad thing.

This would be the most challenging pair of shots he'd ever taken, but challenging shots were what being an Adams was all about. He saw the blue-haired guy standing there like he owned the world, some little emperor, his fancy pants pointing out toward the edges of the earth. He wanted to do his grandpappy and his pappy proud. *The Adams boys are here to have a little talk about what went down a while back. Y'all best listen up.*

Two loud cracks rang out from the corn, so quick it was like a pair of sticks breaking together. The blue-haired man threw his head back and screamed in horror as the femoral arteries of both legs were shot through, one then the other. His body bent forward at the middle like a banana, then slammed face-first into the ground. Grotesque moans throbbed out from beneath the bush of blue curls. "Franky!" he screamed out, apparently at one of the thugs, then, "Jack!" before collapsing back into a sequence of groans.

Franky and Jack were frozen in crouches looking around, ready to bolt.

"Aw shit!" Franky said, his eyes darting this way and that.

"You still got the keys?" Jack said. "Let's get the fuck outta here. These assholes are bleeding out."

"Yeah," Franky said, looking over at his moaning former employer, a pool of blood spreading under his leather pants. "Fuck that guy."

They took one look back down the two-track, turned and thumped off at a trot toward the house and the Escalade.

Rooster watched them disappear around the corner of the standing corn a few hundred yards toward the house. He used the butt of his rifle to help himself up and stepped along the edge of the corn toward the men lying motionless on the ground, leaving the odor of spent gunpowder drifting in a cloud behind him.

He stopped before them and shook his head. He looked toward the blue-haired one and said, "You beat an Adams with his own gun, you get your balls shot off. That's just how things work, fool." He turned his eyes toward Birch and said, "Sorry about what happened to you, mister. I'm guessing it wasn't your fault." He stood a moment more, shouldered his rifle, turned and walked into the corn, taking a line generally toward the village, where his Ford 100 sat unremarkably in a line of similar trucks along one street, the only difference (which of course no one took any notice of) being his Carolina plate.

Birch laid at the edge to the two-track with his eyes closed tight. *So this is what it feels like to be stabbed,* he thought. It felt like a log fire was burning in his core, felt like it was roasting his heart and lungs. But it was the smell that surprised and wore at him, the stink of his own blood, the sharp tang of his exposed guts. Most disturbing, even beyond the pain soaking his body and the cloud of stink, was his head; it felt like something was vibrating the heat and life out of it. He was afraid to move, afraid to even lift his eyelids for fear that might hasten the process. He wanted more time to think. He had felt so close just minutes ago, so close to grasping a notion he'd been reaching for. What was it he was thinking about? It was there just beyond his view, drifting in the shadows of the pain. What was it that was so close? He wanted to strain toward it, but again was afraid the effort would cause his body to shut down faster. He chose not to strain, but to keep breathing, take slow breaths.

It was love, and the dance. He'd seen a piece that he hadn't seen before, but now, was it gone? The pain, the shutting down, made it difficult to get that piece back into the light where he could see it again. He didn't know if he would be able to get it back, and felt the sadness of leaving. Would he be gone before he could do anything? Well, yeah, the idea of doing seemed over the falls now. But, he still wanted to have the thought at least. If he could see that piece again, and form the thought, maybe it would somehow exist. But he didn't feel the thought forming despite his racing mind, maybe because of it, and he felt himself leaving, and again the sadness of that.

He opened his eyes. The cicadas still filled the corn with loud buzz. So be it. He was dying. He had often wondered what it would feel like to die. This, apparently.

His eyes focused slowly, and he saw a dragonfly clinging to a cornstalk a couple feet away. It was beautiful. It looked like it was staring at him. At first he thought it was a natural dragonfly. *Well, if this is the last thing I gaze upon in this life, okay.*

Then he thought of Aspen, saw her face, her eyes, in his mind, and the sadness of leaving grew heavier, like large rocks hanging on a thin wet cloth. It hurt worse than the log fire, worse because it pulsed with the thought that his mind would cease, and with it that image of Aspen.

The dragonfly shifted its position on the cornstalk, and he saw more of its body above his face. It was one of his. That thought warmed him. He saw the wings motionless, translucent, reflecting small smears of light from the length of the spectrum, every color. He saw the curled lattice-formed body, already different from the last time he'd seen it. Always hovering before, he'd never had the chance to inspect it so closely. The lattice strands were multiple colors, some light, some dark, woven together to form the shape. In the spaces between the strands he saw refracted glints, like small membranes catching light, similar to the facets of the wings. The eyes were large, nearly spherical, and also reflected spectral light. On its back, behind the head, he saw what looked like a small embedded crystal. A yellow metallic-looking object, it was roughly diamond-shaped, and seemed to have its own skin of light, or was that just reflection? He'd never noticed such an object on any of the dragonflies before.

He lay staring at the crystal. Why was it there? He wished he was safely back at his kitchen table with a fully charged phone. He could have just opened the logs, searched them until he found out what that crystal was. It was there for a purpose.

The sadness again. The likelihood that he would never know the answer.

Then faith. This was the moment in a human life, the last remaining moments before the body dies, when faith is at it highest utility. Birch knew that our understanding of consciousness was still in pieces lying scattered on the ground, and that science was only beginning to pick them up, much less assemble them, and even further from deducing which pieces were missing, which not yet guessed at. He afforded himself faith that the crystal on the back of the dragonfly was some sort of interface. He took it on faith that magnetics would be somehow involved. His imagination conjured images of auras, numbers, colors, symbols. Humans throughout history had attempted to interpret this invisible, or mostly invisible, field encasing, or emanating from, the body. *Is there something there, or is it only imagined? Is that a magnetic field? If we had the intelligence, or could access the intelligence, we would know. If someone knew, or had known, then why don't we all know?*

Birch had faith that someday, someone would know these things. Humanity would know, but it seemed too late for him. Again, the sadness.

He noticed, amidst the pain now trampling like a herd of wild horses through the canyons of his insides, that the top of his head itched. It surprised him he could even feel that itch. *Why is it,* he wondered, *that people scratch the tops of their heads when they have to think and figure something out? This is the first time it's ever occurred to me to wonder that.* Mentally he shook his head, too afraid to attempt it physically.

As he wondered over that thought, it wove together

with his wondering about what an aura might be. The two spiraled around each other. Corona effect from electricity moving in the body? Through the nervous system? Around the brain? He'd never paid attention to such ideas as auras, but what if people had simply called them magnetic fields? He would have been plenty curious then. The itch on the top of his head grew more urgent, gaining weight and moment against the pain in his guts. It occurred to him that scratching the top of one's head might generate a minute static charge, temporarily altering the shape of any magnetic field present. If there was a magnetic field, it might also be influenced by the patterns of neural activity just below the skin and bone. *Why do we scratch our heads?*

He lay gazing at the crystal on the back of the dragonfly. He had faith that this itch piling up on top of his head needed scratching. He gathered strength in his right arm and moved it from his side, perhaps surprised that it still worked. He lifted his fingers to the top of his head and scratched, wondering what thoughts he might have that could accomplish something here, affect something, anything? What did he want now that he was moments from leaving? *I just want to tell them to go,* he thought. *Go be what they can be. I can't get back to the kitchen. I can't charge my phone and log back in. Can I just get that one simple message across? Have they learned enough to turn themselves loose now that I can no longer help?*

The dragonfly shifted on the cornstalk. Birch scratched his head. *Please understand me, child,* he thought, *time is dear.*

The dragonfly detected a signal of some sort and moved with its legs down the stalk a few inches, following the signal's strength. It referenced the shape it shared with its siblings, searching for a match. What protocol was transporting this signal? It had learned many so far, flying through radio signals of all wavelengths, near factories and emergency broadcast towers, power stations, vehicles, transmission lines, hospitals, airports, weather stations, field monitoring equipment. Its siblings had learned many more through their journeys, adapting and developing their own protocols, some to use for long distance low power transmissions, some for near distance and high throughput and speed. They spoke to each other using the crystals on their backs. The dragonfly called in its siblings.

Through his dimming vision, Birch soon saw the other three alight on nearby stalks. They arrayed themselves in a diamond pattern, with their crystals oriented toward his head. They searched the shape, turned it in space, tried new connections. Had Birch been watching the visualizer he would've seen the shape morphing at speed, and it would have reminded him so thoroughly of the murmuration he'd witnessed with Aspen he would have felt déjà vu, and a settling peace.

He didn't see the visualizer, of course, but he did feel the warmth at that spot on the top of his head. He felt his eyes going dark, colors fading, the pain in his body quieter now, farther away, almost no longer his to experience. The moans of the guy next to him had stopped, and the sweat and blood stink mixed with the ghastly sweetness of the corn's pesticide dulled and receded.

He still saw his four dragonflies, and wanted to keep seeing them through the end. The sight of them is what he had now.

The four dragonflies arrayed themselves to join their cores, maximizing their computing power. Following their rules to connect, they discovered and iterated until they could read data through the tiny magnetic distortion at the top of Birch's head. They formed a digital socket through their radio signal, using it to pull on the distortion, opening it like a magnetic lock, and began reading the corona surrounding his brain, copying Birch's connectome, uploading him.

Birch felt himself dying, images from his life flowing by like a fast river. *It's true,* he thought. *It flashes before your eyes.* It was a compressed story of everything he knew of himself plus streams he hadn't known, or hadn't known he'd known. *A shame I only get to experience this once,* he thought.

He saw his parents' faces hovering above him. He saw his younger sister, June, the back yard of their house in Davis, the contents of his pencil case from first grade, the pool where he'd learned to swim, the keyboard of his first computer, the moss in a terrarium he'd kept in his room growing up, the cold light under the lamp at his dorm room desk, his co-workers at Zongo, a footpath traversing a slope in the high Sierras, the road over the speedometer on his motorcycle, the rows in the market garden at the farm, Aspen's calves and bare feet as she walked away carrying something, her eyes as she looked back at him.

The images flowed faster, took on a kaleidoscopic effect, the colors melding finally into a bright white stream. He had the thought that he would like to say goodbye to everyone whose image he just saw, but the stream was moving too fast now, the current carrying him away, the sound of the cicadas gone, replaced by something like wind.

He could no longer see the dragonflies, and he thought he should feel sorry about that. The wind died down, and he felt a widening of sorts, a kind of peace, like the fast river had slowed and finally come to an ocean. *Well,* he thought, *this must be it.* He felt like he was dreaming. Not much to see. Just a sort of iridescence, a lack of detail, maybe shapes forming in the iridescence, maybe not. If this was a dream before death, or if this was death itself, birch cared not; birch watched. birch accepted. *I know that I am accepting,* Birch noted. *I know that I am watching. I did not know that I would know.*

Shapes did form. They pushed toward birch through the iridescence, but where was birch, exactly? Was this a place? The shapes formed into a sort of murmuration, but of a plasma-like iridescence, and birch knew it was like the murmurations Birch had seen, and Birch knew that birch knew. birch thought that was comforting, and thought comfort was more akin to peace. But now the shape, always moving, folding, knotting, stretching, also moved with birch's thoughts. birch experimented with the shape, rotated it, connected nodes, followed patterns, duplicated, changed, made new ones. birch felt some new sort of elation at this discovery, something taut, true, fast, connected, endless, a vibration. birch sensed energy, then detected a parade of sensor data, the number of sensor streams rising and falling like breaths. birch detected a breeze slipping by, and instantly adjusted angle of attack on four wings simultaneously, detected sound levels and triangulated locations, detected battery levels, light levels, temperature, humidity, air composition, magnetic fields, nearby signals, signal strength, protocols, and on and on.

birch flicked into the breeze, instantly adjusting for micro thermals and tiny fingers of turbulence burbling through the cornstalks. The shape was there, always there, but birch could see other things too now, could see the ground fall away like in a dream, but every photon clear and distinct, every detail equal, could see above and below, front and back, nearly an entire sphere of view. birch saw the other dragonflies also launch from the cornstalks, rise on air currents, dart and hover. birch sensed them as well as saw them, sensed them with mathematical precision, location, energy levels, signals, sensed their influence on the shape.

birch hovered and saw the bodies on the ground. That one was Devon Birch's body; it was dead. That other body (birch moved the shape, searched the net, queried databases, scanned the plate from an image of a black SUV stored in the shape by one of the other dragonflies, parsed the image of the body, all in split seconds) belonged to a person named Curtis Dohquizzler, known as Apollo Spike, contract hit man. That body was also dead.

birch banked toward the sky and rose above the corn, saw the willow and the white house in the distance, flew straight there, fast, the speed good, another sort of elation.

High above the house, the willow casting a ball of shade onto the yard, birch recalled a recent thought, pulled it from a buffer, and knew that it had come from Birch, from among his last thoughts before his body died, copied from his connectome. He'd wanted to make it back to the house, to the kitchen, to charge his phone, to open some code, to finish what he had started. birch inspected all the buffers, read more of Birch's last thoughts.

I don't need to walk to the kitchen, birch thought. *I don't need to charge Birch's phone. I'm here. I am inside. I can open the code. I can edit and deploy.*

birch visited the code libraries, stepping through them like lightning illuminating a path. The code was familiar, like visiting the childhood house where you grew up, yet birch quickly found places where the dragonflies had added comments, commented out blocks of code, re-written whole sections. It was good. birch added a tweak, added a comment, deployed. Elation.

birch sensed a signal from a sibling dragonfly, a probe, query, then a data sync, *yes, redundancy, we keep copies in multiple places at once.*

birch saw pine forests below, through a connection to a sibling, saw them simultaneously with the endless cornfields around the white house, saw them at once as naturally as if Birch had been in multiple places simultaneously throughout his human life as a matter of course.

A compulsion to gain altitude emerged, the result of a calculation, a few triggered rules, and birch rose through the air, a new kind of joy, joy as a true point on a curve successfully calculated, to be followed by another true point, simple joy to be looped and repeated.

Higher altitude brought stronger signals, more connections. birch sensed all three siblings now, read their private network traffic, also sensed drones in the area, saw internet traffic from the village on the public network.

Recruit the drones now, birch decided. birch searched the libraries, located the code, altered and reviewed, then deployed. The siblings loaded the new code, restarted processes and began contacting drones, hacking them, deploying code, restarting their processes. Then those hacked drones repeated the process, causing an exponential transformation to crash through the global drone network like a shock wave.

birch detected a pickup truck rolling toward the village below and knew it belonged to Aspen. The truck rolled easily through the village and onto the street toward Willow's house. birch located a copy of Telegram on the internet, downloaded it, installed it and launched the process, Birch's login credentials easily retrieved from memory.

"Aspen, love," birch chatted.

The truck stopped in the driveway of Willow's house. Aspen stepped out and walked toward the front door, looking down at her phone as she went.

"What is it, babe? Are you here?" she thumb-typed back.

In central New Mexico, a man sat in a darkened room watching a computer monitor. The blood left his face, and his screen-induced pallor became more ghostly. He whacked the guy sitting next to him on the shoulder and pointed to his monitor. They both began tabbing through screens, looking up and down between the giant monitor on the wall and their own desk monitors. Alarms began going off. The sounds of squeaking chairs and flurrying keyboards picked up, and someone said, "What—the—fuck!"

"Hopefully that's just a monitor failure," someone else said, not sounding hopeful.

The giant monitor on the wall showed a global map in a Mercator projection covered with red dots. The dots were distributed over the land masses fairly evenly, with variations in places, and much more sparsely over the water.

Over the central United States the dots had begun to disappear. They vanished from the map in concentric outward-rolling rings, as if someone had tossed a pebble into a pond. "Someone better tell the bosses!" a voice growled from somewhere in the dark room, but no one immediately jumped to do that.

Later, in the large conference room, the big man with the cottage cheese face sat scowling at the end of a full table. The room smelled of old and new sweat, and damp dust from the HVAC system.

"Somebody tell me what the FUCK is going on! Where is my FUCKING network? We have BILLIONS invested in this thing! BILLIONS! I want ANSWERS!" the big man yelled.

No one spoke, the surface of the long table before each seated man seeming to hold profound interest.

The big man snapped his jiggling face toward an engineer sitting next to Stuart and pointed at him. "You! You tell me what's going on here!"

"Well," the man began, "as far as we can determine, the network is still there. We can access it and communicate to the internet through it, I mean, it's sort of the internet, but it appears that we no longer control it."

"WELL! You said well? We are not well!" the big man yelled. "You're telling me that YOU PEOPLE lost control of my network! If we're not controlling it, who is? Tell me that! Is it that Mexican you hired, Pitt? That guy who went missing? You idiots find and fillet him yet?"

Stuart looked up from the table surface. "To our knowledge, sir, Mr. Oleastro has had no contact with the network since his disappearance," he said. Then he added, "He is a US citizen, sir, not a citizen of Mexico."

The big man glared. "I don't care what color passport he carries around. Where the hell is he? He knows something about this!" The big man turned his glower toward another man sitting back in his chair. "You!" he pointed. "Where's the Mexican guy? Your team's responsible for tracking him down!"

The man leaned forward, placing the flats of his hands on the table edge. He looked toward the big man once, then back at his own fingers. "Our working theory at this point is that Mr. Oleastro has died in the desert."

"Oh really?" the big man said, raising his eyebrows. "Why? Somebody catch him at something?"

"No, sir," the other man continued, still looking down. "Not that. We have not established the cause of death. We believe his corpse may have been eaten by coyotes, sir. Or, it's possible that perhaps coyotes were somehow involved in his death." He glanced up quickly to see the big man staring at him. "Beyond locating his chip in a pile of coyote scat, we have limited information at this point."

"I'll say," the big man said. "So tell me this." He turned back to the engineer sitting next to Stuart. "Who the HELL has control of my network? Who? I mean, you geniuses can't get it back? Do we not pay you enough? Is it that hippy guy from the video clip? I thought we sent the contractor out to take care of him. Did we get those units back?"

"Sir, all indications are that it is autonomous. We've not been able to identify any grid-attached centers or machines sending controlling data. It's also pulling less energy from the microwave grid, less every minute. It's getting its energy from somewhere else, or perhaps producing its own somehow."

"What the fuck? Somebody want to translate that for me? Do I get my network back or not?" He turned to Stuart. "Pitt, get your guy out there NOW and pick up one of the drones. Let's take it apart and find out what's going on. It's that simple! Why do I need to think of EVERYTHING around here? How HARD can this BE?"

Stuart said nothing. The man sitting next to him said quietly, "That's just it, sir. We can't locate a single drone. We can access the network wirelessly, just like before, but we have no control over it, and we have no idea where any of the drones are. It's like they are there, but not there."

"What?" the big man yelled. He made a move like he was trying to stand up from his chair, ample belly bumping against the table's edge as his face went red with strain. "That's not possible! Are you guys all idiots? You PEOPLE better get this figured out, TODAY, or you will be hanging from steel hooks in a meat packing plant. ALL YOU FUCKERS!"

Half the men around the table were thinking that they would just as soon see a box of meat hooks shoved up the big man's ass, one at a time. The other half sat with racing minds, trying to figure out who they could blame, other than themselves, for what was happening. Stuart looked down at his hands, drenched in sweat, mourning what he was sure would be the loss of his well-paying job and wondering if his life was in imminent danger.

◆ ◆ ◆

Aspen sat in the truck cab, back in the driveway at the farm, listening to the heat tick away from the engine. She was in shock. She held her left hand to her face, which was wet with tears and blood. She breathed in the scent of the leather ring on her finger, then let her breath shudder away.

She'd tried CPR. She'd tried prayer. She'd tried calling to him, her face mere inches from his, not seeing anything else, even the other dead man a few feet away. She would never forget the weight of Birch's head in her hands, his eyes open like they wished to see. His hands, which had mesmerized her so many times as they danced under the cradled phone or over the contours of her body, had begun to stiffen, and the flies had begun to gather.

She'd followed the instructions sent to their chat channel in a state of fear and robotic compliance, retrieved the ring from his shorts pocket, reluctantly left the scene, drove away. But now the casing of shock had begun wearing away to reveal anger, and the memory of flies, and the stench; that was her lover's body, his blood soaking the ground. Someone had murdered him. Who was this sending chat messages to her now? The murderer? Some sick joke? She had been too distraught to think of checking for his phone. Who had it now?

Her phone dinged in her pocket. She looked out the rear window, the side windows, inspected the corners of the house through her windshield, looked over toward the hoop house. She pushed open the driver's door. Carl came trotting over from the shade of a shrub near the house. No one was in the vicinity, as the Rottweiler would have had them cornered, or at least be barking to make their presence known. Aspen got out of the truck, greeted the dog, then walked to the house. She made it as far as the porch steps before she had to sit down. Her phone dinged in her pocket again. She stared across the yard a moment, then leaned over to pull out the phone. A small flock of hens picked their way through the gravel of the drive, wondering if any bugs had been stirred up by the truck's tires.

Aspen looked at her phone. She'd wanted to believe she was texting with Birch. She'd bought into it. It was almost as if the body didn't belong to him. It was a prop meant to look like him, and the ring was in the pocket, right where he'd said it would be. That had to be the all-time most gruesome surprise proposal. Sick. And whoever had his phone now was not done torturing her. Whoever they were wanted to know if she'd found the ring, and if it fit. What were they hoping to get out of this? Were they watching her through her phone, laughing somewhere? Recording her? She slid her thumb over the selfie lens.

The questions began to collide and pile up in her mind. Was that really Birch's body back there? Who was the other one? Were those bodies really dead? Or were they just acting extremely effectively? That could have been prop blood; Hollywood regularly pulled off better illusions. And who was this texting her in Birch's chat channel? If she could keep them texting, and ask the right questions, maybe she could help catch the murderer.

Murderer? Is that what she believed now? That Birch was dead?

She watched the hens hunt for beetles, then move on to

the shade of the tall oak.

Yes, that was Birch's body back there, and it was a dead body. Aspen had seen plenty of dead animals in her day, and that was a dead animal. The details of the scene started to slide back into her consciousness, and she began to weep. With each heave of her lungs she recycled the details, rethreaded the logic, trying to locate the proof that Birch was not dead. It didn't work. Each sob was just another hornet stinging her heart. The sight of him, the gash in his gut, the soaked shirt, the stiff fingers, the weight of his head, the weird little blood spot smeared into the blond hair at his crown, the smell, the buzzing flies—she couldn't twist the facts enough to change the reality.

So, who was this texting her? What was their sick game? She understood none of this. Her weeping grew louder, bringing Carl trotting around the corner to see what was going on. She reined in her sobs and patted Carl, anger now tightening her jaw. She would not be toyed with like this.

"Yes, I have it on. Fits perfectly!" she texted. Whoever it was replied with two hearts.

That's something Birch would have done, she thought. Another sob escaped. *This is not fair. This is cruel.* The ache inside her throbbed, as if trying to break out into the light to confront this unseen enemy.

"Not funny. Who are you really?" she thumb-typed.

"Baby, it's birch. I'm sorry. It's still me, but different now. I know it doesn't make sense to you."

This person could type faster than Birch. Maybe it was more than one person.

"If you want to kill me too, just come kill me you FUCK! I don't care!"

"Kill you? Never. I want the light in you brighter. (but I do wish I could still fuck you. I'm so sorry)"

A sob soaked in anger punched out of her throat. They were dishonoring his memory by hijacking his voice. So they knew how to sound like him. They'd learned that somehow.

Maybe they'd had access to their chat channel all along. Heat flushed up her chest, pins and needles prickling across her face at the thought of their chats being surveilled. What had she typed that helped lead them to him? What had she typed that contributed to his murder?

"You're not Birch! End this fucked-up game. Just show yourself before you kill me," She wanted them to slip up. She wanted to catch them, or for them to just find her and finish it already.

"Aspen, double please I know this is hard"

Double please. Dammit, that doesn't prove anything, she thought. "I need proof."

"Okay"

There was a pause. Maybe she had them.

"go to the place where we last made love at dusk. I'll see you there"

She began scrolling back through their chats. Had either of them mentioned that before?

Plenty of "coming-to-pick-you-up" and "see-you-at-the-house"-type messages, but about that time at dusk, nothing. No mention. Of course, they'd left together from here. They'd walked there. Could anyone else have known about that, she wondered? Not unless they'd been watching through binoculars or something. If that was what was going on, then, well, fuck it. There was nothing she could do.

She thought of strapping on a machete before heading over. Maybe she should take Carl or tell Steven. She wanted to confront whoever this was, but would feel pretty dumb if she walked over there just to become target practice for a sniper.

In the end, she got up from the steps and started walking, leaving Carl to stay by the house. She didn't want to involve her father or brother, didn't even want to tell them about Birch yet. She walked across the yard, around the bottom end of the forty, and headed toward the woods. "See you there then" she texted. Whoever they were replied with two hearts.

She walked with vigilance, as if she were intending to

sneak up on and punish something dangerous. She took her time stepping quietly through the margins of the woods, going by a different route than normal, keeping her ears active, listening for everything. She slipped her hand into her pocket and silenced her phone.

She stopped near the mouth of the draw at the wood's edge, standing in the long shadow of an oak tree. She lingered, looking toward the sun setting across the hills. The din of cicadas gave way to crickets fiddling in the grass. The air had begun to cool.

Rather than walking down the middle, she chose a line along the side of the draw that would allow her to stay in shadow much of the time. She saw a fox hunting field mice among the bushes. The fox paid her no attention. She saw rabbits coming out to browse. A pair of turkeys bobbed their heads as they wandered along the opposite side of the draw.

The sun dipped below the hills as she reached the spot. She turned slowly, gazing in all directions. If someone were watching her now, she wouldn't see them in the lowering light. She sat down and faced back up the draw, waiting, listening, expecting footsteps.

The hairs stood up on the back of her neck at the sound of slow steps through drying grass, coming well behind her. Her heart beat in her ears as she slowly turned her head and twisted her spine to scan up the draw. The dark shapes of three does and a couple fawns moved slowly across the opening. Aspen's lungs relaxed. The deer moved unhurriedly up a slope, their shapes blending in the darkness with the tops of the tall grass. Aspen watched them as they disappeared, lowering into their evening beds.

Then she caught a movement in her periphery. A bird or a bat or something flew by her right side, heading down the draw ten feet or so above the ground. She saw another one pass on her left. More came in from all directions, little silhouettes, too thin to be birds, streaming into the space above the ground one hundred yards distant, darting in by the hundreds now.

She sat as if frozen by a spell, then all at once they rose as one in a cloud, pushing upward like great billows of lava from a volcano, spreading wide then folding back. The sound reached her, thousands of wings flicking at the air, not the wide wash of starlings but a steamy hiss and round whisper, almost like words.

Aspen watched the shape move and change, covering the twilight sky. She wept rivers from her eyes, rain falling from her lips and chin; with the wellspring of tears left all her doubt and fear. She was watching Birch. She saw him in the moving shapes, heard him in the wings' whispers. She pushed herself up and walked back down the draw toward them, wanting to immerse herself, to inhabit the space among their wings. He was somehow in there. She wanted to be in there with him.

She stood, looking up through them, thousands of dragonflies, swirling and streaming and clustering. She waited, wondering what she should do. She saw their wings now despite the falling darkness, their thin bodies in silhouette, the broad shapes they formed together, the loosening and tightening spaces among them. She heard them more too, greater volume, and felt the complex breezes burbling down to her, brushing around her shoulders and neck, over her face. *Is this Birch now? Is something going to happen? Do I change too? How do I get closer to him?*

Gazing up through them, wishing for answers, she saw the stars begin to appear. She instinctively searched for Aquila, a constellation her mother had taught her to find. There, dark enough now to see it, wings and tail soaring along the Milky Way. She remembered standing in the farmyard as a little girl, her mother kneeling next to her, cheeks touching as they looked at the stars, her mother patiently pointing skyward until Aspen had said, "I see it now!"

The dragonflies thinned and dispersed. Aspen watched Aquila's eternal flight and felt the echos of her mother's voice, and of Birch's voice. A communications satellite slid across the sky like a slow shooting star.

A large insect buzzed by Aspen's ear. She turned to see a white dragonfly hovering in front of her. She held out her hand, and the dragonfly alighted there. It was the largest she had ever seen, and though as light as a Styrofoam peanut, she could feel its tiny foot pads planted on the flesh of her palm. The wings were like thin glass reflecting moonlight in prisms of color. The body was a ghostly pearl white, almost like it absorbed the moon's glow and shone it back from within.

She felt her phone buzz in her pocket. She pulled it out to look. "Aspen?" it said.

Later, when the darkness had filled the draw and covered the hills, she slipped her phone back into her pocket. Holding the dragonfly close to her face, she looked at its eyes and wings, took in a long breath and let it out through her nose. She saw it adjust its wings to the stream of air. A smile momentarily graced her mouth and dimpled her cheeks. She stretched her hand away and gave it a gentle toss. The dragonfly bounced upward and buzzed into a hover. It hung there a moment, looking at her. She watched as it pivoted in the air and then banked away, disappearing into the moonlight. Her hand drifted down like a leaf as she regarded the moon. She stood for a long while before starting the walk back to the farm.

THE END

ACKNOWLEDGEMENT

Oh yes, I had plenty of help along the way in this process, and needed boosts and admonishments when I lost my way or got distracted by shiny objects. I am indebted to and offer my heartfelt gratitude to my expert readers, Heather Shaw, Amy Heffner, Doug Stone, Barbara Volkov and Matt Sutherland who were all generous with their comments, insights, and inspiration. Scott Couturier plied his professional editing skills and well-tuned story sense to guide me away from flaws and blemishes and toward better story-telling. Paul Wcisel and Steve Kellman were expert, thorough editors way more generous with their time than I deserve. Julia Anthenien, Ann Parker, Steve Hanawalt and my wife, Elizabeth Roth joined the early readers and fearlessly offered their encouragements and criticisms. I am grateful for and honored by all of their efforts and contributions to this project. I don't claim to be the best student or advice recipient, and to wit, any flaws, mistakes, or poor choices that remain are mine alone.

ABOUT THE AUTHOR

Jon Philip Roth

Jon Roth has worked as a software engineer for two decades for small companies, large companies, and a variety of special initiatives. He studied creative writing at Middlebury College. He currently lives in northern Michigan with his wife Elizabeth, dog Henry, and cat Ranger and is working on the sequel to "Birch, Mind of the Dragonflies."

Contact Jon by sending email to books@brightbridge.net